Heart of Oak

Also by Alexander Kent

Midshipman Bolitho
Stand Into Danger
In Gallant Company
Sloop of War
To Glory We Steer
Command a King's Ship
Passage to Mutiny
With All Despatch
Form Line of Battle!
Enemy in Sight!
The Flag Captain
Signal – Close Action!
The Inshore Squadron
A Tradition of Victory
Success to the Brave
Colours Aloft!
Honour This Day
The Only Victor
Beyond the Reef
The Darkening Sea
For My Country's Freedom
Cross of St George
Sword of Honour
Second to None
Relentless Pursuit
Man of War
Band of Brothers

Heart of Oak

Alexander Kent

WILLIAM HEINEMANN : LONDON

Published by William Heinemann Books 2007

2 4 6 8 10 9 7 5 3 1

Copyright © Bolitho Maritime Productions 2007

Alexander Kent has asserted his right under the Copyright, Designs
and Patents Act, 1988 to be identified as the author of this work

First published in Great Britain in 2007 by
William Heinemann
Random House, 20 Vauxhall Bridge Road,
London SW1V 2SA

www.randomhouse.co.uk

Addresses for companies within The Random House Group Limited
can be found at: www.randomhouse.co.uk

The Random House Group Limited Reg. No. 954009

A CIP catalogue record for this book
is available from the British Library

ISBN 9780434013517

The Random House Group Limited makes every effort to ensure that the
papers used in its books are made from trees that have been legally sourced
from well-managed and credibly certified forests. Our paper procurement
policy can be found at: www.randomhouse.co.uk/paper.htm

Typeset by SX Composing DTP, Rayleigh, Essex
Printed and bound in Great Britain by
Clays Ltd, St Ives Plc

Contents

v

The stirring story of the life and times of Richard Bolitho is told in Alexander Kent's bestselling novels.

1756	Born Falmouth, son of James Bolitho
1768	Entered the King's service as a midshipman in *Manxman*
1772	Midshipman, *Gorgon* (*Midshipman Bolitho* and *Band of Brothers*)
1774	Promoted Lieutenant, *Destiny*: Rio and the Caribbean (*Stand into Danger*)
1775–7	Lieutenant, *Trojan*, during the American Revolution. Later appointed prizemaster (*In Gallant Company*)
1778	Promoted Commander, *Sparrow*. Battle of the Chesapeake (*Sloop of War*)
1780	Birth of Adam, illegitimate son of Hugh Bolitho and Kerenza Pascoe
1782	Promoted Captain, *Phalarope*; West Indies: Battle of Saintes (*To Glory We Steer*)
1784	Captain, *Undine*; India and East Indies (*Command a King's Ship*)
1787	Captain, *Tempest*; Great South Sea; Tahiti; suffered serious fever (*Passage to Mutiny*)
1792	Captain, the Nore; Recruiting (*With All Despatch*)
1793	Captain, *Hyperion*; Mediterranean; Bay of Biscay; West Indies. Adam Pascoe, later Bolitho, enters the King's service as a midshipman aboard *Hyperion* (*Form Line of Battle!* and *Enemy in Sight!*)
1795	Promoted Flag Captain, *Euryalus*; involved in the Great Mutiny; Mediterranean; promoted Commodore (*The Flag Captain*)
1798	Battle of the Nile (*Signal – Close Action!*)
1800	Promoted Rear-Admiral Baltic. (*The Inshore Squadron*)
1801	Biscay. Prisoner of war (*A Tradition of Victory*)
1802	Promoted Vice-Admiral; West Indies (*Success to the Brave*)
1803	Mediterranean (*Colours Aloft!*)

If my voice should die on land,
take it to sea-level
and leave it on the shore.

Take it to sea-level
and make it captain
of a white ship of war.

Oh my voice adorned
with naval insignia:
on the heart an anchor,
and on the anchor a star,
and on the star the wind,
and on the wind the sail!

RAFAEL ALBERTI
(*translated from the Spanish by Mark Strand*)

Just for you, Kim, with my love

1

Face to Face

The Falmouth-bound coach hesitated at the brow of a low hill, its wheels jerking and spinning against yet another ridge of frozen mud. The horses, four-in-hand, took the strain, stamping with frustration, their breath steaming in the pale, misty sunlight. They, more than any, were aware that their part of the journey was almost over.

It was February and still bitterly cold, as it had been since this year of 1818 had first dawned. Longer than that, many would say along Cornwall's southern approaches. Trees like black bones, as if they would never throw a leaf or bud again; slate walls and the occasional farm roof like polished metal. The coachman, big and shapeless in his heavily caped coat, flicked the reins. No urgency, no haste; he knew his horses and the road as he knew his own strength. His passengers and baggage took second place.

At the rear of the coach, the guard, equally unrecognizable under layers of clothing and an old blanket, wiped his eyes and stared across the straining horses and saw a flock of gulls rise from somewhere, circling, perhaps looking for food as the vehicle rolled past. The sea was never far away. The horses were changed at the authorized stables, but he and the driver had been with the coach all the way from Plymouth. He shifted his buttocks to restore the circulation to his limbs and felt the pressure of his gun beneath the blanket. The coach carried mail as well as passengers, and the crest emblazoned on either door proclaimed risk as well as pride.

Up and around the bleak waste of Bodmin Moor he had seen

1

a few ragged, scarecrow figures still hanging at the roadside. Left to rot and the ravages of the crows as a warning to any would-be robber or highwayman. But there would always be some one.

He saw the coachman raise his fist. Nothing more. No more was necessary.

Another stretch of broken track. He swore under his breath. Somebody should get the convicts out of their warm cells to repair it. There were no longer any French prisoners of war for such work. Waterloo was almost four years ago, becoming nothing more than a memory to those who had been spared the risk and the pain.

He banged on the roof. ''Old on below!'

One of the passengers was a young woman. The violent motion of the coach, despite its new springs, had made her vomit several times. It had meant stopping, much to the annoyance of the man with her, her father. She was with child. Lucky to have got this far, the guard thought. The horses were slowing their pace, ears twitching, waiting for a word or a whistle. He saw some farm gates, one sagging into the ground. Did the farmer not know, or care? He loosened the case containing the long horn, to announce their approach. The last leg. . . .

There was a frantic tapping on the roof. She was going to be sick again.

The horses were getting back into their stride, the wheels running more smoothly on the next piece of road. They would be thinking of their stables. The tapping had stopped.

He raised the horn and moistened it with his tongue. It was like ice.

Inside the coach it was not much warmer, despite the sealed windows and the blue leather cushions. There were blankets too, although with the motion it had been hard to keep them in place.

Midshipman David Napier wedged his shoulder into his seat and watched the passing trees reaching out as if to claw at the window, the paler shapes of a house or barn looming in the background.

It was not his imagination: the sky was already darker. He must have fallen asleep, despite his troubled thoughts and the

2

swoop and jerk of the vehicle. He had forgotten how many times they had pulled off the road, to change horses and take a few steps to ease mind and body. Or to allow the young woman who sat opposite him to find refuge behind a bush or tree.

And her father, his impatience, even anger at each delay. They had stopped overnight at a small inn somewhere outside St. Austell. Even that seemed unreal. A hard bench seat and a hasty meal, alone in a tiny room above the stableyard. Voices singing, and drunken laughter, ending eventually in a mixture of threats and curses, which had only added to Napier's sense of loss and uncertainty.

He winced, and realized he had been gripping his leg beneath the blanket. The deep wound was ever ready to remind him. And it was not a dream or a nightmare. *It was now.*

More houses were passing, some in shadow. A harder, firmer road, the wheels clattering evenly, and then the sudden blare of the horn. Louder this time, thrown back from solid walls.

He licked his lips and imagined they tasted of salt. Twice he had seen the glint of water, the land folding away, final.

The other passenger, who had scarcely spoken all the way from Plymouth, jerked upright in his seat and peered around.

'Are we there?' He sniffed and stifled a cough. A thin, stooped figure, dressed in black: a lawyer's senior clerk, he had disclosed. He carried a leather case, heavily sealed, probably documents, and obviously not intended even for his own eyes.

'Coming into Falmouth now.' Napier watched the buildings, some already showing lights.

The clerk sniffed again. 'Of course, you sailors always know your way about, don't you?' He chuckled, but seized the case as it threatened to slip from his lap.

Napier stared through the window. The coach had passed a church in Plymouth; he vaguely remembered it from that last visit, when their ship, the frigate *Unrivalled*, had come home to carry out repairs, battle damage from the Algiers attack, and to be paid off. And forgotten, except by those who had served in her. Those who had survived.

Like her captain, Adam Bolitho, who, despite the strains of

3

combat and command and the stark news of dismissal, had kept the promise he had made that day in Plymouth.

Fore Street, and the tailor's establishment, where Napier had barely been able to believe what was happening. The tailor beaming and rubbing his hands, asking the captain what he required.

Your services for this young gentleman. Measure him for a midshipman's uniform. So calmly said, but with one hand on Napier's shoulder, which had made it a moment he would never forget.

This was not the same uniform; he had been fitted out again in Antigua, where the old Jacks said you could get all you needed, if you had the money in your purse.

His first ship as a midshipman, the frigate *Audacity,* had been blown apart by heated shot from the shore artillery at San José. The memories were a blur. The roar of gunfire, men screaming and dying . . . then in the water . . . the madness, men still able to cheer as the flagship had closed with the enemy. To attack. To win. Captain Bolitho's ship.

He had scarcely had time to get to know most of *Audacity*'s company. Like a family. The navy's way. Those you would fight for . . . he thought of the dead midshipman on the beach, when he had dragged him ashore after the bombardment. And those you would always hate.

He closed his mind to it, like slamming a door. It was in the past. But the future?

The coach was slowing, taking a wide bend in the road. In his mind's eye he could see the old grey house, anticipating the warmth and the welcome. Wanting to feel a part of it, like one of them. Like a dream.

He touched his leg again. Suppose a dream was all it had been?

Doors opening, horses stamping on cobbles, snorting as men ran to unfasten the harnesses, some one waving, a woman hurrying to throw her arms around the girl who had been so sick. The lawyer's clerk gesturing to the guard, saying something about baggage, but still clinging to his sealed case.

Napier peered up at the inn sign. *The Spaniards.* Again, like a voice from the past.

The horses were gone, the coach standing abandoned. He

saw his midshipman's chest on the cobbles with an inn servant stooping to look at the label.

The guard joined him. His burly companion had already vanished into the taproom.

'End o' the road. For us, it is.' He glanced around. 'You bein' met? It's no place to stand an' freeze!'

Napier felt in his pocket for some coins.

'No. Can I leave my chest here?'

He did not hear the answer. He was trying to think, clearly, coldly. He would walk to the house. He had done it with Luke Jago, the captain's coxswain. The hard man, who had taken him out to *Audacity,* and shouted his name as if he were enjoying it. *'Come aboard to join!'*

He felt now for the warrant with its scarlet seal of authority, which the young flag lieutenant had given him as he left the ship at Plymouth two days ago.

'Come along. We haven't got all day!'

Napier turned and saw the foul-tempered passenger beckoning to his daughter. He had remarked loudly on Napier's arrival that it was hardly fitting for a mere midshipman to travel in the same coach. The coachman had been unable to conceal his satisfaction when Napier had showed him the warrant bearing the vice-admiral's seal.

The girl brushed some hair from her forehead and smiled at him.

'Thank you again for your kindness. I shall not forget.' She reached out and put her gloved hand on his arm. 'I am glad you are safe.'

She could not continue, but turned away and walked deliberately past her father.

'No need fer me to fret about *you*, zur.' The guard dragged off his battered hat, his weathered face split into a grin. *Something to tell the lads. . . .*

A smart carriage, almost delicate compared to the stage, had halted, and a woman was stepping down, assisted by her own straight-backed coachman. People were turning to watch as she, slim and elegant in a dark red cloak, hurried to greet the midshipman.

Napier felt the arms around his shoulder, a hand on his face, his mouth. The tears against his skin.

She was saying, 'A tree across the road . . . Francis had to fetch help. I prayed you'd still be here!' She tossed her head like a girl, but the laugh he had always remembered would not come.

Napier could feel the warmth of her embrace, her pleasure and her sadness. He wanted to tell her, to explain, but his voice came out like a stranger's.

'Lady Roxby, it all happened so quickly—'

But her hand was touching his mouth again and she was shaking her head, her eyes never leaving his. 'Aunt Nancy, my dear. Remember?' She kept her voice level as she called to the coachman, 'A hand here, Francis. Easy, now.'

But Francis needed no such caution. He had served in the cavalry, and had not forgotten what the exhaustion of war looked like. And he had already seen the dark stain of blood on the midshipman's white breeches.

She stood by the carriage while Napier climbed with effort to the step. She was aware of the faces at the inn windows and on the street, discussing and speculating, but they could have been completely alone. She had last seen him as a boy, proud but shy in his new uniform, before he had left to join his ship. She had learned most of what had happened from the letter which had reached England in a fast courier brig from the Caribbean; the rest she could guess or imagine. She was a sea officer's daughter, and the sister of one of England's most famous sailors, and had soon learned that pain and glory usually walked hand in hand.

Napier was gazing back at her, his eyes filling his face.

'I— I'm so sorry. I didn't mean it to be. . . .' But Francis had edged past her and was easing the boy into a seat.

'He'll be all right now, m' lady.'

She nodded. 'Thank you, Francis. You may take us home.' *Home.*

Luke Jago, Captain Adam Bolitho's coxswain, stood beside one of the tall windows and stared down into the street. The carriage, and a carrier's cart which had brought him and some personal belongings here had already departed, and after the endless journey from Plymouth it was like being abandoned, cut off from everything he knew or could recognize.

The street was deserted and, like this house, too quiet to be alive. The buildings directly opposite were faceless and imposing. He took his hand from the curtain and heard it swish back into position. Like the room itself: everything in its place. Overpowering. The ceiling seemed too high, out of reach. He thought of the flagship, *Athena*; even in the great cabin aft, you had to duck your head beneath the deckhead beams. Below on the gun decks it was even more cramped. How could these people ever understand what it was like to serve, to fight?

He relaxed very slowly, caught unaware by his own resentment. The house felt empty, probably had been for most of the time. *Everything in its place.* The fine chairs, glossy and uncreased, a vast marble fireplace, laid with logs but unlit. There were some flowers in a vase by another window. But this was February, and they were made of coloured silk.

Above a small inlaid desk there was a painting; he was surprised it had escaped his notice as he had entered the room. A portrait of a sea officer holding a telescope. A young captain, not yet posted, but Jago could still recognize Sir Graham Bethune, Vice-Admiral of the Blue, who had left his flagship in Portsmouth in such haste, as if staging a race with the devil.

He sat down very carefully in one of the satin chairs, and tried once again to marshal his thoughts. Jago had a keen brain and usually a memory to match it, but after the battle with the slavers at San José and the murderous battering from their shore-sited artillery, one event seemed to merge with another. Leading his boarding party to retake the schooner, and seeing the woman standing on the scarred deck staring past him at *Athena*, as if she were beyond pain, and her blood had been unreal. In action, memory can play many tricks. But Jago could still hear her calling out, as if with joy, in those last seconds before she fell dead.

The return to Antigua, the victors with their prizes, and the total, unnerving silence in English Harbour which had greeted them. Some of their people had been killed in the action and been buried at sea; others had been landed at Antigua and were still there under care.

Jago was hardened to sea warfare and its price. The long years of war with France and Spain were only a memory now, and they were at peace, although some might not see it that

7

way. To the ordinary Jack, any man was an enemy if he was standing at the business end of a cannon, or holding his blade to your neck.

But that passage to Antigua still haunted Jago's mind.

A calm sea and light winds, lower deck cleared, and all work suspended on spars and rigging alike.

Jago had been in all kinds of fights, and had seen many familiar faces, some good, others bad, go over the side. But this was different. Her body stitched up in canvas, weighted with round shot, and covered with the flag. *Our flag*. Even some of the wounded had been on deck, crouching with their mates, or propped up against the hammock nettings to listen to the captain's voice, speaking the familiar words which most of them knew by heart.

And yet so different. . . .

Even the regular thump of the pumps, which had not stopped since the first crash of cannon fire, had been stilled.

And Bethune, their vice-admiral, had stood facing the infamous Lord Sillitoe. A victim or a culprit; it remained undecided, and somehow unimportant at that time and place Jago had later seen recorded in the master's log. The date and their position in the Caribbean when Catherine, Lady Somervell, was buried at sea.

He remembered Adam Bolitho's face when the grating had been raised, and they had heard the splash alongside. Sailors often thought about it, even joked about it on the messdeck. Not this time.

At Antigua there had been new orders waiting. Sillitoe, a friend of the Prince Regent, it was said, had been handed over into the custody of the commodore there, who had been promoted to rear-admiral while *Athena* and her consorts had been under fire.

Jago had kept close to his captain throughout the remainder of the campaign; if you could call it that, he thought darkly. Pulling his company together again, visiting the wounded, and often at odds with Bethune. The latter shouting and thumping the table and drinking beyond his capacity and his normal caution. Some said Bethune had been in love with Catherine Somervell. But Jago knew that she had loved only one man, Sir Richard Bolitho, who had been killed on the deck of his

8

flagship following Napoleon's escape from Elba. Jago had seen her in the old church at Falmouth, when all the flags had been at half-mast, and *Unrivalled* had fired a salute. It had been Richard's name she had been calling when she had fallen dead. More like a greeting than a farewell, or so it seemed, looking back. . . .

Somewhere a clock chimed. Two horsemen were trotting unhurriedly past the house. Dragoons, by their cut, he thought. *Officers*. His mouth tightened. Nothing else to do.

There was something else that still puzzled him. *Athena* had anchored at Plymouth only briefly before proceeding on to Portsmouth, which she had left less than a year ago. Bethune had insisted on breaking the passage, apparently to send some urgent despatches by courier.

Even then, the captain had found time to speak to the men being discharged or put ashore to have their wounds treated. The lucky ones. . . .

And the boy, now a midshipman, who had somehow managed to swim ashore at San José after *Audacity* had exploded. His own captain had been killed, cut in half by a red-hot ball from the battery, but one of his lieutenants had seen fit to write a short report on David Napier's courage and determination in supporting another midshipman and getting him to the beach, where the Royal Marines had found them. Only Napier had survived.

Napier would be in Falmouth now. At the Bolitho house, with the green hills behind and the sea below. Something Jago had also shared in his own way.

Captain Adam Bolitho was at the Admiralty right now, not all that far from this room. It was hard to fix your position, he thought, here in London anyway. It must be somewhere over and beyond those faceless houses. Bethune lived here when it suited him, and had used to ride across the park in a leisurely fashion to his offices.

Athena was being paid off. Another victim, like *Unrivalled* after her battle at Algiers. He recalled the silent bundles being slipped over the side for that last journey, and controlled his anger. That was the way it was. The sea was all he knew. He stood up and faced the door. *And all he wanted.*

But it was not one of the household staff, or even Lady

9

Bethune, not that she would deign to meet him. It was George Tolan, Bethune's servant, although the word didn't do him justice. Always smart and alert in his distinctive blue coat, and obviously at ease with his lord and master. More like a companion or a bodyguard, with the bearing of a soldier or a marine. Jago had seen him in *Athena*'s cabin, pouring wine or something with more bite to it, holding the glass or goblet to study it beforehand. No fuss, not like some. And when the guns had belched fire from *Athena*'s ports and reeled inboard in recoil, he had seen the other Tolan, crouching but unafraid in the fury of battle.

A good man to have beside you, but one you would never know.

Tolan was glancing around the room now, and, Jago guessed, missing nothing.

'I have told the kitchen to prepare a meal for you. A drink would not come amiss, I imagine, after all that bustle.'

If he was disturbed or irritated by the long journey from Portsmouth, the storing and checking of Bethune's personal gear at every stop along that endless road, he gave no sign of it. He probably knew Bethune better than any one.

Jago shrugged.

'No telling how long the Cap'n will be with their lordships.' He looked at the portrait on the wall. 'I can't fathom what there is to yarn about. It's over. We done what we was ordered. That's it!'

'Not so simple this time, I think.'

'Cap'n Bolitho had his last ship taken from him. Paid off. Now *Athena*— God, she's only a few years old!'

Tolan watched him. 'Launched in 1803, I was told. Sounds old enough to me.'

Jago exclaimed, 'Good Kentish oak, too!' and broke off as if he had just heard the remark. 'Not for a *real* ship. Hell's teeth, Our Nel's *Victory* was forty years old when she stood in the line at Trafalgar! They don't know what they're about, their bloody lordships!'

Tolan seemed to be considering something.

'You care about your captain, don't you? Something deeper than duty, loyalty. You're not a man who's easily taken in. I like that.' He smiled with sudden warmth, like offering a handshake, Jago thought afterwards. Dropping his guard, something rare with him.

Tolan said, 'Now I *will* fetch that drink,' and looked up at the portrait. The young captain. . . . 'For both of us.'

Jago stood at the window, grappling with the words, and what lay behind them. *Deeper than duty, loyalty.* It was not something he would ever consider, if he was being true to himself. After the flogging which had scarred his mind as well as his body, he had made himself shun even the slightest hint of friendship.

Perhaps it was trust?

The room was empty once more. He had not even heard Tolan close the door behind him.

He was on *Athena*'s deck again, as if it were yesterday. Now. The seamen breaking ranks slowly, reluctant to return to their work. The empty grating by the gangway, the unfolded flag barely moving in the breeze, the canvas-wrapped body already on the seabed.

But all he could see clearly was Adam Bolitho's face as he had turned away from the side. Their eyes had met, and the words had been quietly spoken, almost an undertone. Excluding every one else.

They're together now. Nothing can harm them.

It had troubled him deeply.

There were sounds, voices, on the stairway: Tolan bringing his master's wine, or maybe something stronger. He felt his mouth crack into a grin.

'There'll be other ships.'

He realized that he had spoken aloud.

Just say the word, Cap'n.

'If you would wait in here, Captain . . . er . . . Bolitho.' The Admiralty porter held the door open. 'Should you require any assistance. . . .' He did not finish it, but closed the door silently behind him.

Adam Bolitho stood a moment to get his bearings, or perhaps to prepare himself. After all the haste and uncertainty, this sudden stillness was unnerving. A table, three chairs, and one window: it was more like a cell than a waiting room.

Like most serving officers, he had not visited this, the seat of

Admiralty, more than a few times throughout his whole career, and he had always been impressed by the orderly confusion and purpose. Clerks carrying files of papers, criss-crossing what were still to him a maze of corridors, opening and shutting doors. Some remained closed, even guarded, while strategic conferences were in session; others, partly opened, revealed the materials and tools of command. Huge wall charts and maps, instruments, rows of waiting chairs. It was hard to imagine the immense power, and control of the world's greatest navy, being wielded from within these walls.

He walked over to the table. On it was a precisely folded copy of *The Times* and beside it a goblet and carafe of water. So quiet, as if the whole corridor were holding its breath.

He moved to the window, impatient now, refusing to acknowledge the strain and fatigue of mind and body. He should have known what it would do to him. The bitter aftermath of the action at San José, 'skirmish' as one news sheet had dismissed it, and the long passage home. Plymouth and then Portsmouth. He rubbed his forehead. Mere days ago. It seemed like a lifetime.

The window overlooked an enclosed courtyard, so near the opposite wall that you had to press your head against the glass to see it. The other wall had no windows. Storerooms of some kind? And above, trapped above the two walls, was the sky. Grey, cold, hostile. He stepped back and looked around the room. A cell indeed.

A carriage had been sent to Bethune's house to collect him for the journey to and along Whitehall. He was met by a clerk who had murmured polite comments about the weather and the amount of traffic, which, he was told, often delayed important meetings if senior officers were trapped in it. The constant movement, the noise. Like a foreign country. *Because I am the stranger here.*

From there he had been handed over to the porter, a towering, heavy man in a smart tailed coat with gleaming buttons, whose buckled shoes had clicked down one passage-way after another as he led the way. Like a ship of the line, with lesser craft parting to let them through.

There was one picture on this otherwise bare wall. A two-decker, firing a salute or at an unseen enemy. Old, and probably Dutch. His mind was clinging to the inconsequential detail. Holding on.

All those faces, names. Not even a full year since *Athena* had hoisted Bethune's vice-admiral's flag. *And I became his flag captain.* And now she was paid off, like all those other unwanted ships. Their work, and sometimes their sacrifice, would soon be forgotten.

. He recalled the longer waiting room he had seen briefly in passing. So like those redundant ships that seemed to line the harbours or any available creek: a final resting place.

Officers, a few in uniform, waiting to see some one in authority. Need, desperation, a last chance to plead for a ship. Any ship. Their only dread to be discarded, cast from the life they knew, and ending on the beach. A warning to all of them.

There were nine hundred captains on the Navy List, and not an admiral under sixty years of age.

Adam turned abruptly and saw his own reflection in the window. He was thirty-eight years old, or would be in four months.

What will you do?

He realized that he had thrust one hand into his coat, the pocket where he carried her letters. The link, the need. And she was in Cornwall. Unless. . . . He jerked his hand from his coat.

'If you would follow me, Captain Bolitho?'

He snatched up his hat from the table with its unread newspaper. He had not even heard the door open.

The porter peered around the room as if it were a habit. Looking for what? He must have seen it all. The great victories and the defeats. The heroes and the failures.

He touched the old sword at his hip. Part of the Bolitho legend. He could almost hear his aunt reminding him of it when they had been looking at his portrait; he had been painted with a yellow rose pinned to his uniform coat. Lowenna's rose. . . . He could see her now. *Andromeda*. He heard the door close. Cornwall. It seemed ten thousand miles away.

There were fewer people in this corridor this time, or perhaps it was a different route. More doors. Two officers standing outside one of them. Just a glance, a flicker of eyes. Nothing more. Waiting for promotion, or a court martial. . . .

He cleared his mind of everything but this moment, and the

man he was about to meet: John Grenville, still listed as captain, but here in Admiralty appointed secretary to the First Lord.

He remembered hearing Bethune refer to him as 'second only to God'.

The porter stopped and subjected him to another scrutiny, and said abruptly, 'My son was serving in *Frobisher* when Sir Richard was killed, sir. He often speaks of him whenever we meet.' He nodded slowly. 'A fine gentleman.'

'Thank you.' Somehow it steadied him, like some one reaching out. 'Let's be about it, shall we?'

After the cell-like waiting room, this one seemed enormous, occupying an entire corner of the building, with great windows opening on two walls. There were several tables, one of which held a folding map stand; another was piled with ledgers.

Captain John Grenville was sitting at a vast desk, his back to one of the windows, framed against the meagre light. He was small, slight, even fragile at first glance, and his hair was completely white, like a ceremonial wig.

'Do be seated, Captain Bolitho.' He gestured to a chair directly opposite. 'You must be somewhat weary after your travel. Progress has cut communication time to a minimum, but the human body is still hostage to the speed of a good horse!'

He sat cautiously, every muscle recalling the journey from Portsmouth. During the endless halts to change horses or rest them, he had seen the new telegraph system, mounted on a chain of hills and prominent buildings between the roof above their heads to the final sighting-point on the church by Portsmouth dockyard. A signal could be transmitted the entire distance in some twenty minutes, when visibility was good. In less time than it would take a courier to saddle and mount.

The winter light was stronger, or his eyes were becoming used to it. He was aware, too, that they were not alone. Another figure almost hidden by a desk on the far side of the room stood up and half-bowed, the light glinting briefly on spectacles perched on his forehead. Like Daniel Yovell, he thought.

Grenville said, 'That is Mr. Crozier. He will not disturb us.'

He leaned forward in his chair and turned over the papers

14

arranged before him in neat piles.

Adam forced himself to relax, muscle by muscle. There was no tiredness now, no despair. He was alert. On guard. And he was alone.

'I have, of course, read all the reports of the campaign conducted under Sir Graham Bethune's command. Their lordships are also informed of the operational control of the commodore, Antigua,' one hand moved to his mouth, and there might have been a trace of sarcasm. 'Now *rear-admiral*, Antigua. It slipped my mind!'

Adam saw him clearly for the first time. A thin face, the cheekbones very prominent and the skin netted with tiny wrinkles, perhaps the legacy of some serious fever early in his service. Keen-edged, like steel. Not a man who would make a mistake about somebody's promotion. Especially at Antigua.

'As flag captain, were you ever concerned that the conduct of operations might not be completely satisfactory?'

So casually said. Adam felt the clerk's close attention, and sensed his pen already poised.

'I have submitted my own report, sir. *Athena*'s log will confirm the ship's total involvement.'

Surprisingly, Grenville laughed.

'Well said, Bolitho, like a good flag captain!' He leaned back in his chair, the mood changing again. 'You are not under oath, nor are you under suspicion for any cause or reason.' He held up one hand as if expecting an interruption; like his face, it was almost transparent. 'We are well aware of your record as a King's officer, both in command and while serving others. You are not on trial here, but we are dealing with diplomacy, something more nebulous than the cannon's mouth, or the rights and wrongs of battle.'

'No captain can be expected to contradict. . . .' Adam broke off, and continued calmly, 'Given all the circumstances, the vessels at our disposal, and the weather, I think we acted in the only way possible. Good men died that day at San José. Slavery is an evil and a brutal thing. But it is still highly rewarding for those who condone it.' He turned unconsciously toward the half-hidden desk. 'And it costs lives, even if it *is* dismissed as a skirmish by those who apparently know otherwise!'

15

The bony hand came up slowly. 'Well said, Bolitho. I hope your ideals reach Parliament. Eventually.'

He turned over more papers, and when he spoke again it was as if his thoughts had been rearranged with them.

'*Athena* is paid off, and her people moved to other ships when suitable, or to continue their lives ashore. As is the way of the navy. Your first lieutenant has elected to remain with *Athena* until she is given over to other work,' a cold eye briefly across the desk, 'or disposed of.'

Adam said nothing, recalling the stern, unsmiling features of Stirling, the first lieutenant. Unmoved, unshaken even in the heat of battle. A man he had never understood. *But was I to blame?*

Grenville stood up suddenly and walked to the nearest window. He wore a plain, perfectly cut blue coat, and it was easy to see him as a captain again.

Over his shoulder he remarked, almost offhandedly, 'You had Lady Somervell buried at sea. That was *your* decision, I believe?'

Bethune must have told him, or the First Lord.

Adam stared past him at the overcast sky. He could see them now, as if it had only just happened. Bethune and Sillitoe staring each other down. The hatred, and something that was stronger than both of them.

He said, 'She's free now, sir.'

He looked over at the clerk. The pens were still in their standish. Unused.

He said quietly, 'What of Sillitoe, sir?'

Grenville's shoulders lifted slightly.

'Others, far higher than their lordships, will have the disposal of him. Be sure of that.' He turned and regarded him steadily. 'And what of you, Bolitho? Do you have plans?'

Adam was on his feet without realizing it. 'Another ship, sir.' Like all those others in that waiting room. Refusing to admit any doubt.

Grenville looked at a clock on the mantel as it chimed delicately. He pulled out his watch, as if it were a signal. The clerk had risen from the desk and his eyes were on the door.

Grenville smiled, but his eyes gave nothing away.

'I heard that you intend to be married?'

16

'I— am hoping—' He stared down as Grenville seized his hand. The fingers were like iron.

'*Then do it*. Bless you both.' He turned away. 'Be patient, Bolitho. A ship will come.'

The door was open, and instinct told him another visitor was waiting for an audience with this man, so frail and so powerful. Always on call to the First Lord himself; he would forget this meeting before that clock chimed again.

He saw that Grenville had turned his back on the door and was looking directly at him. He could feel the force of his gaze like something physical.

He said, 'I hold a certain authority here in Admiralty. Some would describe it as influence. But I have never forgotten the truths that make a sailor.' He gestured around the room, dismissing it. 'To walk my own deck, to hear the wind's voice above and around me— nothing can or will replace that.' He shook his head, impatient or embarrassed. 'I had to *know*, Bolitho, to be certain. Now be off with you. The chief clerk will take care of your requirements.'

Adam was in the passageway, and some one was handing him his hat.

'This way, sir.' A different porter, and the door was shut. As if he had imagined it.

But the words lingered in his memory. *I had to know, to be certain.*

He touched the sword, pressing the weight of it against his hip. He did not see the same two officers turn as he passed them.

The old captain had seen all the faces of command. The blame and recrimination as well as the huzzas of triumph when an enemy's flag dipped through the smoke of battle. And when pride vanquished the doubt, and the fear.

He could still feel the iron grip on his hand. *Then do it!*

To see her again, to be with her. *Walk with me.*

It seemed to take an eternity before the chief clerk was satisfied. Questions, answers, papers that needed a signature. Then it was done. On his way to the entrance hall, he passed the main waiting room again.

All the chairs were stacked at one end, and two men were mopping the floor in readiness for another day. A door opened and slammed, but neither looked up from his work.

17

The doors of Admiralty were opened, and the air like ice. It was pitch dark on the street outside. But there were carriages, and men's voices passing the time of day. One would take him to Bethune's house.

But all he saw was the officer who had just emerged from the sealed room. The last interview of the day. One of many. . . . Perhaps after the long wait, he had been offered some hope. *How many times?*

Then suddenly he swung round and stared at Adam's uniform and the gold lace, caught momentarily in the light from the porters' lodge, and then, openly, at his face. Not envy. It was hate, like a raw wound.

'This way, Captain Bolitho!'

He followed the porter down the steps and into the cold darkness. Like a brutal warning. Something he would never forget.

The coachman jumped down from his box and lowered the step with a flourish.

''Ere we are, sir. 'Nother cold night, by the feel of it!'

Adam stamped his feet, looking up at the house. The coachmen employed by the Admiralty certainly knew their business: he would never have found his own way back to this place. Even so, it seemed to have taken far longer than his journey to Whitehall. Perhaps the coachman had taken a more indirect route, on the off-chance that his passenger might request some amusement after his day's dealings with their lordships.

It had been another world. Glimpses of a London he would never know: people standing around braziers in the street, waiting for their employers or merely for companionship. On one corner a whore, on another a tall, ragged man reciting poetry, or preaching, or perhaps singing. No one had appeared to be listening.

He felt for some coins, fumbling; he was more weary than he had thought. There were lights in most of the surrounding windows, but not at this house.

'Thank 'ee, sir!' The coachman's breath was like smoke in the lamplight. 'I 'ope we meet again!'

Adam turned as the front door swung open. He must have handed him more than he knew.

'Welcome back, sir! I was beginning to think you had been held up somewhere! Perhaps literally!'

It was Francis Troubridge, Bethune's young flag lieutenant, still impeccably dressed, his uniform as neat as when he had boarded the stage at Portsmouth.

There was something odd about the house, though; something wrong. Baggage in the entrance hall, still covered with a waterproof sheet.

He swung round and saw Jago emerging from the shadows beneath the great, curving staircase, grim-faced, eyes steady. Anticipating the worst and ready for it.

'No squalls, Cap'n?' And then, reading his expression, 'I *knew* it, an' I told 'em as much!'

They shook hands, a hard grip, as if to settle something. Like those other times, when even survival had been in doubt.

'No ship yet, Luke. But no squalls either.'

Troubridge watched and listened and made a mental note of it. The captain and his coxswain; but it went far deeper than that. He had learned a lot. He was still learning.

Adam was looking up the stairs.

'It's very quiet. Where is everybody?'

Troubridge said, 'Sir Graham has gone. To join Lady Bethune. . . . It was all very sudden.'

Adam rubbed his cheek with his knuckles. Not like their arrival: Bethune had slammed through the house as if fired by some demonic energy, barking instructions and questions at Troubridge or his frog-like secretary and rarely waiting for a reply from either. More like the vice-admiral Adam had come to know and not the moody, despairing man, often the worse for drink, who had spent most of his time in his own quarters during *Athena*'s final passage to Portsmouth.

'Did he leave word for me? I am relieved of duty until further orders, but he must have known that.'

'He knew.' Troubridge bit his lip. 'Lady Bethune left before him. I thought she was pleased at the turn of events.'

Adam sat down on a carved, uncomfortable chair, and thought of the slight, white-haired Grenville. *Some would describe it as influence.*

He looked directly at the flag lieutenant.

'Forgive me. I intended to ask. What will you do?'

19

Troubridge looked vaguely around the gracious hallway.

'I am going to visit my father. He will doubtless know soon enough what has happened.'

So many memories. Troubridge, the aide who so adroitly fended off any problem or difficulty that might trouble his superior, any day, at any hour. And the Troubridge who had become a true friend in so short a time. Here, in London, when he had been at Adam's side as they had burst into that sordid studio where Lowenna was fighting off an attack. Jago had been with them. What had Sir Richard called his closest friends and companions? *My little crew.* Or as he had heard another describe them, *We Happy Few.*

Troubridge had referred to 'my father'. He was Admiral Sir Joseph Troubridge, well known and respected in the navy. A veteran of The Saintes and the Glorious First of June, as a lieutenant he had been a friend of the young Horatio Nelson. And now he was leaving the Navy List to take up a prestigious appointment with the Honourable East India Company, 'John Company' as it was nicknamed.

Troubridge's future would be in safe hands.

But like the Admiralty waiting room, it was no solution.

Troubridge smiled for the first time.

'I will let you know. I once asked that you might accept my service in the future, if there was any chance.'

Adam gripped his arm.

'You will always be my friend, Francis. Be sure of that. And Lowenna's, too.'

A door opened and Tolan appeared in the hallway.

He said to Troubridge, 'Your carriage is here, sir,' but he was looking at Bolitho. 'I have already had your things taken down.'

Troubridge sighed.

'They are closing the house, Captain Bolitho. Sir Graham will no longer be staying in London, I fear.' He added briskly, the flag lieutenant again, 'You are leaving tomorrow. I had word from Whitehall. I wish you Godspeed and good fortune.' And to Jago, 'Keep a weather eye on the Captain, will you?'

They shook hands again.

'Until the next horizon, Francis.'

They heard the sharp clatter of wheels, and Adam imagined

20

the eyes at other windows along this quiet street.

Jago said, 'There'll be some grub soon, Cap'n. You must be fair starvin'.'

Adam turned from the door. Troubridge had been waiting for him. In case he was needed.

He saw that Tolan was still standing by the stairs.

'When are you joining Sir Graham?' He must be truly drained. Otherwise he would have understood.

Jago said harshly, 'The vice-admiral's *lady* told him to sling his hook! That's the bald truth of it!'

Tolan said, 'I can deal with it.'

Adam sat again. The floor had shifted like a heaving deck, and his legs had almost buckled beneath him.

It was over. He tested each thought before it took shape. *Tomorrow I will go home. To Falmouth. To Lowenna. If. . . .* He stopped it right there.

'I would relish something to drink, if you please. To swallow today's doubts, and the regrets.' He paused. 'If you care for it, Tolan, we can make you welcome at Falmouth.'

Jago was nodding, unsmiling. Tolan could only stare at him with incomprehension, his normal composure shaken.

Then he said, 'I'll make sure you never regret it.'

Jago had recognized the signs.

'I'll go with him, an' bear a hand.'

Adam barely heard him. He would fall asleep here and now unless he took a grip of himself.

So quiet. No call to arms, no rattle of drums and stampede of running feet. The knot twisting in your stomach. And the fear you could never show when you were most needed.

He touched the letters inside his coat. Spoke her name.

He knew that somehow she would hear him.

2

Alive Again

The girl named Lowenna winced as her hip jarred against a small table, but she made no sound. She was more aware of the silence, and the floor that was like ice under her bare feet. She could not even remember getting out of bed, and yet her whole body was shivering, and she knew it was not only the cold.

The room was in complete darkness, and yet she thought she could discern the outline of a window, which had not been visible before. *Before when?* Nancy Roxby, Adam's aunt, had stayed with her for most of the day, making sure she was not alone even for a walk along the headland, where the wind off Falmouth Bay had been like a whetted knife.

She composed herself, running her fingers through her long hair to free it from beneath the thick shawl, which she did not recall taking from the chair.

The house was quiet. Still, as if it were listening. She pulled the shawl closer and felt her heart under her hand. Still beating too fast. The end of a nightmare: *the* nightmare. But why now? The long struggle was over. With the care and persistence of her guardian, she had won, although she shuddered now at the memory of pain and brutal violation, her pleas and screams only inciting worse attacks. Sometimes she seemed to hear her father's voice, sobbing and imploring them to stop, as if he were the victim.

She walked toward the window, her feet soundless, calming her mind as she had taught herself to do. Nothing could soil this day. Adam was arriving in Falmouth. *Today.* It was not a dream, or some cherished hoard of memories, it was real. Now.

She untied a cord and dragged open the heavy draperies. It was still dark, with only a hint of grey to distinguish the land from the sky. Not even a star, nor had there been when she had crossed to this window during the night. *Or did I dream that, too?*

What was Nancy doing, she wondered. She had been born here, in the old Bolitho house, the daughter of another naval captain. She gripped the cord until it hurt her fingers. *Like Adam.* Nancy, always busy with the affairs of her own estate, and much of the time with this one. She had two grown children and two grandchildren, who lived somewhere in London. Her husband, the formidable Lewis Roxby, was dead, but she seemed unbreakable. A gentle woman, but firm when necessary, she was nearly sixty years old, and always surprised that she could still turn a man's head when she passed.

Lowenna found a handle and carefully forced open the window. There was no wind, but the air took her breath away and touched her hair like frost. As if she were naked.

She closed it, but not before she had heard a voice below the wall around the drive from the stables. They were up and about, preparing for the arrival of the Bolitho carriage. How did they know? The roads in February could be treacherous, even though Young Matthew, as they still called the senior coachman, was said to know them better than any one.

Adam would be collected from an inn on the outskirts of Truro. She shivered again. Perhaps not far from the Old Glebe House, where she had posed for Sir Gregory Montagu and found her courage and her pride again. And where life had changed, when Adam had been directed through Montagu's big, untidy studio. It had been fate: good fortune or destiny, who could tell? And how much of those two years since their meeting had they shared? Weeks, or only days? Now was not the time to reckon them.

She found the lantern near the door and opened its shutter. It was not much of a light; somebody would deal with it later. Like everything else in this house.

When would she stop being merely a visitor here and become a part of it? Like the midshipman who had once been Adam's servant. He was here now, and this was his only home. Or did he still regard it as a refuge? *Like me.*

Most of the time this house was empty but for those who

cared for it, and the ghosts of vanished Bolithos whose portraits lined the landing and hung in the fine old study. And the latest portrait of Adam, who was adamantly not a ghost, gazing from the canvas throughout the months of his long absence, wearing the yellow rose on his uniform coat. *My rose . . .* Montagu had asked for her advice: the portrait had not been quite right, not to his satisfaction. They had discussed it, and together they had found what was lacking: that elusive smile. Now it *was* Adam.

She glanced at the window again. Brighter? Yes. She allowed herself to smile. Not a dream. He was coming home. *And I am not afraid.*

If only Montagu had lived to see and share her hopes and happiness, but he had never recovered from the terrible injuries suffered in the fire which had destroyed the Old Glebe House. The Last Cavalier, Adam had called him. Always alert, dedicated, and passionate. Ageless, with his neat, rakish beard; even the paint-daubed smock he usually wore could never conceal his courtly charm. It was so easy to imagine a rapier replacing the brush.

She had been his ward, and he had saved her life. *After I tried to end it.*

She thought of the last time she had been with Adam, at the old boatyard where Montagu had often gone when he wanted to work on a painting undisturbed. They had been alone, and became the lovers in fact that they had been in name.

I was not afraid.

She could hear Montagu's voice, almost the last words he had spoken to her before the doctors had turned her away.

Destiny, my girl. Fate.

How many times had she clung to those dying words.

She heard some one whispering outside the door, the clink of glass or metal. It was time.

'Thank you, Gregory. So much.' She could see him clearly, turning from a new canvas, a quizzical smile above the jaunty beard. The Last Cavalier.

Nancy, Lady Roxby, waited until the doors had closed behind her and held out her arms, her eyes shining with pleasure and emotion.

24

'It is so good to see you, Adam!' She hugged him, imagining the smell of the sea on his clothing, her face cold against his. 'You must be tired out!'

Adam released her and looked at the girl, still standing in the arched entrance, surprised and a little unnerved by the warmth of the welcome.

It had been mid-morning when the carriage, with Young Matthew on the box, had swung around the curved drive and pulled up beneath the leafless trees. 'Grand to have you home again, Captain Bolitho!' His cold-reddened face had split into a grin, and other figures had appeared as if to a signal. Some Adam knew only by sight. Others had always been part of his life, like old Jeb Trinnick, who had been in charge of the Bolitho stables as long as any one in the family could recall. And there were faces he did not recognize, and some far older than when he had last seen them.

In this mood it had been overwhelming, although he should have been prepared for it. A Bolitho was back from the sea.

Smiles, shouts of greeting, others running to calm the horses. And Nancy leading the way, smiling, close to tears as he had known she would be. And then he saw Lowenna at the foot of the steps.

Less than a year: only a dog watch, the deepwater Jacks would say, but not to those who were always left behind.

He had held her, his hands on her waist, how long he did not know. As if they had been quite alone. She had turned her head very slightly and he had felt her shiver, or brace herself as she said, 'I've waited. . . .'

He bent to kiss her cheek, but she had turned her face suddenly, and he had kissed her mouth. Like that other time. . . . *Let them think what they like.*

And now they were here. Some one was whistling; the carriage was moving away from the entrance. He heard a dog barking somewhere and a girl laughing, cut off sharply as if admonished by one of her superiors.

Lowenna unfastened the cloak from her shoulders. It was the same old boat cloak, cleaned and patched a few times. All those vigils along the headland or a beach somewhere, watching for the first sign of a ship. *The* ship.

He said, 'There's so much. . . .'

She reached out and touched his lips. 'Hold me.' She let her arms fall. 'Just hold me.'

Nancy watched them and then turned away, her heel catching on her own cloak, which she had thrown in the direction of a chair. 'I must do a few things. I've arranged your room.'

She picked it up. Neither of them had heard her. She was moved, and disturbed also, that she could still feel envy and loneliness.

When she glanced back, Adam's arms were around Lowenna without apparent pressure or insistence. One of the girl's hands clenched slightly into a fist, and she knew that he was stroking her hair.

There was a tang of woodsmoke in the cold air: fresh fires being lit. Nancy rubbed her eyes. She was *not* going to cry, not today.

The old house would be alive again.

Luke Jago stood back from the chair and wiped the scissor blades on a cloth.

'There, smart as paint. Good enough for an admiral.' He grinned. 'One on 'alf pay, anyways!'

David Napier glanced across at the old desk, where the chair he had been occupying usually stood. It had been replaced by a larger version, more accommodating to Daniel Yovell's portly shape. Even the desk seemed to have changed, with all the familiar ledgers and accounts but some leather-bound files as well, and a neat pile of dockets weighted with a large conch shell.

Even now, if a floorboard creaked or a door banged open, Napier still expected to see Bryan Ferguson, the one-armed steward of the estate.

Jago was dusting hairs from his sleeve.

'Better get yer shirt on. I seen a lad breakin' ice at the pump just now.'

Napier smiled. It was something to say, to help him in his own hard fashion. Jago could read your thoughts, if you let him.

It was stifling in the estate office, and the stove was roaring like a furnace. Even the cat, which was usually close by, had apparently found it unendurable.

He regarded himself in the spotted mirror that hung over a bookcase. His skin was still brown from the Caribbean sun. He balanced, tentatively, on the wounded leg, and tried to take his weight evenly on both, as the surgeon had insisted.

'Thank you. It looks fine.'

'A good seaman can turn 'is wits to anythin', given the chance.'

Napier could hear the surgeon again. *It could have been much worse.* That was probably what they had told Ferguson when they had taken off his arm at The Saintes.

It was sometimes impossible to remember the order of things. *Audacity* reeling under the bombardment of the great guns invisible on the shore. The captain cut down, and the deck exploding around them as the heated shot turned the lower hull into hell. Men dying, others still standing to their guns, until they had no escape but the sea.

He heard some one call out, and the clatter of wheels. Yovell had gone down to speak with one of the local carters. He seemed able to deal with everything: an admiral, a captain, and now a Cornish estate. He felt his hair again. *Good enough for an admiral.* And so it was. He was happy to be back with Jago after his brief service in the frigate: Jago, who hated officers. Jago, who had insisted on taking him out to join. . . .

Jago was at the window. 'Lot of new faces since we paid off *Unrivalled*. The Cap'n'll be thinkin' as much, I reckon.' He turned. 'Th' big day today, eh? Th' Cap'n an' his lady will be on their way to see the G—' He had been about to say 'God bosun'. 'Preacher, round about now.'

Napier pulled on his shirt, and saw the coat with its white collar patches lying across a chest. Twelve days since he had arrived here, with the wound reopened and the former cavalryman bandaging it in the carriage. *It could have been so much worse.*

He had never known such a welcome. They had even given him his own room, which looked out across fields. *You've seen quite enough of the sea for a while, my lad!*

Except when he slept, and the stark, flaming nightmare came back. He had not served in *Audacity* long enough to know many of her people, but, as always, her captain stood out. Twenty-eight years old, 'the same age as my ship', he had said.

27

A good officer, with a quick eye for efficiency or otherwise, but never preoccupied or too superior to offer advice or solve some problem. They had died together.

And now Captain Bolitho was going to the church with the girl with the long dark hair. Beautiful. . . . He could not have put it into words, or told any one. That first night in the room, she had come to him, soothed him as she might have calmed a child, driving away the shame he had felt as he had awakened screaming from a ship exploding, masts falling in flames like broken wings.

She had whispered, 'I understand.' And backed away, her last words lingering. 'I understand. Our secret.'

Napier had been there when the captain had arrived home, had stood and watched with all the others and seen him reach out for her. She had looked directly at the midshipman. Perhaps in some strange way, they had helped one another. *Our secret.*

Jago was saying, 'You'll have to look yer best, see. There's to be some sort of Up Spirits for all hands tonight.'

Jago never used his name, and had only called him 'mister' in front of others on the long passage from Antigua to Plymouth. Was the barrier, the old resentment, still lying in wait?

'What will *you* do?'

He shrugged. 'Oh, me an' old Dan Yovell will likely have a glass or two. Mrs. Ferguson,' a slight hesitation, 'Grace'll serve up somethin' extra grand just for us.'

It needed no words. They had only met Bryan Ferguson a few times, in welcome or farewell. Always here. He thought of *Audacity*'s captain, and the others he had seen put over the side. At least Grace had been with her man almost to the very end.

In his mind he saw the girl with the long dark hair. She would be a sailor's wife. Would she be comparing their lives?

He heard Yovell's voice and that of some one else, and a horse being led across the cobbles.

The door banged open, the air bitter.

The newcomer was tall, erect, authoritative. Napier recalled seeing him once or twice before. Not young, but one who took care of his appearance.

28

'God, it's like a bakehouse in here!' He laughed. 'Sorry to disturb you!'

Yovell closed the door quietly and padded to the desk. 'This is Mr. Flinders, from the Roxby estate. We lend one another a hand from time to time.' He frowned slightly, allowing the gold spectacles to drop on to his nose. 'This shouldn't take long.'

Flinders glanced at the hair clippings around the chair.

'Not very ship-shape, I'd say!' He laughed again, too loudly. 'Don't this lad have work to do?'

Yovell opened his mouth but said nothing as Jago reached over to pick up the jacket, and held it across Napier's shoulders.

'Why don't you ask *him*?'

Flinders stared at Jago and then at the white patches.

'Of course— sir. I was forgetting— so much on my mind at present.' Like magic, Napier thought; the strong teeth, the grin, was back.

Yovell pursed his lips.

'I have the details of the slate delivery. We can save money, by my estimation.'

Flinders bobbed his head. 'Course. Good thinking. There are bound to be changes on both estates. I shall always be on hand to help if I'm needed.'

He looked at Jago. 'You're Captain Bolitho's man, right?'

Jago seemed to relax.

'His cox'n. *Right?*'

Flinders peered out of the window as a horse was led back across the stable yard.

'I must go, er, Daniel. Thought I should come by. You'll need all the help you can get with a new *lady* in the house.' He ducked his head to Napier. 'And good day to you, young sir.' He turned his back on Jago and strode out of the office.

Jago breathed out slowly.

'Wouldn't trust that one within half a cable of a woman I cared about!' He shook his head at Yovell as if he might dispute it. 'Ashore or afloat. His sort's always the same when women are on hand. Like a rat up a pump!'

Yovell looked meaningly at Napier and made a point of shuffling his papers.

'You've made an enemy of that one, Luke. But you already know that.'

Jago touched the midshipman's jacket again.

'Let's go an' test that leg o' yours. We need some fresh air anyways after that little lot!'

Napier looked back from the door and found Yovell's eyes on him, a fresh quill neatly grasped in his teeth, outwardly shocked by Jago's crude comment. Disapproving.

But he winked.

They stood side by side, very aware of the silence, the only sound their steps in the aisle as they walked from the main doorway. The sky had cleared during the morning, right across the bay. So bright that here in the chill of the parish church of King Charles the Martyr it took time to distinguish shadow from substance. Light filtered from the arched windows and reflected on the ranks of pews, and burnished the great cross and candlesticks on the high altar.

In one of the chapels faded banners and flags were on display, mementoes of old ships and the men who had fought them. Lowenna had told him of the time she had been here with Nancy and by chance they had met Thomas Herrick, his uncle's oldest friend. What twist of fate had brought them together?

And the pew where Lowenna had been sitting on that other day, their hands daring to touch, with no one to warn or discourage. When they had driven back to the old house, and his recall to duty had been waiting.

And the day when this same church had been packed to overflowing, to remember and to mourn Falmouth's most famous son, Sir Richard Bolitho. The flags had been dipped, while out at her anchorage the frigate *Unrivalled . . . my ship* . . . had fired a salute. Catherine had been beside him.

Adam touched her hand and felt her pull off the glove, her fingers warm and responsive. No words. Because they had been together so little, some would say. Or maybe there were none adequate for this moment.

Then he turned and looked at her, her hair catching the colours of the light from the stained glass, her dark eyes still in shadow. He heard the rustle of paper, a muffled cough. This great church, so much a part of Falmouth, was never empty. Just a few anonymous shapes, bowed heads seeking some peace, or respite from everyday events. From life itself.

She was dressed in pale grey today, a soft, loose gown, reminding him of their first meeting. Doubt, uncertainty; perhaps they had both been afraid.

He said, 'I *love* you, Lowenna.'

Her fingers moved in his. 'Are we truly here?'

Only a whisper, but one of the bowed heads lifted and cleared its throat.

'So much I want to say. . . .'

Somewhere overhead, in another world, a clock began to chime.

Suppose something goes wrong? She might still change her mind.

They had scarcely been alone together. So many things to be done, and for the sake of appearances, as Nancy had said. She had made light of it, but she meant it.

Lowenna would be thinking about it, with so many reminders of the past on every hand. Famous names, great events, proud as well as tragic, but always the inevitable sadness.

He thought of all the ships he had known. Each one had taken a part of him, and remained a part of him. What would *she* have? Glances, rumours? Like a cutlass on the stone, every version of the story would sharpen with retelling. He reached out and held her shoulders, so that they faced each other. He felt resistance, uncertainty, but before he could speak she whispered, 'Take me, Adam. I don't care. . . .'

They both turned as the voice boomed out of nowhere, like an echo.

'Can you forgive me for keeping you waiting? Time is always at a premium when we most cherish it.'

A big man with bushy white eyebrows, who took their arms in his and turned them toward a door by the chapel, as if, Adam thought, they had been friends for years.

'So let us not waste it, shall we? We will sit a while, and we can consider our options, eh?'

He guided them into a small, spartan room, not unlike the cell at the Admiralty.

The senior curate was bluff, outspoken and forthright.

Nancy had warned him that he might be surprised. This church had had the same rector for over twenty years, but to her knowledge he had never once visited Falmouth. A good and reliable curate was, however, always on hand.

He was saying, 'I have read your letter, Captain Bolitho, and Lady Roxby has kept me fully informed of the circumstances and your proposed marriage. A very good woman, never too busy to offer her assistance for the benefit of our parish.'

He leaned back in the chair, his fingers interlaced across his stomach. Outwardly unconcerned, but Adam sensed that he missed very little.

'The last commission was cut short. I am awaiting orders. . . .'

One hand lifted slightly. 'Your recent exploits are well known. Many would suggest you might expect, even demand some release from duty. We are at peace now. But we must never allow ourselves to become complacent or unwary again.' The massive eyebrows wrinkled. 'We in the Church must also stand to our guns, as it were, and be ready.' He stared up at the arched ceiling and intoned, ' "God and the Navy we adore/ When danger threatens, but not before." ' And chuckled. 'I don't recall who said that, but it is still, sadly, true.'

He looked intently at Lowenna, and then at Adam.

'I cannot promise an early wedding, but I will do what I can. This church is always open if you need help or comfort. I shall send word when we are able to confirm a date.' He gestured to some small, velvet-covered books. 'We will join in prayer before you go.'

The bell was ringing somewhere overhead, and there were whispering voices outside the door, and echoes from the body of the church.

The curate held out his hand.

'A pleasure, Captain. I would have spoken to you before, at Sir Richard's memorial service, but my time was not my own.'

The handshake, like the smile, was genuine. How had he managed to remember, and mark him out? So long ago, and among so many people. He watched the big hands take Lowenna's.

'I hope we shall meet again very soon. Love is not always

32

the most patient of messengers.' He nodded. 'I knew Sir Gregory Montagu quite well.' Adam saw her tense, her chin lifting slightly, as if she were suddenly on guard. 'Sometimes our views and concepts were at odds, but he was a man among men. Sorely missed.'

Adam heard her murmur something and wanted to interrupt, but when he saw her face he knew there was no need. She said quietly, 'He saved my life. Now I know why.'

They stood outside the little chapel and looked along the nave. Nothing had changed; only the sunlight had shifted.

They began to walk slowly down the aisle, toward the entrance, where Francis was waiting.

There would be people coming to the house this evening, some strangers, curious or with minds already biased. She gripped his arm. Her eyes were no longer in shadow, and she was smiling with a radiance he had not seen before.

She reached up to touch his face.

'Take me home, Adam.' Three figures walked past, stepping aside to avoid them. They could have been invisible. 'Time is an obstacle. It is not an enemy.'

Francis had the carriage door open and watched them coming down the steps. It was going to be a long day, but he would tell his wife all about it when he got home, if she was still awake.

He was aware of some passers-by who had stopped to stare or smile. She looked so much the radiant bride.

Together.

3

A Name to Remember

Rear-Admiral Thomas Herrick walked slowly across the familiar entrance hall, and then hesitated as if to reassure himself. Somehow it was different from the picture he had fixed in his mind. A fire was burning brightly and to one side he saw a half-opened door. The library, shelved books rising from floor to ceiling. And beyond that, the curving staircase. The portraits.

He turned. 'I'm sorry, my dear. What did you say?'

He remembered the servant who had ushered him through the front door. A round, open face: a local girl with a poise that marked her as one of Grace Ferguson's assistants.

'Lady Roxby is not here, sir.' She seemed to know the time, although he saw no clock. 'She'm due back directly. If you would care to sit a while, I can fetch you something.'

Herrick jammed his hat beneath his arm and saw her eyes rest on his pinned-up sleeve. It never failed; so why did he still resent it?

'A drink, perhaps?' She shifted from one foot to the other. 'A dish of tea, maybe?'

He ventured, 'Some ginger beer? The last time I was here. . . .'

Her smile widened immediately. 'You be easy, sir. I recollect when you last came.' She gestured toward another room, facing the sea. 'You'll be snug in there.'

'Thank you, Jenna, that would suit very well. I'm sorry to intrude without warning.' But she had already gone, pleased to be doing something, and that he had recalled her name.

Something else he had learned over the years. *It is sometimes all they have.*

He looked toward the portraits, remembering who had taught him that.

He walked to the other room and halted by the door. Like an intruder. He should have sent word, or been here last night, when other guests had been invited. Maybe he should leave now, go back to The Spaniards where he had left his baggage after the journey from St. Austell. Less than half the distance from Plymouth, but it had felt longer. He thought suddenly of the conference he had been asked to attend. Asked? There had been no choice. But it had been an opportunity to keep abreast of naval affairs, perhaps the last he would get.

He had found himself at a big house on an estate near St. Blazey. They were all senior officers, or had been; most of them seemed to be retired. They had met to discuss the merits of reallocating work from naval dockyards to local, civilian contractors. With their lordships' blessing, it might become a matter for Parliament. *Might.*

Suppose Nancy had already forgotten or withdrawn her offer concerning the management of the estates. She had made light of it. *Like running a ship. You will soon get the feel of things.* Like Ferguson, who had taken to it instinctively, and the portly Yovell. Ashore or afloat, he always seemed able to rise to every challenge.

He retraced his steps across the hall and stood staring at the newest portrait. Adam, illegitimate son of Hugh Bolitho and Kerenza Pascoe. Roll back the years and it might have been Richard. Something in the expression, but not the dark eyes. How was Adam facing up to his own future? Two ships taken from him, *Unrivalled* and now *Athena*. How could any serving captain accept it?

He glanced up the stairs. He knew this house well, had been a guest here in the past. Its silence was heavy with memory. Adam's place was at sea. Until. . . . He recalled the men who had sat at the conference table with him. Complacent, even condescending. Impossible to compare with others he had known, and had fought beside, regardless of the odds, or the rights or wrongs of the cause.

'Here you are, sir.' She was back, with a tankard balanced on a tray.

Ginger beer. What would they have had to say about that in the kitchen?

He would have to sit and think it all over again. There was nobody else now to consider.

Her memory was never far away. His Dulcie. . . . In his mind he often saw them together. He sighed a little, and his hand moved as if to brush some dust from his uniform, except that he was no longer wearing the King's coat. Dulcie had died of fever when he had been at sea; she had been nursing prisoners of war. He picked up the tankard and gazed at it. Always the link. Adam had been the one who had carried the word of Dulcie's death to him, just as he himself had carried the news to Richard that his first wife had been killed with their unborn child.

'He's in here, sir.'

Herrick swung round, caught off guard, angry that he had allowed the past to distract him.

A man stood by the study door, looking toward him; the girl Jenna was hovering nearby.

A heavy jacket with shoulder-capes, and riding boots, one mud-streaked. Not young, not old. Herrick thought he was mistaken, but there was something familiar about his face.

He strode across the polished floor.

'Rear-Admiral Herrick? So glad I was in time.' He held out his hand, then paused to wipe it on his breeches. 'I'm James Roxby. My mother told me you might be paying her a visit. Hoped you would.' The palm was hard, and Herrick could see the likeness now, the same gestures, the confidence. He was looking at the tankard and the girl explained, 'Ginger beer, sir.'

'After that ride, I think I'll venture something stronger!'

They laughed.

Herrick wondered why he had not remembered. It was not like him. James Roxby was a highly respected surgeon in London. Nancy had joked about it, saying her son occasionally came down to the West Country on a pilgrimage, or to escape his patients.

'I hear that you have only just arrived.' He did not wait for

36

an answer. 'Some one taken your things? This is no way to greet an honoured guest!'

Herrick said, 'I left them at the inn. I didn't know. . . .' He broke off, feeling like a fool. What had he expected?

'Somebody will go and get them.' Head on one side, and Herrick could see him in his professional role without effort. Then he nodded. 'She's coming now. She'll get you settled.' He almost grinned. 'My mother gives all the orders around here!'

He turned. 'Comfortable, are you?' He did not look at the empty sleeve. There was no need.

But Nancy was here, her eyes moving between them.

'Thomas, this is a lovely surprise!' She tossed a bag on to a chair, and a parcel to the beaming Jenna. 'We were very concerned!'

Herrick made to take her hand but she gripped his shoulder and turned her face toward him. 'Makes it simply perfect.' He kissed her cheek, and she laughed. 'For me, in any case!'

Herrick watched her, her smile, the warmth he had never forgotten.

'I'm sorry I missed the reception for Adam . . .' He faltered. 'And Lowenna.'

She shrugged. 'You would have hated it. *They* were wonderful, but I expect it was an ordeal for them.' She sat, facing him. 'And what of you, Thomas?' She was leaning forward, her eyes never leaving his. 'You are looking so well— we'll not let you escape so easily this time!'

Herrick said, rather stiffly, 'I am finished with active service. I might be offered some temporary appointments, but. . . .' It was nobody's concern. *Except my own.*

But she was laughing, one hand to her mouth, shaking her head.

'So sorry, Thomas, *dear* Thomas! I remembered what you said to me when we last met!' She shook her head again. '*I can pay my way*, do you remember saying that?' She calmed herself with an effort. 'I loved you for it!'

Her son stood up. 'I'll arrange to have the gear collected from—' His eyebrows went up. 'The Spaniards, wasn't it?'

Herrick saw the mask slip, heard the keen, incisive voice. The surgeon again. No wonder sailors feared them. Hated

37

them. There was no one else to blame, not when you were pinned on your back, helpless, waiting for the blade.

But he felt his mouth lift into an unaccustomed smile. It had been so long. Nothing else mattered.

'I've never forgotten it, Nancy.' Like hearing somebody else.

She dabbed her eyes with a lace handkerchief.

'Adam and Lowenna are down at the waterfront. They'll be back soon.' She laughed. 'It's *perfect*!'

More voices, this time Grace Ferguson, one hand holding a bunch of keys. Straight-backed, smiling at him. Altered in some way, but otherwise as he remembered her whenever they had met.

She said, 'Good to have you with us, sir. Like old times.'

They must all believe that.

Then they were alone together and Nancy said softly, 'We shall make them *better*, Thomas. No more heartbreaks— it's never too late.' She examined his face, feature by feature. 'Don't mind James. Sometimes even he can forget he is a surgeon and be human again. Until his fingers start itching for his saw.'

Grace Ferguson paused to rearrange something below the stairs, and listened to their sudden laughter.

She remembered when Herrick had first come here, to this house. The young lieutenant with blue, blue eyes and an uncertain frown. And *she* had been even younger than the girl Jenna.

She thought of the empty sleeve, and began to search abruptly through her keys. There was no value in looking back.

Adam held Lowenna's arm while some fishermen trundled a barrow loaded with tangled nets along the jetty. It was always busy here, boats being unloaded by hand under the sharp eye of local buyers, and a few larger craft using tackle to shift their cargoes directly ashore. Not very different from when he had first seen it as a youth, and he had always remembered it.

She smiled, face fresh in the cold salt breeze, eyes bright with interest and excitement. Sharing it with him, unconcerned or unaware of the attention from idlers and labourers alike.

But he tightened his grip as two men with arms linked, obviously full to the scuppers, as Luke Jago would have said, lurched aside with elaborate respect as they passed.

'Greetin's, Captain, an' yer lovely lady!'

Lowenna said, 'The deck looks very lively today.'

The two seamen stared at her and then fell laughing in each other's arms. There were grins and nods throughout the crowd.

Adam murmured, 'You are wonderful. For a second, I thought. . . .'

But she was shading her eyes against the hard light, the moment already past as she watched a vessel moving slowly clear of others moored close by.

'Your world, Adam. And I want to be part of it.' She laughed as some gulls swooped down on a few fishheads thrown on the water. 'Look, they're happy, too.'

When she looked at him again her face was serious.

'I saw you watching that ship. A brig, isn't she?'

'Yes, she is. Clever of you. Most people would not know.'

But she did not smile.

'I saw it in your eyes. An understanding. Almost . . . a hunger.' She thrust some of her hair under her cloak. 'Am I right?'

He stared across the choppy water. The brig was already under way, topsails and jib filling slightly to the brisk offshore wind. Too far out to hear the sounds of a vessel coming alive, the squeal and clatter of blocks, the measured stamp of bare feet. But he could have been there on her deck.

He said, 'Small and handy, fourteen guns. Very like *Firefly*, my first command. She taught me all I know.' He took her arm again, unconsciously. 'And you *are* a part of it. Since that day. . . .' A great chorus of laughter mixed with jeers scattered his thoughts, and he saw a group of onlookers pointing or gesturing toward the brig, shaking their heads in disgust.

'What is it, Adam?'

I should have known. Been prepared. The time of year did not matter, nor the weather. There were always the old hands, men who had once served in ships of war, and now were unable to stay away from the life which had brutally rejected them. Missing an arm or a leg, permanently scarred, there was not a whole man amongst them.

39

There was a distant squawk from the brig's speaking trumpet, doubtless her first lieutenant yelling threats at a small boat carelessly pulling across the bows. It was common enough in confined waters. But somehow a necessary reminder to survivors like these.

'That showed 'em, eh, Cap'n?' More laughs, and hostility too. It was different at sea. So different. The risk and the danger were ever present. The toast to 'absent friends' was supposed to soften the harsh reality.

He could feel her hand on his arm, very still, like a small creature, listening, waiting.

He said, 'We'll walk to the end of the jetty now that we've come this far.' Suppose they all stood firm. To prove something, take some cheap revenge.

'Everything in order, Captain Bolitho?'

Adam had not even seen them approach. Two uniforms, gilt buttons; one was wearing a sword. Authority, from the revenue cutter he had seen earlier when they had reached the waterfront.

'Thank you, yes.' He touched his hat and saw the other man respond. He felt her fingers tighten on his arm as he added, 'We are amongst friends here.'

They walked on, the way suddenly cleared. Nothing was said; there was only a smile or a brief nod of recognition here and there, and once a hand reached out as they passed.

'I shall not forget that, Adam.' She turned and looked at the moored vessels, and the brig, which was under more sail and leaning slightly on a new tack. 'And neither will they.'

Together they paused to look up the slope toward the town. The square tower of the church was just visible above the surrounding roofs.

Adam thought of the imposing curate and said, half to himself, 'God and the Navy we adore.'

She pressed his arm.

'I cannot wait. Is that so wrong?'

They walked back along the jetty. The onlookers had vanished.

Absent friends.

David Napier walked steadily toward the house, his feet

avoiding the loose cobbles by instinct; they were already familiar, after so short a time. He paused, noting the wind's direction as sunlight lanced off the Father Tyme weathervane. He had walked as far as the little coastguard cottage where a dog always rushed out to bark at him, and there had been no more pain in his leg. He had not even been out of breath. He had seen a few people on his way, most of whom he had come to recognize, or thought he did. It was wrong to pretend, deceive himself, but he could not help it. While he lived here, it was his home. His life.

It could have been so much worse. But every day it was getting better. He raised his foot and took his weight on it. Surely by now. . . .

'I 'eard tell you was up an' about when the cock crowed, young David. You'm missing walking that deck, my son!'

Old Jeb Trinnick was standing at an open stable door, a mug of something gripped in his hand. Tall and fierce-looking, with only one eye, he would take no arguments from any one. But this morning his habitual grimace seemed to be a smile.

A boy called something and he turned away, scowling now. 'Never gets a bloody minute!'

Napier smiled. Jeb Trinnick would have it no other way, from what he had seen and heard.

Perhaps it was the best way. When you were trying to forget, afraid of what might lie in wait. Crying out in the night, even here, where there was nothing to fear.

Our secret.

He had never known any one like her. Lowenna meant 'joy' in the old Cornish tongue.

What must it be like? Really like? When they were together. . . .

He looked up toward the windows of the estate office. Yovell never probed or asked questions, and might even be called secretive, but he cared enough about those he worked for. He could almost hear him saying it. *Otherwise, my boy, I wouldn't be here.*

It was warm in the office, but not the oven it had been when Jago had been acting the barber. The cat was back in its usual place, and Yovell was at his desk.

41

'Ah, here he is. Mister Midshipman Napier in person!' He said it lightly, but Napier was staring at the man with him, a courier, booted and spurred and dressed in a heavy riding coat. He must have ridden up to the house from the main road. 'He has a letter for you.'

He peered over the spectacles at the courier. 'And Mrs. Ferguson will no doubt give *you* something to keep out the cold.'

The courier grinned at Napier.

'I'd take kindly to that,' and walked to the door, spurs jingling, his duty done.

'A letter— for me?' He tried again. 'Is it— my mother?'

Yovell said kindly, 'Sit you down. It might be a mistake.' He slid the letter across the desk, his hand resting on it, as if to give him time. 'But it's addressed to you right enough.'

Napier took the letter and the knife he had always seen Yovell use, here and aboard *Unrivalled*. So long ago.

There were several addresses and directions, all scored out, the final one reading *In the care of Captain Adam Bolitho, Falmouth*.

Yovell said, 'Open it, David.' His spectacles had slipped, but he did nothing to adjust them. 'I shall be here.' He did not elaborate.

Napier slit open the envelope and pulled out the letter. His mind barely kept pace with the meaningless details, the lines of copperplate script and the remains of a broken seal. Like drops of blood. His hands were steady, but his mouth was completely dry.

My dear Mister Napier,

At the earliest opportunity it is my wish to speak with you in person, to offer my gratitude and heartfelt thanks for your courageous attempt to save the life of my only son Paul, after the loss of Audacity.

No written words can convey my true feelings when the news reached me of his death, and your determined efforts on his behalf.

Napier moved the letter; it was shaking, blurred. Tiny, unreal sounds intruded. A horse on the cobbles, a man

42

whistling, breaking off in a fit of coughing. His eyes fell to the foot of the page.

I look forward to the day of our meeting.
I am, believe me, yours sincerely,
Charles Boyce, Rear-Admiral.

'Drink this.' Yovell had come around the desk and was leaning over him.

Napier sipped at the glass and coughed, and felt Yovell's hand on his shoulder. A latch clicked and he heard him snap, 'Not now! Find somebody else!'

Perhaps that did more than anything to steady him. But his vision was still blurred. Like drowning.

He said, 'I didn't even know his name. He was Boyce, that was all I knew.'

Yovell's hand moved slightly. 'You are doing well.' He raised the glass again. 'And his father is a rear-admiral, no less.'

Napier hardly heard him. 'We never shared anything aboard *Audacity*. There were six of us in the gunroom. There was always trouble. . . .' He halted, shocked that all he could recall was hate. He touched his leg, without realizing that his hand had moved. The ship heeling over, explosions muffled and terrible as the sea burst into the hull. The screams, wild and unreal, others trying to cheer as *Athena* surged past, all her guns firing. Then the emptiness, drifting fragments, boats too far away to help. And through and above the smoke, sunlight touching the crest of a hill. Too far, too late. It was all he had.

He saw that Yovell was gazing at him, behind the desk once more.

'You've had quite a load to carry on your back, young David.' He gestured to the letter. 'Some I heard, some I guessed. And you, I know.' He gave his owlish smile. 'The rest can wait. But for the courier's untimely visit, you might never have received this. Not for a while, in any case.'

Napier said, 'I wondered why. . . .' and saw Yovell's irritation as more shouts came from the stables, and then Jeb Trinnick's harsher tone brought an instant silence.

Yovell folded the letter and pushed it discreetly across the desk. Then he said, 'It seems impossible to keep a secret in this place. The courier brought word to Captain Bolitho. It was his main purpose in coming, otherwise. . . .' He unlocked a drawer and dragged it out until it was pressed against his stomach. 'We will talk again soon. Together we shall think of a suitable response to Rear-Admiral Boyce.'

Napier saw the long, buff-coloured envelope, another, unbroken red seal.

He heard himself ask, 'Is he recalled?'

Yovell seemed preoccupied, patting his pockets.

'I do not expect *you* to betray a confidence.' He peered around for his hat. 'That was unfair, and uncalled for. . . . Stay a while, if you wish. This, I fear, must not wait. Damn their eyes!'

Napier watched him in an awed silence. Mild enough, but from Yovell it matched a hardened seaman's crudest oath.

The door slammed and there was silence. Napier folded the letter slowly and replaced it in the torn envelope. *He was a bully, a coward, and a liar.* Aloud or to himself, he neither knew nor cared. He thought of the dark-eyed girl who had tried to drive away those same bitter memories.

Our secret. Now she would be separated from the man who was her life. He thrust the letter into his coat.

Our captain. Nothing else mattered.

She sat in one of the high-backed, matching chairs, her hands clasped in her lap, only her eyes moving as Adam Bolitho strode restlessly about the study. The fire in the grate had all but died, but the door was closed; they would not be disturbed. Her cloak was still lying across the old chest by the window, where she had thrown it when they had arrived back from the harbour.

She had been expecting it, dreading it, but surely not so soon?

She said only, 'When?' and saw him twist the envelope in his hand. 'Is it a ship?'

He turned toward her, with the same expression she had seen when Yovell had brought the letter. And before that, when they had walked from the stable yard and the eyes had watched them pass. He had known then.

He took her hands in his and stooped to kiss her hair.

'I am required to report to Plymouth.' He looked away, fighting it. '*Again.*' A piece of charred wood fell amongst the ashes and he saw her eyes reflect the leaping flame. He thought of the letter, complete with its stamp and seal of Admiralty. It was not a command. *Upon receipt of these orders*, or *to proceed with all despatch*. Curt and to the point. You became used to such brevity; you were not expected to like it. This was unreal; he could see him, hear his voice. John Grenville, still listed as captain, secretary to the First Lord. Second only to God. Like another world, and yet he remembered him better than many he had known for years.

'I am ordered to attend a meeting with certain senior officers. Captain Grenville apologizes for the abruptness of this summons.' He saw the question in her eyes. 'That was stupid of me, Lowenna. You do not know him. He is already at Plymouth . . . his last active duty, to all accounts.' He was making no sense, and he gripped her hands as she rose from the chair. 'I wanted anything but this!'

She waited, giving herself time. This was their life, or would be.

'Down by the harbour, Adam, I told you I wanted to share it, be a part of it.' She put her arms around his shoulders. 'A part of *you.*'

They walked to the old chest, and Adam lifted her cloak so that she could read its carved inscription, the motto of the Bolitho family. *For My Country's Freedom.*

She murmured, 'Remember the curate, Adam. The second part. "When danger threatens, but not before."' She paused. 'And I'm prepared for that too, God help me, if need be.'

There were voices, perhaps guests. He said, 'We must tell my aunt.'

She had seen that look in his eyes when the little brig had been getting under way. The captain. A man apart.

He walked to the door, pausing once to glance back at the room, the books and the paintings. The past. He heard Grenville's voice again. *Be patient. A ship will come.*

She slipped her hand around his wrist, and the gold lace on his sleeve.

'I am ready.'

But as he held open the door, she touched her breast. It was as if her heart had stopped.

4

Yours to Command

The clerk held open the heavy door with one hand while he snatched a coat from a chair with the other.

'If you would wait here a moment, sir. I was told to conduct you directly you were announced.'

Adam Bolitho walked into the spacious room; it was as if nothing had changed. The same paintings, the great windows with their sweeping views across Plymouth Sound, and the narrow balcony where only the determined would brave the cold easterly wind. It only needed Valentine Keen, that youthful admiral, to make an appearance and the clock would turn right back to the year when Adam had taken command of *Unrivalled*.

'I will inform Sir John of your arrival.'

Adam turned abruptly, but the door was closed. He must have misheard, or the clerk was wrong. *Sir* John Grenville? He looked toward the table near the door, at the candle burning beside a pile of envelopes, the wax and official stamp ready for use. Documents of some importance. . . . The clerk was not likely to have made a mistake.

Restlessly he walked to one of the windows and touched the glass. He could feel it quivering to the thrust of the wind, the chill of the March forenoon. Not that you would know it inside the massive walls of Boscawen House, the admiral's residence. Even the candleflame was unflickering. He gazed out at the Sound and the open sea beyond, blue-grey like a shark, waiting, and found himself stretching to drive away the knots of tension, the ache of travel in the last two days. Bad roads and sleeplessness, even when Young Matthew had stopped at some forgettable inn in the middle of nowhere. Why should it be like this? It was his life, the only one he knew. He looked at the candle again: fresh, and only recently lit. Even the clerk had been caught unprepared, and tried to hide his heavy coat from view.

He moved slowly toward a mirror behind the big desk, where he had once seen Gilia, Keen's wife, primp for a moment before hurrying away to deal with one of their many visitors; pushed some loose hair from his forehead and tugged at his crushed neckcloth, his eyes pitiless, as if he were assessing some unreliable subordinate.

It had been different this time because of Lowenna, and because they had wanted it so.

He touched his lip; it felt bruised from the force and the pain of their last embrace. There was no mark.

He made himself return to the window, his back painfully straight. There was an expensive telescope mounted on a brass tripod beside the heavy curtains. When a man-of-war was about to make the final approach, and the guns boomed out in salute to the flag above this building, the admiral would be able to watch every change of tack or manoeuvre to the last moment. And every captain would know it. . . .

But there was only one sail moving today beyond the masts and crossed yards of anchored shipping. A heavy, low-hulled Dutchman, lee-boards lowered to hold steerage way in the lively breeze, her scuppers no doubt awash with the weight of her cargo. Carrying copper, clay, tin or local flint, and now heading for home; they were regular visitors to this southern coast, the war long forgotten.

He thought of the ragged figures on the Falmouth water-front, the grip of her fingers on his arm. Only three, four days ago. *They* would never forget.

'Bless you, Bolitho! Up with the lark, eh? And I thought I was an early riser. You've taken everybody aback!'

He strode across the room and seized both of Adam's hands in his. Hard and strong, despite their apparent frailness: exactly as Adam remembered him, heard him, when he had read his brief message to Lowenna.

'I must congratulate you, sir. I only just discovered—'

48

Grenville waved it aside. 'They only thought fit to inform *me* a few days ago. Proud moment, of course.' He looked briefly toward the window and the telescope. 'Another way of saying *you've run your course, we don't need you any more*. Not unexpected, but all the same. . . .' He faced him again, the momentary shadow gone from his face. 'You must be tired out with this constant bustle. Eaten anything yet?'

He glared as the door opened. The clerk had returned.

'I don't wish to be disturbed.' He gestured to the candle and the pile of envelopes. 'They can wait, all day if need be. Pass the word to the piermaster.'

The clerk bobbed his head. 'I must remind him about the boat, Sir John.'

Grenville retorted, 'The boat will *be there*.' The door closed. 'Many apologies, Bolitho, but time is an old enemy, pressing ever closer. I know that only too well.'

He smiled, and it transformed him. 'I have been thinking about you. Wondering if your lady will ever forgive me for dragging you away from her after so brief a reunion. But on this occasion there was no choice.' He reached out and touched the telescope, without seeing it, Adam thought. So full of energy and enthusiasm. How could he himself contain his true feelings, say that it had been like having a door slammed in his face? Worse. . . .

'She knows it was necessary, Sir John.'

The swift, penetrating glance again, which seemed to see and say so much. They had met only once, and his slight figure had been framed against another sky and the sprawling, smoky backdrop of London. And yet. . . .

Grenville said, 'All those ships lying out there, the flagship and other great liners. England's "sure shield", or so many of our leaders still believe.' He tapped the telescope. 'But times are changing, too fast for minds which will not progress. With the flagship's people alone I could crew three frigates— a whole *squadron* of frigates if I spread my net a little wider.' He sighed, and allowed his hands to fall at his sides. 'No more speeches, Bolitho. Do you know of the *Onward*?'

Adam shook his head. There was no point in pretending; Grenville could see right through you. Loved, admired or hated, his loss would be felt far beyond an empty desk at the Admiralty.

'I'm not surprised. You were too busy with your "skirmish", as you described it, to keep track of matters here.' He looked toward the sea, perhaps picturing her as he spoke. '*Onward*'s a new frigate, thirty-eight guns. Launched last year, private yard, brought here to Plymouth for completion, armament and—' He shook his head impatiently. 'You know chapter and verse when a new ship is commissioned. And there are plenty I'd like to forget, believe me. Delay after delay, all with excuses to match them!' He regarded him steadily, as he would have watched an unknown ship, assessing her strength or ability.

'When Pellew, Lord Exmouth, carried out his attack on the Dey of Algiers, and when most people claimed he was attempting the impossible, ships against well-sited shore batteries, you were there with him in *Unrivalled*. Later, in his report to their lordships, Exmouth wrote of you, "Bolitho is a true frigate captain". Praise indeed from one of our greatest.'

He smiled. '*Onward* can be a ship to make us both proud.' Somewhere in the far distance a solitary cannon or coastguard signal disturbed the stillness, but his eyes remained fixed on Adam's face. '*Take her*, Bolitho. She's yours to command!'

Afterwards, Adam could not recall who spoke first, or if there were no words.

There were muffled voices beyond the door, some one giving a discreet cough.

Grenville said quietly, 'The Admiral wishes to see you, but he is human enough to take his turn.' He touched his arm. 'Come, we will walk down to the boat together. The formalities can wait a while longer.'

The door was open: there were unknown faces, the glint of gold lace, somebody calling out congratulations, smiles, sharing the moment in their own way.

Adam took a grip on his emotions, distancing himself, regaining control, as if he were at the heart of a sudden squall or a call to arms.

Grenville was holding his arm, pausing only to greet or wave to some anonymous figure. As if it were his day. His ship.

He heard himself ask, 'Do we meet the present captain, Sir John?' and Grenville turned and faced him as if surprised.

50

'His appointment was not confirmed.' He was waving somebody aside, his eyes on the stairway. 'In your home county they have a saying, my friend, that bad news rides a fast horse. You will hear all about it soon enough. Captain Richmond is dead. You will appreciate why I. . . .' He changed the subject abruptly. 'You are *Onward*'s first captain. Don't fail her.' The transforming smile again. 'Or those who believe in you, eh?'

He felt the air now, like ice on his lips. Hands were offering him his cloak, but something made him wave it aside. He saw Grenville's nod of approval.

'*Your* day, my friend!'

There was a launch waiting at the pier, a lieutenant raising his hat in salute, some spectators loitering expectantly.

Grenville said, 'Do you have any one with you?' and then seemed to shrug. 'I need not have asked!'

Adam saw Luke Jago already in the sternsheets, as if he belonged there.

'My cox'n, Sir John. It was his wish to be here.'

Empty words. Jago had insisted. *My place, Cap'n*. And even though they had hardly spoken during that gruelling journey, he had been very aware of the tough, silent companionship.

Grenville was saying, 'Backbone of any ship— mine was, anyway.'

Adam saw a young woman peering down from one of the windows, on the floor beneath the room with the telescope. She was waving, and at a distance she might have been . . . He looked away.

The hardest part begins now.

'Attention in the boat!' The lieutenant stood at the foot of the familiar stone steps, the launch lifting and dipping on the choppy swell below him. A well turned-out crew, arms folded and facing aft. For them this was mere routine.

The helmsman stood by the tiller bar, and beside him Jago was already on his feet. Grenville was moving briskly toward the boat, his face hidden, and it was then that Adam felt the full impact of what this moment must mean to him.

'Allow me, Sir John.' He stepped over the gunwale and into the sternsheets, barely able to keep his balance. He saw the helmsman's surprise, and knew that the lieutenant had turned.

It was one of the navy's oldest customs. A captain always boarded any boat after every one else, and was the first to leave, so that he would never be unnecessarily delayed or inconvenienced.

He felt Jago reach out and steady him, and managed to grip his hand, and heard him mutter, 'Well spoken, Cap'n.' He of all men would know what he had done, and the significance of his gesture.

Grenville was following now, and the lieutenant was stiffly at attention again.

For today, at this moment and with all honour, a captain was going out to his ship.

The launch pulled steadily and unhurriedly toward the spread of ships which lay across the main anchorage, oars rising and dipping like wings. Other boats going about their business were careful to keep clear, conscious of the passenger who wore a captain's bright epaulettes, or of the crest on either bow signifying the admiral's own authority.

Luke Jago gazed along the boat between the banks of oarsmen, all eyes astern, or watching the stroke. A smart enough crew, but how would they perform in open sea, in the teeth of half a gale? He looked away. It was force of habit. *A ship will be judged by her boats.* The hard way, or the easy way, the old Jacks always said. Or you'd feel the touch of a rope's end, just to jog your memory.

He saw a big two-decker, a seventy-four, anchored apart from all the others. Waiting to be hulked, or for the breaker's yard, mastless and stripped of rigging, gunports empty. He glanced at the captain's shoulders and saw his head turn, as if remembering *Unrivalled* when they had returned here. Those same stone stairs. . . . He could almost hear some one saying, 'Never look back.' But he had. He could still feel the pain.

Now another two-decker, in stark contrast, standing rigging freshly blacked-down, ensign and jack streaming in the offshore wind, and men working about her decks, some pausing to watch as the launch pulled abeam. A seaman by the entry port, and an officer training his telescope to make sure that his ship was not about to receive an important and possibly unwelcome visitor.

52

Breathe easy, matey! Jago saw the captain's hand shifting his sword away from his leg, unconsciously, his mind miles away, probably still in Cornwall with the woman he was going to wed. And no wonder. Or was he troubled by the speed of this new appointment? He had hardly uttered a word on the journey to Plymouth, even when they had stopped at some poxy inn for a piss and a glass of grog. More like a burial vault. . . .

He almost smiled. The captain had felt it badly. *Forgive my poor company, Luke.* How could you turn on some one like that? Like the handshake as he had stepped, and as a result all but fallen, into this launch. Jago had seen them staring. He was still getting used to it himself, and to his own response. Just a little while ago, he would have said it was impossible to change. *Bloody officers.*

He saw the one called Grenville gesturing toward another ship.

'I served in her! Twelve, no, fifteen years back. I can't believe it!' Jago saw him touch Bolitho's arm, and recalled that unexpected gesture when Grenville had been accorded the honour of taking precedence over the captain. It never made much sense to Jago, but he had seen what it had done for a man who seemed all-important anyway, an intimate of their lordships. But he had witnessed it, shared it, and thought he understood it. This was Grenville's real world. *Like the rest of us.* And he was going to lose it; and the captain knew, and he gave a damn.

Grenville gripped Adam's arm again.

'There she is! Larboard bow! Isn't she a beauty?' There could have been just the two of them in the launch, Jago thought. 'They must have all worked watch-and-watch to have made her so!'

The lieutenant signalled to the helmsman and the tiller went over. Jago saw figures on the maindeck, some running, and a little group already assembled by the entry port. How low and sleek she looked after *Athena*. . . . There were barges alongside, deep in the water, and carefully fendered away from *Onward*'s new paintwork. Loaded with ballast which must have been removed when the new artillery had been hoisted aboard. Jago could remember all those other times: tackles, orders, back-breaking labour, the sweat and the curses. *Poor old Jack!*

Some of the gunports were open, black muzzles already visible. *Onward* was showing her teeth.

Impossible to guess what the captain was thinking now. A new ship. The proudest, and perhaps the loneliest, responsibility any man could grasp.

'Boat ahoy?' They were still half a cable from the ship, but the challenge was clear enough.

The helmsman looked over at Jago. 'Yours, 'Swain!'

Jago cupped his hands and shouted, *'Onward!'*

Adam saw the long bowsprit and tapering jib-boom sweep directly above their heads, and the figurehead, perfectly fashioned, a naked youth with one outstretched arm across a leaping dolphin, his other hand gripping a trident. A beautiful work of art. He felt a sudden sense of disloyalty, *Unrivalled*'s figurehead clear in his mind.

'Bows!' Oars scraping across the thwarts, the bowmen on their feet, a boathook poised and ready.

Onward's side loomed over the narrowing strip of lively water. 'Oars, *up!*'

Twin lines of blades, water running down over the seamen's arms and legs. The moment they all hated. A tot of rum would put things right with them.

Adam got to his feet as the hull lurched against fenders; two sideboys were already in position to ease the initial impact. He had never forgotten the story of the captain who had been tipped overboard when joining his first ship. It was probably true.

Grenville had remained seated but was looking up, studying him.

Adam reached for the hand-ropes and saw the entry port. He was shivering, but it was not the coldness of wind or sea. This was no time for doubt, or to lose your nerve. Like hearing his uncle's voice, recalling all those other ships. *Remember this. They will be far more worried about their new captain.*

He took a deep breath and stepped clear of the launch, and on to the stairs that mounted the tumblehome. It seemed no distance at all after *Athena*.

The bark of commands and the piercing shrill of boatswain's calls, and he felt his feet on the deck, careful to avoid the piles of cordage that awaited stowing as he faced aft, touching his hat. The ship seemed to rise up and around him, standing rigging like black glass, loosely brailed canvas stirring in the wind as if *Onward* were about to get under way.

Seamen and a few Royal Marines at attention, facing the entry port. Beyond them, groups of riggers and dockyard workers standing amidst the litter and disorder of their efforts.

A lieutenant had stepped forward, his hat in his hand.

'Welcome aboard, sir. I'm Vincent, sir. I am the senior here.'

The first contact: some said the most important.

An alert, intelligent face, younger than he had expected. Or was he still seeing the stolid and remote Stirling, *Athena*'s first lieutenant?

'Thank you, Mr. Vincent.' He looked along the deck. 'Most people will be thinking I could have chosen a more convenient time!'

Vincent responded with a firm handshake, and the suggestion of a smile. Brown eyes, as dark as Adam's own. What was going through his mind? Rumours or reputation? Maybe he was making comparisons with the man who had died.

He stood aside as Grenville came through the port, hooded eyes everywhere.

'Sir John has told me you've all worked with a will since the ship commissioned. She does you credit.'

Vincent said, 'We could not have done it without your support, Sir John.'

Plain, almost matter of fact, as Grenville would appreciate.

Another boat was coming alongside, and a harassed-looking seaman called, 'For you, Sir John!' But his eyes were on the new captain.

Grenville said curtly, 'I was expecting it, although I might have wished for better timing!' He strode back to the entry port, and Adam saw a lieutenant hovering with a heavily sealed package. He noted the twist of gold lace and thought of Troubridge. This must be the admiral's flag lieutenant.

Grenville said, 'I shall deal with this in the chart room.' He lifted his hand. 'And I *know* where it is.'

Vincent seemed to breathe out slowly.

'If you would care to come aft, sir,' and frowned as two

seamen ran ostentatiously to drag some filthy canvas away from the deck. 'The galley fire is lit, and you will be more comfortable in your quarters.'

Adam followed him. A new captain, a senior official from the Admiralty, and now a message from the admiral. It was enough to throw any first lieutenant into a panic. Vincent was hiding it well.

Behind him, he could hear the hammers and winches resume, the squeal of tackles as more stores and equipment were hauled aboard. A ship coming to life.

He heard some one shout and Jago's curt response. 'I'm with the Cap'n!' His guard was up, until he was good and ready to let it down.

Adam climbed on to the ship's larboard gangway, which linked forecastle to quarterdeck. Beneath him on the maindeck he saw the remaining rigging still to be hoisted and lashed into place, although to the casual onlooker it might seem a meaningless tangle. The real work, however, was finished, stays and shrouds taut and in place, running rigging, braces and halliards piled in coils or hanging like strange creeper in a forest.

Vincent was careful to point out stretches of wet paint, and any undried pitch that might cling to the shoe of an unwary visitor.

Adam looked down at the nearest eighteen-pounders, lined up behind their ports, breeching ropes taut. On parade. The quarterdeck was surprisingly clear, even spacious after the litter and confusion elsewhere. He paused for a moment, his eye taking in the big double wheel, and up and beyond, against the washed-out sky, the finely raked mizzen mast and yards, sails loosely brailed. A seaman was sitting casually astride one of the yards, a marline spike glinting in his hand. He seemed to freeze as he realized that one of the figures peering up from the deck below was his captain.

Down the companion ladder: less light here, with most of the screens in position to separate these quarters from the rest of the ship. Somebody was planing wood, one of the carpenter's mates, making a last-minute adjustment to ensure nothing would jam and refuse to move when required.

Vincent opened a screen door and stepped aside.

'Your quarters, sir.'

A strange sensation, almost recognition. Very like *Unrivalled*'s great cabin, but because it was empty it seemed double the size. The stern windows curving from quarter to quarter were the same, the anchored ships and passing small craft shimmering through the wet glass like some unfinished tapestry.

He felt his head brush one of the deckhead beams and found himself smiling. That, at least, did not change.

Vincent said, 'I apologize for this gear, sir. I told the bosun's mate to deal with it!'

Adam turned, and saw the 'gear' he had referred to. Some large leather chests, brass-bound, expensive and, he thought, new.

They must have been brought aboard to await their owner, whose name was clearly painted on one of them. Captain Charles Richmond.

'Did you know him?'

'Scarcely, sir.' The question seemed to startle Vincent; a full minute passed before he recovered from it. 'He was away much of the time. Awaiting final instructions. Most of the dockyard people were still in control, you see.'

Adam nodded. He *could* see. 'The first lieutenant stood guard, eh?' He walked aft to the broad stern window. 'How did he die?'

Bad news rides a fast horse.

'Captain Richmond was staying with friends here . . . there was something he had to arrange before he joined us. There was so much for the rest of us to do anyway.' He half turned and looked at Adam. 'Nobody offered us any explanation. I was told that some one had tried to break into the house, and there was a fight.'

'Robbery?'

'So they say, sir. Whoever he was, he got clean away.'

Somewhere, a boatswain's call brought all movement to a standstill.

'More stores coming alongside, sir. It shouldn't take long.'

Adam sat on the bench seat below the stern windows. *A first lieutenant's work is never done.* But this was something else. Vincent had been glad of the interruption, had not wanted to be drawn into the past, no matter how recent.

57

He leaned forward and stared at the largest chest. *It is not my concern.* He turned the label over. To be returned to an address in Exeter. . . .

He ran his fingers through his hair, feeling the salt and roughness. He was too tired to think beyond this moment and the ship.

The screen door opened and Grenville peered in.

'You look quite settled and at home here.' He held out the thick envelope. 'For you.' He did not take his eyes from it as he handed it across. 'The day after tomorrow, you will read yourself in. The admiral will be in attendance.'

He paused, briefly lost in memory.

'She is your ship, my friend. Anything you need, now is the time to make yourself heard.' He looked at the baggage as if he were seeing it for the first time. 'Not dead man's shoes, like some I've known,' and seemed to dismiss it. 'You'll be remaining on board, no doubt. Go through the ship's books. It may be your only chance.'

But the smile would not come. He stood by the door again, looking around, perhaps prolonging it.

'Your lady will wait for you. Be fair to her.'

Then he swung round. 'Stay here. The first lieutenant will see me over the side.'

The door shut, and Adam heard his voice as he spoke to some one by the companion, possibly Jago. He clenched his fist, slowly, until he felt his nails drive into his palm. They had not even shaken hands. And yet he could feel it, like that very first time.

A boat was bearing off from the chains, the sounds muffled here in the great cabin, a shouted command, and then the creak of oars for the long pull to the land.

Stronger than words. He knew they would never meet again.

5

'Under my Hand'

Lieutenant Mark Vincent crossed the quarterdeck and gripped the hammock nettings firmly with one hand. The splicing, like the cordage, was hard and new. Untried, like the ship. He stifled a yawn, not daring to calculate the hours he had walked, measuring every inch of planking with his footsteps, on this day alone.

He stared through the shrouds toward the shore. Seven bells of the afternoon watch had just chimed from the forecastle, but it could have been night, the land already a shapeless dark blur, interspersed with tiny lights and the stronger glow of a beacon.

Only the sea gave any sign of movement, with an occasional boat making slow progress against the restless current. Plymouth: at the end of another long day, it could have been almost anywhere.

Vincent squared his shoulders and moved away from the nettings. He was tired and could admit it, but a first lieutenant was never free to reveal it. Not a good one, anyway. He smiled to himself. Like hearing a lecture from the past.

How different *Onward* had looked when he had been pulled around her yet one more time. Fully rigged, and every stitch of canvas neatly furled, she was a living ship now, after the months of endless work and inspection. A few blows, too, when nobody had been watching. A man-of-war any one would be proud to serve. To command. . . .

He heard another boat thrashing away from the side, the oars cutting the water, raising small spectres of foam. Voices called out, some almost regretful; friendships had been made among riggers and dockyard hands and the ever-growing numbers of seamen and marines.

He could hear the sharper tone of Rowlatt, the master-at-arms, no doubt keeping a watchful eye open for any petty theft. Souvenirs, the dockyard mateys might call them; Rowlatt's vocabulary was less euphemistic. How easily the name fitted the voice now. Vincent could remember when he had started with a list and trained himself from that first day aboard, putting faces to names and eventually a name to each voice. Somebody yelped with pain in the gathering darkness. *Most of them, anyway.*

He faced aft and stared up at the mizzen yards and standing rigging. He could walk this deck now without even glancing down for the treacherous cleat or coaming that could lay anybody, officer or man, ignominiously on his face. He had laughed at so many others in his early days with the fleet. . . . Vincent was twenty-seven years old. *A lifetime ago.*

A boatswain's mate was pacing slowly back and forth, his silver call glinting in the glow from the cabin skylight. Captain Adam Bolitho was down there in his quarters, with his piles of signals and books, wading through them, interrupting Vincent only with brief questions or scribbled notes.

Captain Richmond's personal belongings, which had never been unpacked, had gone ashore. Dead man's shoes, he had heard old sailors call them— and more of Bolitho's gear had been brought aboard. Vincent still found it difficult to accept the inevitable. Richmond had scarcely visited the ship since she had been commissioned; Vincent had been in charge from that first handing-over signature, had even seen himself there in the great cabin. In command.

Onward was a fine ship; Bolitho was damned lucky to have her.

'Boat ahoy?' The challenge rang loud and clear. Vincent walked to the quarterdeck rail and peered down at the entry-port. Another visitor, even now...?

The reply echoed back across the water. *'No, no!'* and he relaxed slightly. No officers aboard, then, so probably only stores. It was a wonder the boatswain and his working parties could find any more space.

Another voice. 'You, there! Take these new hands to their messes if the purser has finished with them!'

'Been done, sir!' It was tired and resentful.

'Why wasn't I told? I'm not a mind-reader!'

Vincent swore under his breath. Hector Monteith was *Onward*'s third and youngest lieutenant. *We all had to begin somewhere. . . . but was I like that at his age?*

He moved into deeper shadow. *At his age.* Seven years ago; but at moments like this, it could have been only last week. It was even the same month, but bright sunlight had been turning the sea to glass, and the enemy sails had filled the horizon. They called it the battle of Lissa now: the last sea fight against such formidable odds.

1811, and he had been serving in the frigate *Amphion*, his first ship as lieutenant. How they had survived, let alone scored a decisive victory against a force of French and Venetian men-of-war, seemed a miracle.

Many had fallen that day, friend and foe, but he had lived.

And relived it, again and again, the fire and thunder of those rapid broadsides. Eighteen-pounders, like these shining new guns lining *Onward*'s sides, which might never fire a shot except in training and drills. And always uppermost in his memory: *I felt no fear.*

He heard quick, light footsteps across the new planking and brought himself back to the present.

Monteith was slim, with a round, boyish face. But for his uniform, he could still be a midshipman.

'More stores coming aboard, sir. And three items of baggage for the captain.' He waited, his head to one side, a habit he no longer noticed.

'Have the baggage taken aft immediately, if you please. We don't want some ham-fisted Jack dropping it between decks.'

'I've details the hands already, sir.'

The formality irritated Vincent, although he could not have said why. A first lieutenant was not at liberty to cultivate favourites or offer privileges.

One ship. One company. . . .

He was reminded of the second lieutenant, James Squire. The contrast was complete. Big and powerfully built, he was some years older than Vincent and had risen from the lower deck, an achievement still rare even after all the years of war. Squire had been serving as a master's mate when he had been chosen to join a surveying vessel under the charge of the famous explorer and navigator Sir Alfred Bishop. He had obviously more than proved his worth and ability. Promotion had followed.

It was hard to draw him out on the subject of his experiences, or the skill of transmuting unknown depths and treacherous waters into the distances and soundings on a chart. Squire was strong and confident, but remained at a distance, perhaps still feeling his way. *Like the rest of us.*

'The captain wants us all aft as soon as the hands are dismissed. It's the last chance we'll have before the admiral and his merry men come aboard, so if you can think of anything—'

Monteith thrust his hands behind him, another little habit Vincent tried, unsuccessfully, to ignore. It usually happened when he was speaking pompously with a seaman, no matter how experienced he might be.

'The captain has a fine reputation. I've met several officers who have served with him. Wounded, taken prisoner by the Yankees and escaped, and then there was the time. . . .' He swung round. 'Don't you *know* better than to interrupt an officer when. . . .'

Jago stood his ground, and spoke to Vincent as if Monteith were invisible.

'The Cap'n sends his compliments, sir, an' would you join him when you are able?'

'I'll come directly.' There was an outburst of angry shouts from forward and he added, 'Deal with it, Mr. Monteith. Call me if you need me.'

Monteith would rather choke, he thought, and knew he was being unfair.

He fell into step with the coxswain. A hard man to all accounts, he sensed, but a good one to have protecting your back. Such a short time aboard, and he had already made his mark.

'You've been with Captain Bolitho a long time, I believe?'

He felt Jago's cool gaze. 'A while now, sir. This ship an' that.'

Curt enough, but characteristic. Vincent smiled privately. They had a saying about it, like everything else in the fleet. Between every captain and his ship's company stood the first lieutenant. *And his coxswain.*

Down the companion ladder, his eyes noting the changes. A Royal Marine at the screen door, boots coming together smartly as they moved into the lantern light. Newly spliced hand-ropes, a reminder that even this would be a lively expanse of decking in any sort of sea.

The sentry tapped his musket on a grating.

'First lieutenant, *sir*!'

He could not remember the marine's name. Not yet. . . .

The great cabin had completely changed, and with the dividing screens folded away seemed much larger. Most of the piled books and papers had gone, and an opened log or diary lay on a small desk Vincent had not seen before.

There were furtive noises coming from the hutch-like pantry that adjoined the captain's sleeping quarters: it would be the cabin servant, Morgan. Vincent had made that choice himself.

'Thought you might need an escape before the others joined us.'

Bolitho came out of the shadows and stood framed against the stern windows, flickering lights passing back and forth across the sea behind him like moths.

The same warm handshake, as if they had just met. He gestured to the table.

'Some cognac, will that suit?' He grinned as Morgan hurried from his hiding place, a tray balanced in both hands. 'I feel as if I could sleep for a week!'

Vincent watched the cognac swirl and move to the motion. He had chosen Morgan with care. A man of some experience, but still human enough to hear and report any conversation which might be of interest elsewhere.

'Can I help in some way, sir?'

Bolitho faced him again, his eyes in shadow.

'You have, Mark. You *do*.' He picked up a goblet. 'As always, this is the hardest step.'

There were candles on the cabin table and he held the goblet to their light, hesitating, his mind still lingering on questions and doubts. Then the strain seemed to fall away. 'To us, Mark. And those we are leaving behind.'

They touched glasses, but Vincent barely noticed the taste. Leaving behind? They had not even finished with the watch and muster bills yet.

'I did hear that you were about to be married, sir.' He broke off. 'My apologies, sir. I did not intend. . . .'

'It does you credit. Here, in this cabin, you may speak as you will. No misunderstandings!' He looked toward the darkening windows and said, 'God willing, I *will* marry soon. It asks so much of any woman. And in exchange. . . .' He said nothing for a moment. 'About tomorrow. I should like to walk through the ship with you. Before the admiral comes aboard.' He moved across the cabin, speaking his thoughts aloud. 'To the people, I am still a stranger. That will change. Any ship's company deserves to share the pride as well as the responsibility. Pride, Mark— what we can create together.'

The mood changed. 'I looked at the punishment book today. A captain I once served told me that it reveals the true strength or weakness of any ship's company, and in particular her officers.'

He looked at the screen door.

'You've done well during your time aboard. Not an easy role in a new ship, with a company as mixed as flags in a locker.' He smiled again. 'Let's have the others join us.'

Vincent saw Morgan hovering, half in and half out of the pantry. He, at least, was ready; Vincent had not realized that, during their conversation, the other lieutenants and warrant officers had been waiting.

Adam called, 'Morgan— you're from Swansea, right?' He was looking critically around the main cabin. 'More candles, I think, can you do that?'

Morgan seemed surprised or pleased, it was hard to tell.

'Good as done, sir!'

In the growing light Vincent noticed a tall-backed chair facing aft by the stern windows; it must have come aboard in one of the last boats. Not new, quite the opposite: he could see scars and stains on the green leather. Well used, a place to rest between watches, even snatch an hour's sleep when you were expecting to be called. A captain's chair; Bolitho's chair.

He became aware that Adam Bolitho was watching him, waiting, but relaxed. Then he smiled, as if recalling something private, intimate.

'So let's be about it, shall we?'

Midshipman David Napier found himself crossing an enclosed courtyard, and heard a gate clang behind him. Around the corner of the guardhouse would be the jetty, and then he would see the ship. As he had pictured it in his mind, again and again, as if to reassure himself. He wanted to stretch his arms until the muscles screamed, stamp his numbed feet, anything to drive away the strain and confinement of the journey from Falmouth.

It had rained all the way without pause. Like being shut in a box, reeling from every rut and jolt between Cornwall and Plymouth.

He looked at the sky, now hard and clear, without warmth. Somewhere along the way the road had been flooded: another delay while Francis had searched for an alternative route, little more than a cart track. Ex-cavalryman though he was, even he had been at a loss for curses.

He had recovered by the time they had reached the last barrier, and found a porter to carry the midshipman's chest.

Just a grin, and a pat on his shoulder. Maybe Francis understood better than many what it meant. The need to make it brief. No time to brood or regret.

'Can I 'elp you— sir?'

A tall Royal Marine, scarlet tunic unnaturally bright in the harsh sunlight, had appeared from nowhere.

Napier held out the creased warrant, his fingers stiff from clenching it in his pocket.

'I'm joining *Onward*.'

He felt the marine's eyes giving him a quick, disinterested look from beneath the brim of his smart leather hat. *Just another middy. Be giving all of us hell before you know it.*

'If you'll just wait 'ere, sir. I'd best tell the sergeant.'

Somewhere there was a clock striking. It went on and on, and Napier thought he could smell cooking. He swallowed hard.

'Well, where the hell has *he* been? On the moon?'

65

Then the sergeant stepped into the courtyard, the same warrant gripped in his hand.

'You were logged to arrive earlier, *Mister* Napier.'

It sounded like an accusation.

'The road was flooded.'

The sergeant brushed biscuit crumbs from his immaculate tunic with the warrant.

'We've all been on the hop since dawn. The admiral, see? Nothing but the best!' He relented slightly. 'There's another young gentleman waitin' to join *Onward*. Tell the piermaster.' Then, brusquely, 'Best we can manage till we get the word.'

Napier felt his ankle turn on a loose cobble, expecting the pain, the warning. Nothing happened.

And he had not even thought about it. All those miles. The lurching and the unending rain. . . .

'This way, sir,' the marine was muttering. 'Probably all over by now.' He did not offer an explanation.

Napier took off his hat and loosened his hair. He could smell perfume on his cuff. *Elizabeth*. He flinched almost guiltily, as if he had spoken her name aloud.

The room was long and narrow, and had been used for stores. There was a solitary, barred window at one end, with a shaft of sunlight playing across a few crude chairs and an empty bookcase, which did nothing to make it welcoming. He realized that some one was standing beside the window, half hidden in shadow, his elbow resting on the sill.

Napier heard the marine's boots clicking away, then there was silence.

He said tentatively, 'I was told that you're joining *Onward*. So am I. But I got here so late— it was not my fault. The weather. . . .' He moved closer to the window. 'I'm Napier. David Napier.'

'I was delayed, too.' An even, unhurried voice. Disinterested? Wary? Impossible to tell.

He tried again. 'They say the admiral is on board. I suppose we shall have to wait until we're told what to do.'

The figure had moved slightly, and Napier saw the sunlight playing across his own midshipman's chest. So bright and new, like his uniform, and everything else.

The voice said, 'My name is Huxley, by the way.' A pause.

66

'Simon Huxley.' The shadow moved again. Restless, impatient, waiting for something. On edge.

Then, 'Not your first ship? I thought perhaps. . . .'

Napier clenched his fist, and pressed it against his hip.

'No. I was in *Audacity*.'

Nothing else would come.

'*Audacity*? I read about it in the *Gazette*. Heated shot from a shore battery. Your captain was killed, wasn't he?'

Napier said quietly, 'A lot of them died that day. But I could swim.' Like an apology for being alive.

Huxley reached out and tapped his shoulder. 'Luck or skill. Fate decided in your favour, David.' He dropped his arm; the gesture had taken them both by surprise. 'I can't swim a stroke!'

He had moved further into the sunlight, turning as boots tramped along the road outside, perhaps from the jetty.

'I shan't be sorry to get aboard, to be doing something useful.'

Napier studied him. A year or so older than himself, with a serious, thoughtful face. *Onward* might be his stepping-stone to promotion, or oblivion. What most midshipmen joked about, and dreaded.

He said, 'Were you held up by the weather?'

Huxley did not reply immediately. The marching feet had faded away and it was so quiet in the long, narrow room that he could hear him breathing.

'No.'

'I'm sorry. I didn't mean to pry.'

'I went to visit my father. *Onward* might be under sailing orders. Rumours, but there may be some truth in them.' He swung round and stared at the door, listening, but there was nothing. 'I wanted him to know. . . .'

'Is he unwell, Simon?'

Napier could not see his eyes.

'He is confined to quarters.' He paused, as if waiting for some reaction. 'And awaiting trial by court martial.'

'My God, I'm so sorry.' Napier felt shock, pity, anger, and something else he could not explain. He had known Simon Huxley for a matter of minutes. *But I am his friend.*

Huxley said bitterly, 'I thought everybody knew about it!'

67

There were voices outside.

Napier said, 'We can talk about it later. A new ship, remember? A new beginning for us both.'

The door banged open.

'Boat's waitin', gentlemen.' A pause. 'When you're ready, o' course.'

Neither of them noticed the sarcasm. Just a handshake. It was enough.

Captain Adam Bolitho walked past the Royal Marine sentry and into the cabin. Quiet now, and almost spacious after the ceremonial of the forenoon. The admiral and his retinue had returned ashore; the trill of calls and the blare of a trumpet still seemed to hang in the air to mark their departure. His cocked hat was lying on a chair by the desk, but he did not recall tossing it there.

He should be used to it after all these years. Listening to those same words or hearing them issuing from his own mouth, as so many of those aboard today would know them too, by heart. *Willing and requiring you forthwith to go on board and take upon you the charge and command of captain in her accordingly. . . .* He recalled some of the younger faces staring up at him from the maindeck. There did not seem many in this new company.

He groped to remove his sword belt and a voice checked him.

'Allow me, sir.'

It was Morgan. He must have managed to stay hidden during all the 'stamp and bustle', as Jago had called it.

Adam unbuttoned his coat.

Morgan was waiting, the old sword held in both hands. 'I thought a drink might be in order, sir?'

Adam smiled, and felt his jaw crack. 'It is, and thank you.'

'Went very well, we thought, sir.'

Preparing himself for the days ahead. Where did they find men like Morgan, or *Athena*'s cabin servant, Bowles? And what was *he* doing now?

'The admiral seemed pleased.'

Morgan laid the sword across the high-backed chair, his eyes darting around as if planning a proper place for it.

'Fine old blade, sir.' He stood, swaying easily to the movement of the deck, as Adam walked right aft to the stern windows. 'In your family for years, they say.'

If you want to know all about a captain, just ask his cabin servant, he thought.

He peered through the salt-misted glass across the anchorage. He had seen the other ships nearby, the telescopes on their decks levelled at the admiral's smart barge and accompanying boats. Critical but envious too, no matter what they said between decks. A new ship, and a frigate above all else.

There was a sudden burst of cheering. Morgan had opened the cabin skylight an inch or so, and the din seemed to fill the whole poop.

He beamed. 'Splice the mainbrace, sir! Hitting the right place, I'd say, see?'

'They've earned it.' No doubt the purser thought otherwise. Vicary, that was his name. A stooping, desiccated, humourless man: one of those he had met for the first time yesterday evening.

Morgan had placed a goblet on the table. 'Cognac, sir. Came aboard today. The guardboat brought it.' He paused, and laid an envelope beside it.

Adam opened it and saw the ribbon, the same colour as the one she had given him, and her writing, like the letter he always carried.

From the Last Cavalier. There was a smudge, kiss or tear. She was with him.

'Thank you.' He looked away sharply at the water astern, still reflecting the hard light. A few boats were moving or loitering nearby, friends, relatives, hoping for a glimpse or a wave.

It would only make it worse when the anchor broke free and *Onward* put to sea. Worse than this? How could that be?

The sentry tapped his musket beyond the screen.

'Officer o' th' watch, *sir*!'

'That'll be Mr. Monteith, sir.'

Adam saw Morgan's reflection briefly in the sloping glass windows. He was scowling. Then he hurried to the door.

He picked up the card and read it again before slipping it into his pocket.

Voices now beyond the screen. Monteith. . . . When he had boarded *Onward*, the young lieutenant had been with the side party. And yesterday here in this cabin, with his fellow lieutenants and all the senior warrant officers. Young and very attentive, eager to answer questions about his duties, and today when he had been introduced to the admiral, different again. Anxious, almost shy.

He put down the goblet; it was empty. Monteith presented another face completely in the punishment book. There were several entries, mostly for trivial offenses, when a sharp reprimand from a senior seaman or a quick slap when nobody was looking would have sufficed. Nothing serious, but wrongly directed they could end at the gangway with two dozen lashes. Or worse. Vincent must have been aware of it, but had offered no comment when they had discussed the ship's affairs.

Charge and command of captain. It would always be the invisible line between them.

He shook himself mentally. He was letting it grow out of all proportion. He was too tired to think clearly.

'Mr. Monteith wishes to have a word with you, sir.'

Morgan was holding the door half open. It sounded like 'insists'.

'My apologies, sir. I understood that the first lieutenant was here.' He bit his lip. 'He left word that I was to call him if—'

Adam said, 'As you can see, Mr. Vincent is *not* here. Can I help?'

Morgan strode past, heading for his pantry, and said meaningfully over his shoulder, 'If you need me, sir?'

Monteith pulled out the papers.

'Two midshipmen have just come aboard.' He frowned slightly, his head on one side. 'To join. They were overdue, and the first lieutenant wanted to be told when— *if* they made an appearance.'

Adam turned away. David had done it. After his experience he might have been forgiven for not wanting to return to sea. But he had recovered his strength and his resolve.

'I understand one of them has served with you before, sir?'

Adam took the papers and opened them. He could feel

70

Monteith's eyes flicking around the cabin, noting his captain's untidy appearance, the empty glass on the table.

He knew he was being unfair, and said abruptly, 'There has been flooding in Cornwall, roads blocked. It does happen.'

'Quite so, sir.' A pause. 'But the other midshipman was already *in* Plymouth.'

Adam looked up from the papers, the fatigue suddenly gone. This visit was no accident.

'Midshipman Huxley was delayed for personal reasons. The first lieutenant will know that.'

'As I thought, sir.' He dropped his eyes confidentially. 'But as officer of the watch I considered it my duty to confirm it. The word is that Midshipman Huxley's father is awaiting court martial.'

Beyond the door the sentry rapped his musket again.

'First lieutenant, *sir!*'

Morgan bustled past.

'No peace, sir.'

The door opened on a separate little drama. A seaman below the companion, a mop in his hands, a marine checking his musket in readiness to relieve the sentry. And Lieutenant Vincent staring into the cabin, barely able to contain his anger.

Monteith finished, 'For losing his ship!'

Vincent cut in, 'I am very sorry, sir. I was in the sick bay—one of the new hands has had a fall. Not serious, but—' He controlled his voice. 'I *left word* where I would be.' He had not looked at Monteith. There was no need.

Adam unclenched his hand slowly, deliberately, and withdrew it from his pocket. A small thing which should never have happened. And tomorrow it would be all through the ship.

He said quietly, 'Losing a ship is an indescribable experience, because it never leaves you. It happened to me.' He barely recognized his own voice; it was cool, almost matter of fact. 'Like a terrible storm. You ride it or you go under, with the ship. But you never forget.'

'Boat ahoy!' The challenge from the maindeck was faint, almost inaudible amongst the shipboard sounds. It could have been an echo of those lost voices.

Then he heard the shrill of a boatswain's call, and running feet, very much alive.

71

'Carry on, Mr. Monteith.' He did not look at him. '*Onward* is a private ship, no admiral's flag flying at our masthead, no chain of command while we wait to be told what to do. We depend on ourselves.' He felt the deck tilt very slightly beneath him, as if she were stirring. 'Upon each other.'

When he turned Monteith had gone, almost running to deal with the arrivals.

Vincent said, 'The wardroom has asked if you will be our guest,' and faltered. 'If you would feel inclined to. . . .'

The tension had gone; it was like being set free.

'I will be honoured, Mark, although I have a feeling that it might be delayed a while.'

Vincent thought he understood. The captain was back.

In his little pantry Morgan waited until the screen door had closed, then poured himself a small tot of rum and sipped appreciatively.

Tomorrow it *would* be all through the ship.

6

A Proud Moment

Luke Jago climbed down from the boat-tier and examined the gig closely. His gig. Oars stowed, lashings in place, *equal strain on all parts*. Probably its first time out of the water since leaving the builder's yard.

'Fair enough, Robbins. You can fall out now.'

The big seaman knuckled his forehead, grinning. Praise indeed from the captain's coxswain, who was impossible to please.

Jago hardly noticed. Just words, but they mattered. Anybody could pull an oar after a few attempts, and a threat or two. But the gig was special.

He stared along the maindeck, quieter now after all the working parties and inspections, as if a King's ship had never weighed anchor and put to sea before. All those years, different ports or anchorages he could no longer name or recall, and you never got used to it. Doubt, anxiety, resentment. All and none of them.

He saw Joshua Guthrie, the boatswain, indicating something on the mainyard, jabbing the air with a massive fist to make his point to one of the new hands. A born sailor, Guthrie had entered the navy at ten. Now he seemed ageless, scarred and battered, his nose shapeless from fights ashore as well as in the line of duty. He could control the deck with a minimum of effort, using only a powerful, carrying voice and a cuff if the offender was near enough. His girth had increased over the past few years but only a fool would see it as a soft plank. *Like punching a bloody oak tree*, as one seaman had discovered.

But even Guthrie could not hide his mood, and to those who knew him well, his excitement.

It had started this morning, even as both watches of the hands were mustering for working ship, the stink of the galley funnel carrying on a fresh north-easterly. A few lights still twinkling from the dark mass of land, faint shouts and calls from other ships nearby. Another day.

Then the challenge from the gangway. *'Boat ahoy?'*

Early, but not unknown in Plymouth, major naval port that it was.

Jago had recognized the boat immediately: the same one which had brought him and the captain out to *Onward* for the first time, with that senior officer from the Admiralty. But it was not stores, or some officer begging a free passage after a night ashore with one of the Plymouth whores. He had seen the sudden activity at the entry port; even the first lieutenant had been there.

Guthrie had been close by with one of his working parties and had called back softly, 'The admiral's speaking trumpet is among us!'

The flag lieutenant had come aboard, a tall, foppish young officer who seemed to wear a permanent look of disdain and impatience. It was hard to picture him serving in any seaman-like capacity. 'Flags' had walked past the side party and marines without even a glance and continued aft with Lieutenant Vincent beside him.

Jago contained a smile. All the bluff and tight lips meant nothing if you had trust. The launch had been coxswained by the same man as before. He had followed the flag lieutenant up to the entry port and seen Jago, and remembered him. Just the hint of a grin, mouth barely moving, eyes still on the officers.

'Sailin' orders, matey! Best o' luck!' And he was gone.

Secret orders, like the heavily sealed envelope he had seen in the flag lieutenant's hand, never remained confidential for long in the 'family'. The conference of officers and senior warrants called unexpectedly in the great cabin, and an announcement by the first lieutenant, had confirmed it.

Tomorrow forenoon *Onward* would be leaving Plymouth. Senior hands of messes would report for instructions.

Jago had heard one of the seamen joke, 'Write your wills, while you still can!'

It was all they had been told. All they needed to know.

He looked aft and astern past the great ensign curling lightly in the breeze. *Onward* was swinging to her cable, so that the land seemed to be edging out around the quarter, like a protective arm.

Secrecy meant very little in a seaport like this one. People would know. Some worrying, dismayed at the news. And others who would see it as a release, or an escape.

Jago rarely thought beyond the moment, taking it at face value.

He saw Morgan the cabin servant standing by the quarterdeck rail, something white in his hand. A letter, or letters, for that last boat ashore. Jago eased his shoulders, and straightened the smart blue coat with its gilt buttons. For him there would be no letters. He had nowhere else to go.

But it felt so different. In war, every flag was an enemy, each encounter a chance of battle or worse.

He turned and saw three midshipmen up on the larboard gangway, watching an old schooner passing slowly abeam. One of them was David Napier, his teeth flashing white in a grin. No regrets in that one. Glad to be leaving. Would he change with maturity, and become just another officer?

It was stupid, absurd. As if it mattered. He must be losing his grip. Getting past it. . . .

The bell chimed out from the forecastle, and his mind responded automatically. Time to report to the carpenter to settle the question of some boat repairs. One of the busiest men in any new ship, he hated to be kept waiting.

It was as if he had spoken his thoughts aloud. *Past it. . . .* Napier must have run from the gangway to reach him so quickly. No sign of discomfort, let alone pain, a far cry from those early days of his recovery. And so at ease now in his uniform. Hard to remember him as the attentive, often over-serious cabin servant in *Unrivalled*.

'Settled in, have you?' Jago gestured toward the slow-moving schooner. 'I seen you with your mates, getting along— or can't you tell yet?'

Napier shrugged. 'We're all finding our way.' He was

frowning now. 'I've been wondering about you, Luke. *Onward*'s not a big ship, not like *Athena*— but I never seem to see you. And we're sailing tomorrow. I wanted to ask you. . . .' He halted, and touched his long-buttoned coat. 'It's not because of *this*, is it?'

Jago hesitated as two seamen hurried past, unwilling to be overheard, angry with himself for not anticipating this. *Never get too close to them. You of all people shouldn't need to be told.*

He looked at him steadily, giving himself time. What he said now would matter. Napier was not just another 'young gentleman', thinking only of himself, reckoning his chances.

'The Cap'n came down and spoke to all of you midshipmen, right?' He said it slowly, wanting it to reach him. '*All* of you, David. But don't you think he was wanting to share the moment just with you. 'Cause you're special?'

Some one called, 'Mr. Falcon is yellin' out for you, 'Swain, you'd better jump about!'

It had slipped Jago's mind. He reached out roughly and gripped Napier's arm, and felt him start a little with surprise.

'No favours, David— leastways you never show 'em, or you're finished. Others look to *you*, or very soon will. . . .' He shook his arm, hating his inability to express it, as if they were strangers. 'Think on it, David. One day you'll meet some fine well-bred young lady who's got her eye on a likely King's officer. She might even be an admiral's kin, no less.' He waited for a smile, a flicker of understanding. There was neither.

'I've been looking for you, man!' The carpenter.

Napier watched them go to the boat-tier, Falcon gesticulating with some sort of rule, perturbed about something.

He touched his sleeve, still feeling Jago's grip: strong, like his presence and his convictions. Always at a distance of his own making, but he could see right through things. When others turned aside, or spluttered excuses.

'Are you coming, David?' That was Huxley. He must have seen Jago speaking with him, might even think it was gossip about his father and the forthcoming court martial.

He began to climb back to the gangway, his mind lingering on Jago and what he had been trying to say. He had seen and done so much, and had suffered in some unknown way which had scarred him as deeply as blade or ball. Maybe only the captain knew.

Jago understood the necessity of distance. *No favourites.* He stood on the gangway and felt the ship moving beneath him, as if eager to leave. To be free.

Was anybody?

He looked toward the boat-tier but Jago and the carpenter had vanished.

A man apart and alone. Trusted but feared. Who missed nothing.

He shivered, remembering his comment about some fine, well-bred young lady. An admiral's kin. . . . Just a rough allusion to make his point, as if he had witnessed that moment in the stable yard at Falmouth. The young, impatient Elizabeth very upright in her riding habit, staring at him, tapping her crop against one boot. 'Leaving now to exchange all this for a *ship*?' Serious or mocking, he was never certain. Despite the new uniform and his experiences in the Caribbean, she still regarded him as her cousin Adam's cabin servant, and treated him as such.

She had waited for him to walk toward her, and he remembered how much he had *wanted* her to see that he was no longer limping.

She had watched his approach with cool eyes.

'It may be a while before you come to visit again.' A slight crease of the clear, pale forehead. 'To stay. . . .' She seemed to have been coming to a decision. He had heard the horses stamping on the cobbles, impatient to begin the long haul to Plymouth.

'Write to us, when you feel inclined.' She had pulled off her hat and let her long chestnut hair spill over her shoulder. 'You may kiss me, if you wish.'

He could still feel the touch of her cheek, her hair falling between them. There were others in the yard, and the sound of somebody hammering metal on an anvil.

He had felt her turn very slightly, and the warmth of her breath across his mouth.

'So that you'll remember me.' A hand pressing the back of his neck. Their mouths joined. No sound: even the horses were still.

She had walked away, toward the old grey house. She had not looked back.

An admiral's daughter.

He told himself it was only a dream. She would be the first to shatter any illusion he might cherish. Maybe Jago knew something, and was trying to save him from making a fool of himself. He thought of the kiss again. *Or from breaking my heart.*

'What's this, *Mister* Napier? Day-dreaming, are we?'

He did not need to turn to recognize the third lieutenant's sarcasm.

'On my way, sir!'

'Remember in future, *Mister* Napier. Promotion requires skill, not popularity!'

Monteith was already striding away, eyes everywhere, gesturing meanwhile to a seaman who was untangling some halliards.

Another sailor working nearby said quietly, but loud enough for Napier to hear, 'God knows best!'

Napier looked out to sea, embarrassment and irritation melting away, then he felt himself smiling. Thanks to the unknown sailor.

He looked then at the shore, the high ground beyond the old fortifications and the houses. Day-dreaming. Monteith was right. Only a kiss, and nothing more. Her way of saying good-bye, ending something that had never begun. It would soon pass and leave him in peace.

He waved to his new friend Huxley and hurried aft to rejoin him.

But she was still with him. *Elizabeth.*

Adam Bolitho walked through the cabin until he was right aft by the stern windows. There were no lights here, so that the sea and sky beyond seemed almost bright, and alive. He had been unable to sleep and had been shaving by candlelight long before all hands had been called to breakfast and clean, while the anchorage was still as black as pitch.

He had spent much of the night watches lying in the old bergère, as so often in the past, unsettled, going over every last detail. Something he knew was a pointless exercise.

His mind had never seemed to rest. Once in the night he had found himself thinking of Vice-Admiral Sir Graham Bethune, and the portrait of him he had seen at the house in London. Wearing the uniform of captain, not even posted, as Jago had commented. Had he been any different as that young man? And what would become of him now without the authority, the power of command?

He walked forward again and stood beneath the skylight, still dripping from overnight rain. He had heard it when the restlessness had driven him to leave his swinging cot; he had left the blankets turned down, but doubted if Morgan would be deceived.

Morgan seemed capable of anything, had even managed to have Adam's seagoing coat repaired; the tear above one pocket, the result of one of many unofficial inspections throughout the hull, was barely visible.

'One of the sailmaker's crew, sir.' He had almost winked. 'Used to be a tailor until circumstances changed at home!'

Adam slipped his arms through the sleeves. It was not an old coat. But how many leagues, how many days and nights had it shared? Immortalized now in the portrait painted by Montagu, much against his own wishes, to satisfy his aunt. *Naval Officer With Yellow Rose.* When he had met Lowenna. Fate. . . .

Feet thudded across the deck overhead, and some one slipped and fell. The planking would be treacherous after the rain, especially for landmen or the over-confident.

He felt his pockets, impatient with himself. *Sailing day.* It was like hearing some one shouting it aloud.

Full morning now, the great cabin laid bare in the daylight. Vincent would be here soon to make his report, and step aside.

He glanced at the desk, its polished surface empty. He could feel the little book in his pocket, her last letter tucked inside like a talisman. A link.

The ship seemed quiet again after the usual bustle of cleaning the messdeck and securing unwanted gear. He picked up the old sword and loosened it in its scabbard. So many times. So many hands. *And always, you, Uncle.* Seeing him in other ships, other cabins. He laid it across the green leather chair, deep in thought, and flinched as eight bells chimed faintly from the upper deck.

He looked again around the cabin, familiar even after so brief an occupation, thought of the room across the water, the expensive telescope at the window. The admiral watching these final preparations with his dandified flag lieutenant hovering at his side, ready to offer some suitable apology if things went wrong. And in London, a note would be made on one of those great charts. Routine. *Onward* was under orders, to take despatches to the Flag Officer, Gibraltar, and to join the Strait Squadron. Bald and simple on the page.

He recalled the faces at that hastily convened meeting. Relief, surprise, anticipation, excitement, each man seeing it from the standpoint of his own responsibility. But, for the most part, they were still strangers to him. Some said it was better that way.

Gibraltar. He had last been there in *Unrivalled*, on passage home after the bloody encounter at Algiers under Exmouth's flag.

He heard the sentry's musket tap quite gently on the grating outside the screen door.

'First lieutenant, *sir!*'

Something made him pause and turn back, deliberately. He could almost hear Richard Bolitho's voice. *They'll expect to see it, Adam.*

He picked up the sword and strode toward the door.

He paused at the top of the companion ladder with one foot on the coaming. After the dimness of the cabin, the sky seemed dazzling, making a lie of the keen winter air. He could feel Vincent close behind him, silent now, mentally reprising his report in case he had forgotten some vital detail, like every first lieutenant with a new captain. Lower deck cleared, capstan manned. . . .

Routine. The quarterdeck and both gangways filled with seamen and marines. The capstan with all its bars shipped and ready stood like an intruder.

He saw the sailing master, Tobias Julyan, his feet apart, a telescope tucked loosely under his arm. He was speaking to the helmsmen on either side of the big double wheel, nodding occasionally, outwardly at ease. Adam liked what he had already seen of him. A midshipman, slate held in readiness to

80

jot down a signal or report one from elsewhere, stood nearby. He had a set, serious face: that was Deacon, the senior 'young gentleman' aboard, and due for examination when the next Board became available. Before this he had been serving in the flagship. He was fortunate to have been given *Onward* in these uncertain times. Luck, favouritism, skill? *We shall soon know.*

Adam walked forward, and felt men move aside to clear a space by the quarterdeck rail.

He looked up at the masthead pendant, flapping loosely in the breeze one moment, then taut as a lance the next. Once clear of the land it would be lively enough. He glanced along the deck to the forecastle: more men mustered in parties, each with a senior hand in charge. Landmen and the newly joined, the 'waisters', useful for adding their weight to the braces, or lending another ounce of muscle to the capstan.

And right forward, almost in the eyes of the ship, was Squire the second lieutenant. A true professional, but not an easy one to know. A man for whom charts and navigation were allies and not enemies; it was obvious why he had been given a commission after his service with Sir Alfred Bishop. From the lower deck . . . the old hands always insisted that it brought out the best, or the very worst.

Vincent was saying, 'Quarter-boat is towing astern, sir, with a crew standing by.'

'Better to be safe, Mark.' He did not see his surprise at the use of his name. It seemed to break Vincent's concentration.

'I am sorry, sir. I forgot.' He stared abeam as the guardboat pulled slowly across the bows. 'There was one man missing at the last muster.'

'Deserted?' Adam concealed his impatience. It was not so long ago that any man would run when a King's ship came into port or dropped anchor close by and the hated press gangs had been put ashore, and a blow over the head was the only conversation. Most of *Onward*'s company, however, were either skilled seamen from other ships, or volunteers, with reasons as varied as their histories.

'A good man. Harris, one of our best coopers. Must have happened during the dog watches.'

'When the last fresh water lighter shoved off. Yes, I heard the commotion.' He stared at the sea and did not notice

Vincent's expression. *The Captain's down aft in his cabin. He won't know anything. . . .* 'List him as missing. The officer of the guard will know what to do.'

He grasped Vincent's arm, suddenly impatient to be gone. 'A fair wind, so let's not waste it! Make our signal to the Flag.'

He saw the bunting jerk up the halliards and break out to the wind; the signal party must have been poised with the flags already joined.

'Your glass, sir?'

Adam turned, the faces and shouts of command held at bay. It was Napier.

'Well, David?'

The boy waited, frowning slightly with concentration as he took the telescope.

He answered simply, 'I'll not let you down, sir.'

Adam reached out as if to grip his shoulder, but saw his face. Like a warning. He let his hand fall and said only, 'You will be up forrard with the second lieutenant. Stay close and wait for his orders.'

The midshipman stepped back and touched his hat.

'Aye, *aye*, sir!'

'Signal from Flag, sir!' The pencil was squeaking loudly on the slate. ' "Proceed when ready!" '

Adam walked aft again. 'Man the capstan!'

He shaded his eyes against a shaft of reflected sunlight and looked at the shore, and the overlapping rooftops. The admiral would be observing them, but what of that other captain? Grenville, *who gave me this ship.*

'Heave, lads!' Guthrie now. 'Put yer bloody backs into it, *heave*!'

Sir John Grenville would be there. And he would be alone.

More men ran to the capstan, chests pressed to the bars, arms cracking with strain.

'*Heave*, lads, *heave*!'

A gaunt figure in a shabby blue coat had climbed on to a hatch cover, a violin gripped in big, reddened hands. Some one raised a cheer, and Guthrie the boatswain yelled, 'Step out, me lads, an' make yer feet *tell*!'

Others shouted encouragement, and there was a loud, metallic click as the first pawl fell into place. The capstan was starting to turn. *Click.* The fiddle brought more shouts, cheers as well, when some of the scarlet-coated marines piled arms and ran to lend their weight.

Adam watched the helmsmen. One was already gripping a spoke, but his foot was tapping the deck in time with the fiddle.

He recognized the fiddler now as *Onward*'s senior cook. Without his long apron he was a completely different man. And the tune was familiar, but he could not give it a name. He half smiled. Not 'Portsmouth Lass'. That, he would never forget.

He could imagine the long, sleek hull beginning to move, clink by clink, toward the embedded anchor. Muscle and sweat. A contest known to every deepwater sailor.

And the nippers below in the cable-tier, mere children most of them, guiding and stacking the cable, and trying to clean off the mud and filth as it came inboard.

A ship coming alive. He swung round and saw Vincent bending to speak with some one at the companion.

'Stand by, on deck!' Sharper than he had intended, but the next few minutes would be vital. There would be many eyes watching today, and many ready to smirk or sneer at *Onward*'s new captain. *Afraid of his own shadow.* But too much confidence could be a killer. No matter how many times these men had been trained to scramble aloft until they knew every hand and foot hold, and the feel of each sheet and stay, this moment of truth was the real test. If some one slipped and fell overboard, it would still be possible for the quarter-boat to cast off and rescue the unfortunate seaman. But one false step aloft. . . . He glanced at the maintop. There was no second chance.

'Standing by, sir!'

The capstan bars were revolving like a great human wheel. And, yes, faster now, the pawls' movement steady and unbroken. Then Lieutenant Squire's voice along the full length of the deck.

'Anchor's hove short, sir!' He had not even cupped his hands.

'Loose the heads'ls!'

Adam clenched his fist. *Too soon.* He listened to the capstan and imagined the ship thrusting above the anchor.

He looked directly ahead, at an old seventy-four which had arrived in Plymouth yesterday. Her shrouds were full of sailors, and he saw the glint of telescopes on her poop.

'Ready on the helm, Captain.' Julyan the master, and beyond him one of his mates, with a book open in both hands. All staring forward, their eyes on Squire. All but one. Luke Jago stood at the foot of the mizzen, arms folded, indifferent to the figures already high above him, some clawing their way out along the yards, dark shapes against the sky.

Adam saw him raise his hand, a gesture no more than a man would make brushing off a fragment of oakum. Then a nod, even as the cry came from forward. *'Anchor's aweigh!'*

The capstan was moving quickly now, men running to join those already hauling the braces, taking the strain as the great yards began to swing, canvas spilling to the wind as *Onward* broke free from the land.

Another quick glance at the anchored two-decker. As if she were under way and altering course toward them. But no sails were set, and only the people in her shrouds were moving to observe the new frigate's departure.

Adam strode forward, stepping over the unshipped capstan bars, even as men ducked past and around him to clear the deck.

He studied the compass, his body leaning slightly with the ship, feeling it, living it. More hoarse shouts, the clatter of tackles and the stamp of running feet as others answered the demands of wind and rudder.

The topsails, free of their yards at last, were already hard-bellied in the offshore wind, flinging down the night's rain like pellets. *Onward* was answering, her masthead pendant throwing a hard shadow across the topmen as they dragged and kicked their way to safety, calling to one another in a mixture of bravado and relief. Julyan watched the jib as it filled and shook, some of Squire's anchor party pausing to stare up even as they continued to make fast the great anchor to the cathead, the sea suddenly alive and breaking beneath them.

The land was sliding away across the quarter. Adam heard Guthrie again, voice like a trumpet, and could imagine him unmoving, his men running and weaving around him.

More hands to the braces now, some slipping, pushed or cursed by those who stumbled over them.

Adam sensed Julyan's eyes on him, covertly, not wanting to be seen.

'Meet her!' He wiped some spray from his face and heard the wheel go over. The helmsman was angled to the deck, his head thrown back as he, too, watched the sails, the canvas slapping and refilling while the bows continued to swing.

Faces, voices intruded. Impatience, anger. 'Catch a turn there, Johnson!' A muffled response, then, *'Well, do it, whatever your bloody name is!'*

Some one's foot caught on a snaking length of rope; he fell, the breath knocked out of him, but was still able to offer a mocking bow to the man who pulled him upright.

Adam peered at the tilting compass.

'Steady!' He rested his hand on the shining brasswork; he had seen a young sailor polishing it with great care at first light.

'Sou' east by south, sir!'

He looked abeam and saw a fishing boat altering course to stand well clear, some small figures crouched beneath the tanned sails, one or two waving. Some of the anchor party were waving back. David Napier was standing beside the massive Squire, looking up at him and laughing. Still an adventure, then, even after the horror of *Audacity*.

'We could let her fall off a point, sir.'

Adam lifted the telescope and wiped the lens on his sleeve.

Julyan was a good master, and *Onward* was his ship also.

'Well spoken.' He waited for the wheel to swing over once more, the fishing boat vanishing astern.

Vincent was beside him now. 'All secure, sir.' He was looking up at the masthead pendant. 'Wind seems steady enough.' He shaded his eyes and stared forward, then he raised his hand. 'The foc'sle party can fall out. The anchor's catted and secure for sea.'

Then he smiled, for the first time. 'A proud moment.'

Adam steadied his telescope and saw waves breaking on the rocks, harmless, almost delicate at this distance. But many a luckless sailor knew otherwise at close quarters. Penlee Point. He moved the telescope, and the silent crests and the land fell away.

A few faces loomed in the glass, and then the quivering jib

and staysails. And unseen beneath them the leaping dolphin, the youth with his outstretched trident.

He waited for the bows to lift. A beginning, and yet so final.

He could hear Vincent's words. *A proud moment.*

The open sea.

7

Written in Blood

David Napier reached out to steady himself but dropped his arm as the deck lifted beneath him. He was becoming accustomed to the motion of a ship again, and *Onward*'s sudden changes of mood. Five days since they had weighed anchor and Plymouth had merged into the coastline and vanished. It was as if the elements had been waiting for them. Strong winds and rough seas the further they drove into the Western Approaches had made rest a luxury, and sleep impossible, with the pipe for all hands to shorten sail or man the braces for yet another change of tack shrilling every hour, and *Onward*'s people up and running.

Five days, and still no sight of land nor any other vessel. Sea and wind, and he was pleased that he had been able to ride both without fear. He did not allow himself to think much about *Audacity*, but she had been a smaller frigate. A good beginning for any young gentleman.

He looked at the door across the narrow passageway: *Onward*'s wardroom. Only a few paces from the midshipmen's berth, but as one wag had remarked, it could take a lifetime to reach it.

Onward carried six midshipmen, and yet they scarcely knew one another. Learning their duties and their own parts of ship, and the foul weather, had made certain of that. Even off watch or in rare moments of peace, they were still strangers. Deacon, the senior in the gunroom, spent most of his spare time reading manuals on navigation or gunnery and making notes in his log; he was also in charge of the signals crew. The

87

prospect of the examination for promotion obviously weighed heavily on him.

At the other end of the scale, Midshipman Walker, who was twelve years old and in his first ship, seemed to be continually seasick or recovering over a bucket, as he was now. Napier swallowed. He had never suffered seasickness, but there was always a first time.

Simon Huxley had remained friendly, and helpful when they were allowed to work on charts together, but he was still reserved, thinking constantly of his father and always anticipating any slur or criticism, real or imagined.

The wardroom door opened to his knock, and a messman, some silver tankards gripped insecurely in one hand, regarded him impassively.

'Can I help?' The merest pause. 'Sir?'

'Lieutenant Squire sent for me.'

The messman looked over his shoulder.

'He can't see you just yet, Mr. Napier. If you wait, I'm sure he'll not be long.'

Napier nodded. He could hear voices, one raised. The deck tilted sharply and a tankard slipped from the messman's hand and clattered across it.

Napier stooped instinctively and retrieved it.

'No damage.'

The messman gave him a long, measuring look.

'Thank you, sir. You shouldn't—'

Napier wondered what he would think if he knew he was speaking to some one who had been a cabin servant, and had waited at table. But the messman had disappeared.

He heard Squire say something and then the other voice.

'Thought you should be *told*, that's all! Some might think you'd forgotten you was one o' them, and not that long ago, neither!'

The speaker strode past Napier without a glance. *If he even saw me.*

Squire came to the door.

'Ah, there you are, boy. Come in and rest easy. We'll be changing tack soon— all hands again, eh?'

Napier followed him, still thinking about the man who had just pushed past him. He had seen him about the deck often

88

enough, a burly, hard-faced boatswain's mate. Fowler: the name had stuck in his mind for some reason.

Some one who must have known Squire while he was still on the lower deck. An old grievance, or perhaps he wanted a favour. . . .

'I've changed your present duties for gunnery drill. Mr. Maddock agrees. Starboard battery. All experience is needed in a new company like ours.' He seemed unperturbed by whatever had happened. 'The captain intends to increase the gun drill. He's not satisfied, as it stands.' He opened a pad and studied it.

Napier was gazing around the wardroom, home to the officers, with its spartan comforts, small, screened sleeping quarters, chairs and tables: their only private space and refuge after long hours on watch or handling the ship under every imaginable condition, even in the heat of action. He felt his skin crawl. Like that last time. *Beat to quarters.* The squeal of trucks, the guns being run out. Ready to fire.

He clenched his fingers into fists.

'How's the leg, by the way?'

'It's fine, sir.' As if he had read his thoughts. His fears.

Squire gestured vaguely. 'Lady Luck was with you that day.'

Napier watched him, head bent over the pad, scratching notes, apparently relaxed. No secrets in a frigate, they said, and it was true.

He heard the familiar trill of calls, the thud of feet in that other, real world.

'All hands! All hands!'

They left the wardroom together and almost collided with another messman.

Squire asked, 'Where are you going? Didn't you hear the pipe?' and the man lifted a bucket.

'Young middy's spewin' 'is guts up again, sir!'

'He'd better get over it. Otherwise. . . .' He left the threat hanging in the air as he strode heavily to the ladder.

Afterwards, Napier wondered if he had welcomed the interruption.

Adam Bolitho leaned back in the chair and stretched both

arms above his head. Had he been alone he would have allowed himself to yawn, but his mind was still clear and alert. It was almost noon, and the shipboard sounds were intruding once more after the squeal of trucks and gun-tackles from the starboard-side eighteen-pounders. With the hull still tilting under a brisk north-westerly, it had taken every muscle to haul each gun up to its port, and he had not needed to be within earshot to be aware of the curses aimed in his direction as they had obeyed each command of the drill. Rammers and sponges, and more sweat with handspikes to train or traverse toward an invisible enemy. He had not forgotten, and he had probably cursed his captain then as bitterly as the rest of them.

He saw a shadow fall across the table as Lieutenant Vincent moved away from the stern windows. After the gales and roiling cloud it was almost unreal to see the sun, and feel a hint of warmth through the thick glass. Not that either of them could see very much through the layers of caked salt.

He could picture the chart, the calculations, and the nagging doubts that stayed in company. He should be armoured against them, but wind and sea were always waiting to ambush an arrogant captain.

Vincent said, 'We'll sight the lights of Cadiz tomorrow. The next landfall will be the Rock.'

The other figure stirred at the table, closing his much-thumbed log book.

'Sunday, praise the Lord, we can celebrate in church!' Tom Maddock, *Onward*'s gunner, gave a rare grin. 'With plenty of time for more drills!'

Adam heard sounds from the pantry. Morgan would be standing by; he was getting used to his ways, knowing his captain was eager to meet his officers to discuss, and perhaps criticize, their progress in working up this new company.

And it had not been easy. In the Bay of Biscay they had been forced to hoist and manhandle the quarter-boat inboard to avoid it being swamped or torn adrift in a steep following sea, 'as solid as a cliff', one topman had observed. Guthrie the boatswain had left no room for doubts. 'If you goes overboard in that, you'll need to swim the rest of the way to Gib!'

But nobody did, although a good many had taken a thrashing

from *Onward* for their efforts. *A sailor's lot.* A bandage, a tot of rum and a slap on the back cured many ills.

Morgan had come into the cabin, a tray with four glasses already prepared. Adam rubbed his eyes, the fatigue washing over him.

'Gentlemen, I forgot. I've asked the surgeon to join us.'

Maddock said, 'I'd best get back to my duties, sir. I have to fix the skead on one of my carronades.'

Adam waved him down with a smile. *My carronades.*

'Take a glass beforehand.'

Maddock sat and opened his log book again.

It was nothing personal. Maddock shared the wardroom with Murray the surgeon, but their shipboard work, and their worlds, kept them apart much of the time. Most sailors felt the same. Share a tot and a joke together and then one day there was the barrier, and the dread.

He returned his thoughts to Gibraltar. Ten days since they had left Plymouth. Not like the last time in *Unrivalled*, when they had returned there after Algiers. Only eight days from the Rock to Plymouth Sound. But that had been different. . . .

He said suddenly, 'You were at Trafalgar, I believe?'

Maddock looked up.

'Aye, sir, gunner's mate in the old *Spartiate*, seventy-four, Cap'n Laforey.' His eyes crinkled. 'Different times then.'

Reading his mind.

He watched Morgan pouring the wine, deep red and tilting in the glass, then holding quite still before moving again. *From the Last Cavalier.*

Sunday, when the anchor dropped, what would she be doing? Thinking? Walking near the old church, or along the headland. Waiting for a ship. Never sure.

Morgan murmured, 'He's here now, sir.'

Gordon Murray, the surgeon, glanced around the great cabin.

'Celebration, is it?' A quick nod to Morgan, and he sat down, a trim, slightly built figure, unlike so many of his calling, and light on his feet like a dancer, or a swordsman. 'I was delayed, sir.' The fourth glass was being filled, tilting to the motion. 'Hard to think with all the damned din on deck. Two men injured.' His eyes flicked to Maddock. 'But they'll live. I hate to think what they would do if those guns ever fired in anger.'

He shook slightly, but the laughter remained silent.

Adam waited, trying to read Murray's face: strong features dominated by a hooked nose, and piercing, pale eyes. Hair flecked with feathers of white, as if he had dodged through a flurry of snow. Murray looked directly at the pantry door and said loudly, 'Would you fetch my bag from the sick bay?'

As Morgan departed, he added, 'Not for me to give orders to your servant, sir!'

Adam said, 'Tell me.'

Murray turned on his chair and looked over at Vincent.

'You reported a man missing, just before we weighed.'

'Ned Harris. It's in the log. Have you heard something about him?'

'More to the point, Mark, I have found him, or two of my people did. Came straight to me.' He moved a hand dismissively. 'Be all over the ship before a dog can bark. I did what I could.'

Adam said, 'Where?' And the inner voice. *You knew.*

Murray turned back, his nose training around like one of those guns.

'Sail room, sir. I wanted some spare canvas. Harris was out of sight . . . and down on the orlop, there are many other smells.'

Vincent exclaimed, 'How did it happen, for God's sake?'

'He was stabbed.' The pale eyes remained very steady. 'Five times, to be precise.'

Vincent returned to the stern windows and rested his hand on the salt-patterned glass.

'He was a good man, what I knew of him. Popular, too.'

Maddock said, 'So the killer is still among us.'

Adam stood up, fatigue gone, a new, grim energy coursing through him. Whatever the cause, greed, debt, a moment's uncontrollable fury, a man was dead. Unknown to some, a messmate to others.

'Clear lower deck, Mark. I'll speak to all hands.'

It was little enough, but it was right that they should know. And the one man among them who would stand alone.

Morgan had returned.

'They said you had your bag with you, sir.' But he was looking at Adam.

Vincent said, 'Had he been robbed?'

'Searched, I believe, but nothing taken.' And to Adam, 'No sign of struggle.'

Adam looked toward the screen door as if it were invisible, seeing the ship in his mind. Afternoon watchkeepers at their stations on and above the deck, the men they had relieved hastening to their messes, eager for a hot meal, gossiping about the day's events, and most of all the prospect of landfall. No longer a rumour or a pencilled cross on the sailing master's chart, but the conclusion of their first passage as one company.

Vincent asked, 'Shall I pass the word, sir?'

Adam listened to the murmur of sea and wind, the occasional thump of the tiller-head.

'Let them eat first.' He looked at the others. 'Thank you, all of you, for your help.'

He walked aft again and watched the broken crests following in silent procession. Then he said, 'Can't you tell? They know already.'

But he was alone.

He stood by the quarterdeck rail in the last moments of *Onward*'s final approach, tasting the smoke on his lips. The silence of the anchorage after her salute and the measured response from the battery ashore was profound, almost unnerving. The gulls settled again on the water.

He looked at the anchored men-of-war, their paintwork and checkered gunports reflected with the gulls; some had already spread awnings against the hard sun. Fewer than on those other visits, but impressive enough. The pale buildings ashore were partly hidden in mist or gunsmoke; impossible to compare this to the wind and chilling rain of England's winter.

He had seen the gunner pacing slowly inboard of each port as the salute had shattered the morning stillness, mouth barely moving in the chant he used to time every explosion, hand ready to signal instantly to the next crew if there was a misfire. There was not. Maddock might well be smiling now, he thought. Between the bangs he had thought he heard what sounded like church bells.

He shaded his eyes, and saw the anchor party standing together, the new hands staring at the towering Rock, others doubtless trying to identify the ships.

The wheel moved slightly; even that seemed loud. *Onward* was barely making headway, with all her sails clewed up except topsails and jib.

'Guardboat, sir!'

'Very well.' The flash of a glass, somebody watching their approach. Like so many others for whom *Onward* would represent news from England, from families, from a lover. Births, deaths, promotion, hope, disillusionment. The guard-boat had slowed above its own image, oars tossed.

'Stand by forrard!' He heard the order being passed, the voice cracking, bringing a grin from the second helmsman. It was Midshipman Walker, the one who had been seasick since they had weighed at Plymouth. There was hope for him yet.

He saw Lieutenant Squire by the cathead, gesturing sharply, no time left for errors. David Napier would be with him, the whole panorama of ships and craggy landscape laid at his feet.

It felt like that for me.

He turned and gazed up at the masthead pendant, moving listlessly now, and his eyes passed over the Royal Marines paraded by the quarterdeck carronades, their officer, Lieutenant Gascoigne, standing rigidly, staring straight ahead. A splash of colour aboard *Onward* for the telescopes. . . .

'Lee braces there! Hands wear ship!'

More shouts, and somebody laughed or coughed.

'Tops'l clew lines!'

Adam heard the slap of canvas, and a few curt words from the boatswain. He saw the cook, in his apron and without the fiddle, stooping to duck out of sight.

'Helm a-lee.' And she was turning, very slowly, the long, tapering jib-boom like a pointer, the masts and yards of the nearest ship passing across it.

Another voice, not loud but terse, and the obedient response from the boat-tier. Luke Jago would not be distracted. The gig would be out and alongside as ordered. No matter what.

Adam faced forward again, felt the air like warm breath on his face as *Onward* turned into the wind.

'Let go!'

94

He thought he saw Squire's hand slice down, then the burst of spray as the anchor hit the water, men running while the cable quivered in pursuit.

The compressor was already checking it, slowing and taking the strain.

The yards were secured, all canvas brailed or furled, seamen scurrying down the ratlines, the less cautious sliding straight down backstays.

Vincent was with him now.

'All fast forrard, sir!' He was grinning, as if all strain had dropped away with the anchor.

Another voice: Deacon, the senior midshipman, grim-faced, and very conscious of the moment.

'Signal, sir!' He had to clear his throat. 'From *Flag*!'

Adam heard Julyan the master remark, 'He's in a bit of a bloody hurry.' He looked away as Adam walked past him.

'What is it, Mr. Deacon?' Some one had handed him a telescope.

Deacon said steadily, 'From Flag, sir. *Captain repair on board.*'

Adam trained the glass, taking extra seconds to refocus it. The flagship swayed across the lens and steadied, her name, *Tenacious*, clearly visible across her counter.

He said quietly, 'Thank you, Mr. Deacon. That was perceptive of you.' He heard Jago shouting orders, the squeal of tackle. He knew.

'Sir?' He turned back and saw that, as Deacon pointed out, the flagship should have been flying the colours of a rear-admiral. She was not. A commodore's broad pendant had replaced them. Permanent or temporary, but there had been no hint of a change in command when he had spoken with the admiral. Promotion, or away on some diplomatic mission? He looked over at the canvas canopy by the boat-tier. Or, like the murdered cooper Harris, beyond the concerns of this world.

Morgan had come on deck, with the sword and Adam's boat cloak in readiness. He looked like a man who had been offered an affront.

'I'm told it's urgent, see? You would not wish to squander the time donning your best uniform, I thought, sir?'

'Thank you.' He held out his arms so that Morgan could

95

fasten the belt. The commodore must have had hours to gauge *Onward*'s approach, if he was interested. Was this urgency just a show of authority?

Vincent was saying, 'I'll have all boats lowered, sir. Mail ready to go ashore.' His eyes also moved to the canvas canopy. 'What about Harris, sir?'

Adam brought his mind back with an effort.

'A shore burial will be necessary.' He gazed up at the towering rock, cloud streaming from its peak. The gateway. 'We could lose a hundred men in the King's name and not raise an eyebrow. But one poor devil. . . .'

'Gig's alongside, sir!'

Adam tossed the boat cloak back to Morgan. 'Not this time.' He touched one of his epaulettes. They, at least, were still untarnished.

He walked to the ladder, aware of their eyes, some familiar, others still unknown. At the mainmast truck the pendant was coming to life again in a light breeze, and a few small figures were still working in the top, pausing to peer down as he strode toward the entry port. The boatswain was touching his hat, an evil grin on his battered face.

'We'll show the buggers, sir!'

And Rowlatt, the master-at-arms, glaring at such informality.

Two midshipmen. Huxley, who had joined the ship with Napier, and the one called Hotham, whose father was a clergyman. There was a story there, and he could imagine the comments in the gunroom. Or maybe not so much these days. After all, Nelson's father had been a man of the cloth.

A squad of Royal Marines, and the boatswain's mates by the port, one caught in the act of moistening his call on his tongue. There were suddenly a dozen things he wanted to point out to the first lieutenant. *When I step into the gig, he is in command.*

Vincent murmured, 'I have the weight, sir.'

Adam raised his hat, the calls shrilled and the muskets slapped down in salute, within a cloud of pipeclay. Something every captain took for granted. As his right.

He nodded to one of the side-boys as he rested his hand on his shoulder, then stepped out and into the gig.

Jago was standing in the sternsheets, hat in hand, eyes

everywhere. He, more than any one, probably knew the truth.

'Cast off, forrard! Out oars! Give way *together*!'

Jago eased the tiller slightly and watched the oars dipping and pulling, all eyes on the stroke and none on the captain. Given time, he would knock them into a fair crew. He glanced astern and saw *Onward*, already bows-on, one of those clumsy-looking local craft with the big lateen sail hovering close by. Ready to barter, or steal anything they could lay hands on.

He looked over the stroke oarsman's head and measured the distance. So many times, but always different. Some could find you dreaming and carry you past the ship or landing stage. Or an oarsman, no matter how experienced, could 'catch a crab' and throw the stroke into a shambles.

He stooped to listen as the epaulettes moved slightly, and he heard the captain remark, 'I can think of better ways to spend the first day in harbour, Sunday or not!'

The stroke oarsman grinned, but kept his eye on the tiller. Some of the others shared it even if they were out of hearing. He always seemed to have that way with them. Did *he* know it, he wondered? He saw the sunlight flashing from the flagship's high stern windows and on the gilt gingerbread scrollwork around her poop. *Must have cost a fortune.*

Figures on the gangway now, telescopes raised. He scowled. *Bloody officers. Are they all blind?*

'Boat ahoy?'

He bellowed back, '*Onward!*'

He felt almost proud, but it would end up with bloody knuckles if anybody knew what he was thinking.

The bowman had hooked on, and the gig nudged against the rope fenders below the entry port. After *Onward*, the flagship's side and tumblehome seemed like a cliff.

Only seconds, and their eyes met. The hint of a smile.

'Squalls ahead, Luke.'

Then he was gone.

The lieutenant stood aside, one hand holding the door half open.

'Commodore Carrick will not be more than a few seconds, sir. Something urgent has come up.'

It was only a temporary cabin, with screens to separate it from the admiral's quarters in the poop; there were a few chairs, and an open port that looked across the main anchorage and its array of ships. *Onward* lay somewhere on the opposite quarter, out of sight, and the knowledge gave him a peculiar sense of loss.

He looked at the deck, where the painted canvas had been rolled back to reveal deep scars in the planking. A gun had once been run out through this port, or been hurled inboard on recoil after firing in drill or deadly earnest. *Tenacious* was a veteran, at a guess about twenty years old. A third-rate two-decker, with much of the heavier hull structure he had first seen as a midshipman in his uncle's old *Hyperion*.

The lieutenant had made him welcome enough, but had been careful to keep him apart from the ship's officers after his formal reception on board. He wore the twist of gold lace like Troubridge and was probably the rear-admiral's aide, and he had Troubridge's easy way of making conversation with a stranger. Without listening to or answering direct questions, Adam noticed.

His comment about the new commodore, for instance. When Adam had asked about the suddenness of the appointment he had replied airily, 'A fellow Cornishman, sir. You might know him.' And that was all.

Of course, the flag lieutenant was probably more concerned about his own immediate future. Commodores were not usually entitled to official aides, during what was often only a temporary promotion. He recalled Troubridge's cheerful warning: *the higher we climb. . . .*

'Captain Bolitho, sir?' Some one, the flagship's equivalent of Morgan in a well-cut velvet waistcoat and nankeen breeches, was regarding him from the other door, face sweating in the sunlight from the open port, as if he had been running. But it was humid between decks, and no awnings were rigged on deck, nor windsails to bring some relief to the messes below. Maybe the commodore considered the flagship's outward appearance more important than the comfort of those who served him.

He stopped the thoughts like a cable brake. They had not even met. If it began badly today, it would be of his own doing.

'If you will walk this way, sir.'

A Royal Marine sentry stepped smartly off a grating to open the main door to the great cabin, and Adam was aware of the quick glance. Another visitor, a little piece of news to pass on to his mate in the 'barracks'.

He thought of *Onward* again. So short a time, and yet he could not imagine going back to another ship of the line like *Athena*, or this, the flagship.

People ashore might ask him what was the difference.

This is the difference.

Commodore Arthur Carrick was standing with his back to the door. All the screens had been raised, to offer an immediate view of the anchorage and the spread of land beyond. The quarter windows were partly open, and there was the suggestion of a breeze.

Carrick turned toward him unhurriedly, casually even, his hands folding a document of some kind, which he held out toward the flag lieutenant.

'You will see that I've struck a couple of names off the list. I can't abide either of them. You would know that if you had been with me. . . .' He broke off and smiled directly at Adam, almost as if this were an unexpected meeting.

A lean, bony face with a high forehead, hair cut quite short in the style affected by younger members of the wardroom. He waited for Adam to reach him. 'You are welcome here, Captain Bolitho. I saw you anchor. Does my heart good to see a fine new frigate joining the squadron.' He did not offer his hand, but used it to pass the document to his aide. 'Stronger than anything faster, faster than anything stronger, isn't that what they say?'

A fellow Cornishman, the lieutenant had said. There was not much of it in his speech. More of a drawl, clipped only when he wanted to emphasize a point. But the face was Cornish, and Adam was reminded of his aunt's description of some one. *Looks like a real pirate.* Between forty and fifty, although he might have been any age.

He was saying, 'I shall read your report as soon as I'm able, Bolitho, but do you have any particular news for me?'

Adam realized that a chair had been placed beside him, and the lieutenant had disappeared.

Carrick sat by a table and rested his elbow on the edge.

'Hear quite a lot about you, Bolitho. Not one to waste words, I'm told.' The quick smile again. 'I like that.'

'One of my ship's company died when we left Plymouth. His body was found only two days ago.' Carrick had shifted very slightly, his chin resting in his hand. His eyes were very steady. Still.

'Two days? The corpse had been well hidden, I take it? You'd have nosed him otherwise.'

'He had been murdered, sir. In my report—'

'I'll read it later. A shore burial, then. That'll bring a few complaints.' He had turned as if to listen to something, and Adam saw his eyes in the filtered sunlight, more grey than blue, and hard as iron. They rested on him once more. 'I may require more details.' He paused as the servant placed a tray with glasses and a decanter on the table. Then he said, 'Rear-Admiral Aylmer was required to haul down his flag, the sudden return of an 'old illness'. We're still not certain.' He seemed to dismiss it. 'But you were Sir Graham Bethune's flag captain. You know all about the whims and fancies of senior officers, I have no doubt. We must be patient.' He gestured brusquely to the servant. 'Not for me— I am seeing the governor shortly. But Captain Bolitho will require refreshment after his hectic morning.'

Adam said, 'I have to see the governor myself, sir.'

'I know. But this is far from being a duty. A social matter.'

The wine seemed sour, but he knew it was tainted by his own anger. Resentment.

Carrick spoke again.

'So many changes, Bolitho. New minds, fresh diplomacy. Too many seem able to forget the wars and the sacrifices. Some of us find it a hard lesson to learn.' He tapped the table, and the smile was back. '*Onward* is now part of the Strait Squadron. I know your reputation. Lord Exmouth spoke well of you after the Algiers campaign. Peace or war, loyalty means everything to me.' He regarded him steadily. 'Your uncle, Sir Richard, had he been spared, would certainly recognize today's enemy.' He stood abruptly and gestured toward the side. '*Treachery*. It should be up there on the Rock, carved in stone where every one in his right mind can read it!' He glared as some one tapped hesitantly on the door. 'Before it's written in blood!'

Adam was on his feet and saw Carrick's eyes drop to the sword at his side.

'You will receive more detailed orders tomorrow, after you have seen the governor.' Then he called, '*Come in, man*, if you must!'

He turned back with a shrug and a hint of the smile, and said, 'So . . . let's be about it, shall we?'

8

One Company

Lieutenant Mark Vincent closed the cabin door behind him and inhaled deeply. A few steps from the wardroom on *Onward*'s lower deck, but it would turn any volunteer's head away from the sea for good. It was allocated to the captain's clerk, and in size was probably no smaller than his own, but whenever he came here he felt stifled, trapped. There was hardly a space left uncovered or unstacked with ledgers and log books, and no natural lighting but a glimmer through a small vent. How the clerk managed to prepare and study his written work, as well as sleep and enjoy any escape from shipboard life was impossible to imagine.

As first lieutenant it was sometimes necessary for Vincent to delve into these logs and muster books, or arrange an official report which, when beautifully penned in the clerk's stylish hand, was destined for some similar claustrophobic cave in flagship or headquarters ashore.

Henry Prior, the clerk, was sitting behind his table, left hand on an opened ledger, the right shading a candle, which he had just fitted to one of his several lamps. A small, neat person, bright-eyed and usually wearing a half smile, discreet to the point of secrecy, he was certainly no gossip. Vincent had heard the captain's coxswain remark of him, 'Like trying to open an oyster with a feather!'

And as far as he knew, Prior was the only man aboard who had served with the unfortunate Captain Richmond, who had arranged for his appointment while *Onward* had still been in the builder's yard.

Vincent turned his head to listen to the twittering call from boatswain's mate somewhere in the upper hull. *My ship.* The captain was still ashore with the commodore, or perhaps at the governor's residence again. *Could I have taken command?*

Prior said, 'These are ready for signature, sir,' moving some papers across the table.

'So that *I* can carry the blame if they're not accurate.'

'I have checked them myself.' Fussily, Prior shook the paper cuffs he wore to protect his spotless shirt, as if to dissociate himself from the contents. 'I believe the captain is returning aboard today, sir?'

Vincent tried to push all the other demands and duties to the back of his mind. Perhaps orders had arrived and *Onward* might be free to sail again. The uncertainty or indifference from on high was oppressing every one. And the captain? Sometimes he felt that a barrier was still there. As if Bolitho were waiting, watching for something overlooked.

'I had better do my rounds.' He stretched, and felt his knuckles touch the deckhead. 'Send word if. . . .' He realized that Prior was getting to his feet, glancing possessively at the desk as if to mark everything in its place.

He said, 'I'll leave *you*, sir. Mr. Monteith, you will recall.'

Vincent sighed.

'I'm never allowed to forget him!'

The door closed, leaving him entombed with the logs, but for a few seconds he heard the sounds of thudding feet and a voice calling somebody's name. A living ship. He repressed another sigh. *A first lieutenant's lot. . . .*

Monteith came into the cabin, hat wedged beneath his arm, his eyes not leaving Vincent's face as he stood stiffly opposite the table.

Vincent said, 'This could have waited. Later, perhaps, in the wardroom.'

He saw Monteith's chin lifting slightly, his free hand pressed against his side. Scarcely moving even as the deck swayed uneasily beneath them.

Monteith said, 'I made an official complaint, sir. And as my first lieutenant, I expected you to support it.'

Vincent felt cool air coming from somewhere. 'Close the door, will you?' So calm, but he could feel the anger growing.

Coming up the back stairs, as he had heard the gunner say on several occasions. He sensed the hostility and the confidence, too. Always ready to seize upon the smallest breach of discipline or effiency. He recalled the captain's comments after examining *Onward*'s punishment book.

Trivial or not, Monteith's charges of slackness or insubordination were usually well founded. *I should have seen it. Stopped it at the very beginning.*

He said, 'We have all been very busy. Many of us still are,' and saw Monteith's fingers clench more tightly at his side. 'You gave one of the hands an order— Willis, maintop— which he failed to carry out. Am I correct?'

'To reeve some new halliards, as I put in my report. When I went to examine the work I discovered that my order had been ignored. Willis told me it had been countermanded by another officer.'

'And you are certain of this?'

'Lieutenant Squire told me himself.' He squared his shoulders. 'Admitted it. I saw their faces.'

'And you want an explanation?'

'An apology. In writing.'

'You are determined about this?'

'It is my right, sir.'

There was a tap on the door and it opened a few more inches. It was one of the master's mates.

'What *is* it, Mr. Meredith?' He relented immediately. 'As you can see, it is not convenient.'

The eyes flickered between them.

'A ship's headin' for the anchorage, sir. Mr. Julyan said to inform you.' He glanced at the young lieutenant. 'Looks important, sir. She's a Frenchie.'

The sailing master was not the man to waste time on idle observations. And in any case. . . .

'My compliments to Mr. Julyan. I shall come up right away.' He waited until they were alone again and turned back to Monteith. 'Leave the matter with me. Ours is a small wardroom. I see no reason to make a storm out of this— what do you say?'

Monteith nodded curtly. 'It was my duty to bring the matter to you first.'

Vincent was reaching for his hat but stopped in mid-movement.

'First?'

Monteith stepped back from the table, almost casually.

'I shall see the captain, *sir.*'

Vincent waited until the cabin was empty again. Something stupid and unnecessary had caused this to happen. *And I should have seen it.*

There was another tap at the door.

'I *said* I was coming up!'

But it was Prior, the half smile apologetic.

'I saw Mr. Monteith leaving, and I thought. . . .'

'Forgive me, the cabin is yours again. I am learning a lot of things today. Mostly about myself.'

They both looked up as the first echo of a gun salute quivered against the hull. The newcomer, paying her respects to the governor and to the flag.

Vincent hurried up the ladder and into the hard sunlight.

Another bang. *Onward* was a new ship. She had no memories.

He saw Julyan standing by the compass box, arms folded, staring across the anchorage. He was surrounded by some of the duty watchkeepers, and others who had come on deck to pass the time and gaze at the incoming ship. But Julyan could have been completely alone. He did not even blink at the next crash and the echo that followed it.

Vincent shaded his eyes. When he reached him, Julyan was speaking as though to himself.

'She's the *Nautilus*, forty guns. Maybe more now.'

'So you know her?'

'I did.' He glanced up at the ensign, which was barely moving. 'New frigate, she was. First commission, an' her last, under this flag.'

A ship taken by the old enemy. It was common enough in the war at sea, on both sides. Like Maddock the gunner: the *Spartiate*, in which he had served at Trafalgar, had been a French prize taken by Nelson at the Nile.

Julyan unfolded his arms.

'The new flag won't change things, y' know. Or people.'

He might have said more, but a midshipman called, 'Gig's

105

shoved off from the jetty, sir! *With the captain!*'

Vincent touched his hat.

'Thank you, Mr. Deacon. Warn the side party and the master-at-arms.'

When he looked again, the French frigate was partly hidden by a big two-decker, sails still moving slowly beyond the rigging and furled canvas.

So the captain was coming back, and life would be on course again.

But all he could hear was Julyan's voice. *The new flag won't change things. Or people.*

Perhaps he was still brooding over Monteith's arrogance, or his own inability to deal with it. But it sounded like a threat.

Adam Bolitho slumped down in the green leather chair and kicked off his shoes.

'When I bought these in Plymouth, the shoemaker swore they would suit every sort of wear. Damned fellow had never heard of Gibraltar!'

He leaned back in the chair and tried to relax. To recover. Luke Jago was at the stern windows, both hands resting on the bench seat.

'Glad that lot's behind us, Cap'n.' His jaw cracked into a grin. 'Don't know how you do it, an' that's a fact.'

Adam stifled a yawn. 'Go ashore if you want to, Luke. You've earned it ten times over.'

Jago jerked his thumb at the screen door. 'I'll pipe for Morgan. He'll fetch you something.' The yawn was infectious, and he did not trouble to hide it. 'Sounds like another busy day tomorrow. Feet up with a tot of somethin' will do me!'

Adam unclipped his sword and laid it on the deck beside the chair. Through the windows he could see the lights ashore, and those on vessels at anchor. After the activity and urgency it was strangely peaceful now, with no boats moving. And if there were, they would be carrying senior officers or their guests. He thought of all the faces he had seen, hands he had shaken, and names he had tried to remember, since Jago's gig had first taken him ashore.

He stood up, swinging both legs from the chair, impatient with himself. There were stars above and below the Rock, and he knew he would fall asleep if he broached to now.

The skylight was partly open and he could hear a violin playing somewhere, then laughter and feet tapping in some lively jig. Were the French aboard *Nautilus* also enjoying some sailors' dance, and yarning with their mates like these men?

We are at peace now. With a stroke of the pen, and an ocean of blood. What was it like for the Frenchman's ship? Hemmed in by all the old foes. . . .

It took more than a pen to make peace.

He moved to the desk and touched the paper he would use for his next letter. How long had it been? He could see her holding it, opening it. Would it bring them closer, or would their still unreachable horizon withdraw even farther?

The door opened and Morgan padded into the cabin.

He said cheerfully, 'I expect you can still find a space for something, sir?' and placed a tray carefully on the desk. 'Does me good to see you back aboard, sir. We all wondered—'

Adam walked slowly through the cabin, the deck cool under his stockinged feet after the stairs and steep, cobbled streets, the hours of standing, the endless formalities.

'Some wine, I think. The first lieutenant is coming shortly.'

Vincent had met him at the entry port on his return. Eager to know the news, and *Onward*'s fresh orders. Or was he?

Morgan opened his little pantry and pretended to examine some of the bottles he had selected earlier. The captain looked drained. What did they find to argue about, when all these top officers put their heads together?

Now, when I get ashore. . . . He was still smiling to himself when the sentry rapped on his grating and announced Vincent.

Adam sat by the desk and gestured to another chair.

'Rest easy, Mark. You've been doing all the work in my absence.'

Vincent looked around the cabin.

'It feels right now, sir.'

Adam nodded. Then, 'I'd better tell you. We are sailing the day after tomorrow, in company with *Nautilus*. A matter of diplomacy, if you like.'

'Is that an order, sir? From the commodore?'

'Far higher than him, I'm afraid!'

Morgan was replacing the cognac with wine.

'Thank you. You can go and pipe down now.' Then he said, 'When I was in *Unrivalled* and we took part in the Algiers attack under Lord Exmouth, we learned quite a lot about another enemy stronghold. Aboubakr, some two hundred miles further along the coast. The French have always had a lively interest in the place, to base their own ships for use against *us*, and to control the local rebels. And now we are to support them.' He shrugged. 'Better the devil you know.'

He stood up and paced restlessly to the windows. 'A show of solidarity, nothing more.'

Vincent said, 'A dangerous game at the best of times.'

Adam looked at him keenly.

'Is something wrong, Mark?'

Vincent took a book from his pocket and said, 'A complaint has been made by Lieutenant Monteith, sir.'

Adam moved closer and touched his sleeve.

'Tell me. This is our ship. What we *make* her.'

Vincent kept the book in his hand. 'It was more than likely a simple misunderstanding. Squire countermanded an order after Monteith told one of the hands to reeve some new halliards.'

'And Monteith jumped to the wrong conclusion. Then it *was* a misunderstanding. Squire has a blunt way of doing things. It happens.' He smiled. 'Whatever they say on the lower deck about their officers, we can *all* make mistakes in our haste.'

Vincent said stiffly, 'It was a formal complaint, sir. I had no choice.'

'As first lieutenant, you did as you thought fit. Loyalty and obedience are yours by right. But respect is something else, and much harder to achieve.'

Vincent stood up.

'If that is the end of the matter, sir?'

'In two days' time we shall be at sea. Many will envy us. So let's remember that, shall we?' He walked back to the desk. 'We are the fortunate ones!'

But the door had closed. He knew he had failed.

Luke Jago nodded companionably to the sentry and pushed his way past the screen door. He was never questioned or refused entry. He could not even recall how or when it had begun; it remained something unspoken.

It was cool in the great cabin, or so it seemed after the dusty offshore wind. Even out in the anchorage, you could still taste sand in your teeth.

There had been all the usual bustle and argument of preparing for sea: the purser and his crew bringing aboard fresh stores and fruit from the harbour, with lists to be checked and a few clips with a rope's end or starter to move things along. Now the working parties were resting, enjoying a stand-easy, with a welcome smell of rum in the air. And tomorrow. . .

Morgan was leaning inside his pantry, sipping something from a mug. They were comfortable with one another now.

Jago remarked, 'The Cap'n's in the chart room. Don't want to make a bloody mess of things in front o' the Frogs, do we?'

Morgan considered it. 'Bit of a goer, isn't he?' and Jago grinned.

'You won't find him draggin' his feet when a mob o' forriners is watchin' every move!'

Morgan judged the moment, and put a mug down in front of him: it was raw rum.

'What about women? He's a post captain, after all, and not married, is he?' He wagged a finger. 'I've seen that painting he keeps so safely stowed in his sleeping quarters. Enough to make your hair curl!'

Jago took time to swallow his drink.

'The Cap'n's goin' to tie the knot when they gets a minute.'

Morgan looked across the cabin and dropped his voice.

'Not like some I've known. I shouldn't speak ill of the dead, but Richmond,' he jerked his head, 'you know . . . he was a real woman-hunter and no mistake. And one lady in particular, I was told.'

'Local girl?'

'Not she. Her husband was always away. A shipbuilder.' He patted his counter. 'Built this fine lady, for one.' There were voices from the skylight, and the marine sentry clearing his throat. '*She* got what she wanted, right enough.' He laughed coarsely. 'In more ways than she bargained for!'

Then he hurried to the door and for a few seconds longer

Jago was alone in the great cabin, remembering that first day aboard, when he had seen Richmond's effects packed and ready to be sent home to his widow.

Dead man's shoes.

He saw Bolitho walk into the cabin, and that he was limping slightly.

Also, that he was quite alone.

The morning was clear, with none of the haze which had obscured the Rock. *Onward*'s decks, swabbed clean at dawn, were already bone-dry, and the air was hot.

David Napier stood watching the hands being mustered beneath the mainmast truck, where the tackles and falls for hoisting boats were laid out in readiness. The twenty-eight foot cutter, their biggest boat, was about to be brought aboard for the last time before sailing.

Napier plucked at his heavy coat and wished he could strip off his uniform, like the men around him. He knew it was not so much the heat but something else in the air: excitement, the thrill of being part of it. Something he could still not explain.

He saw Huxley, the other midshipman stationed here, staring at the shore, perhaps hoping for some final boat to come with mail. Was his father still awaiting the court martial, or had its verdict been passed? He caught his eye and gave Napier a strained smile. Little enough, but it meant something to each of them.

He shivered, tasting the fat pork and biscuit crumbs from that early midshipman's breakfast. Even that had been part of the adventure: their ship being ordered to some strange place named Aboubakr, of which nobody seemed to have heard and which nobody could spell, although Julyan the master had assured them they would all know it beyond endurance when he had made them memorize the charts. Deacon, the senior midshipman, had suggested Julyan was as much in the dark as any of them.

He could hear Guthrie the boatswain rapping out orders to the cutter's crew alongside. Working parties and individuals seemed to revolve around him like the bars of a human capstan, although the bars themselves were still lying in ranks, waiting for the command.

Napier stared up at the braced yards, their sails still neatly furled as if trimmed to an invisible measure. He saw figures on the quarterdeck; they too were looking aloft, one gesturing as if to make a point. Vincent, the first lieutenant, seemed to be everywhere. Friendly enough with the midshipmen, and encouraging when it occured to him, but sometimes you had the feeling that he was never really listening. As Hotham, the clergyman's son, had said, 'You don't need to listen when you're next in command!'

He thought of the captain. The hardest part was getting used to the screen which was now a physical and figurative barrier between them. He was able to appreciate and accept it; it was necessary, for both their sakes.

He often thought of Falmouth, which he had been encouraged to regard as his new home, and of the girl who had helped him overcome his fear and the nightmare of *Audacity*. He thought, too, of Elizabeth, which was stupid of him, he had told himself often enough. But he did think of her.

'Ah, Mr. Napier. Time on your hands? We'll have to change that!'

It was Lieutenant Squire, big, powerful, and always apparently at ease. Old for his rank, but most officers were, who had made the longer passage by the lower deck. He looked like *somebody*, Napier thought, as if the solitary epaulette was perched on his shoulder by accident.

'Ready when you say the word, sir.'

'The cutter's coming aboard now.' He waved his fist to the nearest party of men and grinned broadly. 'You take charge. You have to begin some day!'

Napier did not move. He had watched the process several times, and he knew the order of things. But the cutter was a large boat, the maid of all work. It could load and carry stores, land parties of armed seamen and marines, shift a complete anchor for kedging the ship from one part of an anchorage to another. He found his brain was suddenly quite clear, and his nerves were steady. *Or carry a poor murdered sailor ashore for burial.*

'*Haul taut*, lads! Marry the falls!' He could hear the slither of cordage, the slap of feet, blocks taking the strain. But his mouth was dry as dust.

Another voice. 'Hoist away, handsomely, lads!' It was his own.

A hand brushed his arm as if in passing.

'Well done, young Napier. I've got it now!'

The great shadow, black against the sky, as the cutter swung evenly up and across the deck. He felt droplets of sea water splash his face and throat like shards of ice.

'Avast hauling! Secure those lines! Jump to it!'

Napier turned. The cutter's crew were leaping down to the tier, lines hauled into position and secured. Even the boat's coxswain, Fitzgerald, a tough seaman who hailed from Donegal Bay, was beaming with satisfaction, or relief.

Squire was already studying another list, but he looked up from it and said briefly, 'Just remember. It gets harder!'

Napier saw Huxley grinning over at him and waving both fists in congratulation. Some one yelled, 'The Frenchie's shortenin' 'er cable, sir!'

'Man the capstan, lively there!'

Napier saw the boatswain's mate, Fowler, lash out with his starter at one of the young hands, then strike the man across the shoulder even as he threw his weight on the nearest bar. He could see blood on the bare skin from the force of the blow. He glanced uncertainly at Squire, but the lieutenant had turned to watch the French frigate.

Doesn't he care?

Napier stared aloft, but the sun blinded him. He had seen the topmen spread out along those yards, canvas billowing and punching between them.

Squire had hurried to his station in the eyes of the ship, and when Napier joined him above the cathead the wet cable was already jerking inboard like some endless serpent. One of the forecastle hands paused for breath and shouted, 'The Frenchie's aweigh! *Onward*'ll show her a clean pair of heels when she makes a run for it, eh, lads?'

Pride and, Napier thought, animosity too. Maybe that was why they did not use the other frigate's name. She might be a prize, but she was still one of their own.

The shrill of more calls, and Guthrie's voice carrying above them all.

'Anchor's aweigh!'

He saw Squire watching the glistening cable as it brought the anchor firmly to the cathead. He could feel the deck moving, and caught a glimpse of other ships, still at anchor, apparently shifting their bearings without a stitch of canvas spread.

Hotham had dragged off his hat and was waving it wildly in the wind, his voice lost in the din of canvas and rigging. If the clergyman could see his son now. . . .

Squire was looking across at him.

'My respects to the Captain. Tell him, all secure!'

Napier hurried aft, dodging braces, halliards and running figures aware of nothing but the task in hand. He saw Monteith shouting to some men clawing their way up the weather shrouds, still dwarfed against the Rock, although he knew *Onward* must be well clear of the anchorage.

Monteith exclaimed, 'Are they damned well deaf?'

Guthrie ignored him and repeated the same order, which they heard without effort. Monteith swung away, gesturing irritably to some one else. Guthrie spared Napier a quick glance and muttered, 'You'm learnin' today!'

The ship was under way, upper deck already clearing of cordage and tackle, men still climbing aloft as more canvas was spread.

Napier waited below the quarterdeck rail as the marines of the afterguard clumped away from the mizzen braces, somehow keeping in step.

Lieutenant Vincent called to him, *'Speak up!'*

'I— I was told to report to—'

Two men ran between them, and another limped past, a bloody rag tied around one knee.

Then, suddenly, the captain was there, looking down at him.

'I saw the signal.' They could have been alone. 'It was smartly done, and in half the time.' Some one was trying to attract his attention, and the big double wheel was going over again. How many times, how many decisions, until each link in the chain of command was answering as one? 'You did well, David. I am proud of you.'

Julyan the sailing master had joined him now. There was no more time.

Napier dropped lightly to the deck, and might have caught

113

his scarred leg against a stanchion. But he felt nothing.

'Mr. Squire wants you, double-quick!'

He hurried toward the forecastle again, braced for the next task. Squire was waiting.

'Muster some waisters to clear up this deck, and get all loose gear stowed and ready for rounds.' His eyes moved swiftly across the starboard bow. 'We don't want our French friends picking any holes in our coats!' He was smiling, but serious enough.

Napier hastened to a ladder and hesitated, one foot in mid-air as he stared aft toward the quarterdeck.

The captain was no longer in sight amongst the figures busy at halliards and braces. But his words remained very clear in Napier's mind. *With him*.

9

Articles of War

The chart room door closed, and Julyan the master touched his hat in apology.

'I'm a bit adrift, sir.' He peered over his shoulder. 'I had to be certain of a couple of things. But they know where I am.'

Adam said, 'Find a place for yourself. I'll not keep you long.'

Three lieutenants and Guthrie the boatswain left little room beyond the table, with its array of charts and reference books.

'We should make a landfall today, later in the dog watches, if the wind stays kind to us.' He tapped the open log. 'And *these* observations prove to be accurate.' He saw Julyan smile, and felt the tension dissipate. 'I have made a rough plan of the anchorage and the approaches, from what little information we have of them.'

He saw Squire nod. He would have had plenty of hazardous moments during his surveying voyages. *A lead-and-line and a lot of luck*, as one old hand had described it.

Adam looked at each of them in turn. 'We shall remain in company with *Nautilus* until she is received without unrest or opposition, as is anticipated. We will take no unnecessary risks.'

In company. But the other frigate had been scarcely in sight when the masthead lookouts had first reported her at daybreak.

A shift of wind overnight, or had her captain spread more sail deliberately? But what would be the point? If there had been an unexpected breach of the peace, it would already be too late for argument without a real show of force.

115

He heard the squeal of gun trucks, the occasional shouts of command as some of the forward eighteen-pounders began another painstaking drill. Maddock had already told him he had cut two minutes off the time it took his crews to clear for action. Not much, some would say, but it could be the margin between opening fire or being dismasted.

Only a few days since they had weighed at Gibraltar, and some three hundred miles. They had done well, even if they did damn his eyes every time they manhandled a gun up to its port.

Be prepared. The next ship they sighted might already be at war: an enemy. *How would you know?*

He had seen the telescopes trained on them from *Nautilus*, and not only during the gun drill. Curiosity, or perhaps they too were coming to terms with the new alliance. Something decreed by those who had never experienced the numbing horror of a broadside or the steel of an enemy at close quarters.

He knew that Vincent was staring at him, but looked away as their eyes met.

'Study the plan. You will see some fortifications on the north-east side. Not like Algiers, or some we've encountered.' He tapped the diagram, and recalled Jago and Morgan spreading these sketches on the table for him.

He looked at Squire. 'I want the second cutter lowered when we make our final approach. You will be in charge. Crew to be armed, with rations for two days in case of trouble. And remember, James. No heroics.'

Squire nodded but made no comment.

He turned to Guthrie, who seemed unusually subdued, perhaps a little overwhelmed because he was being consulted with the others.

'Your best lookouts, and the most experienced leadsmen in the chains. Arms will be issued, but not on display. Am I making sense?'

Guthrie beamed. 'I'll watch every mother's son, sir. Leave it to me!'

Julyan punched his massive arm. 'Watch *all* of 'em!'

Adam waited, and then said, 'Tell your people what you think fit. We might know more at first light tomorrow. Any questions?'

116

'The fortifications on the plan, sir?' It was Gascoigne, the lieutenant of Royal Marines, quiet and oddly unobtrusive despite his scarlet tunic. 'If there *is* resistance, should we expect a battery of some description?'

Adam looked past him at the old-fashioned octant hanging near the door. It belonged to Julyan, and was probably the first instrument he had ever owned or used. *With men like these. . . .* He answered, almost abruptly, 'The ship comes first. The Royals would be landed.'

That was all. It was enough.

Adam looked directly at Vincent. There was no more time. He was the first lieutenant. If anything should happen. . . .

'Do you wish to add anything, Mark?'

Vincent faced him. The challenge was still there.

'As you said, sir. The ship comes first.'

The chart room quivered, and even the instruments on the table seemed to tremble as the guns were run up to their ports together, like a single weapon. There was a burst of cheering, immediately quelled by the voice of authority: Maddock himself.

Vincent said, 'I was wondering, sir,' and glanced at the others. 'What sort of man is the French captain?'

Perhaps it had been uppermost in all their thoughts.

Capitaine Luc Marchand had been present at two of the meetings Adam had attended in Gibraltar. Others had made the brief introductions, but he and Marchand had progressed no further than an exchange of polite smiles: Commodore Arthur Carrick had made certain of that, with behaviour verging on hostility.

Marchand was about Adam's age, perhaps a year or so older, strong-featured, with a ready, disarming smile and clear greyish-blue eyes. A face that would appeal to any woman. The flag lieutenant had been more informative once the commodore was out of his way.

Adam touched the charts, and his own rough plan laid across them.

'Marchand is an experienced captain, supposedly due for promotion when the war ended. No stranger to English ships. He was serving in *Swiftsure* after she was taken from us, and again at Trafalgar,' he grinned, 'when *we* recaptured her.'

117

Julyan nodded. 'I remember *Swiftsure*. Third-rate. Put up quite a fight against us.' He spoke almost proudly.

Adam waited, then said, 'Does that help?'

Vincent shrugged. 'I doubt he'll ever forget the past.'

The door squeaked open a few inches and a pair of eyes sought Julyan. Nothing was said, but the master seized his hat and swore under his breath.

'Seems they need me on deck, sir!'

He would not leave without good reason, but Adam sensed that he was relieved to have been called away.

He said, 'A good time to end our discussion. You may carry on with your duties.'

Vincent remained by the table as the others departed.

'I understand that there is a seaman listed for punishment? I read your report before this meeting. Asleep on watch and insubordinate. Tell me about it.'

Overhead, the gun trucks began to move again. Closer this time: Maddock was about to exercise his next division.

Vincent said, 'His name is Dimmock. Foretop, long service— over twenty years. Never had any trouble with him before.' He paused as though surprised by his own words, as if they were some excuse or admission. 'We were hard-pressed for trained, experienced hands when we were commissioning. Landsmen and young boys were the first to come forward.' He added with something like defiance, 'I trusted him.'

Adam listened to the drill, the creak of tackle, an ironic cheer as something miscarried. Like another world.

'Dimmock.' He spoke the name, but no face came to his mind. 'He was never rated for promotion.' It meant nothing; there were many like him in the King's service. The old hands, content or resigned, and the hard men who steered their own course, if they were offered the chance.

Vincent said suddenly, 'A stand-over could be ordered, sir.'

Adam recalled Thomas Herrick, his uncle's oldest and most loyal friend; could hear his words. *Discipline is a duty, not a convenience.*

'It happened during your watch and you feel responsible, as he was a man you trusted. But it could have been at any time, with some one else left to take action.' Vincent seemed about to protest. 'He had been drinking beforehand, I gather.'

118

'He was not drunk, sir.'

It was common enough through the fleet. The only crime was being caught. And Vincent was an experienced officer; he did not need to be told. The old Jacks could even joke about getting a checked shirt at the gangway. Few ever remembered the reason. But afterwards, the blame always lay with the captain.

He raised his eyes from the charts.

'You gain nothing by delaying it. Tomorrow forenoon, all hands to witness punishment. Inform the surgeon, will you?'

'Right away, sir.' He half turned as if to listen. 'The gun drill has stopped. I hope it's achieving results!'

Adam watched him leave and heard him call a greeting to some one as he passed, as if uninvolved. Like those first days. Still a stranger.

Several hours later, at the end of the first dog watch, as predicted, the masthead lookout sighted land. On deck every telescope was trained across water like blue glass, ruffled occasionally by an uncertain wind. The French *Nautilus* seemed to hold the last of the sun on her topsails and rigging, her hull almost hidden in shadow.

A fine landfall. Even Julyan could not hide his satisfaction. But as he watched the captain walk to the quarterdeck rail and press both hands against it, he wondered what he was thinking. Planning for some future command with no admiral breathing down his neck to torment?

Meredith, one of his master's mates, was calling to him and he turned to give his full attention. But not before he made a careful observation. The quarterdeck was busy with hands on watch, and others waiting to man the braces and change tack. And in the midst of it at the quarterdeck rail, their captain, who wanted for nothing, was completely alone.

Midshipman John Deacon laid his dirk and folded crossbelt on top of his chest and relocked it. He glanced at the others.

'A formality, so do it.'

David Napier thought about it. It was every midshipman's dream and nightmare, even if he managed to conceal it. That first real step, the King's commission. . . . But the examination before a selected Board came first. Deacon already spoke like a lieutenant, without even knowing it.

He saw the messman murmuring instructions in the ear of his young assistant, a boy. *As I was.* Gesturing to the canvas that concealed cleaning gear and the bucket, in case their youngest midshipman might need it. Walker had been luckier of late, but wind and sea had been more considerate.

He sat down at the mess table opposite Simon Huxley.

'What are you studying at this early hour?'

Huxley frowned at him, then seemed less defensive. 'I made some notes about this place we've been plotting on the chart through every watch, thanks to our Mr. Julyan.' He smiled, and it made him a different person. 'Aboubakr seems to have changed hands many times in the last fifty years alone. Slavers, missionaries, pirates, and invaders under a whole fistful of flags. So who's next, I wonder?'

Napier remembered the first hint of land, then the darker outline, hills and deeper shadows linking where there had been only the edge of the sea.

'I heard them say it's a good anchorage. That's what gave it value. Prosperity, too.'

Huxley murmured, 'For some, anyway.'

Deacon had joined them.

'We shall show ourselves and pay our respects.' He slapped his palm on the table. 'Then back to Gibraltar for new orders.' Then he turned and said unexpectedly, 'Captain Bolitho sponsored *you*, David. When the day comes for you to face up to the Inquisition, his name and reputation should carry some weight.' Napier considered it, surprised by this revelation. 'That was wrong of me. But every day now I ask myself . . . if I shall be . . . ready.'

Another shadow moved across the table: Charles Hotham, usually a bright spirit in the gunroom, and popular on deck with most of the hands despite glaring mistakes during gun drill and work aloft. Guthrie the boatswain had been heard to forcefully comment, 'Better for all of us if you'd followed the Church instead of Neptune, Mister 'Otham, *sir*!'

He said in an undertone, 'How long now?'

Napier patted his arm. What they were all thinking. Avoiding it.

'I was the one who found him, you see? I wanted to settle it somehow, but he. . . .'

120

'All hands, clear lower deck! Hands lay aft to witness punishment!'

Huxley said kindly, 'You did your best.'

Deacon was already at the door, clearly recovered from his moment of self-doubt.

'Lively, now! It's not the end of the world!'

The upper deck was already crowded. It was rare to see both watches and all the special dutymen gathered at once. Some stood together, messmates, or because they shared a hazardous perch aloft strung out along the yards, making or shortening sail when a firm grip and a timely shout could save a limb or a life. Some of the forenoon watch were in the shrouds or ratlines, framed against the sea or sky as if trapped in a giant web. Others were grouped between the eighteen-pounders, those stripped to the waist showing scarred, tanned or sun-burned skin commensurate with their service.

The Royal Marines were lined across the quarterdeck, in full uniform, facing forward, swaying in unison as *Onward* ploughed unhurriedly through reflected glare and infrequent bursts of spray.

Vincent, the first lieutenant, stood on the larboard side of the quarterdeck by the gangway, one hand shading his eyes as he received reports from each division and section. It was still early, but like the marines he wore full uniform, and was beginning to sweat in the heat.

Despite all those present it seemed unusually quiet, only the sounds of cordage and canvas, the creak of timber or spar, breaking the stillness.

The midshipmen were crowded together by one of the quarterdeck carronades, opposite the gangway where a grating had been rigged upright. Close by, but separated by years and experience, the warrant officers had already assembled. The backbone in every man-of-war: no ship would sail, fight, or even survive without them. Tobias Julyan, as sailing master, had grown to know them in the long months since *Onward*'s commissioning. In their faces now he saw resignation, even impatience, as might be expected from men who had seen almost every aspect of a sailor's life.

From where he stood Julyan could hear the occasional creak of the wheel, beyond some of the hands on watch, and saw the helmsman in his mind's eye, a good man, not the sort to let his attention stray from the compass.

He looked at the rigged grating and felt his mouth go dry, and glanced at the midshipmen. Youngsters, full of hope. They looked to *him* now. That other memory should have died, with so many others. But at times like these. . . .

Over twenty years ago. He had been as young as the seaman at the wheel. Some of the older hands still yarned about the Great Mutiny in the fleet at the Nore and Spithead. France was poised to invade, and the horror of the guillotine and the fear of revolution was stark and very real.

Reason had triumphed eventually, and guilt been admitted by both factions, quarterdeck and forecastle. Julyan remembered one captain who had ordered a man flogged because he was slow to obey an order: *showing disrespect to an officer*, he had claimed. And there had been others . . . maybe there had always been others . . . who would treat a pressed man like scum, even though he had been torn bodily from the arms of his family or lover and dragged aboard.

One mutineer had been sentenced to four hundred lashes, and to be flogged through the fleet. Julyan could see it now. Hear it. The procession of boats, crewed by witnesses from each vessel at anchor that day, pausing at each rated ship while a proportion of the punishment was awarded alongside. Four hundred lashes. How could that *thing* have survived?

Some movement made him turn his head and he saw that one of the midshipmen had crouched down behind the carronade. The youngest, who was always being sick. He had heard them joking about it. *Even if the ship was in dry dock!* The youngster next to him had leaned over and put his hand on the boy's heaving shoulder. It was Napier, the one who had survived *Audacity*. Sponsored by the Captain. Somehow it was seemly. . . .

'Attention on the upper deck!'

Like a little parade. Rowlatt, the master-at-arms, and the ship's corporal, with the prisoner lurching between them. Two boatswain's mates, one carrying the tell-tale red baize bag which contained the cat. Lastly Murray, the surgeon, to ensure that the prisoner did not lose consciousness.

122

The surgeons must have been deaf and blind that other, terrible day.

High above them some one called out: a topman needing assistance from his mate. Nobody looked up.

Adam Bolitho walked to the quarterdeck rail, his coat heavy in the heat and already clinging to his shoulders. Would he never become hardened to the demands and the doubts? He was no longer that young and often unsure commander in his first ship, the one he had evoked for Lowenna during their last waterfront stroll in Falmouth. Would she believe him if she could see him now?

Vincent was making his report, but his back was to the sun, his face in shadow and impossible to read.

Adam looked the length of the ship, at the upturned faces and the figures in the shrouds, silhouetted against the sea and sky. Some were still strangers, others emerged from obscurity with names and voices, a living force.

He looked down at the prisoner for the first time.

'John Dimmock, you are accused of neglect of duty, that you were asleep on watch.' He sounded hoarse, and wanted to clear his throat. Some of the silent onlookers would not be able to hear him. '. . . and that you showed contempt to a superior officer.'

Dimmock was staring up at him intently, his eyes red-rimmed as if from heavy drinking. Smuggled rum from messmates, despite the risk of discovery.

'Have you anything to say?'

Dimmock seemed to straighten his back. 'Nuthin'!'

The master-at-arms gripping his wrist hissed, 'Nothin', *sir*!'

Adam stepped back slightly and said, 'Carry on.'

Behind him he heard some one take a deep breath. It was Luke Jago. Always the same, every time he saw or heard the ritual of punishment. Jago had been flogged in error. The officer responsible had been court-martialled and dismissed the service in disgrace, and Jago had received a written apology from an admiral and a sum of cash which had amounted to a year's pay. But he would carry the scars of the cat to his grave.

'Seized up, sir!'

Adam felt the Articles of War pressing against his side, against the old sword. Jago's way of telling him. Of sharing it.

He removed his hat, and knew others were following his example. Dimmock was stripped to the waist and pinioned against the grating. There was a tattoo of some kind on his right shoulder, faded now and probably acquired when he had been a much younger man, as was the habit of landmen and raw recruits, as an act of bravado or when awash with too much rum. It was usually regretted afterwards.

Adam took the Articles of War from Jago and spread the final page: Article number thirty-six. He had heard it read aloud often enough, and could remember reading these same words for the first time.

'All crimes not capital, committed by any person or persons in the Fleet. . . .' Once he felt the deck tilt more steeply, with the responding slap of canvas. The wind was dropping, or had shifted slightly due to the nearness of land. But his voice remained level, unhurried. *'. . . shall be punished according to the Laws and Customs of such cases used at sea.'* He closed the folder. 'One dozen lashes.'

One of the boatswain's mates had pulled the cat-o'-nine-tails from its bag and shook it so that the tails fell free, but his eyes were on the captain, not the prisoner.

Adam replaced his hat.

'Do your duty.'

The man's arm swung out to its full extent and the cat struck Dimmock's bare back with a sickening crack.

'One.' The master-at-arms had begun to count, his voice matter-of-fact.

Jago had been watching a strange, dark-winged seabird he did not recognize as it swooped past the foretop, but felt his eyes drawn relentlessly to the gangway and the figure tied to the grating. Under a spell, unable to escape, like the prisoner. He could feel it like that day, the force of the blows driving the breath from his lungs, his body unable to move or to yield against the grating. And then the pain. Like nothing you could believe or describe.

'Two.'

There was blood now, the force of the lash opening the flesh as if by the claws of a beast. Jago could recall the blood nearly choking him. He had bitten through his lip or tongue. The surgeon had stopped the flogging to examine him, but only

124

briefly, and the ordeal had continued. He remembered his own half-mad sense of triumph when the last blow had fallen across his torn and blackened body. Hatred had saved him then, and for countless days afterwards.

'*Three.*'

Jago saw the captain's fingers on the hilt of his sword. His hand was tanned, but the knuckles were white from the force of his grip. Jago had known captains who would order two or three dozen lashes merely for spitting on the deck.

'*Four.*'

The boatswain's mate faltered, the cat swinging in mid-air and blood spattering his arm, while Rowlatt twisted round, mouth open and ready for the next count.

An explosion, like distant thunder, echoing and re-echoing across the unbroken water. But sharper, and drowned by the shouts and confusion as men stared outboard or at each other, then, inevitably, to the figure in blue with one hand on his sword.

Adam leaned over the rail and tried to see beyond the starboard bow, but the headsails made it impossible. *Nautilus* should be in sight. Otherwise. . . .

He saw Vincent striding to join him, his face alive with questions.

Adam said, 'Marchand's emergency signal. Pipe the hands aloft and get the courses on her. The wind's dropping, so let's use what we have!'

He heard a groan from the gangway. It helped to focus his thoughts.

'Cut down the prisoner and have him taken below.'

The master-at-arms called, 'What about the punishment, sir?' Confused, even indignant. 'Less than half, sir!'

Adam stared up at the masthead pendant. *Not much. But enough.* As if he were telling the ship, or himself.

'Send some good eyes aloft, Mr. Vincent. The best you can muster. Give him a glass, mine if it saves time.' He knew he was speaking too fast, and why. He looked at Rowlatt, who was still standing by the blood-splashed grating. '*Ended!* We have work to do.'

Jago saw his face as he made his way to the companion.

Preparing himself for whatever lay ahead. But Jago had

known him longer than any one else aboard, and was gripped by what he had just witnessed. Like Dimmock the prisoner, the Captain had been cut free.

10

Under Two Flags

Midshipman David Napier climbed steadily up the foremast ratlines, his hands and feet working in unison, the deck already far below him. He felt the sun on his neck and shoulders as the foretop loomed over him, and he arched his back to swing out and around it. He could still remember all those first attempts, when he had scrambled up the shrouds with the other boys and midshipmen. The sailor's way, around the futtock shrouds, all toes and fingers like a monkey. It still made him hold his breath until he was up and reaching for the next challenge.

The deck was angled beneath him, less crowded, only the duty watch standing by the braces and trimming the freshly set courses.

The first lieutenant had told him to join the masthead lookout. 'And don't drop that glass, or you need not come down again!'

To break the tension, perhaps in the only way he knew.

The grating had been lowered, and two men were scrubbing it clean. The prisoner who had been flogged had already vanished below.

Napier had heard a marine say in an undertone, 'His lucky day, I reckon.'

He gripped the barricade of the foretop and stared across the blue water. The land appeared sharper now, with shadows marking inlets, and the harder wedge of headland beyond.

And he saw the *Nautilus*, apparently hove to, sails loose and aback, poised above her own shadow.

He recalled hearing the third lieutenant, Monteith, remark, 'This is where we part company, and good riddance!'

He took a deep breath and pulled himself on to the next stretch of ratlines. *Don't look down. Don't count every step.* It helped expunge the sound of the lash from his memory. The gasps of agony. He had witnessed floggings before, had sensed the hostility of those around him. *Us and them.* And it was still there: he had just passed a seaman coiling some halliards. The man had deliberately looked away.

He felt his ankle twist, his foot jerk sharply from the ratline. He had almost forgotten the pain, the numbing shock that seemed to burn into his leg like fire, or the surgeon's knife.

His shirt was plastered to his back. Sweat, fear. Some one called out, but he could not speak or breathe.

'You all right down there?' Then again, more sharply, 'Don't move! Don't even blink! I'm coming!'

He lost track of time; maybe he had fainted. He was lying on his back with some one kneeling beside him. Naked to the waist, skin tanned like leather: one of the topmen. He could see the heavy scabbard at his belt, the sort favoured by professional seamen for knife and marline spike. He felt him gripping his breeches, the cloth tearing like paper.

'*Jesus!* What did this to you?'

He had turned slightly, and Napier saw his face, young and open, in his twenties; he had been in the navy since he was twelve. Napier struggled to sit up, to clear his throat.

'*Tucker.* I thought for a minute. . . .'

'That's me.' He had his arm around his shoulders. 'I'll fetch help.'

Napier shook his head. 'Not yet, David. I have to look at something.' It was like a fog lifting from his mind. They had first met when Tucker had asked him if he would read a letter he had received, as he could neither read nor write, and they had discovered they shared the same Christian name. Little enough, but it had been a bridge between the *us* and *them.*

Napier had written two or three letters for him after that, and in exchange Tucker had taught him the finer points of ropework and splicing. But most of all, they had talked. Tucker was an orphan, and had been signed into the navy by a relative of some kind. The easy escape. Something else they shared.

He was on his feet, gripping Tucker's arm, swaying with him like two drunks after a run ashore.

He said, 'I must use the glass. Now, before it happens again!'

Tucker watched him doubtfully. 'If you say so. Sir.'

He glanced down to the foretop again: the other seaman had gone. He looked back at Tucker, who was unfastening the telescope. Would it have made a difference?

Tucker said, 'Fine piece of work,' and rolled it expertly in strong fingers. 'What's this writing say?' and when Napier told him, 'God Almighty, the same name as the Captain!'

'It belonged to his uncle. Did you know him?'

Tucker smiled, but there was sadness in it.

'Who didn't?'

Napier steadied himself against the barricade. 'The Frenchman fired a signal, hove to for a rendezvous. We're standing by in case of any local disputes.' He sucked in his breath; the pain was coming again. 'That was how it was explained to us.'

'Never thought I'd be asked to worry about *them*! A broadside's always done the talking before!' He crooked his elbow to train and steady the telescope like a musket: a true seaman. 'There's *Nautilus*. No extra canvas set.' He shifted the glass. 'And there's another sail, fine off the headland.' He did not take his eyes from it. 'Is that what you saw, before you fell?'

Napier nodded, mind still grappling with it, as if it were a badly finished painting.

Tucker murmured, '*Got you*, my beauty!' Then, 'She's a schooner. French colours. Some sort of signal hoisted.'

Napier took the weight on his leg once more. No pain now, but he knew it was weeping, like the first time he had walked without a crutch. He could hear the surgeon's warning: *he'll always have a limp*. He had beaten that, too. . . .

'You can report to the quarterdeck . . . sir. It'll be hours before they get close enough to talk. The schooner's not under full sail, and the boat she's towing will slow her down even more.' He closed the telescope with a snap. 'Sailors— I've. . . .' He did not finish. 'They need more sail. Soon as the wind dropped, they should have done it.' He stared across the water, the telescope held loosely at his side. 'I've spouted more than enough!'

Napier sensed his uncertainty, felt it, like a barrier.

'What is it? It might be important.'

Tucker looked down at the torn breeches, flapping open in the warm breeze.

'Here, let me fix that before you present yourself to the gold lace, eh?'

But he was gripping the telescope again, his fingers running over the engraving.

'It was a while back, four, maybe five years. I was with the prize crew in a schooner— she was a Frog, too. Lively little craft after a two-decker of eighty guns. But she needed all hands when the call came to make or shorten sail.' He unslung the glass and offered it abruptly, perhaps before he could change his mind. 'This schooner don't seem to be carrying enough men to do the job.'

Napier moved to the barricade and peered down at the deck, and the forecastle where he had listened and learned from Lieutenant Squire and felt the rough camaraderie of the men around him.

He heard Tucker call after him, 'Watch that leg o' yours!' And then, 'They might not believe you!'

Napier turned stiffly and peered up at him. There was still no pain.

'*I* believe *you*, David!' He lowered himself on to the ratlines, which seemed to be vibrating, shivering in his hands. Like the sudden mutter of canvas. A note of urgency.

He swung himself through the shrouds and felt the deck beneath his feet. He could not believe he had moved so fast.

'Have you been relieved? I did not hear any such order!'

It was Monteith, still wearing the sword and coat he had donned to witness punishment.

'I have to see the captain, sir.'

'Do you, indeed? By whose authority?' He was looking at the torn breeches, even smiling, as he rocked back on his heels. 'And you hope to become a King's officer!'

A shadow had loomed between them. Murray, the surgeon.

'I'm going aft, Mr. Napier.' But he was looking at the lieutenant. 'We shall see the captain together.' He watched as

130

Napier released his grip on the rigging, then added quietly, 'And after *that*, you and I will have a little talk. That is an order.'

Monteith glared as some seamen paused to watch or listen.

'I would have dealt with it!'

Murray put his hand under the midshipman's arm. 'I am glad to know it, Hector. And by whose authority?'

Napier could sense the animosity between them, but it meant nothing to him. He hesitated and turned to look up at the masthead, the long pendant whipping out and holding the wind. Suppose. . . . He tried again. The topman named Tucker, another David, who had served aboard a schooner. A prize taken from the enemy. . . . It was not making sense.

He stumbled, but some one else had taken his other arm.

'Easy, my son!' It was Jago.

'Where to?' Another voice.

'Cap'n's quarters. It'll save time.' A chair had come from somewhere. 'Make things a bit easier as well.'

It was quieter now, and airless. Some one propping him up, another tugging away the torn breeches. A scarlet tunic moving to close a door, some one moistening his parched mouth.

'Nice and easy, David. You're going to be all right. Be sure of that.'

Napier opened his eyes and stared into his face. The captain. Another voice in the background. The surgeon.

But the captain said, 'Just now, David, you spoke of a ship. A schooner.' He felt the hand on his bare shoulder. Like that other time. His leg. . . .

'Tell us what you saw.' The hand moved slightly. 'Tell *me*.'

Lieutenant Vincent strode across the quarterdeck and touched his hat.

'No change, sir. The schooner's holding the same course. No extra sails set.' He breathed deeply. It had been a long time since he had climbed to the masthead and down again, with so many eyes judging his progress.

He looked up, eyes slitted against the glare. 'Wind's serving us well enough at present.'

Adam glanced along the deck, at men off watch who would

otherwise have been in their messes, in groups or wandering beneath the taut canvas and the criss-cross of rigging. All waiting.

And the familiar figures, aft by the compass and wheel. The master and his mates, Midshipman Deacon with the signals party.

He said abruptly, 'Did you speak with Tucker?'

'A good hand, sir. He recognized the schooner's mood, something many would have missed.'

Adam looked up at the masthead pendant.

'Send for the gunner. Time is running out.'

Vincent hesitated. 'But *Nautilus* is making the rendezvous, sir. And she could outshoot and outsail that schooner, even if it were some kind of trick!' He looked away, then back. 'Mr. Maddock is standing by.'

Adam faced him. 'The rendezvous is supposed to be at Aboubakr, not at sea, in open water. And yes, *Nautilus can* outshoot and outsail that schooner— she'd be a challenge even for us, if it came to that. . . .' He broke off. *And if I am wrong?* He could see the doubt on Vincent's face.

'You wanted me, sir?'

Onward's gunner held his head slightly to one side as if he were afraid of missing something; he was almost deaf in one ear as the result of his trade, although few would have guessed it. Short and squarely built, he had the brightest pair of eyes Adam had ever seen in any long-serving sailor.

'The schooner that lies ahead is making for *Nautilus*. I believe she intends mischief of the worst kind. If the wind holds, and with your help, I will stop it.'

Maddock was nodding, his mind already busy. 'Bow-chasers, sir?'

Adam shook his head. *Like stamping a seal on my own court martial.*

'No. We will begin as soon as we are within range. *You* will lay and fire each gun yourself, understood?' He turned to Vincent. There was no time left for argument. 'In a moment you will clear for action. Have the hands piped to quarters, no drums or show of force. They'll know soon enough.' Their eyes met. 'This is what I intend.'

Luke Jago nodded to the Royal Marine sentry and walked

132

past the screen door and into the great cabin. All these months, years even, and he still expected some one to dispute his right of entry. *The coxswain's privilege.* Some tried, but they only did it once.

There seemed to be people on deck everywhere, unwilling to go to their messes, when usually one watch would be below, washing down the noon meal with a healthy wet or even a mug of the sour red wine called Black Strap. He could feel the tension like something solid. A fight was one thing, but. . . .

He, at least, knew what was coming.

Morgan, the cabin servant, stood with his hands on his ample hips and exclaimed, 'What say you, Luke? Fit for a post-captain, isn't it?'

The midshipman was standing by the broad stern windows, wearing a pair of seaman's trousers and a clean shirt.

Morgan added, 'Those breeks would almost fit *me*, but he can rest easy until this lot's over and done with!'

Napier bent his knee and balanced on one leg. He smiled and said, 'I'm all right!'

Jago breathed out. When he had seen the boy being brought aft, half carried, his face like chalk beneath its sunburn, he had thought the worst.

He glanced past him into the glare on the empty sea astern. It was unreal. Eerie, Prior the captain's clerk had described it. It was a new term to Jago, but it suited.

Onward was holding her course toward the two small shapes on the horizon, one motionless and the other barely moving. Except that they were closer now, the schooner on the starboard bow. As if they might eventually collide. He scowled. If they ever reached that far before the wind dropped completely.

It was five hours since the prisoner Dimmock had been released from the grating, and taken moaning below. Since Napier had climbed aloft with the captain's telescope and collapsed. He had seen that cruel wound again when they had stripped him here: as bad as that first time when a few had turned away, and shaken their heads.

Five hours. They could have sailed from Plymouth to Falmouth Bay in that time.

Morgan looked in the direction of his pantry. 'If you want something, Luke, have it now.' He made a mock bow. 'No

133

charge!' Then the mood changed. 'They just gave the word to douse the galley stove. You know what that means.'

Jago pushed the thought aside and said roughly, 'When all this is over, you can get some new middy's breeches made up here on board, right?'

'Indeed, yes. Jeff Lloyd,' grinning, 'another Welshman, see?'

'Him that patched up one of the Cap'n's coats? He was well pleased.'

Morgan winked. 'He's a craftsman right enough. Did some work for our late and lamented Captain Richmond, God rest his soul.' He looked toward the screen door as if he were listening. 'Jeff Lloyd's good, right enough. But don't trust him with your—'

There was a rap at the door.

'Ship's corporal, sir!'

The man peered around the door, his eyes everywhere but on the occupants. Like most visitors to this sanctuary.

'Hands to quarters, sir,' he said to Napier. There was a bloodstain on his jacket; he had helped cut the prisoner from the gratings.

The door closed, and Morgan said softly, 'So, now we know.'

Jago looked over at the midshipman. 'Ready?' He heard the thump of feet, some running, and the muffled scrape of screens being lowered. They would be here soon, and this would be a cabin no more, but a part of the ship. This silent clearing for action, without the urgent rattle of drums and the shrill of calls deck to deck, somehow seemed more threatening.

Napier stood by the long, high-backed bergère, and touched its worn leather for a few more seconds.

I lay here.

He lifted his chin.

'Aye, ready!'

Adam Bolitho climbed on to the nettings and trained his telescope across the tightly packed hammocks; even through his sleeve, they felt hot in the strong sunlight. Behind him, the ship was quiet again, as if it had been only another drill or exercise. Waiting for a verdict, before being dismissed.

He gripped the telescope, so familiar to his hand now, like an old friend. He could sense Vincent standing nearby, had felt his disapproval when he had been told to clear for action. Perhaps they all shared his doubts about their captain's judgment.

He took a deep breath, focusing it, and saw the schooner spring to life in the powerful lens. Scarred paint, and the patches which were different shades of canvas in her sails, hard-worked like the vessel herself. He blinked, waiting for the image to steady once more. There were some figures in a group, almost midships. And one in uniform further aft near a small deckhouse or companion. Probably the schooner's helm. Her colours were vivid against the sky, but the signal, whatever it was, had been hauled down.

Vincent said, 'Maybe they'll lower a boat, sir. They can *hail* each other, if she stays on course.'

Adam lowered the glass. He had seen the boat towing from the schooner. Some kind of galley, probably a local craft. He had seen plenty of them at Algiers. It was closer to the schooner than before. Under her quarter. . . .

The thought was like a hand on his shoulder, shaking him. The boat was not a threat. It was a means of escape.

He raised the telescope again. *They are watching us right now.*

'Bring her up two points to larboard.' He dropped to the deck as the order was repeated, and the big double wheel began to respond. He stared forward, seeing the faces at each gun peering aft, and Maddock standing just inboard of the first eighteen-pounder. He was ready, no matter what he might be thinking.

'Nor' east by east, sir.'

Adam watched the schooner slowly change her bearing as *Onward* responded to the rudder. His mind told him it was Julyan's voice. Taking no chances.

'Open the ports!' He was at the quarterdeck rail but did not recall moving. There was no turning back. *My decision.*

'Run out!'

Maddock's drills had not been in vain. Along *Onward*'s starboard side, the eighteen-pounders thudded against their ports. Showing her teeth. . . .

135

Maddock was staring aft, one hand raised against the pitiless glare, the other on the shoulder of his senior gun captain.

Adam watched the schooner, almost abeam now as *Onward* settled on her new course. It was as if *Nautilus*, and the headland, did not exist.

'On the uproll!' Like counting the seconds. *'Fire!'*

The forward gun recoiled, its crew leaping aside, handspikes and sponge ready, as if they had been doing it all their lives.

The crash of gunfire was still echoing over the water. A jagged burst of spray showed the fall of shot, directly across the schooner's bows.

Vincent said sharply, *'Nautilus* is making more sail!'

'That woke 'em up!' Jago's voice. Adam scarcely heard them. Men were running along the schooner's deck, and some were already down in the boat alongside.

He raised the telescope, cursing the time it took to focus. The schooner was still under way. The solitary figure in uniform was standing where he had last seen him. Closer now, but partly obscured by drifting gunsmoke.

The image seemed to hold him in a vise. The man by the helm had not moved because he was tied upright, helpless. Probably dead. And it could not be gunsmoke at that range.

He leaned on the rail and saw Maddock turn.

'Fire!'

Maddock might have hesitated, but only for a few seconds. Then he was stooping at the second gun, gesturing almost unhurriedly to his crew, until he was satisfied.

Some one gave a wild cheer as the ball slammed into the schooner's side. More smoke, and Maddock's voice, strong and clear.

'Lay for the foremast an' fire on the uproll! *Ready!*'

Adam did not hear the order to fire. It was as if the sea had exploded in his face. But the picture remained starkly before his eyes, as it had been when the telescope was jolted from his hands.

Men in the boat, struggling, fighting to cast off from the schooner's side, knocked over by others leaping down to join them in a panic which distance could not hide. One figure running in the last moment of sanity before bursting into a

136

human torch, arms and legs flailing as he pitched into the sea alongside.

And then the explosion, bursting through the schooner's deck: a giant fireball blasting masts and sails into ashes, the heat enough to sear the skin at a cable's distance.

Fragments were splashing around the stricken vessel, some ablaze and breaking up, burning on the water so that the sea became a final torment for those still alive.

Men stood by their guns staring at the smoke, the debris still falling so near. Some one cried out as another explosion rebounded against the hull, like a ship running aground. Final. But muffled this time, no searing glare.

The schooner, or what remained of her, was on her way to the bottom. And through it all the wind was holding, cool after the inferno.

Adam picked up his telescope and cradled it in his arm.

'We will heave to, Mr. Vincent.' He rubbed his forehead with the back of his wrist. 'Fall out guns' crews.' To his own ears, he sounded like a stranger. Calm. Dispassionate.

'Boat's crew, sir?' Guthrie, the boatswain.

Adam licked his lips. They tasted of smoke and sudden death.

'Have them standing by.' He raised the glass with both hands, knowing that others were watching him. 'But there's little chance.'

He felt the deck tilt uneasily as *Onward* turned into the wind, headsails flapping and filling again in confusion.

He moved the telescope slowly, giving himself time, allowing his hand to steady. And there was *Nautilus*, topsails braced and full on a fresh tack, gangway and lower shrouds alive with tiny figures. Gunports still closed, as Maddock and his crews would notice. The silent witness.

He thought of the French captain, Marchand. How he must be feeling even as he watched the ever-spreading litter of charred remains and ashes. Seeing again the fireball which would have been *Nautilus*. His ship, his men. Himself.

Vincent was beside him. 'No survivors, sir.' His voice seemed hushed, as if he were dazed by the swiftness of near disaster. *Treachery*. Perhaps the commodore was right. 'But for you. . . .'

137

He said nothing more.

'There's your answer, Mark.' He did not trust himself to raise the telescope.

Midshipman Deacon shouted, '*Nautilus* is dipping her ensign, sir!' He was staring around at the others. 'The Frenchman's saluting *us*!'

There were cheers from the upper deck. Adam turned deliberately toward the other frigate and raised his hat in acknowledgment. Marchand would see, and understand.

Vincent asked, 'Shall we go ahead?'

Adam held the hat to shade his eyes. Or hide them.

'As ordered. Under two flags.'

Lieutenant James Squire reached the quarterdeck and paused to stare abeam at the land: no longer lines and figures on a chart, but real and alive. He prided himself on his vision, and even without a glass could see the shades and depths of colour of the coastal waters, spray shining on a spur of rock or fallen cliff which marked the entrance to the bay; tiny figures by the water's edge; a track or rough road leading inland, and a lone horseman raising a trail of yellow dust, soon lost from view over a ridge or bare hillside.

Local people, caught in the crossfire of war or revolution, and hardened enough to gather and watch a vessel blowing apart, destroyed in its own trap.

He glanced across the deck where the marines of the afterguard, some by the hammock nettings, were leaning on their muskets. Grim-faced after what they had witnessed, contemplating the fate they might have shared. The senior midshipman by the flag-locker, silent and unsmiling: the same one who had shouted with such wild excitement to the deck at large when *Nautilus* had dipped her ensign in salute. And the young topman who had been sent for by the captain, cornered now by some of his mates, grinning, but still mystified by whatever he had said which had proved so significant. He looked aft again, and saw the captain with the master and his crew by the compass box, and another midshipman writing on a slate, teeth gritted against the sound of the squeaking pencil. He saw the land moving aside, the bay slowly opening beyond the bows. Some small houses, white and hazy in the sunlight. He pictured the chart, and the captain's own rough map; how he had made light of the possible inaccuracies and flaws in their information, even if it had come from the admiral. And all the time he must have been confronting the real danger, which only at the last minute they had all glimpsed for themselves. And he had still found time to thank a common seaman. For doing his duty, many would say.

Squire heard some one laugh and thought, *And we are alive.*

'Boat's crew mustered— sir.'

It was Fowler, boatswain's mate, tough, experienced, and ruthless. Years had passed since they had served together, yet it was all so clear. Even just glancing around, here and now. Stowing hammocks together. Hauling on the braces or lying back with all their strength to run out a gun, like today. Then he had taken the irrevocable step from messdeck to wardroom, and even fame in a minor way when he had been chosen to join the voyage of exploration under Sir Alfred Bishop. And then *Onward*, a new frigate when so many shipyards were empty, and men crying out for work. And a captain of repute: who would not envy him?

When Bolitho had assigned their duties upon arrival here, and given him charge of the cutter as guardboat and liaison with the French, Squire had been pleased and surprised.

But Fowler couldn't leave it at that. *Gave it to you to spare his precious first lieutenant, or one of his favourites. Can't you see that?*

Their eyes met, and Squire said, 'I didn't know you were coming.'

Fowler looked over at some seamen by the boat-tier.

'I "volunteered". Need somebody to keep an eye on you!' And he laughed.

'You watch what you're saying. Or one of these days—'

'You'll *what*?'

'Bosun wants you!' A seaman was peering up from the gangway.

Fowler grunted. 'Tell 'im I'm with the second lieutenant!'

Squire walked to the side again as more of the bay opened out across the bow. The fortress above the anchorage reminded him more of an old monastery than a place fought over for more than a hundred years. *Nautilus* was turning into the wind, her anchor catted and ready to let go.

There were people on and above an embrasured wall. The battery. The captain had been right, and brave to follow his instinct.

He heard Fowler threatening some one who was too slow for his taste.

It went through his mind yet again.

He saved me from disgrace. I was a coward, and others paid for it.

'Ready below, Mr. Squire!'

He raised his hand and smiled, outwardly at ease.

But the other voice persisted.

I want him dead.

Lights were already burning in the great cabin, although it had been daylight when he left the upper deck. Adam rubbed his eyes and threw his hat on to a chair. Men were still working throughout the ship, replacing screens, dragging chests and furniture from the holds. The cook was trying to rekindle his galley fire; the anchor was down and there were lights across the water, above the ancient fortress and its battery.

Just in time.

He had passed a party of seamen restoring hammocks to the messdecks. Some had grinned, and one had called after him, 'You showed 'em, Cap'n!'

And yet, only hours ago, he had seen the cold hostility in their eyes as one of their number had been flogged.

Morgan was here, as if he had never moved.

'Visitor, sir.'

It was Murray, the surgeon, come to make his own report.

'No injuries, sir. A few cuts and bruises, but only from preparing for the worst.' The keen eyes were assessing him. 'Dare I suggest that our captain find time to rest his limbs? Richly deserved, if I may say so.'

Adam knew that Morgan was already nodding on his feet. *If I close my eyes. . . .*

'I have to visit *Nautilus* before nightfall. I don't want to be fired on by one of the guardboats, especially ours!'

He heard the clink of glass. Morgan had roused himself and

was preparing his own remedy. But if he gave in to it now. . . .

'How is—' He had to grope for the name; he was in worse condition than he thought. 'Dimmock?'

'He'll live.' Murray might have smiled; it was difficult to see in the half light. 'Slept like a log throughout the whole episode, too full of grog to know or care.'

Adam heard voices, Jago talking to the sentry. What did he think about being called at this hour to take the gig across to *Nautilus*? He had not left his side all day, except when he had been here with young David.

'Midshipman Napier. . . .'

Murray was ready for that. 'I'm satisfied. Surprised, too, I must confess. A word of advice for some one, however. If a masthead lookout is required urgently, let young Napier wait a while before he puts up his hand again.'

Adam felt his dry lips break into a smile.

'I'm grateful. For all you've done.'

Murray looked toward the stern windows. The sea was flat and unmoving, molten gold in the dying light.

'I keep thinking of those poor devils today. My trade requires of me both impartiality and compassion.' He turned back, his face in shadow. 'But I thank God for our survival, and the quick wit of the man who kept us alive.' He thrust out his hand. 'Be proud!'

Adam could still feel the palm, as rough as any seaman's, long after the door had closed behind him.

The cabin seemed to swim in the dimness. What of tomorrow? And the next decision? He could see his small desk, replaced exactly where it had stood; Morgan might have measured it. The blank sheet of paper was lying in the centre as before. He could almost see the words flowing from his pen.

My darling Lowenna. . . .

The door opened and he turned away, abandoning her once more.

'Are you ready, Luke?'

'Gig's alongside, Cap'n.'

Proud.

11

Refuge

George Tolan eased his back against the hard seat and felt the cart swaying around a bend in the lane, like a jolly-boat in a lively sea. Every muscle ached; he had given up counting the days and the miles. And the doubts.

He glanced sideways at the driver. His name was Dick, and he had described himself as a carter. He must have overheard him asking directions to the Bolitho house when he had been left by the coach at the Spaniards Inn.

Friendly enough. 'I'm goin' that way m'self. Tes some far to walk with that great bag!'

Captain Bolitho might have been making a gesture, nothing more, no matter what his coxswain had insisted. They would both be at sea now in any case. And this was Cornwall, not London or some familiar port. Even the air was different: clean, indefinably tinged with the sea. He watched the passing colours in the hedgerows, foxglove, vetch, campion; the carter named them for him. Then, 'You'll be a stranger in these parts?' Tolan had felt the warning. It had never left him, despite moments when he had begun to believe that he was safe. Out of reach.

He thought of Sir Graham Bethune, the vice-admiral he had served from his time as captain. Servant, aide, unofficial bodyguard: as close as any one could hope to be, while he had still been needed.

'Workin' up at the old house, then?'

Tolan said, 'I think so, yes.'

He nodded. 'Be seein' Mister Yovell, I s'pect. Nice old

stick, but sharp as a tack, so watch out!' He laughed and flicked the reins. 'Don't tell he I said so. I does a good bit o' trade at the Bolitho house!'

Tolan loosened his coat. The sun was warmer than he had expected, *or is it me?* They might slam the door in his face, of course, as if he were some vagrant. Bolitho would have forgotten all about their last meeting, although the flag lieutenant, Troubridge, had done his best, providing Tolan with a warrant for travel by coach as far as Plymouth, and even for the final leg of the journey as an outsider with a few other passengers, swooping along narrow roads with branches almost brushing their heads.

He saw the sea again, dark blue, and hard in the reflected glare, a few whitecaps weaving a pattern closer to the land. Like claw marks.

There was a small white-painted cottage now, a man with a long clay pipe standing to wave as the cart clattered past.

'Coastguard.' The carter pointed to a cluster of trees, dark green against the road and the sea beyond. Bent, but surviving the worst this storm-lashed coast could offer.

Tolan saw the house. Journey's end. He had learned the hard way: hope had to be proved. And it was dangerous.

He relaxed the hand which had been gripping his knee. Hope could be fatal. . . .

Past some gates and turning now into another lane. People, a boy leading an unsaddled horse across cobbles. Some one polishing a smart landau, turning without curiosity at the sound of the cart.

Stables, and some kind of tower, a weathervane turning to flash in the sunlight. Doves taking flight as the wheels braked to a halt beside a water trough.

Dick the carter murmured, 'Watch this un, my son.' But he smiled and raised his battered hat. 'Good day to 'ee, Miss Bolitho!'

Tolan caught a brief glimpse of the girl as she strode toward the house, in riding habit, a crop swinging from her hand. She ignored the greeting.

'I pity the poor devil who tries to make his way with she!'

Tolan jumped down to the cobbles and reached into his coat pocket. The carter shook his head.

'Nay, tes my pleasure, this time.' He winked. 'We'll meet again!'

Tolan picked up his bag. One step at a time. No stupid mistakes. Like the girl who had walked past. He had not even seen her face, but he had been reminded of his sister. Where was she now; had she married? *Would she think of me without shame?* Something like panic gripped him for a moment. Had he expected to stay safe, living a lie forever?

Some one touched his arm. 'Nobody looking after you?' and laughed. 'Sorry to make you jump!'

Tolan faced him, calm again, on guard. 'Mr. Yovell?'

'I'll take you to him.' Over his shoulder, 'Come a long way, have you?'

Tolan followed him; the carter was already talking to somebody else, but raised his hat casually as he passed.

He replied, 'Far enough,' but he thought it went unheard.

His guide said, 'There 'tis. He'll be in the office.' He smiled and went back into the yard.

Courteous. No questions. So far, just as Luke Jago had described. He swung round as he reached for the door handle and almost collided with a young, fair woman wearing an apron. She stared at him, startled.

'I'm sorry— I didn't know—'

Upset, angry; it went deeper than that.

Tolan reached inside his coat, making no sudden movement.

'I was told to see Mr. Yovell.' He saw her breathing slow, one hand thrust some hair from her forehead. 'I'm George Tolan.' There had been voices beyond the door. Now there was silence. 'From London.'

Her eyes were still fixed on his face. He had learned a great deal about people and their reactions during the time he had been serving Bethune. You didn't last long if you were too slow to measure up: his own words on more than one occasion. And this girl was. . . .

She bent her head slightly, looking away at last.

'I b'lieve I heard about it, zur.'

He said quietly, ' "George" will suit.'

She gestured to the door. 'He'm in there,' and seemed to tense as the voices resumed. 'I have to go. My place is in the house.' She turned, but something made her say over her shoulder, perhaps out of mere politeness, 'Jenna is my name.'

The boy who had been leading the horse was coming back, and she took the opportunity to hurry away.

Tolan rapped on the door and pushed it open.

Daniel Yovell was standing by a desk, facing him as he stepped into the office. Even this seemed familiar, because of Jago's descriptions: the shelves and ledgers, and a few framed prints and maps on the wall, one awry because the door had been slammed shut once too often. Even the stove, unlit now, where Jago had shared a wet from time to time with this neatly dressed, corpulent figure.

Yovell held out his hand.

'Take a seat. You are George Tolan, if I am not mistaken.' He plucked a pair of gold-rimmed spectacles from his forehead and laid them on the desk. 'We had word you would be arriving.' He permitted himself a slight smile. 'Eventually.'

Tolan touched his coat again.

'I have a letter. . . .'

'Later. Captain Adam gave us all the details. The rest we can deal with in our own good time.' He moved a file of papers as if to cover something, a Bible or prayer book, Tolan thought. Strangely, that fitted, too.

Yovell was saying, 'We function here not unlike a ship of the line. Requiring loyalty, honesty, and no fear of hard work. How does that suit you?'

Tolan saw his irritation as another door banged, and he recognized the second voice he had heard. A tall man, built like a prizefighter, about his own age. What Jago would call full of himself.

Yovell said, without warmth, 'Leaving, are you?' and did not wait for an answer. 'This is Mr. Tolan, who is staying with us a while. Mr., ah, Flinders is steward of the adjoining estate, Roxby's. Lady Roxby is Captain Bolitho's aunt, as you will discover.'

Tolan could feel the eyes, and the questions.

Yovell added smoothly, 'Mr. Tolan was an aide to Vice-Admiral Sir Graham Bethune.'

'An' you'll know some good stories to tell, I expect?' Flinders turned toward the door, 'I shall send—' He seemed to be listening to something, and changed it to, 'I shall *bring* the estimates for those repairs, and we can fix a price.' He looked directly at Tolan this time. 'There was a deal of talk about your Sir Graham a while back. Had a real eye for the ladies, I hear. An' not just an eye, neither!' The door slammed behind him.

Daniel Yovell replaced his spectacles and studied the newcomer. What next? Nothing was ever straightforward.

But he said, 'I believe you were speaking to our Jenna just now. A local girl, very respectable. Mrs. Ferguson's right hand these days.'

Tolan said nothing, recalling the carter's amiable warning. *Sharp as a tack, so watch out!* He was right.

So it had been Flinders who had upset the girl. Used to getting his own way. A bully, and possibly a lecher. Nothing new, but not to be ignored.

'I shall take you over to the house and introduce you to Mrs. Ferguson. She'll be glad of some help, I daresay.' He did not elaborate. 'Then I shall find you a corner to call your own.' Again that calm, owlish gaze. 'While you're with us.'

Tolan picked up his bag and followed him into the yard.

He felt the sun on his face and breathed the warm air with an odd sense of relief. Captain Bolitho had kept his word.

One of the stable hands looked over and gave him a grin. He quickened his pace. Yovell was holding open a door for him.

So cool and still after the noise of the stable yard. And right or wrong, it was his decision. There was no turning back.

Lowenna looked down at the portmanteau open on the floor, and touched the gown carefully folded on the top. She had worn it on their last day together.

It was too late now. She had said she would go.

She walked to the window and stared out across the terrace, toward the sea beyond. The letter had been brought by messenger from Mark Fellowes, Sir Gregory Montagu's closest friend. Two days in London, three at the most. The will had been settled; there were more papers to sign. Fellowes would take care of everything, even a carriage and accommodation in both directions. He was a good man, and a friend still, despite their mutual loss.

She looked around the room. Impersonal, perhaps deliberately so. She was still a visitor here, while work was being done on the roof of the Roxby house where she was officially in residence. As Nancy had said, 'For appearance's sake. Give all the busy tongues something else to wag about!' She felt herself smile.

When Adam came home. But when would that be? How long before. . . .

Nancy was in Bodmin, on family business. She had asked her advice on the proposed trip to London.

'Better to do it yourself, my dear, rather than involve yet another lawyer looking to line his purse!'

It had made sense. But that was then.

There was a light tap at the door.

'Just looking to see if you needs any help?'

It was Grace Ferguson's girl. Friendly, feminine, efficient, and always ready to offer a hand or pass the time of day when she felt it was welcome.

'Have *you* been to London, Jenna?'

She clapped her hands together. 'Never been out of Cornwall— Lowenna.' She hesitated. 'We'm surely going to miss you.'

'I shall be back before you know it. Who was that I saw you talking to earlier? I didn't see him leave.'

Jenna reached out to adjust a curtain.

'A man called Tolan. Mr. Yovell knew all about him.' She did not look at her. 'Served with Captain Adam and an admiral.'

Lowenna smiled. Adam had told her about Tolan, a loyal servant to Bethune, and discarded without a thought. Like the flotsam on the beach where she sometimes walked.

'What was he like? Did he seem a nice person?'

'I s'pose.'

Lowenna crossed to the window again, touching the girl's arm gently. She should not have asked. Jenna had been sent out to work when she was very young. Walking home late one night, she had been raped by a soldier from the local garrison, although no one was ever charged or convicted. She had borne a child, which had lived only a few days.

It might have been me. And the brutal aftermath, the rumours, the whispers that would never die. *There's no smoke without fire.*

147

But now she was here, safe and cared for.

Like me.

'If you needs me. . . .' The door closed softly.

Lowenna stared out at the sea, at a tiny sliver of sail unmoving on the shimmering water. Probably a fisherman coming in to port to sell his catch. Like that last time: the idlers on the waterfront watching the comings and goings of every vessel. Critical, but wistful too.

The only life they knew. Now only memories remained.

She thought of Jenna, and the new arrival, Tolan. Making new lives, starting again. They were to be envied.

She remembered Adam's face, his pleasure when she had recognized the vessel leaving Falmouth on that last day. Would he recall that? *I want to belong, to share it and play a part, not just be a privileged possession. A rose in his lapel. . . .*

She thought of Nancy again: the daughter, sister, aunt of naval officers, and descended from generations of others, she understood better than many the iron grip of ships and the sea on those who had served and been rejected by them. Like Rear-Admiral Thomas Herrick. Herrick would be such a good partner for the widowed Nancy, but pride or something fiercer stood in his way. And John Allday, Sir Richard's old coxswain, who had held him in his arms as he had died, and who was now the popular landlord of The Old Hyperion inn over at Fallowfield: he had in spirit never left that same deck. Dan Yovell, Bryan Ferguson, so many others: no wonder this old grey house held such strength.

She stared at the tiny sail again. It had barely moved.

Tomorrow, then. She was afraid and she was determined.

She said aloud, 'Walk with me.'

No longer alone.

Thomas Herrick climbed down from the carriage and peered around, recovering his bearings, aware that Young Matthew had already left his box and was murmuring something to his horses. Careful to display no undue concern for his passenger, but always ready, in case he was needed.

He would never forget that other visit, the first time they had seen him with the empty sleeve, and his own outburst. 'I'm not

148

a cripple, for God's sake!' And his instant apology, ashamed that he had turned on a friend who could not answer back.

His companion on this short journey, James Roxby, had already descended and was speaking with two men on the drive before the imposing house. As old or even older than the one he had just left, but sprawling and a little shabby, and built on several levels, enlarged as required over the years. It must have seen many changes, and dominated an estate which was one of the largest in this part of the county.

Herrick recognized one of the men. Flinders had been steward of the estate for a good many years. Tough and competent: he would have needed to be, to satisfy his late master, Sir Lewis Roxby. 'The King of Cornwall', as people still called him.

He saw them turn, and James Roxby smiled.

'This is Henry Grimes.' He waved his hand vaguely. 'He is putting the old house to rights for us.'

Herrick had already noticed the gaping holes in one of the many rooftops, with workmen, stripped to the waist, crawling through them. All very industrious, and well aware of them. Like hands working ship, he thought, when an officer made an unexpected appearance on deck.

'This is Rear-Admiral Herrick, a visitor.' He did not introduce Flinders.

Grimes was small and wiry, with grey hair pulled back in a tight, old-fashioned queue. Keen, brilliant eyes, which Herrick sensed missed nothing. He felt the familiar pain in his shoulder and realized he had straightened his back, out of habit, at the mention of his rank.

Grimes smiled broadly. 'Glad to know you, sir.' He did not offer his hand. 'I've been trying to explain about timber to my people— like talking to blocks of wood these days, if you'll pardon the expression! But *you'll* understand what I mean. When I first started work in a shipyard, timber was of the finest quality, from the *Growth of England*, they always insisted.' He shook his head. 'The way things are going, there won't be an oak left standing in the country!'

'How have you managed here?' Roxby sounded impatient, perhaps thinking of the final bill.

Herrick turned to watch as a young woman appeared by a

builders' shack carrying a tray of glasses and mugs, and laughing as some of the men stopped work and gathered around her.

Grimes was saying, 'They're breaking up an old two-decker down at the yard. Her old timbers are still rock-solid, despite her thirty-odd years.'

Herrick said nothing, and did not ask the ship's name, afraid he would know her, and remember her as she had been.

What did I expect?

Like that last visit to Plymouth: this time he had seen the admiral himself. He could hardly recall the preliminaries, and, in fairness, the admiral had not enjoyed it either.

He had ended it by saying, 'You will shortly be receiving a formal appreciation from their lordships, and I feel certain that if your services are ever required in the future. . . .'

Like hearing the door slam in his face, for the last time.

He had wanted to tell Nancy about it. But how could he?

Grimes was saying, 'Ships today are mostly fir-built, Baltic pine and the like. On active service they'll last eight, ten years at the most.'

Some one called him away, and Roxby remarked, 'Talks too much, but he knows his trade.' He lowered his voice. 'This place is far too big. My late father was always too busy to give it the proper attention, and I want my mother to be free to enjoy her life, not be tied to the estate and the constant demands of farmers and tenants.'

Herrick waited. He knew James Roxby was well respected in London; he had a fine mind and was ambitious, where many would be content.

But this *was* her life. Could he not understand?

Grimes the builder was back, with sawdust in his hair.

'When we've cleared the old ballroom, we can give you a better idea.' Then, 'You have another visitor.'

Herrick thought he sounded relieved.

Flinders spoke for the first time. 'Came lookin' for work— Dan Yovell's dealin' with him. Another—' He bit it back, and Herrick saw him avert his eyes. *Another lame duck,* he had been about to say.

He watched the new arrival as he spoke to Young Matthew, before striding toward them.

150

Roxby said, 'Fellow's on foot— must've walked all the way from the house!'

Flinders scowled as two of the workmen pulled the servant girl's apron strings and made her protest, still laughing with them.

'Used to be a marine, served with Captain Adam, I heard.'

Tolan crossed the last few yards, his eyes moving between them and settling on Roxby.

He held out a sealed envelope, then glanced at Herrick and knuckled his forehead. 'Sir!'

Roxby said curtly, 'Some one is coming to see me tomorrow,' folding the envelope and jamming it into his pocket. He nodded to Tolan. 'Thank you for that. Speak to them over there, and tell them to give you refreshment.'

Flinders said, 'I'll deal with *him*, sir,' but stopped as Grimes the builder said to Tolan, 'A moment.' Smiling, but quizzical. 'Don't I know you?'

Tolan faced him without expression. 'Where did you serve, sir?'

Grimes threw back his head and laughed. 'I was wrong! The only ships I served were the ones I helped to build. A long, long time ago!'

Roxby tugged out his watch.

'Must be getting back. My mother will return this evening, before it gets dark on the roads. We can tell her what we've been doing.' He glanced around, but he and Herrick were alone. 'I consider it important. I believe she will, too.'

Herrick walked beside him to the carriage. Even now Roxby was opening a sheaf of papers and frowning over the figures. Tomorrow he might be the surgeon again, but at this moment, Nancy would recognize her husband. *The King of Cornwall.*

Roxby looked up at Young Matthew.

'Shall we wait for the fellow who brought the message?'

'Already gone, sir. Cut across the fields, I reckon.'

Herrick looked in that direction. So near the sea, but you could not catch a glimpse of it from here. He reached up to pull himself into the vehicle and thought he saw Young Matthew smile.

As the carriage rolled out on to the road, it halted for a herd of cows meandering toward a wide gate, and a red-haired

151

youth turned to raise his stick like a salute; he had recognized the crest on the door. Herrick ran his hand along the polished sill. Richard would have used this vehicle whenever he came home from sea. And that last time, when he had left here to hoist his flag above *Frobisher.*

He could see his face, the smile. Sometimes he imagined the resemblance in Nancy, sometimes in Adam, something in the bone structure, or a gesture, or in the voice.

The carriage was slowing, Young Matthew calling to the horses as they topped the brow of a hill. Herrick leaned forward. Here was the sea again, a blue that recalled the Mediterranean. . . . What would Richard say if he knew his true feelings for his sister?

He looked over at Roxby, but he was already immersed in another document.

That last visit to Plymouth, and the admiral's condolences, were blurring, out of focus. Like some distant memory. Like those times with Richard.

Ahead lay not defeat, but a challenge.

He smiled to himself. *So let's be about it!*

'As you can see, my dear, the house is much as Gregory left it.'

Mark Fellowes paused at a bend in the grand staircase and waited for her to join him.

Lowenna looked down at the entrance hall, with its open door. The clatter of carriage wheels coming from the street seemed very loud in the silence. *His* study, its door half open. A pale rectangle on one wall where one of his favourite paintings had hung.

It was strange to hear him named without his title. But Mark Fellowes had been his friend since. . . . It was lost in shadows.

But the house was *not* as he had left it. She ran her fingers along the carved banister. It was dead.

She followed him across the broad landing. Quieter now. Hard to believe that this was one of the busiest streets in London.

She was surprised that she was not tired after two days on the road, with only brief halts for rest and refreshment. True to his promise, Fellowes had ensured that she was watched over

152

all the way by a soft-spoken agent engaged by the lawyers dealing with Montagu's affairs.

Her escort had not been so quietly spoken on one occasion. They had stopped at an inn for the night, and somebody had called after her. She was not even sure what had been said. He might only have been the worse for drink. But in an instant her unassuming escort had the offender pressed against a wall, and she had heard the level voice take on a very different tone. The other man had fled.

When she had thanked him, he had merely shrugged. 'Goes with the contract, miss.'

Then a day with the lawyers. Papers to be signed, and it had been unsettling to see his familiar signature. Discreet enough, but she had seen the curious stares from the younger members of the staff and known they were trying to guess the nature of her relationship with Montagu.

She still found it hard to accept that he should have considered her in such a private matter, when he had already given her so much. Her very life had been his gift.

Even Mark Fellowes, who was used to more unconventional associates, had been unable to hide his surprise.

'Five hundred pounds!' He had beamed with genuine pleasure. '*And* the harp.' It was a replacement for the one which had been damaged beyond repair. She wondered if he remembered her last visit, when she had refused to pose with it.

She lifted her chin. She would keep her promise. Then back to Falmouth.

It was only a promise, not a debt.

And she would have something to contribute to their future. Adam would understand. So unalike, and yet he and Sir Gregory had become fast friends. Together they had created Andromeda. . . .

More stairs, completely quiet now. The whole house standing between the real world and Montagu's creation.

Fellowes said, 'John Fielding is an artist of renown. I believe you have worked with him, and Gregory, of course.'

She nodded. He seemed unsure, even nervous. It was not like him. Most people would think him easy-going, untroubled. An artist in his own right, he came from a wealthy family, which must have helped in this precarious profession.

He said, 'He has brought his patron,' he cleared his throat, 'his client, with him. He already owns two or three of your studies.'

She looked at the big double doors, and remembered the long, bare room beyond, windows on one side, a walled garden below. Recalling his patience, his kindness. And his moments of frustration and anger, throwing brushes and palette in every direction. 'It does not *speak* to me, my girl!' But it never lasted very long.

She halted. There were voices, one of them a woman's.

'Do I know him?'

He was looking at a clock, which had stopped.

'A name in the City, not *our* world. Meyrick. Lord Meyrick.'

It meant nothing. She touched her gown, testing herself. Tomorrow it would be behind her.

'I think we should go in.' He took her arm. 'Together.'

The voices were silent now, but she did not notice them, only the long, littered table with its chalks and crayon, pads that still bore Montagu's notes and preparatory scribbles. The canvas, propped where it held the light without reflection. A plain stool, and the harp.

Mark Fellowes was greeting the artist, John Fielding, older than she remembered, but the same almost casual stance, which she had soon learned was to put his subjects at their ease. No mean feat in some of the studios to which Sir Gregory had conducted her. He must have had great faith in her, when she had none.

Lord Meyrick was not what she expected. Tall, with an athlete's body in expensively cut clothes. A bony, hawk-like face. A countryman, perhaps once a soldier.

'With all respect to the late Sir Gregory Montagu, his paintings do not do you justice.' His voice was low, almost soft. Unlike the hand that took hers and brushed it against his lips.

Lowenna saw the woman who had accompanied him, lounging in one of the tall gilt chairs. *Not comfortable enough to encourage sightseers*, Montagu had said dryly.

She turned her attention to the canvas. Her own face, gazing

154

out at her, the rest roughly sketched from the painter's imagination. It gave her time. The woman was hardly what she had expected, either, even as a casual companion.

Meyrick was saying, 'I have another fine likeness of you, one of his most explicit, I believe. "The Rape of Helen".' He laughed. 'I felt only envy!'

She said, 'But there was nothing that. . . .'

Mark Fellowes moved the harp slightly.

'While the light is so favourable, I think we should begin.'

Meyrick gave a slight bow.

'Please do. I am all attention.' To the woman he said, 'Be *patient*. You need not have come here.'

John Fielding was already stooping over the table, selecting and discarding brushes.

'You will recall where everything is kept, Lowenna.'

Fellowes called, 'I shall be back in a moment,' and the doors clicked shut.

Lowenna walked behind the screen and looked from the window to the sheltered garden below. All green now, with few flowers, overgrown and uncared for. Like the house. The last time she had stood behind this lovely old Oriental screen, all the leaves had been brown, or scattering in the wind.

She saw the smock draped over a bench and held it to her face. The same one. Even the dried paint where she had wiped her fingers. . . .

She was conscious of urgency, and a determination not to reveal it. The voices were speaking again, but she ignored them, shut them out. It was done.

Her gown folded over the bench, her reticule beside it. She saw herself reflected in the window. The loose smock, the feet bare on the floorboards.

She walked deliberately into the studio, and felt nothing. Like being guided.

When Fielding spoke, and touched her shoulder, it could have been Montagu.

She was sitting on the stool, and if she reached out she would feel the harpstrings. Like that day when Adam had ridden away, after seeing her. Perhaps wanting her even then. She must not think, where was he now?

Shall I always be asking, hoping?

155

'The hair should be *free*, looser. You can change it, can't you?'

The soft hands were on her neck, and she could feel the weight of her unbound hair dragging at the smock as it slipped from her shoulders.

'Like this.' She heard the woman say something, but the hands remained.

Another voice. 'If you're certain, my lord?'

'Very, *very* certain.'

She could feel his breath on her neck where the hair had been pulled aside, then the smock had fallen and she felt his fingers around her breast. She was on her feet, clutching the robe, attempting to cover herself. A laugh, cracking into a gasp and a curse of pain, and the hand was suddenly gone.

Like madness. Or like being an onlooker.

Mark Fellowes bursting through the double doors, a tray perhaps with glasses splintering on the floor. And Meyrick's hand pressed to his eye, reeling from the blow she could still feel burning through her arm, as if she herself had been struck.

Meyrick was shouting, 'You bitch! I should have *known*!' His woman was pulling at him, calling out, laughing or sobbing, it was impossible to tell. 'You can whistle for your bloody money after this!'

Fielding said nothing, standing with one arm across the canvas, as if to protect it.

Mark Fellowes was staring at the doors as they banged together.

'If I had thought for an instant—'

She shook her head. Later, every detail would be clear. She walked to the windows again and stared out at the garden, then at her own reflection. It had to be now, or she might break.

'Finish the painting. For *me*. You will be paid.'

She turned with that new, cold deliberation and returned to the stool and the harp, drew her fingers across the strings, heard the sweet notes in the utter silence. She knew the others were watching her as if unable to move.

She arched her shoulders and felt the smock fall around her ankles.

No fear. His final gift.

156

12

The Longest Day

'Captain, *sir*!'

Adam Bolitho opened his eyes, his mind reluctant to respond. It was too early; he had only just fallen asleep. But the shadowy figure beside the chair was real, the midshipman's white patches visible against the cabin's dim backdrop.

'Thank you, Mr. Hotham. Right on time.'

'Morning watch, sir.'

Adam allowed his body to relax, hearing the muffled sounds of the ship around him, the occasional thud of the rudder head. Four o'clock in the morning. And it would be exactly that: Monteith had been standing the middle watch, and he would make certain that the half-hour glass was turned only when the last grains had run through it. No 'warming the glass' to shorten the watch for those on deck. He could remember being told to do it himself when he had been like young Hotham.

He rolled over and felt the ship come alive beneath him. Slow, uneven; the wind had dropped again. He peered aft at the stern windows. Utter darkness, but in a few minutes his mind would be fully awake, and the gloom would be gone.

A visit to the chart room. The latest calculations on the chart. *Reality*. He felt for his shoes, a foot at a time. No pain. Luke Jago or some mate of his had done a good job of stretching the one that had been too tight.

'Mr. Vincent sends his respects, sir, and do you require some refreshment?'

He felt the deck shudder again, heard the far-off squeal of blocks.

'I think not. It sounds as if Mr. Vincent has other tasks more pressing. You'd better go to him.'

He heard the door close. Hotham would carry it all with him back to the midshipmen's berth. Good or bad. *As I once did.*

He walked aft, his body angled unconsciously to the deck.

Today, he would meet with the purser and discuss his complaint that some of the stores were unsatisfactory. Some one else had doubtless signed for them in Gibraltar when he was looking the other way.

Two hands for punishment: minor offenses, with which Vincent could deal. Gun drill again. Yesterday it had been impossible to exercise the larboard battery at all; the gunports had been almost awash as *Onward*, alive and demanding, had heeled over on the opposite tack.

He stared at the whitecaps beneath the counter. The first hint of dawn lay on the water.

Tomorrow they would anchor at Gibraltar once more. What next? And what had they achieved?

Something broke the pattern, a leaping fish, or perhaps the cook had thrown scraps overboard.

He recalled the explosion, the great spread of wreckage and grisly fragments which had followed. There were no cheers or celebrations, just two ships, dipping flags. How would that look eventually in his report? Would any one care?

He thought of their departure from Aboubakr. Coastal craft in plenty, but keeping their distance. People on the beach and along the headland, others by the battery and its hidden artillery. Friends or enemies?

Nautilus had been lying at her anchor, awnings spread and boats alongside, but her captain would be very conscious of the potential danger. Even now, many of those watching would view him not as a protector but an invader.

During his visit to *Nautilus*, Adam had been aware of the tension as he was greeted. Enemies for so many years, victories too often stained by sorrow and tragedy.

There had been moments when the shadow of the past was put aside. A French seaman had pushed through his comrades and held out both hands.

'M'sieu, you save our ship!' He had broken off, embarrassed or overwhelmed, or because his English had run its course.

But he had grasped Adam's hands in his, and his face had spoken the words which had eluded him.

Their meeting had been brief. Marchand had produced wine and two glasses and together they had drunk a toast which had remained unspoken. Then Marchand had seen him over the side, where Jago had been perched in the gig, unconvinced by this display of friendship.

Marchand had saluted him. And his last words, 'Stronger than wine, Capitaine Bolitho!' still lingered in Adam's memory.

He pulled on his old seagoing coat with its frayed and tarnished epaulettes and walked to the screen door.

There would be new orders at the Rock. To take despatches to another squadron, or to relieve some man-of-war in need of refit or overhaul. Vigilance remained high in these waters, and there was always the possibility of local uprisings which could lead to renewed conflict. Pirates, slavers and smugglers all made their own rules along this endless coastline. Others, like Marchand's masters, saw it as the gateway to Africa itself, a new challenge. An empire.

He was reminded suddenly of Captain Sir John Grenville, when he had last seen him leaving this cabin. *Yours to command.* Grenville had understood the mysteries of policy and diplomacy, and it had cost him the only life he had ever truly wanted.

He heard the clink of metal and saw a Royal Marine corporal straightening his coat, probably concealing a mug of something brought for the sentry. He had been caught out by the captain's unexpected appearance.

'Good morning, Corporal Jenkins.'

He heard him call something in response, and his heels clicking together.

They didn't question the rights or wrongs of being here. Their lives were the ship, and one another.

It was a pity many in high authority did not remember that.

He saw the dark outline of the companion hatch, a sliver of cloud like drifting smoke, and felt the wind across his cheek as he stepped over the coaming.

The tiredness was gone. This was always the same: exciting, challenging. When he had been a midshipman he had heard Sir

Richard saying to some one else, 'If the first moment of the day fails to stir you, you are no longer fit to command.'

The figures of the men on watch taking shape around and beyond him. The towering shadows of the mizzen sails reaching across that same streaming cloud, the yards braced hard around to hold an elusive breeze, flapping occasionally but filling again enough to rouse rigging and sailors alike.

Vincent was by the compass box, his shirt hanging loose and unfastened in the warm air. The helmsman was still indistinct in the predawn gloom, but his eyes came alive in the tiny light when he peered down at the swaying compass card.

A second helmsman straightening his back when he saw that, once again, the captain was an early riser.

Hotham was back at his post by the little hooded bench where his slate and the night log book were hidden.

Adam peered at the compass. West by north. Unmoving.

He said, 'It'll be light enough, soon.'

Vincent was ready. 'I've detailed two good lookouts.' He glanced directly overhead. 'I'll go up myself, sir.' It sounded like a question.

'Do that, Mark. We might have lost him.'

It was hard to fix the time when they had realized that *Onward* was being followed. Probably soon after they had quit the anchorage at Aboubakr. Another schooner, but with extra topsails, which the lookout had noticed. Like *Nautilus* on their outward passage, holding the distance if *Onward* showed any sign of changing tack toward her.

There had been a few small craft sighted, but the schooner was always lagging far astern when the watches changed.

In these waters it was common enough for a vessel's master to keep in company with a man-of-war, more so now that the great fleets were at peace and there was little fear of being stopped and searched. Or worse.

He watched as Vincent leaned across the quarterdeck rail to call to some seamen beneath him. *He thinks I'm too cautious. Afraid it might happen again.* Maybe he was right.

He walked down to the lee side. Marchand had known the master of the schooner which had exploded like an inferno, the uniformed figure Adam had seen, tied and helpless, likely already dead.

Marchand had explained in his careful English, 'He had his own men aboard, not only people from Aboubakr. But his young son would also have sailed with him. They would have forced him to watch what they could do to that boy. But you cannot bargain with the devil!' He had shrugged. 'Or with fate.'

Adam walked aft again and stared at the flapping topsail, barely holding the breeze. He saw Vincent climbing on to the mizzen top, his pale shirt marking his progress. And a seaman twisting round to stare at him, even as he was sliding down a backstay toward the deck. Some one close by muttered, 'There 'e goes! Thinks 'e's a young nipper!'

There was smoke in the air; the galley fire was already drawing, the cook or one of his mates preparing the first meal of the day.

He reached out and stretched every muscle. The ship coming alive. No wonder his uncle had cherished this moment.

Vincent was still climbing, hidden now by canvas and rigging. A good and caring officer, and popular also, or as popular as any first lieutenant could hope to be.

But the barrier was still there between them. They were no closer than on that first day, no matter what they both might pretend.

A handshake was not enough.

Midshipman David Napier paused in the shadow of the boat-tier, looking forward along the deck. It was only an hour or so since all hands had been piped to lash up and stow hammocks and the washing down of decks had been completed. Now the hammocks, lashed and neatly paraded in the nettings, looked as if they had never moved, or *Onward*'s more than two hundred sailors and marines had not slept through the night watches undisturbed. They seemed able to ignore every motion or sound, until the shrill of a call brought them up and running.

The decks were already dry, even hot under the bare feet of seamen mustered into working parties and the others on watch.

He glanced around furtively and stepped on to a bollard, running his hand down his leg. The wound was sore, like the aftermath of a burn. But no real pain. He had been gritting his teeth, preparing himself.

He straightened up, and saw that a seaman had noticed. He grinned conspiratorially and stooped over a length of splicing. Napier shaded his eyes and stared outboard at the endless stretch of blue water. Like a great mirror. There was even a little awning rigged now above the wheel to shade the two barebacked helmsmen as they peered at the compass and watched the set of the sails.

And tomorrow they would anchor off Gibraltar. He had helped to plot the final course on the chart himself. Old Julyan, the master, had frowned sternly to conceal his approval.

'I can see that I shall have to watch out, *Mister* Napier!'

'So here you are! I sent word. . . .' It was Lieutenant Monteith, some papers rolled in one hand. He was faultlessly turned out, untroubled, it seemed, by the heat and sluggish breeze, or the fact that he had only come off watch himself four hours ago. 'I have been asked to arrange something. It has to be done before we reach Gibraltar. I am not convinced—' He looked away, as if he had gone too far. 'I must go below, to the forrard messdeck.' Then, 'I saw you examining your leg.' It sounded like an accusation.

'It's strong again now, sir.'

'Good. We can't afford. . . .' Again, it was left unfinished.

Monteith led the way, walking briskly and without hesitation. Men stood aside or stopped what they were doing as he passed. Some of the looks spoke more loudly than words, Napier thought.

Below deck the ship seemed more spacious, the messdecks opening out, scrubbed tables arranged at regular intervals. Benches and lockers marking each individual mess where *Onward*'s company ate, slept, and lived out their free time below. Away from discipline, except that which they dictated themselves. And sustained by a tolerance and brutal humour no landsman would ever understand.

At one end of the deck was a small working party, with a new timber-framed screen. Falcon the carpenter was overseeing their progress, jabbing a finger from time to time at the men stitching a canvas partition.

Monteith ducked beneath a deckhead beam and unfolded his papers. Napier had noticed on other occasions that he never removed his hat. *Remember, it's their home. Show respect when you walk into it.*

He had never forgotten that, and he had seen Falcon's expression. Like the seamen on deck, no words were necessary.

Monteith said, 'Harris, the man who was killed. He was one of your crew?'

Falcon eyed him warily.

'Not directly. 'E was a cooper, see?'

'No matter. He answered to *you*.' He waved the papers as if it were insignificant. 'We anchor tomorrow and time will be limited. When a man dies aboard ship it is customary to auction his personal effects to his messmates.' He faltered, as if it were completely foreign to him. 'I am informed that, in view of the circumstances, the wardroom and warrant ranks will make a contribution.'

Falcon flicked some wood shavings from his sleeve.

'I scarce knew the man, sir. 'E was aboard when the ship commissioned, and worked ashore in the yard when she was buildin'.' He rubbed his chin. 'But if it's an order. . . .'

Another voice. 'Ned Harris was ashore most of the time, sir. Only just got married. I reckon *she* can do with all the help she can get.'

Napier could feel it. A man they had hardly known, but one of their own. Not killed by accident, or in action. Murdered.

Falcon called, ''Ere, Lloyd! You worked with 'im a few times— what d' you think?'

Napier saw him look up from the deck where he was kneeling. The sailmaker who had been a tailor ashore, and a good one according to the captain's servant. He had turned his hand to making clothes for people in this ship, if they could afford him. He and Morgan got along well, they said. *Fellow Welshman. . . .*

'Never had a lot to say, but he was always short of money, getting his wife settled before he was off to sea.' He seemed to notice Napier for the first time. 'Anyway, if the officers are putting their hands into their pockets. . . .' Laughter drowned the rest.

Falcon held up his fist. 'Show a bit of respect, lads!' But he seemed relieved. 'Leave it to me, sir.'

163

Monteith rocked back on his heels. 'The captain will arrange for the proceeds to be put aboard a courier.' He cleared his throat. 'With a suitable message.'

'I think you're wanted on deck, sir!'

Monteith turned and said over his shoulder, 'Send word if you need advice.'

A voice muttered, 'Pity we ain't collectin' for *'im*!'

Falcon glared. 'It's not stand-easy yet, lads, so back to work with you!' But he winked. Monteith was out of sight.

Jeff Lloyd sat on his haunches and waited for the midshipman to pass.

'Your new breeks'll be just about ready in a couple of days. We can try them for fitting— you just say the word, eh?'

Napier smiled with pleasure. 'That was quick! Thank you for. . . .'

Falcon bared his teeth. 'You'd better jump about, Mr. Napier. I think 'is lordship is callin' for you!'

Jeff Lloyd leaned forward and pressed the canvas very slowly into a tight fold, using all his strength, a simple enough task which he could do with one hand. The laughter and the comments that followed the lieutenant's departure meant nothing. Like getting over a nightmare, trapped and fighting in his hammock. Unable to escape.

The voices had returned to normal, Falcon making a suggestion to one of his crew. Somebody whistling softly as he used his chisel to put a finish on the new screen.

He thought of Napier, bending to thank him for finishing the breeches. A lie. He had scarcely chalked out the seams. But it had bought him time. Just long enough.

He felt his breathing steady again. Or was that all in his mind, too?

He should have been ready, anticipated it. But he hadn't, and after all this time just the mention of that name had made him jump, as if it had been shouted into his face.

He found himself staring aft, past the empty tables and scrubbed benches. A solitary figure in one of the messes was writing very slowly on a piece of paper, tongue poking from one corner of his mouth. Dodging work to try and write a letter, so that it could be taken ashore at Gib. The lifeline.

Beyond the huge trunk of the mainmast, and down another

hatchway. Narrow walkways and storerooms, like the one where they had found his corpse. The waiting had been the worst bit. He had thought they might never find him, maybe believe he was still ashore. Skipped his ship to stay with his new wife. Poor woman, she was better off without him. He had even thought Ned Harris might still prove him wrong; he might suddenly appear. Laughing. . . . Like that last time when he had turned his back, the final threat still on his lips.

Slowly, calmly, Jeff Lloyd reached out and gripped his long scissors.

Afterwards, he had heard that they were searching for a knife. Harris's own blade was still on his belt.

The worst was over. There might always be reminders. Like now, today. Harris's miserable belongings.

He felt his blood pounding again. *He threatened me. Unless I paid him, he would swear himself in as a witness. To murder.*

When he had laughed, for the last time.

Boots thudded past, some Royal Marines on their way to their own messdeck, their 'barracks', carrying pieces of equipment, freshly pipe-clayed in readiness for some ceremonial drill at the Rock. A good enough crowd, but in their own special world. Apart. Two of them spoke his name. Glad to be down in the cool shadows.

'I've been thinkin', Jeff.'

He looked up. It was Falcon, staring after the scarlet tunics.

Lloyd wanted to lick his lips. Bone dry. As if he already knew.

'Most of the lads seem to know you, by sight if nuthin' else. Might seem more proper if *you* go round the messes?' He had his head on one side, unused to asking favours. 'Tell 'em about th' sale of 'is gear. Sound better comin' from you.'

Lloyd stood up slowly.

'Glad to, Mr. Falcon.'

The carpenter touched his arm, smiling.

'Good lad. See me for a wet at stand-easy!'

Lloyd folded his tools with great care. Buying himself more time.

He had been wrong. Ned Harris was still laughing.

Lieutenant Mark Vincent tried to stifle a yawn, and signalled with his free hand to warn the cabin sentry of his arrival. But he was not quick enough.

'First lieutenant, *sir*!'

Vincent said, 'There was no *need*, at this hour.'

In the small, swinging circle of light from the lobby lantern, the Royal Marine might have grinned. Almost.

'Cap'n's still up an' about, sir.'

How could that be? He had just taken over the morning watch when Bolitho had come on deck. That was yesterday. Did he never sleep?

The screen door opened slightly. It was Jago, Bolitho's coxswain.

'I came as soon as I could.'

Jago's eyes shone only briefly in the same swinging light. The unfastened coat and dishevelled turn-out would not pass unnoticed. It should not matter. But it did.

It was after midnight, and apart from the watchkeepers every sane man was tucked in his hammock and asleep. It had been a long day. And tomorrow. . . . He tried to shut it out of his mind.

There was plenty of light in the great cabin, so that the stern windows looked like black mirrors, throwing back the captain's reflection sharply. He was standing by the table, his log book unopened, the pad which usually lay on the small desk beside it, marked at intervals with unused quills. Charts also, including the one they had used at the last conference before Aboubakr.

'All quiet on deck, Mark?' Almost in the same breath. 'Sorry to drag you down aft.'

He moved toward the quarter and stared into the darkness.

'I've been thinking about our shadow. She was still holding station astern at nightfall. And she will be there at first light.'

Vincent waited in silence, unsure where this was leading.

'Whoever planned to disable *Nautilus* must already have estimated her time of arrival.' He spread his hands. 'And known that she was coming to Aboubakr. Such intelligence could only have originated in Gibraltar. But there was no time or opportunity to inform any one that *we* would be in company with her.'

Vincent heard sounds in the pantry. Morgan was standing by his captain, despite the lateness of the hour.

He said, 'Rebellion, sir?'

'Whoever holds that fortress and commands the only good anchorage until Algiers, might determine the future of a nation.' He stretched his arms. 'Given the right allies.'

'The French?'

'Perhaps. When they're ready.' He gestured. 'Take a seat, Mark. We can have a mug of something in a moment.' He moved to his old chair and ran a hand along the worn leather. 'But for us *Nautilus* would be a wreck, and her people dead. What, I wonder, would have been the next move?'

He paused and looked at the deckhead, listening.

'She's sailing well. Running like a good mare with the scent of home.' He smiled. 'You've done her proud, Mark. I shall not forget.'

Vincent watched him, feeling the energy and the frustration driving him. He was by the quarter gallery now, his hand against the glass as if to hold the darkness beyond.

'Landfall today, Mark. If only. . . .'

Vincent could guess what he was thinking. Of the girl who could be sharing it with him.

Adam turned away from the windows.

'They're waiting for our return, at Gibraltar. *As ordered.* You can think me crazy, but I was of half a mind to come about and run down on that damned schooner, chase her inshore and cut her out, to hell with the risk!' He laughed shortly. 'Maybe the wind waited until now, when it's too late, even for a touch of madness!'

'But for you, we would be taking bad news to the flagship.'

'Us, Mark. It was a great deal to ask of a new company.' He glanced at the littered table. 'I heard that they responded well to the sale of Harris's effects. It's little enough, but most of them gave what they could. I only wish. . . .'

Vincent waited, at last knowing why he was here, surprised that he had not understood. All the days and the long nights, the doubts and the first hint of danger. And fear. The Captain had been carrying it, sharing it with no one.

'I flogged a man because he fell asleep on watch, because he was insolent, and maybe had been drinking beforehand.' His

167

hand moved. 'I could call now for cognac and drink my fill, *because I command here*. And yet a murderer walks free amongst us, to blacken the name of the ship. I am *not* proud of it, Mark.'

'We did all we could, sir. Otherwise—' Something fell on the deck overhead and somebody laughed. He must have been standing close to the cabin skylight; another voice was hissing a warning. Then there was silence again.

Adam said, 'Thank God they can still laugh.' He tugged out his watch and held it close to one of the lanterns. 'I've kept you listening to my woes far too long. We've a long day tomorrow. *Today*.'

Vincent walked to the screen door, oddly unwilling to leave. He looked through the great cabin, remembering the envy and resentment he had felt; knowing this was a moment of special significance, and only later would he understand why.

Adam said, 'Get some sleep. You have the forenoon watch. I shall see you then.'

The door was shut and Vincent was outside in the swaying circle of light once more, with the same sentry, his body leaning slightly as the hull dipped beneath them.

He could still see the cabin in his mind. A fresh shirt lying near the old chair. The uniform coat hanging nearby, not the faded seagoing one with its tarnished lace. And no doubt his coxswain would be on hand to shave him when dawn changed those stern windows from black to blue.

This night's conversation was something he would not forget. A privilege, and a warning.

13

Ships That Pass

Commodore Arthur Carrick waited for his servant to close the cabin door behind him and gestured to a chair.

'Be seated, Bolitho. I regret leaving you to cool your heels, but now I am all attention.'

Almost an hour had passed since Adam had boarded the flagship, although he had seen no other visitor arrive or leave before him.

The same flag lieutenant had met him at the entry port, and had explained that the commodore was eager to see him but was extremely busy. That, despite the signal for *Onward*'s captain to repair on board, which had been hoisted even before the anchor had hit the bottom.

Nothing had changed aboard *Tenacious*, although some awnings had finally been spread to protect the upper deck from the sun. Here in the great cabin the quarter windows were open, and there was a slight breeze from the harbour.

He sat in silence as Carrick unfastened the folder, which Adam had checked with care before climbing down into the gig. The guardboat had signalled *Onward* to a different anchorage this time, convenient for the shore, but a longer pull for the gig's crew. Even the urbane flag lieutenant had been unable to hide his surprise when Adam had requested that his men be allowed aboard the flagship, rather than left sitting tired and parched in the sun.

'If you say so, sir.' But it had been done. He had seen Jago's expression, and was glad.

The servant had padded in again and was speaking softly to his master.

The commodore was outwardly relaxed, even casual, his lean, bony features composed. Only the hard blue-grey eyes gave a hint of the man within.

Even the matter of the gig's crew had occasioned a cool jibe.

'Hope they appreciate it, Bolitho. Most Jacks would only take advantage, from my experience!'

He must have sensed a corresponding chill in Adam, and changed the subject.

'Now, in your own time, Bolitho, tell me what happened during your passage to Aboubakr. I will give full attention to your report, but I need to hear it from you in person. I have already gleaned some of the sorry details— even here on the Rock, we are not without news of the real world.' He smiled. 'As they say in our home county, bad news rides a fast horse!'

Then he swivelled round on his chair as if watching for passing vessels or inquisitive harbour craft, and waited.

Adam found himself listening to his own voice, flat and unemotional. The reports from the lookout. The midshipman, almost fainting with pain, managing to describe what he and the seaman had seen and interpreted. And the grim outcome, no heroics, no flags, except the ensign dipping in salute after the smoke had cleared.

Carrick spoke at last.

'*Nautilus* owes her survival to your prompt action. Your gun crews had good fortune.'

Adam recognized the challenge, and felt the iron-cold eyes on him as he pulled a packet from his coat. He could still hear Lieutenant Squire's voice when he had handed it to him: 'A prayer would have helped, but I couldn't think of one fast enough!'

He put it on the table.

'Part of the schooner, sir. Fell on our foc'sle deck. We were as close as that.'

Carrick unwrapped the charred wood and held it to the sunlight.

'Indeed.' He nodded. 'Too close for comfort.'

The servant had returned, and placed a pair of goblets discreetly near the papers and Adam's rough map.

Carrick was saying, 'Some local resistance, or a full-scale rebellion. . . . I can understand why the French authorities will be concerned, and, it is to be hoped, grateful for your initiative. There I trust it will end, at least while I still command the Strait Squadron.' He saw Adam's expression and laughed. 'Rear-Admiral Aylmer is still unwell, although I am informed that he expects a complete recovery, damn his eyes!' The laugh became a cold smile. 'You did not hear that, Bolitho. So, now let us drink to you and your fine ship.'

They touched glasses, although Adam had not seen them filled. If he slept when he went back to *Onward*, he thought, he might never wake up.

'When we last met, Bolitho, you reported that one of your company had been murdered.' He studied his goblet. 'Some petty dispute, maybe? I take it there were no developments.' He did not seem to expect an answer. 'No matter. If I shouldered the blame for every soul who's gone aloft under my command, I would be as sick as my admiral!'

He stood up. Abruptly, like most of his gestures and words.

'I will read your full report, and discuss it with the governor. The next move will be. . . .' He frowned as the flag lieutenant appeared at the door. 'What is it now?'

'You have a meeting with—'

Carrick waved him into silence. 'Slipped me mind, dammit!'

He turned toward Adam just as easily.

'We will meet again soon. You will be informed.' He held out his hand. 'Now, I am certain you have a great deal to do.'

It was a dismissal, and Adam was glad of it. Carrick called after him, 'Your boat's crew should be well rested by now for their pull back to *Onward*, don't you think?'

He strode from the cabin, the flag lieutenant hard put to keep up with him.

'I sometimes wonder why I worry myself sick, when. . . .'

He broke off. It was not the lieutenant's fault.

Two seamen seemed to be waiting for them. One of them, a bosun's call hanging around his neck, blurted, 'Cap'n Bolitho, sir? You won't remember me, but. . . .'

Adam reached out impetuously and gripped his arm.

171

'Logan. Spike Logan. You were with me in *Unrivalled*. Maintop.'

The man and his companion were both grinning and nodding, and some others were loitering nearby, listening.

They walked on toward the entry port, where the side-party was waiting. The flag lieutenant spoke at last, in an undertone, touching his hat.

'Now you know *why*, sir.'

Adam climbed down the side and stepped into the gig, which was already in position, as if it had never moved. He looked around at the crew, sitting smartly upright, arms folded, as if the flagship, towering over them like a cliff, did not exist.

His eyes met Jago's and he smiled, surprised that it came so easily.

'No squalls, Luke.' He sat down facing the stroke oarsman. 'Not yet, anyway.'

Jago tilted his hat slightly against the reflected glare.

'After what *we* done?' He said no more. There was a faint smell of rum on his breath.

Then, 'Shove off, forrard!' He could see faces watching from the high poop with the gilded gingerbread he remembered so well from their arrival here. The flagship's officers. *What the hell do they care?* 'Out oars!'

He counted the seconds, standing with his fingers just touching the tiller bar, as if unconcerned. He contained a grin. *If only they knew.* 'Give way together!'

He waited until he could see *Onward*'s masts, almost delicate against a big two-decker nearby, and eased the tiller until they had moved into line. Then he sat down and watched the stroke, the captain's gold epaulette near enough to touch.

He tasted the grog on his lips. It was good to have mates.

He looked away. *Even in a flagship.*

Lieutenant James Squire walked aft from the companion ladder, his eyes still dazzled by the sun and the vivid panorama of the harbour. He had visited Gibraltar several times in different ships, but he never grew tired of its life and colour.

Within minutes, or so it seemed, of dropping anchor and the captain's departure in response to the usual impatient signal, *Onward* had been hemmed in by boats ready to sell, buy or steal anything available. The master-at-arms and a full squad of marines had their work cut out to keep the decks clear of invaders, however friendly they might appear.

He had heard the boatswain telling some of the youngsters, 'If you gets to step ashore, keep yer 'ands on yer money belt, or it'll go. They can take a tattoo off a man's skin and 'e wouldn't feel it!' From what he had heard, old Josh Guthrie would be one of the first ashore. He could take care of himself.

Morgan the cabin servant stood facing him by an open gunport. Even that was guarded by a spread of netting.

'Do you wish to see the captain, sir?' Self-possessed as always, but sweating slightly. 'He is very hard-pressed just now, only returned aboard a moment ago.'

Squire said patiently, 'It's my watch. *I* received him on board, remember?'

Morgan let out a sign. 'My apologies, sir. We are busy, too.'

Squire stared through the open doors, and beyond the sentry who was peering past the companion ladder, as if he expected to see some intruder trying to reach the lower deck without being seized.

'Guardboat just brought some mail. Mostly official, had to be signed for.' He looked again at the cabin. 'So I must. . . .'

The purser and one of his assistants were there, unrolling a mass of documents, and Prior the clerk, with a ledger almost as big as himself, was edging his way toward the captain. Even the surgeon was present. But it was nothing serious; he was laughing at something the coxswain, Jago, was telling him.

The captain had seen him.

'Mail, James? I saw the guardboat pulling away. I wondered. . . .'

Squire carried the canvas bag into the cabin. *I wondered, too. We always do. And hope.*

They walked aft together. The stern windows were open and the shutters drawn, the wind warm but refreshing. There was haze closer inshore, and dust from the town. Everything else was dwarfed by the Rock.

'I had to sign for these, sir.'

But the captain had not heard him. Adam was not listening.

A heavy sealed envelope, the contents probably written or

dictated weeks ago. *I am directed by my lords commissioners of Admiralty.* . . . And one bearing the familiar anchor and crossed swords, put aboard a courier in Plymouth. The admiral's seal was still bright in the filtered sunlight.

He put them on the bench seat and picked up an envelope uncluttered by seals or official sanctions.

As if the cabin was suddenly empty, the view astern from these windows quite still.

She was here, with him. Like coming alive, all tiredness gone. He touched it again. So many miles, days, weeks.

Always waiting.

Vicary the purser said, 'If you could just glance at these, sir. They will require your approval before I take them ashore.'

Adam laid the letter on the bench seat and reached for the knife Morgan had placed where he could see it.

'A moment.' He slit open the heavy envelope and glanced across each separate section. He could still recall his first command, and the introduction to documents like these; it had been like reading a foreign language. It seemed a long time ago.

He looked at the date, and the perfect script. Official, enclosing a shorter letter, its contents very much to the point. He remembered the face behind the writing, one of the admiral's aides at Plymouth.

More voices. Vincent was here now; he had been occupied with a supply lighter when Adam had returned from *Tenacious*.

'I'm a bit adrift, sir.' He hesitated. 'Is something wrong?'

Adam folded the letter.

'Midshipman Huxley. Where is he, d' you know?'

'Lowering the jolly-boat, sir— I've watched him do it before. I thought. . . .'

'I want to see him immediately. This concerns his father.'

Vincent lowered his voice. 'The court martial, sir?'

'Not guilty.' He wanted to hit out, smash something. Prevent this from happening. 'They were too late. He was found dead in his quarters. Hanged himself.'

Vincent said, 'I'll fetch him. I have always found him easy enough to talk to.' He faltered. 'It's no use, is it, sir?'

Adam picked up the other letter. Her letter. Later. . . .

'Thank you, Mark. But he is one of *my* officers.' He turned and faced the others. 'If you will excuse me, the first lieutenant can deal with the issue of signatures.'

They filed out of the cabin and Vincent closed the door as they left. The surgeon had been the last to leave.

'If you need me?' He knew, or guessed.

Morgan had been waiting by his pantry, sensing the change in atmosphere, wanting to do something. This was his place. But he gathered up the empty glasses and headed for the screen. He would be ready when called. And the captain would know it.

Adam stood by the open stern window and saw another boat pulling slowly beneath the counter, some one holding up shawls or bright clothing, undeterred by shouts from the deck.

It was hot, and he was still wearing the dress uniform coat in which he had boarded the flagship.

He made to unfasten it, but something stopped him.

The slight tap on the grating.

'Mr. Midshipman Huxley, *sir*!'

'Enter!'

He was the Captain.

The two midshipmen sat side by side on the forecastle deck watching the lights on the shore; occasionally one moved, like a star fallen on the water. Overhead, if they looked, the converging pattern of shrouds and stays reached to the sky, yards and spars completely still, resting, like the ship.

There had been music, the lively sound of a violin, laughter and what sounded like feet stamping in a jig, but even that had gone silent. It would soon be time to pipe down; some of the hands were already in their hammocks.

Down by the entry port there was still a lantern burning, an intrusion in the darkness. The glint of metal and a moving shadow showed the duty watch was alert, waiting for one of the boats, or the Officer-of-the-Guard on his endless patrol around and between the anchored men-of-war.

David Napier glanced over his shoulder as a solitary figure walked past: one of the anchor watch doing his rounds, although he would hardly be able to see the cable where it reached down into the black water. They might have been completely alone, sitting where they were in the eyes of the ship. Even the figurehead was invisible, reaching out to another unknown horizon.

Soon they would have to return to the midshipmen's berth. Nothing had been said, and the silence made it worse, if that were possible. They all knew. The whole ship seemed to know.

Once, he had said, 'Would it be better if I left you in peace, Simon?'

No words, but he had felt a hand on his arm and known he was shaking his head.

And then, quite suddenly, Simon Huxley had started to talk.

'I knew what had happened. When the Captain sent for me, I *knew*. I kept going over it, again and again, but I was thinking too much about my own future. . . .'

It had been dark, but not enough to hide the tears on his face. He had shaken off any attempt to restrain or comfort him. Like a flood-gate giving way.

'When I saw him, that last time, in Plymouth, and every one was trying to make things seem better, I should have known. My father had already condemned himself, no matter what any court martial might decide!'

Huxley had got up suddenly and leaned out across the water, and Napier had stood with him, hardly daring to hold him, afraid of what he would do. But in a calmer voice he said, 'Two of his men were drowned within sight of land, and he blamed himself. Even when he was told that the court would find him not guilty, he said, *it won't bring them back to life.*'

They had sat down again, sharing the stillness.

Then Napier had asked, as if he had no control over it, 'What did the Captain say?'

Huxley had said nothing, reliving it for a moment. Then he whispered, 'He treated me like a man, a friend. I knew he cared. It wasn't just words.' He had been unable to continue.

Some one shouted, and another said, *'About bloody time!'*

A boat was pulling out of the darkness, the oars trailing living serpents of phosphorescence.

Napier took his friend's arm gently. 'Shall we go below, Simon?' and felt him nod.

'I'm ready.'

That was all. But enough.

176

Hugh Morgan was still in his pantry when the last boat came alongside. Here, down aft, you could not hear much of it, but there would be some curses and flying fists if they carried their high spirits down on to the messdeck. The ship's corporal would have to deal with it. Rowlatt, the master-at-arms, was still ashore, 'on special duty', they said. He had heard that Rowlatt had a woman in the town. He grinned. She must be blind, or desperate.

He raied his glass and sipped it, savouring it. The good stuff. . . . It had been a long day.

He glanced at the open letter laid on his counter. Long and rambling, from his brother in Cardiff. Older than himself, he was a glass-blower, as their father had been; it was a marvel he had any lungs left after all this time. Six children, too; but they would be children no more. He could always picture Cardiff in his thoughts. . . . *Be like another world to me today.*

It would seem strange to walk those old streets again. But maybe. . . .

He heard a faint shout, then a crack, likely a starter across some one's rump. Otherwise the ship was quiet, the candleflames unmoving. The pantry door was just ajar; he could see the small pool of light over the desk. The captain was still sitting there, a pen grasped in his hand. Like the last time he had crept across the cabin to close the quarter gallery windows. Not much air, but it was better than enduring the insects that tapped against the glass or flickered in the faint glow from astern.

Tomorrow, perhaps, he might go ashore. He had been to Gibraltar a good many times. Different ships and shipmates. He had a friend who worked in the big chandlery, if he was still there. But you had to know your way around, like any seaport. He smiled, sipping the rum. Even the 'gateway to the Mediterranean'.

Women, too, at a price. He gave them a wide berth. Otherwise you could find she had left you with something you would regret, long after you had forgotten her face. And she yours.

In a minute, he would make some excuse and disturb the captain, perhaps persuade him to climb into his cot. It was hard to recall the last time the man had been properly asleep. What drove him? He had known other captains who would have left the work to others, and complained about it afterwards.

He thought of the visit to the flagship; there was always plenty of gossip. How the captain had been kept waiting to see the commodore, after what he had done, and risked, to save the Frenchie from being turned into a giant coffin.

He should be used to it. Morgan had served three captains, and could take the rough with the smooth. This was different. Like today. Perhaps today most of all.

Something which his brother in Cardiff would never understand, as long as his lungs allowed him to live.

The young midshipman standing in the great cabin, which had been suddenly emptied of visitors. The captain with the letter, which was still lying on his desk. Then his voice, inaudible to Morgan. And the youth, *one of my officers*, watching him fixedly, even trying to smile later at something the captain had said, with tears running down his face.

They had walked together to the gallery windows, and he had seen the captain pointing out something, his hand on the midshipman's shoulder, like brothers meeting and coming to know one another again.

He tensed. The pantry door moved very slightly. The screen door must have been opened, although there had been no sound, no shout or stamping of boots.

'Still awake, Luke?' Jago was fully dressed, alert. 'What is it?'

So it was serious.

'Signal for the Cap'n.' He held up some paper. 'Mr. Monteith asked me to bring it— he's a bit busy with a defaulter.' He grinned, but it did not reach his eyes. 'Bloody drunk, more like!'

'Can't it wait?' Morgan pushed a glass toward him, and filled it to the brim.

Jago shrugged. 'The ink's still wet. Must be important.'

They both turned as the pantry door was pulled aside.

'It's impossible to find any peace, even here!'

Then he smiled. Afterwards, Morgan thought it was like seeing a great weight being lifted from him.

'Finish your drinks, please.' He took the signal and opened it unhurriedly. 'And pour one for me.'

Jago watched him narrowly. *So many times.*

'Trouble, Cap'n?'

Adam crumpled the signal. He could see the unfinished letter on his desk.

My dearest Lowenna. I dream of you, always. . . .

'I shall need the gig tomorrow, Luke. Flagship at four bells. Forenoon.'

He lifted his glass. It was still only a dream.

Lieutenant Mark Vincent walked along *Onward*'s larboard gangway, his mind ranging over his list of duties. It was a bright morning, surprisingly free of haze even along the shore, the buildings unusually clear in the sunlight. A steady north-easterly had made all the difference.

He licked his lips, tasting the strong coffee which had been his only breakfast. A wise decision, he thought.

The cook must have broken open a new cask of salted pork for their first day in port. Some people never seemed to heed a warning. A line-up for the 'seat of ease' in the forecastle had resulted, or more drastic measures for those unable to wait. Pumps and brooms had been busy at first light.

He glanced at the empty boat-tier. The boatswain needed no reminder: all the boats were in the water. Clinker-built craft, especially new ones, opened out very quickly if left high and dry.

He stopped and stared toward the main anchorage, and behind him the accompanying footsteps halted also: Midshipman Walker, ready to run with a message, or scribble something on his slate. The youngest member of his mess, and in fact the whole ship, Walker had changed more than any one. He seemed far more self-assured, serious, and more to the point, he had not been seen crouched over a bucket, spewing up his guts. Not even after the pork. Maybe the encounter with the schooner had left its mark. There was always a first time.

He saw Midshipman Deacon with some of his signals team standing by the flag locker, pointing to something and grinning. He held a telescope, although he would be hard put

179

to see the flagship with other vessels anchored across his line of sight, among them a smart-looking brig, undoubtedly a courier, which had anchored very late, when the lights had been showing ashore and the water was like black silk. Skilled or reckless, her commander had taken a calculated risk.

Once again, Vincent asked himself, *what would I have done, if . . . ?* There was always *if.*

The captain's gig would be hooked on and ready; Jago had already gone down to keep an eye on that. A man you might never really know, unless he chose. But if you were in a tight corner, he would always be there.

Vincent ran a finger around his neckcloth. The air was warmer, despite the north-easterly wind. The captain would be speculating about his summons to the flagship. New orders? Running more errands for their invisible superiors? *Not like last time, I hope.*

He took his mind from it and returned to his list. Some defaulters. Nothing very serious, mostly too much to drink. A few hours' extra work would be enough, without any one thinking the first lieutenant was going soft.

Walker said loudly, 'Boat heading this way, sir!'

Vincent turned. 'Are you sure?'

Deacon had also seen it and was training his telescope, without undue excitement. It was not difficult to see him as a lieutenant, when opportunity and luck came his way.

Pulling smartly. Not a casual visitor this time. He walked to the ladder.

'Boat ahoy?'

The reply came back just as smartly. *'Merlin!'*

Midshipman Walker called, 'The brig that came in last night, sir! It's her captain!'

Vincent swore under his breath. 'Man the side.' Some one had handed him a telescope. *Now, of all times.* He adjusted it and saw the boat leap into view, the crew pulling strongly, bowman standing and lifting the boathook.

He settled on the solitary passenger, and tensed. A young face, very young. But in command.

'Shall I pass the word to the captain, sir?'

'He's about to leave the ship. I'll deal with it.'

At the entry port, the side-party was already in position,

boatswain's mates moistening their calls on their tongues, eyes on the approaching boat.

Vincent saw that *Onward*'s gig had been moved to clear the way.

He was calm again, under control. He should get used to it. What did they say about promotion? Not *what* you know, but *who* you know. . . .

The oars were tossed, and the calls trilled in salute.

'I apologize for appearing without any warning. My ship is under orders to sail, but I knew you were lying here. . . .' He looked around. He was even younger than Vincent had thought.

Vincent said, 'I am the senior here, sir. My captain is about to leave the ship.'

'I know. The flagship. I have just been aboard *Tenacious* myself.'

'Francis Troubridge! Of all people! Here, let me look at you!' They all stared as the captain strode amongst them and seized the visitor by his shoulders, and the two bright epaulettes they bore. '*Commander* Troubridge, by God! And rightly so! Well deserved, if people don't know the real truth!'

They both laughed.

'This is Mark Vincent, my right hand.' Then, more quietly, 'So many things I want to know, to ask you.' He took his arm and together they walked inboard, as if they were completely alone.

Jago had appeared on deck, and stood near Vincent, watching impassively.

'Vice-Admiral Bethune's flag lieutenant, sir, in *Athena*. Afore we was given *Onward*.'

And it was all over just as quickly.

Another rough hug, then stepping apart and saluting one another. Friends. Equals.

Vincent watched with the others, and heard the captain call, 'I shall tell her, when I see her!'

Then the boat was pulling away, with Commander Francis Troubridge waving his hat like a midshipman, as if he could not restrain himself.

Jago said, 'We'd best do the same, Cap'n.'

He had seen most things, could take them head on if need be.

181

Ships that pass. Something his father used to go on about, when he was sober enough to make sense.

'I'm ready, when you are.' Adam was looking in the direction of the boat, but it was already hidden by the lateen sails of a Gibraltarian trader.

He thought of the last time they had all been together, in Bethune's London house, captain, coxswain, flag lieutenant, and the vice-admiral's servant, Tolan.

The navy was like that. The family. It meant something, Jago thought. A hand on the shoulder.

Vincent was saying, 'His first command, sir?' But some one called out, interrupting him, as the gig was warped alongside again.

Adam saw Morgan hurrying toward the entry port with the old sword in his hands. There would be some peace in the great cabin for a while. Morgan deserved it. . . . He recalled Vincent's words. Admiration or resentment?

He climbed down into the gig, the salutes ringing in his ears. 'This will not take long.'

Jago turned to look at him. *How does he know?*

He said, 'Do 'em good, Cap'n. Work off some o' that pork!'

As they pulled away from *Onward*'s side and out of her shadow, Adam looked toward the anchored brig, her paintwork like glass in the sunlight. There were tiny figures aloft on her yards, and he guessed the capstan was already manned.

Troubridge was cutting it fine, and under the eyes of the flagship, too. His brief visit had been important enough to him to delay sailing.

To both of us.

His first command. *Like Firefly.* He thought of that last walk on the waterfront, those same reminders.

I shall tell her, when I see her. But who would see her first?

He climbed swiftly up and around *Tenacious*'s tumblehome, and found the side-party waiting.

The flag lieutenant hovered as the salutes were carried out, and then guided him aft with an urgency very unlike his previous visit. As if there was not a minute to spare.

'The commodore is waiting to see you, sir. I shall take you straight to him.'

Adam had already seen a midshipman standing by the flagship's belfry. He was speaking with some seamen, and obviously in no hurry to strike the four bells of the time arranged for this meeting.

He could hear Carrick's voice long before he reached the lobby. The Royal Marine sentry was staring straight in front of him, face impassive. Maybe it was often like this.

'I don't give a saint's damn what he says! Get him here, *now*!'

A lieutenant hurried past without even sparing them a glance. Carrick was standing in the centre of the cabin, feet astride and with his fine coat unbuttoned, breathing hard, as if he had been running.

'So here you are, Bolitho. Not quite what we expected, eh?' He gestured to the flag lieutenant. 'Get something to drink, for God's sake, Flags. That fool of a servant is ashore, damn his eyes!'

'I believe you sent him, sir.'

It was not a wise thing to say, but Carrick apparently did not hear him.

'After all the care and preparation! *Treachery*— remember what I said, Bolitho? There's no other word for it!'

He walked to the side of the cabin, still breathing raggedly, while the flag lieutenant found and placed a full glass on the table. He had already seen Adam shake his head. This was not the time.

Carrick slammed down the empty glass.

'If I hadn't sent you to accompany the Frenchman to . . . to Aboubakr. . . .' He stumbled over the name. 'The trick would have succeeded, and *Nautilus* would be lying in charred fragments, like that piece you showed me! The best bloody thing that could have happened, if you ask me!'

The flag lieutenant waited while Carrick strode to the stern windows and leaned out over the quarter, and said patiently, 'The French government is concerned about the uprising, and is eager to strengthen its alliance with the present ruler.'

Carrick swung round, his face shining in the filtered sunlight. 'They're going to give *Nautilus* to him, for God's sake! A token of trust and solidarity! Like the Algiers fiasco.' He jabbed a finger. 'You were there, Bolitho— you saw the

183

scum who tried to use a just campaign to cover their own crimes! There'll be others this time, you mark my words!' He glared at the door. 'Say that again!'

A voice called, '*Merlin* has just weighed, sir.'

He breathed out very slowly. 'Good. Her commander's a friend of yours, I gather?'

'My last ship, sir.' Adam watched him compose himself, as if it were a physical effort requiring all his strength.

'Well, he's under *my* command now.' The anger was still simmering. 'While *I* am still making decisions here!'

He pointed to a litter of papers scattered across the table.

'I have ships undergoing or awaiting repairs. Captains running damned errands for those who think they know what is needed.' He changed tack just as sharply. 'I was told that *Onward* is taking on supplies?'

Adam felt the flag lieutenant's eyes on him.

'The usual replenishments, sir. Fresh water too, of course. My purser is dealing with our immediate requirements.' Carrick was not listening.

Instead, he asked, 'How soon can you weigh and put to sea?'

Another challenge, and Adam felt an overwhelming desire to hit back, reciprocate measure for measure, despite the consequences.

'Now, if so ordered, sir.'

It was so quiet he thought he could hear Carrick's breathing.

Then, unexpectedly, he smiled. 'That was bravely said. I might hold you to it.' He loosened his coat. 'But two more days should suffice.'

For a moment longer Adam thought he had gone too far, that the meeting was over before it was begun.

Commodore Carrick had turned toward the screen, his voice expressionless.

'I shall want you to patrol that same coastline again. To be ready to act against interference or intimidation, as you see fit. You have proved your skill better than most. I have sent word to Capitaine—' He snapped his fingers. 'Marchand. I think he *owes* us something, eh?'

Adam thought he saw the flag lieutenant raise his brows.

And Troubridge was already on his way to that same hostile rendezvous.

Carrick stared at the papers on his table.

'When diplomacy fails, the cannon usually speaks. That must not happen. You will receive your orders with all despatch.' He thrust out his hand. 'Be ready.'

They walked from the great cabin, this time together.

There was no sign of the brig *Merlin*; the north-easterly breeze was steady, and holding. Troubridge was on his way.

He had been warned: the rest was up to him.

The iron-hard eyes were watching him, perhaps reading his thoughts.

'The next time we meet, Bolitho. . . .' He did not finish it, saying instead, 'I envy him. So be it!' Then he turned and walked away.

Adam made his own way to the entry port, where Jago and his crew would be waiting. Once back aboard *Onward* he would go around the messes, informally, like those other times, asking Vincent to accompany him.

He thought of his uncle, how it must have been.

The people come first.

14

Storm Warning

The carrier's cart wheeled sharply into the inn yard and jerked to a halt.

John Allday climbed down on to the cobbles and took a few moments to recover. It was no distance from the village of Fallowfield and back here to the Old Hyperion Inn. He usually walked it. But maybe not for a while.

Dick the carter waved to him. 'Got some fruit, John— tes all today. I'll trot un round to the kitchen.' He was off without waiting for a response. He was no stranger here.

Allday leaned back carefully, allowing his muscles to unclench. The lane was in poor shape: too many heavy wagons using it, carrying ballast for the new road. It brought more business to the inn; Unis deserved that; but it would be better when things became quieter again.

He looked up at the sign, depicting the old *Hyperion* as he had known her. He was proud of it, and he smiled. *Keep sailing, my girl!*

He felt the heat of the sun across his shoulders, but there was thunder about, a storm blowing in from Falmouth Bay. Rain would stop the farmers complaining. He straightened his back. The stiffness was almost gone.

He looked across the yard toward the open stables. Two or three horses: so there were still some customers, wearing out their welcome. He checked himself. *Where would we be without them? Where would I be?*

A light carriage too, shafts empty, a tarpaulin draped over the box. Some one else thought there was rain on the way.

Jack, their latest recruit since Tom Ozzard had shoved off one night, was rolling an empty cask carefully toward the cellar door. A good lad. . . . He saw Allday and gave him a furtive 'thumbs down'. He had learned a lot since coming to work for them.

So Harry Flinders was here. Allday sighed. He would have to make an effort, for Unis's sake.

She came to meet him, wiping her hands on her apron as he stooped to hug her. So small, but so strong in his arms, as any customer would be quick to discover if he tried to take liberties with her.

She was about to tell him, but he said, 'I knows, my love,' and crossed his heart with a grin. 'I'll stand upwind of him!'

He moved to the door, careful to disguise any fatigue or discomfort from her.

She said, 'That fellow Grimes is here again,' and waited for some comment. 'The builder working on the Roxby house.'

Allday glanced around the kitchen, taking quiet pleasure in the gleam of copper and the ranks of shining pewter. His unfinished model of *Frobisher* stood on one of the shelves, and he was strangely reluctant to complete it. Maybe a slight alteration to the foremast rigging was needed, or the rake of the bowsprit? Something. It had to be right.

Unis knew what he was thinking, although she said nothing. John had intended it as a gift for Captain Adam, but the model of *Frobisher* might never be finished. To him it was not just any ship. It was *their* ship. John's last, and Sir Richard's, where he had fallen to an enemy marksman. But she knew the truth. Like the sea, in his heart he had never left it.

She considered Harry Flinders. John couldn't stand him, nor could most folk, unless they wanted a favour, but if you turned every one away you disliked for some reason, the Old Hyperion would soon be bankrupt.

She said gently, 'Show your face, John. I've got a pie to finish.'

He pushed open the door of the Long Room and summed up the few remaining customers. The tradesmen were at the market, or on their way to Falmouth, but there were still a couple of smartly dressed lawyers he recognized from previous visits. Kept to themselves; probably glad to get away from Truro. Some poor devil would be hanged for their efforts.

'Here he is— ask *him* about it!'

Unis's brother, also named John, gave him a wink as he clumped toward the parlour, clearly making his escape. Only when he walked was it apparent that he had lost a leg, long since, fighting in the line with the 31st Foot. But it had taken years, and all the care and encouragement of his sister, before he had talked about it.

Flinders was sitting in the corner, in what he grandly called 'my usual chair', smiling like a snake as always. Gilt buttons on his waistcoat, almost military. How he loved to be admired, or so he thought.

Allday steeled himself. He had nothing against Henry Grimes, the builder. A fairly regular visitor to the inn since the road had begun, tearing down dwellings which had stood in its path and replacing them when the offers of compensation were made. Always busy, and giving employment to men thrown on the beach when the fighting had ended. He was also working at the Roxby house. No wonder Flinders was being so cosy.

He said, 'How can I help?'

Flinders leaned back, one arm hanging down casually.

'I was telling my friend here that you were with the fleet for a good many years. *You*'d be the one to ask.' He gestured to Grimes, but his eyes remained on Allday. 'The Great Mutiny, twenty or so years ago, wasn't it. Had the whole country squitterin' with fear that Boney would invade, with no ships to stop him! You must have been in the thick of it?'

Allday was surprised, but said cautiously, 'I seen some of it, but I was at sea most of the time in the old *Euryalus*. In '97, it was. A bad time.' He was silent for a moment, reflecting. 'But a lot of us seen it comin'.'

Grimes said, 'I was building ships in them days. Not tearing 'em apart like today, 'cause the country's running out of seasoned timber!' He chuckled. 'But I do remember the mutiny. Some of us were doing repairs aboard one of the ships. An emergency, we were told.' He touched his half-empty wine glass, his needle-sharp eyes suddenly distant, focusing on the past. 'A seventy-four, she was. Nothing unusual.' He slapped the table, so that the two lawyers looked across at them. 'And then it suddenly flared up all around us. We couldn't believe it was happening. Officers being driven from their posts, or treated like they was invisible. The captain— I can see him now— yelling orders, cursing like he was goin' to explode.' He dropped his voice, as if still shocked by the memory. 'Only the marines stood fast, a line of 'em across the deck, when the captain ordered 'em to fire on the mutineers. The officer in charge was about to give the command to shoot.' He hesitated. 'I can remember . . . it was so quiet . . . the men just standing and staring into the muskets. Then, one shot, an' the officer laid with his face blown away.'

Allday said, 'There were a few things like that. Some of us. . . .'

Flinders interrupted, 'It was murder. A long time ago, but you witnessed it.'

Grimes said uneasily, 'Bad times. A lot of men were pressed, an' they hated the navy an' the discipline.'

Allday said: '*I* was pressed. With my old friend Bryan Ferguson, rest his soul.'

Flinders said abruptly, 'Another round.' Grimes was shaking his head, peering around for the clock. Flinders ignored him. 'There's a Rear-Admiral Herrick staying at the house. You know him pretty well, I believe?'

Allday nodded. *The house.* As if he still belonged there. Part of it.

'I wonder what *he'd* have to say if he knew the man who shot down an officer in cold blood was still alive.'

Grimes said, 'We don't know that!'

Flinders waited as the other John strode heavily to their table, refilled the glasses and poured a measure for Allday. A door banged shut. The two lawyers were gone.

Grimes said, 'I can't be sure. What would people say if I was mistaken?'

Flinders shrugged. 'I think Rear-Admiral Herrick should be told. It is his duty.' He turned hard eyes on Allday. 'There are others we should consider, don't you agree?'

He stood up suddenly. There was wine on his immaculate waistcoat, like blood.

He grinned, showing his strong teeth. 'I've got work to do. They'd all fall asleep if I didn't watch 'em!'

He picked up his hat and walked to the door, and Allday

heard him calling out to some one, maybe the dark-haired Nessa. She would be coming back from her walk with little Katie. He would get no encouragement there.

Grimes repeated, 'I can't be *sure*. All those years.'

He was feeling in his purse. Unlike Flinders, who seldom paid.

'Some one you met?'

Grimes looked past him, avoiding his eyes.

'He came to the Bolitho house, brought a letter from Captain Bolitho. Needed work. Dan Yovell seemed to think it was fair and square, and you know nothing slips past that one. But I can't swear to it.' He stood up, shaking his head. 'These times, you can't be certain of anything.' He dropped some coins in a plate and Allday watched him leave. Probably just gossip, and they should be used to that here. And Sir Richard's sister would know or sense if there was some one flying false colours under that roof.

He touched his cheek, remembering Captain Adam's lady, when she had kissed him in front of all those folk after Bryan's funeral.

'What did you make of all that?' His brother-in-law must have had his ear to the door. 'Henry Grimes doesn't seem too certain, specially after a glass or two.' He laughed and tipped the plate of coins into his apron. 'I can think of several bloody officers I could've shot, given half the chance!'

'But you didn't, did you?'

He listened to the horse clattering past the windows.

'You've made up your mind, then?'

'I was going up to the house anyway.' He was surprised that the lie came so easily.

The other John looked at him keenly, but said only, 'Thought you might.'

Allday went out, and he heard him talking to young Jack in the yard; otherwise the inn was silent. Until work on the road stopped for the day.

He looked along the room, at the cheerful prints and polished brasses, and turned to join the others in the kitchen. Nessa would be there. He tried to put the latest piece of gossip out of his mind. It was best left alone, forgotten. But some people could never let things die.

He glanced again around the room, so quiet now, and stooped and touched his wooden leg.

'We won, didn't we?'

For some, it was not enough.

Herrick stood by one of the tall windows watching the steam rise from puddles on the terrace. The rain had been sudden and heavy, but the sky was almost clear again, the sun as brilliant as before. He had heard a carriage: Nancy was back, and he was relieved. Even the best horses could be difficult when there was thunder in the air.

She hurried through the door, throwing off her cape and shaking out her hair.

'Oh, Thomas, you're here already! I so hoped. . . .' She broke off, gazing at the loose wrappings on the floor. 'What's this?' And then, recognizing it, 'She said it was on its way. Thank you for dealing with it, bless you!'

'Special carrier,' he said rather stiffly. 'All the way from London. I hope it was worth it.'

She tugged the remaining wrappings away. The harp had arrived before Lowenna.

She brushed some straw from her sleeve. 'Well, I'm no expert, but it *looks* undamaged. . . .' and turned toward him as he said, 'I would have done that. But—'

She came to him and touched his face gently.

'I *know* that.'

Neither of them looked at his empty sleeve.

Then she said, 'She should be here today. I hope the roads are clear.'

She ran her fingers over the harp, seeing the other, twisted and burned, in the Old Glebe House.

'It belongs here now.'

Herrick said, 'I was early. The storm . . . the builders had to stop work.'

'And I was *late*.' She glanced at the bell-cord, but changed her mind. 'I was over at Magpie Cottage . . . Tresidders'. She's just had a baby.' She shook her head and her hair fell across her shoulder like a young girl's. 'What would you know about that? You sailors are all alike!'

'I don't know what they would do without you, Nancy.'

She said in a low voice, 'Or I without them. The house will be finished soon . . . and I'll be a visitor here once more. So you see. . . .'

'Your son—' he tried to soften it, hearing the austerity in his own voice '—James has great plans for the— *your* estate. Some of it will be used to train and berth young doctors. He says the scheme would be welcome, and successful.'

'He never gives up. Like his father.'

Herrick said, 'I shall have to be moving along, too.'

She took his hard hand in both of hers.

'You belong here with us, Thomas. Can't you feel that?'

He returned her grip, and could not meet her gaze, afraid that he would hurt her, lose her.

She is not mine to lose.

He said awkwardly, 'He's offered me a position there. If. . . .'

She tightened her grip.

'I *thought* there was something. So you see?'

'I shall be getting my pay. *Half*-pay, from now on.'

There were voices in the hall, a dog barking, some one laughing. He had left it too late.

'What *do* you want, Thomas?'

'I want you, Nancy. I have no right, but. . . .'

The door swung open and somebody coughed, perhaps apologized, and withdrew. Herrick heard none of it. She was holding him.

Only her words: 'You have *every* right, dear Thomas!'

George Tolan quickened his pace as the first heavy drops hissed into the long grass at the roadside. He had seen a disused barn close by on one of his previous walks; it would offer some cover until the storm had blown over.

Tolan enjoyed walking, despite, or perhaps because of, his time as a foot-soldier. Even aboard ship he had tried to maintain the exercise, pacing the deck or gangways to the amusement or irritation of the sailors.

There was an inn somewhere; Daniel Yovell had mentioned it while they had been chatting. *Sounding me out.* With Yovell, you could never be sure.

Tolan had already discovered it, a tiny place used mainly by farm workers straight from the fields, but sometimes by the squires themselves. He felt welcome there, unlike his first visit, when he had met complete silence, blank stares, impenetrable dialect, or at best a version of the carter's, 'You'll be a stranger in these parts?'

Like working at the Bolitho house: it had taken time. But he had finally been accepted, and most of them called him by name now. The barriers had come down.

He even worked alongside Yovell in his little office, helping with the estate business and balancing the accounts, something he had learned all those years ago in the grocer's shop while his father had been recovering from a bout of heavy drinking with his mates at Kingston market. He could even think of that now without pain or anger.

But he was always on guard against the casual remark or question that came without warning. *Where did you serve? What ship was that? Did you ever meet so-and-so?* And worst of all, like that day at the Roxby house, when Grimes the builder had said outright, 'Don't I know you?'

He saw the derelict barn and ran the last few yards, heard the hail clattering on the remaining slates. It would not last long.

He thought of the one called Flinders. A real bastard, full of his own authority and enjoyed making a show of it, even at the Bolitho house. Yovell kept his opinions to himself, but Tolan had inferred a good deal from what was left unspoken. Yovell had no time for him.

And the girl named Jenna smiled at Tolan now, whenever they chanced to meet.

He kicked at some loose stones. It was madness even to think about her.

There was another vivid streak of lightning, but the trees screened most of it.

How much could Grimes really remember?

The past was always there, lying in wait like a man-trap even as he attempted to build a new life. To escape.

There *had* been some dockyard workers on board that day, trying to continue their repairs even as the mutiny was exploding around them.

He ducked instinctively as a deafening crash of thunder

brought more slates down from the roof, and simultaneously a flash so bright that he was blinded for a moment.

He seized something, part of the wall, mind reeling to other sounds, the wake of a broadside, the deck shuddering as spars plunged down through the smoke of battle.

It was over immediately, but he could still smell it, taste it, although the sun was already breaking through, and the rain had lessened. Utterly quiet, as if a great door had been slammed shut, or he was suddenly deaf.

He stepped out into the open and across deep pools of rainwater, one of which reflected the sky, steel blue, like a mirror.

He stared down the narrow road, the long grass glittering now in the sun. Storm or no storm, somebody was on the move. A horse, trotting slowly at first and then picking up speed.

But it was not a horse. It was a pony, riderless and moving fast.

Tolan quickened his pace, his mind very clear. He had seen the pony at the house once or twice, harnessed to a little trap. A friend of Daniel Yovell's had used it before. . . .

The scream pierced his deafness, and Tolan was running with all his strength even before the sound died. The lightning had struck a tree. The pony had been dragging the remains of a harness. Some one was hurt. Only a woman could scream like that.

He reached a bend in the road, where he recalled seeing a stream nearby. He jerked to a halt, feet sliding in mud; the only sound now was his own gasping. Taking it all in: the tree split in halves and scorched, still smoking, the remains of the little vehicle crushed beneath it, one wheel lying on the other side of the road.

There were two men by the tree, one on his knees by the wrecked trap, the other holding up something small and gold that winked in the sun. Both men were staring in his direction, motionless, like unskilled players waiting for a cue.

But Tolan saw only the woman lying beside the wreck. A girl, hair caught in one of the branches, the fabric of her gown torn, revealing the pale skin beneath.

He could remember seeing her for the first time, striding past the stables, head in the air. *I pity the poor devil who tries to make his way with she!*

Only a matter of seconds, but it seemed forever before any one moved.

They were roughly dressed, unshaven, vagrants or on the run. He had heard some talk about convicts being used to clear the way for a stretch of the new road.

One said, 'Get on with it— I'll take care o' this 'un!' He was crouching, a blade shining in his fist. The other had hidden the jewellery inside his coat. Tolan saw him bare his teeth as he tore at the girl's clothing, heard him swear as she pushed him away. Her scream was cut short when he struck her again.

Tolan shut it from his mind, the girl, too terrified now to move, the figure bending across her, tearing at her like a wild animal. He watched the other man, feeling his intent, his confidence, seeing the knife, in shadow now, held against his hip. No stranger to violence and the fear it created.

An unarmed man would turn and run.

He moved slightly, the weight on his right foot, saw the eyes move quickly, the blade catch the sun again. He twisted around and threw himself almost to his knees. A split second, and he would have failed. The blade would seal it.

He felt the other man blunder against and over his shoulder, the force of his lunge throwing him aside like a bundle of rags.

Tolan felt a blow in his side, the breath gasping into his face, his eyes shutting out all else.

He twisted his wrist, pulling him down; his own weight and the thrust of his arm would do the rest.

It was like some terrible madness. The sergeant's hard, cheerful voice at the barracks. *Thumb on the blade, my son, and stab upwards!*

He felt him shudder, unable to scream or make any other sound. Choking on his own blood.

Tolan was on his feet, ready for the other one, but he had vanished. There were voices, horses . . . how could he not have heard the wheels?

He staggered and almost lost his balance, but there was a hand on his arm, another taking the knife.

'You did us proud, matey!' He must have kicked the man on

195

the ground. 'We'll see how brave *you* can be at the end of a rope!'

The girl was here too, holding the fabric across her shoulder. Some one called, 'You all right, Miss Elizabeth?'

She nodded, pushing some hair from her face, staring at Tolan with clear, grey-blue eyes.

She said in a steady voice, '*He* saved my life.'

Only then, she began to sob.

Yovell reached out to assist her, but dropped his hands as she exclaimed, 'I am *not* a child!'

And Allday still stood near the sprawled body, holding the knife, and watching the others. It had all happened so fast. He had been with Yovell when the alarm had been raised and troopers had been seen searching in the fields for some escaped prisoners; he had heard their dogs baying like wolves.

He said, 'They'll soon catch the other bastard,' and looked down at the contorted face and empty eyes. 'This one's cheated Jack Ketch.'

He tossed the knife down and took another deep breath. No pain. Nothing.

He saw the little pony trotting around the bend in the road, led by one of the stable boys. Everybody was here, it seemed.

Yovell called, 'I'll see you back at the house, John. You had something to tell me?'

Allday put his hand on Tolan's shoulder, and knew the girl was watching from the carriage window.

'It can wait! Take care of *her*!'

Francis, the Roxby coachman, touched his hat and flicked the reins. Allday wanted to force it from his mind. *It might have been Unis. It might have been my Katie.*

He looked at Tolan; there were bloodstains on the cuff of the smart coat.

'My wife'll soon deal with that.' He gripped his shoulder and felt him tense. 'You an' me need a nice wet!' He grinned. 'An' that's no error!'

They walked to the road together. Once Tolan looked back, but somebody had covered the corpse with an old horse blanket.

A close-run thing, which might have ended with his death. But, like the storm, it was over. He felt the heavy hand on his shoulder: part of the Bolitho legend. He had found a friend.

15

'No Heroics'

Lieutenant James Squire moved restlessly across the quarterdeck until he stood on the weather side, feeling the wind: light
but steady. He had taken over the afternoon watch less than an
hour ago, but it seemed like forever. His shoes were snagging
on the softened deck seams, and he was thankful for the mizzen
topsail's great shadow. He had brushed against one of the squat
carronades in passing: so hot you could cook a meal on it. As
if it had just been fired.

A week and a day since they had weighed at Gibraltar, back
and forth along this same godforsaken coastline, always with a
misty blur as their horizon. And for what? He was accustomed
to the monotony of those long voyages of exploration and
discovery, days, weeks at a time, logging the same course,
often without sighting land or another ship of any kind. But
there had been a purpose to that, and usually a result.

He gazed along *Onward*'s full length. A few hands
crouching, some even lying in patches of shade, if they could
find any. Men off watch, still digesting their meal and
measures of rum. He could feel their mood like something
physical. Boredom and resentment, and more names in the
punishment book as a result. A Royal Marine had been posted
by the fresh-water cask: another sure sign. Men on watch
needed an occasional drink, tasteless or rancid though it might
be, but it would all vanish within a few hours in this heat if left
unguarded.

There was another frigate patrolling this same area, but they
never met. Their only link was maintained by the smart little

brig *Merlin*. They would sight her again tomorrow, then *Onward* would come about and begin all over again.

He walked aft and saw the helmsman straighten his back as he approached.

'East by north, sir.' He hardly glanced up at the taut canvas. 'Full an' by, sir.'

Close to the wind and moving well, the yards braced hard round to catch every puff of wind. But if that fell. . . .

Two midshipmen were sharing the watch, Napier and young Walker, who had not been seasick again, or so he had been told. Squire still thought about the ill-fated schooner. Death at close quarters. *It might have been us.* He remembered the piece of charred timber, and the captain's face when he had given it to him. The same man he had seen fling his arms around *Merlin*'s new commander when he had come aboard for a few minutes, before he, too, sailed to this barren coastline.

He glanced at the tilting compass card but his mind did not register it, nor the helmsman's resentful scowl.

Merlin would be a fine command. Her commander was far younger than most, and the son of an admiral. Nothing would stop his ascent up the ladder of promotion, whereas. . . . Squire walked back again and stood by the quarterdeck rail. He was lucky, and grateful to be where he was; he had told himself often enough. Now, this might well be the end of the ladder. *For me.*

A seaman hurried past, giving Squire a quick grin before he vanished down the poop ladder. Most of them seemed to like him, and the younger ones were not afraid to ask his advice when they needed it. *Unlike some.*

He had never served as a midshipman, and he could still remember some of the comments when he had been promoted directly from the lower deck. 'That's what they did for "Bounty" Bligh, and it didn't do *him* much good.' And worse.

Meredith, a master's mate, cleared his throat.

'Captain's comin' up, s—' and stopped with one hand on the rail, the sentence unfinished. Then Squire heard it, too. Far away, impartial.

'Gunfire, sir!'

He saw the captain look up at the masthead pendant, and

move to the compass box, and heard him say with a dry little mocking note of disapproval, 'And on a Sunday, too!'

It was not something Squire would ever forget.

Then he said, 'To the south-east of us. If this wind holds. . . .' He gestured. 'Fetch the first lieutenant!'

Squire saw one of the midshipmen hurry toward the companion and heard the captain call, '*Walk*, Mr. Napier!' and the boy looked around. 'I want you to stay in one piece.' He might even have smiled briefly. Then he strode to the quarterdeck rail. 'That lookout, Tucker— bring him aft, *now*!'

Squire saw a messenger running along the gangway. Like most of the others on deck, he was wide awake now. He cupped his hands behind his ears, shutting out the regular sounds of canvas and rigging, but the sea was silent. Maybe a ship was testing her guns. Nothing heavy; might even be the brig *Merlin*. Trying to break the monotony of this endless patrol.

''Ere 'e is, sir!'

Tucker had appeared at the top of the ladder, jaw still working on the remains of his meal, his eyes, very clear in a deeply tanned face, fixed on the captain.

The master's mate murmured, 'What d' you reckon, sir?'

I would have waited, to be sure. But Squire said only, 'The captain thinks there's trouble ahead.'

The upper deck seemed suddenly crowded with people. The watch below, off-duty marines, even the cook and his mates. All staring out to sea, then aft toward the quarterdeck.

Meredith, the master's mate, grinned. 'So much for Sunday!'

Adam pointed across the starboard bow. 'I shall alter course directly, Tucker. It will put some more power in the sails— give us an edge.' He felt him start with surprise as he reached out and touched his arm. 'I know what you can do. Take a glass, mine if it suits. But if there's nothing. . . .' He shrugged. 'Take your time.'

Tucker nodded, brushing some dry biscuit crumbs from his cheek without even knowing he was doing it. Every one seemed to be here: old Julyan the master, even the first lieutenant. He saw Napier with some other midshipmen, and the boy smiled and raised a hand in greeting.

'I'm on my way, sir!' He took the telescope and after a slight hesitation slung it over his shoulder. He turned away, then halted. They all heard it. Five or six shots. Unhurried.

Adam stared up at the masthead pendant until the glare blinded him.

'Please God, let it hold!' And to Vincent, 'All hands, Mark. I want every stitch she can carry.' He ran his hand along the rail. 'Let her fly!'

Julyan the master watched him. The captain was speaking to his ship. Maybe nobody else noticed, or understood, but Julyan had served at sea all his life. *Since* . . . he glanced at Midshipman Walker, waiting with his slate . . . *I was your age.* And his oldest brother had been Sir Richard Bolitho's sailing master in the *Black Prince*. Those were the days. . . .

He heard the first shrill of calls, apparent confusion changing to order, and knew he would be needed in the chart room.

He jumped through the hatch, and paused to look up at the sky, and the hard edge of the sea beyond the gangway. He had seen Deacon, the senior midshipman, already heading for his flag locker, and heard young Walker call after him, 'What shall *I* do?'

Julyan closed the chart room door behind him and found he could laugh about it.

He answered aloud for Deacon.

'Just pray!'

Luke Jago judged the moment and hurried across the deck, a mug balanced in his hand. It took some getting used to. He peered up at the straining canvas, topsails and courses like metal. Not since the Western Approaches had she moved like this; not since she had first tasted salt water. The men on watch were angled to the deck, and there were dark stains on the planking where spray had burst up and over the bulwark.

He saw the captain by the compass box, Vincent standing a few paces away. Two helmsmen on the wheel, the quartermaster loitering nearby in case he was needed.

'*What is it?*' Then, 'Forgive me. No call to bite *your* head off, Luke.'

Jago held out the mug. 'Water, Cap'n.'

Adam sipped it. Warm and tasteless, from the cask on deck. It could have been anything.

Jago watched him. He knew him so well. The others around them only thought they did. Moaning all the time about extra work. . . . What else would they be doing in this bloody place?

Adam said quietly, 'Lady Luck seems to have deserted me this time, Luke.' He half turned. 'Stand by to alter course. Two points to starboard.'

The quartermaster had been waiting for that. 'East-by-south, sir. Standing by.'

Vincent remarked, 'I think we'll need more hands aloft.'

Jago swore under his breath. Was that all it meant to him? Everybody hated the third lieutenant, but at least Monteith showed some guts. He felt his dry mouth fold into a humourless grin. *Coming from me, of all Jacks!*

'Deck there! Sail on th' starboard bow!'

Adam stared aloft, the mug rattling unheeded across the deck.

'Well done!' Although Tucker was unable to see or hear him up there amongst the thudding canvas and rigging. He stared across the sea until his eyes watered: lively crests now, not dead calm like all those other days and sleepless nights.

Vincent was saying, 'I'll go aloft myself, sir. This time I'll—' and Jago heard the captain cut him off with a curt, 'I need you here. Young Tucker is doing well. Leave him to it.'

Jago stooped down to retrieve the mug from the scuppers. It gave him time.

Captain Bolitho would have to watch his back.

He touched his belt but the broad-bladed dirk was below, in the mess.

And so will you, matey!

Adam gazed aft again. The same group around the wheel, leaning together as the deck tilted to another thrust of wind, and elsewhere men climbing into the shrouds in an attempt to see what was happening. He shut them from his mind. The lookout had sighted another vessel. Very soon some one would realize that *Onward* was heading toward them under full sail. He thought of the shots. Small guns, but deadly. Probably swivels, which took longer to prime and reload than heavier cannons.

There had been no sound of any resistance. Maybe some luckless trader, caught unawares.

'Deck there! She's a schooner!'

Vincent muttered, 'What about the other one?'

Adam imagined Tucker in his lofty perch, training the telescope.

'T' other vessel is dismasted!'

'Bloody pirates.' That was Meredith.

'Deck there!' And then silence, as if he were feeling the sudden weight of responsibility. 'Schooner's steerin' south-east!'

Jago said, 'Runnin' for the shore, damn his eyes!' But he swung round as Adam drove one fist into his palm and exclaimed, *'Got you!'*

He looked up, gauging the wind. If the schooner had tacked up to windward, *Onward* would have lost her. This time there was nowhere to run, except to hide in one of those small coves or inlets which he and Julyan had marked so carefully on the chart. Vague and dangerous. . . .

He looked over at Vincent.

'We'll hold this course until we're ready to change tack. We can outsail him now, whatever he does!'

He walked to the larboard side again, reaching for his telescope before remembering where it was.

'Here, sir!' It was Napier with another.

Adam felt his mouth crack into a smile. 'You're not going to forget that, are you?'

He trained it across the opposite bow, blurred faces springing across the lens, a sailor shouting or laughing soundlessly, then out across the open sea. Then he found and held the tiny image until his eye felt raw. Stern-on, sails fully spread and filling, the dull shoreline like a far-off curtain beyond. He closed the glass with a snap.

'Too clever this time!'

Squire was the first to speak.

'The same schooner, sir? A pirate, maybe?'

Adam said, 'Bring Tucker down here, and put another good man in his place.' He seemed to recall Squire's question. 'I intend to find out.' He looked toward the bows again. 'But first, some people will need our help.'

203

Tucker came running aft, his bare feet thudding along the gangway like boots. He was not even breathless.

'Same one, sir!' He looked around as if he expected an argument. 'Watched her all the way to Gibraltar— not likely to forget!'

'And the other vessel?'

'Local craft, I reckon, sir, a big dhow of some kind. Dismasted. But they're tryin' to re-rig one of 'em.'

Julyan said, 'Probably after the cargo. Otherwise. . . .'

Adam shut the speculation from his mind. The schooner might still take a chance and run for it, even though the wind was against her. Her master would know this stretch of coast like the back of his hand. But why run and risk capture, when you could shelter and be safe, until the next time?

It could prove to be worthless, but the schooner might reveal something. He thought of the commodore: *bad news rides a fast horse.* Surely it was better than no news at all?

Tucker said suddenly, 'The other vessel bein' a dhow, they're helpless when they tries to claw to wind'rd. No chance at all.' He might have blushed under his deep tan. 'Sorry, sir. Not my place to go on about it!'

Adam smiled briefly. 'Who better?' He saw the surgeon and one of his assistants climbing to the quarterdeck. Murray must have sensed he might be needed.

Vincent said, 'I'll have the second cutter ready for lowering.'

'Jolly-boat, Mark. We shall need both cutters for sterner work.'

He saw the comprehension dawn in Vincent's face.

'You intend to cut out the schooner? Under their noses?'

'Too risky?'

'With respect, sir, it's better than waiting for our commodore to decide!'

They both laughed, then Adam said, 'So be it. Volunteers only.' He turned his back on the misty shoreline, deliberately. 'But first, an act of mercy.'

Midshipman Napier jumped clear as more men threw their weight on the topsail braces, bodies angled to the deck as *Onward* turned into the wind. Nobody fell, unlike in those early days, and hardly an order had to be repeated. He peered up at the reefed topsails, each one fisted and kicked into submission, the boom of canvas drowning out the curses of the seamen spread along the yards. He could see the jolly-boat being manhandled from the tier and hoisted out, ready for lowering. He dashed spray from his face, surprised that it could feel so cold when his shirt was clinging to his skin with sweat.

The jolly-boat was smaller than a cutter or gig, a maid-of-all-work, but he had seen the surgeon in his shapeless white smock, ready to be taken across to the drifting dhow. It would be a rough passage. He had already heard some one shout out to one of the boat's crew, 'Hang on to yer belly, Bert, or ye'll lose yer pork!'

Busy though he was, Guthrie the boatswain found time to retort, 'You'll lose more than that, Barker, my lad, if I 'ears another peep out o' you!'

But somebody laughed.

Napier stared across at the other vessel. One of the big lateen sails was already half hoisted again, but badly torn, the wind exploring the shot-holes. He could see some of the crew trying to hoist a second mast, some one obviously in charge, and not a face turned to watch the oncoming frigate. There were more scars along the hull: canister, he thought.

He smiled self-consciously. *Watching and listening.* He had come a long way.

He thought of the schooner, and his friend David Tucker, who had come aft to see the captain. Surprised, proud. Sharing it.

He had heard the first lieutenant asking for volunteers for some separate action against the schooner, and seen his undisguised astonishment when so many had shouted their names. Napier had been going around the ship with Lieutenant Squire, making a list. Like those other times. . . . He saw little Walker hurrying past with a message. There were a lot of *Onward*'s company who had not experienced those other times.

The arms chest was open, a gunner's mate watching over the issue of weapons. Cutlasses and boarding axes, but no pistols, for fear of a misfire which would ruin any hope of surprise attack, if that was being planned. One wag had suggested it was in case 'Mister bloody Monteith' was taking part, as he would be the first target!

He watched the jolly-boat cast off, veering away from the side, oars in disarray until the first stroke.

Squire was standing by the tiller, swaying easily with each plunge of the boat.

Some one said grudgingly, 'Knows 'is stuff, does that one.'

And another: 'Well, one of us, wasn't he?'

Napier felt a shoulder near his and knew it was Huxley. Still quiet, withdrawn, but they had become closer because of what had happened. In the midshipmen's berth he was usually studying notes on navigation and seamanship, and keeping up his diary, a compulsory burden if eventually he appeared before the examination Board for promotion. Perhaps such relentless activity was keeping the reality of his father's suicide at bay. As if by some unspoken agreement, nobody in the mess ever mentioned it.

Huxley was watching the jolly-boat, the surgeon's white figure clambering up the side of the dhow after two previous attempts.

He said, 'They won't accept any help, David. Except maybe with the repairs.'

'Why do you say that? They might all have been killed!'

He said distantly, 'I heard it somewhere.'

Napier looked over at the dhow again. *Heard it from his father.*

'They're coming back.'

The jolly-boat had cast off, rising to the swell like a leaf in a mill-race, the white smock still upright, one hand raised in salute or farewell.

Huxley asked, 'Have you got a girl, back in England?' He turned to face him with sudden intensity. 'I mean, a *proper* girl, just for you?'

Napier watched the jolly-boat's progress; the surgeon was seated now. But instead, he was seeing her in the stable yard. Aloof, haughty. Unreachable. But she had kissed him, and not like a young girl.

And the lovely Lowenna, who had lain beside him to drive away the fear and the memories. *Our secret.* How could he forget?

'I met some one. . . .'

Huxley shook his head. 'But not . . . *that* way.'

A call shrilled; men were moving again, tackle squeaking as the jolly-boat was hoisted inboard.

'Hands aloft! Loose tops'ls!'

'Man the braces! *Move yerselves!*'

They both hurried aft along the gangway, the sea surging alongside. But Huxley's words stayed with him. He had become used to the brutal and often lurid humour of the lower deck. At first he had been shocked by it, as was intended. This was not the same.

What is it like?

He saw the captain by the rail, speaking to Maddock the gunner, shaping something with his hands, listening, and then nodding in agreement. He turned to watch the sails as the quartermaster shouted a new compass course, and only for an instant their eyes met. The Captain. . . . Napier had seen him in every sort of mood. Angry, resentful, depressed, or at peace, with that rare, transforming smile.

He was smiling now, but some one else was already calling to him.

Napier thought of him with her. Together.

What is it like?

The gunner's mate beckoned with his fist. 'First lieutenant says you should arm yourselves, gentlemen!' He showed his missing teeth in a broad grin. 'Just in case, eh?'

Napier picked up a well-worn hanger. Not intended for display, or receiving an admiral on board. The curved blade had been crudely sharpened on the ship's grindstone. It was like a razor.

He hurried after his friend.

Once he paused and looked for the drifting dhow. Tomorrow they might still be struggling to complete their repairs. But they would be alive, and free.

He tightened his grip on the hanger, his troubled spirit calmed. Accepting it.

It was too soon to think of tomorrow.

Lieutenant Vincent leaned forward on the thwart and stared beyond the measured rise and fall of oars. Despite the muffled looms and thickly greased rowlocks, each stroke seemed to invite disaster. He knew it was only in his imagination, but the sound seemed louder now, closer to the shore. He could even hear the stroke oarsman's steady breathing, see his eyes as he lay back to take another pull, the blade slicing the water, timing every stroke.

No moon, but the sky was paved with stars, giving enough light to mark the contours of the land, which now seemed much more elevated than it appeared on the chart. So close you could smell it. Feel it.

Beside him at the tiller he could sense the coxswain, watching his crew, not merely dark shapes to him but names and personalities. And now a team.

A long, slow pull; the boat was heavier than usual. Full, even carrying four marines, marksmen. One was up in the bows with the musketoon, which was mounted on its own swivel. Like an old blunderbuss, loaded with musket balls, it would be their only defense if they were taken by surprise. To reload would be almost impossible in the dark. But at least it would act as a warning to the other cutter following astern. *If it's still there.* He did not turn on the thwart to look; it would be pointless.

Onward had anchored. It was too shallow to move closer inshore. *The ship comes first.*

He peered abeam. Uncanny: it seemed so quiet after the tension of casting off from the ship's side. He released his grip on the scabbard pressed against his leg. Strain, unease. This was not the time to display either.

Squire was in charge of the other cutter. A good man, experienced, but still a stranger in so many ways. Maybe because he wanted it so.

Fitzgerald, the coxswain, muttered, 'Now, sorr?'

Vincent saw the darker wedge of land moving out and down toward the bow, and thought he could hear the surf above the creak of oars and the rudder's occasional murmur. He lifted his hand. No commands. Fitzgerald had trained his crew well. The blades were still, drops splashing alongside to mark their passage through the dark water.

He exhaled slowly, overwhelmed by a sense of utter loneliness. *Onward* seemed a thousand miles away. It had all been like part of a dream. The captain speaking to the boat crews, and the other volunteers. *And to me.*

'I believe this is important. Otherwise. . . .' He had held Vincent's arm and the dark eyes had burned into his face. 'I shall be waiting for you. No heroics.'

It seemed clearer now, perhaps because of the silence. The stillness. The captain had wanted to be here himself.

How could he leave the ship?

He gripped Fitzgerald's arm. Like a piece of timber. In Ireland he had been a bare-knuckle fighter, or so Vincent had heard.

'*Listen!* The others are still astern!'

Fitzgerald grinned. 'Music to my ears!' He crossed himself with his free hand.

Vincent signalled again and the stroke oarsman leaned toward him. Like a curtain shifting slowly to one side, the brilliant stars reflected on smoother water now, with hardly a breath of sultry wind as the boat thrust ahead. He stood up unhurriedly. A sudden move might wreck any chance of surprise, let alone success. But he knew this was vital.

'Be ready, lads. Stand together!' He saw them leaning on the oars, or squeezing between the thwarts to hear him better. They needed more time to recover from the long pull. But there was no time. 'No quarter!'

He sat down and unclipped his belt. Suppose the schooner had slipped away, even as they were idling with the dhow? How would Bolitho excuse that to the commodore? Or to himself?

There was a splash and a piercing shriek, then a violent flurry of wings close, even under the bow itself.

Vincent saw the oars sliding to a halt, men heaving them inboard as if in response to a spoken order.

The anchored schooner lifted out of the darkness as if to run them down.

Habit, drill, discipline. . . . The tiller was hard over, a grapnel clattered across the schooner's bulwark, while another fell close by in the water.

There were shouts, even as the vessel's bowsprit swept over their heads and both hulls ground together.

Vincent had the hanger in his hand, and could feel some one

pushing him from behind as he reached for the schooner's bulwark.

Something screamed and slithered against his legs as a cutlass slashed past him, and there were more shouts, mingled with curses, as they fought and stumbled across the deck. A pistol flashed, and Vincent felt the ball thud into the planking by his feet.

More blades, and figures swarming up through a hatch by the foremast.

The hanger crossed with a heavier sword, sliding hilt to hilt; he was falling back under his attacker's strength and determination. He felt his breath, the beard rasping against his skin, the great blade forcing him back and down. His foot slipped, perhaps on blood, and he knew his life was over. Like a door slamming.

He tried to twist the hanger, but he was falling.

'At 'em, Onwards!' More shouts, feet thundering as men climbed up from the second cutter and charged across the deck.

Vincent was on his feet again, a sailor offering him his hanger, eyes wild, staring around for another enemy.

Squire picked up the broad-bladed sword and hefted it thoughtfully.

'Hmm. Scimitar. Can take a man's head off.' He leaned toward him. 'Near thing. Are you all right now?'

Vincent was still breathing harshly, haunted by the strength behind the heavy blade.

'Thanks to *you*, James.'

Men were shouting, waving cutlasses or boarding axes, a few kneeling by injured companions, and some who might never move again.

Squire glanced up as a hurrying seaman paused to jab his thumb up before running aft where others were guarding prisoners.

'We've taken her. Thank God!'

Vincent repeated, 'Thanks to you, James!'

Fitzgerald strode toward them, dragging a bearded prisoner, with a boarding axe poised above his head by way of persuasion.

'Caught this bastard tryin' to ditch a box over the side, sorr!'

He took a deep, rasping breath and shook the axe. 'Sure, an' I wonder if it's what we came lookin' for!'

'You may be right.' He looked down at the dead man by the bulwark. Teeth still bared in a grin of triumph when Squire had cut him down.

He asked, 'What's the bill?'

Squire walked to the side to look down into the cutter.

'Two.' One of the seamen signalled to him. 'Now it's three. And a few cuts and bruises. The leech can put those right when we get them back to the ship.'

Vincent felt his mind clearing, as if in response to some command.

'We'll cut the cable and warp her into deeper water. Two boats' crews should be able to move her far enough.' He looked at the huddled prisoners. The same men who had fired on unarmed traders and left them to die. 'I'm sure we can rely on *their* help?' He wanted to smile, to break the tension, but his jaw felt locked, and his hand was clenched and trembling with reaction. 'If it can't be done, we'll sink the bloody thing where she can do no more harm.'

One of the marines was calling to him, 'We can mount the old murderer over 'ere, sir!'

Some one had lifted the musketoon from the cutter and mounted it on an improvised swivel by the main hatchway.

'That was quick thinking.' He could not remember the marine's name. 'Cover the prisoners. And if you have to, use it!'

Squire was already organizing men to pass out a hawser, for towing the vessel once the cable was cut.

One of *Onward*'s seamen was shrouding the three corpses with scraps of canvas. Unhurriedly, as if he were beyond emotion.

Vincent looked toward the dark edge of land and the faint gleam of water marking their escape to the sea. The stars seemed so much paler now, although it had taken no time to board and seize the schooner. Men had died, obeying orders. No questions asked. The old Jacks always insisted, *never volunteer*. But they were usually the first to step forward when the call came.

He tried to clear his throat; his mouth was as dry as dust. A seaman padded past, wrist wrapped in a crude bandage. The blood looked back in the feeble starlight.

'We'll get some prize money for this, eh, sir?' He could even chuckle about it.

They would never know how close it had been. If that startled seabird had raised the alarm two minutes sooner, or some lookout had been posted. . . . *I would not be standing here.*

'Boats ready, sir!'

Vincent waved to the man standing by the cable.

'An extra tot if you can do it in three!' He saw him grin and lift his axe.

The boats had cast off, the towing hawser already trailing in the water.

'Give way!'

There was a thud and he heard the man yell, 'In *one*, sir! Does I get a double tot?'

Vincent felt the deck quiver, and heard the splash of oars as the two cutters took the strain.

Once in open water they might find it harder, but at least there was less weight in each boat now.

Some of the men on deck were waving and shouting encouragement, until a voice silenced them with a few well-used threats.

The cutters were pulling away on either bow, and he could hear Squire calling across to the other boat, where Fitzgerald would still be standing at the tiller like a rock.

A snail's pace, but at least they were moving. . . .

He felt the seaman beside him almost jumping with relief and excitement.

'We did it, sir! We showed the buggers!'

The big scimitar was still lying where Squire had dropped it. But for his swift and brave action, there would be nothing. Vincent would be lying with those three pathetic bundles awaiting burial.

He turned and grasped the seaman's shoulder. It could have been any one of them; it no longer mattered.

He said, 'Yes, we did it, and we did it together!'

He stared up at the foremast, sharper now against the paling sky. The fore-and-aft rig would make it simpler to spread some sail when they had enough sea-room.

He had been given a second chance. He would not allow himself to forget.

'Stand by to cast off!'

And he was ready.

16

Out of the Shadows

'There's a sight to touch your heart!' Captain Adam Bolitho
lowered the telescope and rubbed his eye with the back of his
hand. He trained the glass again, he had lost count of the times,
and waited for the image to steady.

'I prayed for this.' He heard Julyan the master clear his
throat, and realized he must have spoken aloud, his guard
down, and unable to hide his true feelings.

He moved the glass very slowly: figures, even faces coming
alive, working at sheets and halliards, the big sails fighting
back as the schooner butted too close to the wind. The two
cutters were towing close astern, and he had already seen the
uniforms, aft by the schooner's tiller. Vincent was safe, and so
was Squire. He had closed his mind to the harsh possibility that
accompanied every raid or cutting-out attempt. But it was
always harder to accept if you were waiting, and not personally
at risk. The canvas-covered shapes by the bulwark had been
visible when the schooner rolled to the wind. It was wrong to
feel thankful, but, like the flag they had hoisted above the
captured vessel, he was conscious only of his pride in them.

He walked across the deck and trained the telescope over the
opposite quarter. *Merlin*'s topsails were bright against the hard
horizon, holding the first hint of sunlight.

Francis Troubridge was on time for his rendezvous. . . . Now
there was something for him to pass on to the commodore.

He closed the telescope. It might be more than he had
bargained for.

'I shan't tell you again. Now *do it!*'

214

Monteith, losing his patience and his temper. He had been on deck without a break since the ship had dropped anchor, in sole charge. In fairness, he had shown no sign of flagging.

Adam thought of the drifting dhow which had begun the whole chain of events, and the surgeon's description when he had returned aboard after his precarious visit.

Four killed and two slightly injured, by canister shot, as expected. Murray had done what he could, but the dhow's crew had been eager to make their way without further interference, and to bury their dead when the time was right.

Murray seemed to take it in his stride; he was used to pain and death in every guise. He had even served at Trafalgar.

Where was the dhow now, he wondered. Perhaps sheltering in one of the countless coves that pockmarked this coast, hiding places for trader and pirate alike.

They had no choice. Today's enemy might be the law of the land tomorrow.

Julyan had joined him, frowning pensively.

'The schooner's got no anchor, sir. If that wind comes back, they'll have to stay under way.'

Adam looked toward *Merlin*, but without the glass she was a blur between sea and sky.

'I'm sending the schooner to Gibraltar. If they need more proof, she should be enough.' He did not mention the commodore by name. 'She'll need a prize crew.'

He saw the question in Julyan's eyes. '*Merlin* will supply it.' He looked across the heaving water again, patches of sunshine now like drifting sand on the current. 'We shall need all our people before you know it.'

'They're manning one of th' cutters, sir.' That was Jago. Always there, like a shadow.

Adam shaded his eye: Vincent was climbing down into the boat, unlike the last time, with only a minimum of hands at the oars.

He thought of the cabin, still in darkness below his feet. Just to sit for a few moments in the old chair. Or at the little desk, with her last letter. . . .

He pushed away the temptation with great effort, and said quietly, 'When you go below, Luke,' and sensed him moving closer, 'fetch my prayer book, will you?'

215

Jago nodded. He knew who the other passengers would be in the cutter, and was surprised that it could still matter. Count for something. He had seen so many go over the side, good, bad, friend and enemy. But it did.

He waited long enough to see the cutter come alongside and the first lieutenant climb up the ladder which had been lowered for him. They were swinging out a net on block and tackle for the three dead men.

He saw Vincent hesitate as the captain met him by the gangway and reached out to grip both his hands.

'I am so proud of you, Mark. That was bravely done!'

He heard Vincent answer, 'It was Lieutenant Squire, sir. I would have died, but for him.'

The grip remained as the captain responded, 'And *that* was bravely said!'

Jago went below, and nodded casually to the marine sentry as he pushed his way into the great cabin.

Morgan had been standing by the stern windows, and came to greet him. It was never too early or too late for him to be about and busy.

He said cheerfully, 'You look scuppered, Luke, boyo. I've got just the something to liven you up!' He paused in the pantry door. 'I see that they're back. It was a long night.' He waited, testing the moment. 'Have you heard anything, old friend?'

Jago faced him squarely, no longer surprised that they had become so close.

'I think we're goin' to fight,' he said.

Commander Francis Troubridge stared across the water at the schooner.

'Yes, I can muster a prize crew for the run to Gibraltar. I have a master's mate who served in a schooner in "the bad old days", as he calls them.' He turned to look at his own command, a searching gaze which Adam understood and remembered. Like his own first ship, all that time ago. He had been even younger than Troubridge.

He was saying, 'I'll have to see the commodore.' Again, the youthful smile Adam had come to know so well when he had been Bethune's hard-worked flag lieutenant. Only a few months ago. . . .

216

The smile widened to a grin. '*If* he's still in command, of course!'

Adam said, 'I have a report you must deliver to him. I doubt if it will surprise him. But he will not be pleased.'

Troubridge walked with him to the quarterdeck rail. He did not need to be told that this was a matter of urgency. Intelligence and intuition had served him well as a flag lieutenant, and he had needed both under Bethune. *Do this, Flags*, or *Why wasn't I told, Flags?* And Adam Bolitho he would never forget. On deck, under fire, men dying around them. And his face when the smoke had cleared, compassionate and self-critical, always questioning his own performance.

He had seen that *Onward*'s capstan bars were shipped, with extra hands already mustered to weigh anchor yet again.

There was always tension and excitement in preparing to sail. Now he was feeling it more intensely himself, in command of his own ship.

And the familiar sight of corpses sewn in hammocks, awaiting burial. Not like that other time, when they had buried Catherine Somervell at sea, but Adam Bolitho would be recalling it when he did his duty by these three victims of battle.

He asked suddenly, 'What do you intend,' and tried to smile, 'sir?'

Adam saw him glance once more toward *Merlin*, almost protectively.

'D'you have a good first lieutenant, Francis?'

The question seemed to puzzle him, but he nodded. 'He can give me a few years, and I sometimes think he wonders if I'm good enough for the task.' He laughed lightly. 'I shall overcome it, I suppose.'

Adam was watching the schooner.

'I was once told that envy and ambition often walk the same deck.' He turned back to Troubridge. 'I believe *Nautilus* is being handed over to the Aboubakr government as a symbol of trust, and in the hope of future co-operation. France has made no secret of its ambitions in Africa.'

'I was told as much, when *Merlin* was ordered to liaise with you and *Saladin*.'

Adam hardly heard him.

217

'When we went to the aid of a merchant dhow, my surgeon went aboard to offer aid to some of their wounded. One was beyond help, and died while he was there. Murray is a good man— resourceful, too. The dying man gave him a name, and he remembered it. This morning, as dawn broke, my first lieutenant came across from our prize and brought me some documents, which some one had been trying to throw overboard in a weighted bag. Just a few items, some in French.' He paused, and Troubridge bent his head in concentration, listening closely. 'And that same name featured prominently. Mustafa Kurt.'

'But that's not a. . . .'

Adam smiled. 'Originally he was Turkish. I don't know what flag he flies now. I first heard about him after the Algiers campaign. He had been overseeing the Dey's harbour defenses. And it was a damned close-run thing, as Our Nel would have put it.'

Troubridge regarded him steadily. 'And you think this Mustafa Kurt is going to try to overthrow the present power in Aboubakr, and seize *Nautilus*?'

Adam saw Vincent on the gangway, waiting.

'I think he's already there. Has been from the beginning.'

'My God!' He looked again at *Merlin*. 'I'm not letting you sail alone! If it's true, he'll have the whole coast ablaze! D' you think I'd stand by and let you face it single-handed? It would be no mere cutting-out exploit this time!'

Adam took his arm and walked with him to the gangway. *Merlin*'s gig was below the entry port, a side-party waiting to see Troubridge depart.

He said, 'Go now. The commodore must be alerted,' and saw the anguish and indecision on Troubridge's face. 'I can *order* you to leave. But we are friends.'

Troubridge stepped back, dismayed, perhaps shocked. Then he said curtly, 'I shall never forget!' and turned and strode along the gangway.

Adam stood watching the boat pull clear of the side. Troubridge did not look back.

Eventually he knew Vincent had joined him, and said, '*Merlin* is sending a prize crew, Mark. We will weigh anchor as soon as it's done.'

There was an uncertain silence.

'Was it hard, sir?'

'Harder for him, I think.' He looked across at the schooner, a marine's scarlet coat vivid in the sunlight. Guarding prisoners.

Vincent was already calling out names, glad to be doing what he knew best.

And if I am wrong. . . .

Luke Jago had heard most of it, and could feel his initial anger giving way to impatience. He had seen some of the seamen around the capstan looking over at *Merlin,* and muttering to each other as if all hell was about to break loose around them. What did they expect when they signed on?

He realized that Bolitho was looking at him, and called, 'I've brought the book, Cap'n.' He took a chance. 'One of old Dan Yovell's, mebbee?'

Adam nodded, then he said briskly, 'So let's be about it, shall we?'

Gordon Murray stood in a corner of the sick bay, head bowed beneath a deckhead beam while he washed and dried his hands. One finger at a time, slowly and with care. Force of habit: something he now took as a matter of course, rather than necessity. He had learned the hard way, like most naval surgeons. He could still remember when he had caught one of the loblolly boys in his first ship slicing mouldy cheese with one of the surgical knives.

He cocked his head, listening to the sounds above him, and the regular creak and sigh of timbers, could picture the tall pyramids of canvas braced round, as he had just seen them. The ship leaning over, holding the wind. What there was of it.

Down here it was quiet, subdued. Only two men had required treatment after the capture of the schooner, and they had been lucky, despite some ugly gashes. Unlike the ones he had heard go over the side. He was too familiar with that to be moved by it. He thought of the names written on the canvas-wrapped corpses he had seen in the past. *Unless it was some one who. . . .*

He straightened his back, head precisely between the beams. Everything in its place. He heard his assistant speaking to one of the wounded sailors. A good man, Erik Larsson, a Swede who might have made a fine doctor. Notoriously impatient, and sharp with any one he believed to be malingering to avoid working ship, or to gain a few extra tots of grog. No bad thing in a crowded man-of-war. But despite Murray's curiosity, he had made a point of never questioning him, or asking how a Swede had found his way into a British warship. Maybe that was why Larsson trusted him. They trusted one another.

He thought of the dying man aboard the dismasted dhow, wounded in the stomach by grapeshot. It was a wonder he had remained alive as long as he had. Murray had been in several sea-fights, had known the toll so high that there had scarcely been a space left on the orlop for a man to die, let alone receive any treatment.

He could recall the fingers like steel on his wrist, as if every last ounce of his strength had been concentrated in them. Gasping out the name. Nodding, eyes suddenly alive, when Murray had repeated it until he was satisfied. Then he had spoken it one last time, like a curse, with his dying breath.

And later, after Vincent had returned aboard with the documents he had saved from destruction, the discovery of that same name. He had seen doubt and caution in the captain's face, and then the first hint of excitement. Like a huntsman with the unexpected scent of quarry. But it was something deeper and stronger than that.

And now they were under full sail again. It would end nowhere. Or they would have to fight.

He remembered Trafalgar. He had been serving in the eighty-gun *Tonnant*, under Captain Tyler. She had been a French ship, captured at the Nile, like others which were to serve again under new colours. He had heard some of the younger hands voicing their resentment that *Onward* had been ordered to act as escort to *Nautilus* when they had first arrived at the Rock. It was nothing new.

Some one tapped at the door: one of the sailmaker's crew, a huge bundle of loose canvas gathered in his arms.

Murray said, 'Larsson will show you where to stow them. I hope we will not need them.'

He took his thoughts from it. He did not need to be reminded that whatever happened men would die, and others, like this

220

sailmaker, would have to stitch them up for their final journey.

Jeff Lloyd tipped the canvas on to the deck and began to sort and fold the various pieces into matching lengths.

He saw the surgeon go to his desk and begin to write something in a book. *Callous bastard.* He glanced around the sick bay and through to the orlop deck beyond. It was peaceful here, good to be away from the mess and the constant chatter and speculation about chasing after another suspected enemy. Pirate, more likely.

He thought of the burials he had seen carried out almost as soon as the anchor had been catted. *They couldn't wait.* He had known one of the dead men well. Worked on a farm before he had decided to quit and volunteer for the navy. Whistling aboard ship was forbidden. In case, they said, it might be mistaken for a call announcing a vital command or duty. Only a fool would believe that.

But this man had whistled in a gentle, fascinating fashion. Sometimes, maybe in the dog watches, when there was some quiet, he could recall the soft, easy whistle. Like real music. Even the loud-mouths had piped down to listen and enjoy it.

With some of the others he had watched the brig *Merlin*, her arrival after the cutting-out, and then her departure, with their prize as an unlikely consort.

They all had their own thoughts. Lloyd had heard *Merlin* was under orders for Gibraltar again. What then?

To him it meant reaching back to another life, the one that lay in the past. And must remain there. *People soon forget.*

Like the ones they had just buried, and Ned Harris, who had wanted too much to keep his mouth shut. It was shut now.

But he could not prevent himself from thinking of the woman who had changed everything. At the time it had seemed like a secret joke, or a form of revenge when she had encouraged him. Her husband was always away from their home in Plymouth: a shipbuilder, who had interests in other yards. Women too, most likely. She had probably recovered by now, and maybe she had already found a new lover to drive away the boredom.

Or was it deeper than that? She might even think of writing to him. She had done so twice before. He had since destroyed the letters.

She would not dare. Surely she would see the danger, the risk? That night, when her other lover had visited her without hint or warning, he had been there with her.

The shock of recognition had saved him. The fury, and the true realization of danger, had ended it. The other lover had lain dead and bleeding outside the door.

But there had been a witness, who had been working ashore at a local alehouse, repairing casks for the landlord. The witness had been Ned Harris, the cooper.

Lloyd looked down at his hands. Only *she* knew, and had seen it happen. He had thought about it today while the captain had been reading from his prayer book, before they had tipped the three bodies over the side.

If a cruel twist of fate had not brought *him* to the house that night, *he* would have been standing there today, in Captain Bolitho's place.

And now, only she would know this dangerous secret. It would be safe with her. Had to be. They must never meet again.

He smiled. It was better, safer to look ahead. He found he was humming a little tune to himself. One of those his friend used to whistle, before they buried him at sea.

Murray walked past. 'All done? Good lad.'

Jeff Lloyd heard him leave the sick bay, and call out to some one in the passageway. *Another officer.*

He could not help it, but he was rocking back and forth on the deck, and shaking with uncontrollable laughter.

David Napier sat at the table and stared at the writing paper by his elbow. There were only two small lanterns alight in the midshipmen's berth, and the air was stifling. It was about midnight, but he was not tired, nor even remotely sleepy. There was no point in worrying about it, he thought, he would be called in a few hours for the morning watch. And no sense in slinging a hammock; all hands would be called early this coming day, and the nettings would have to be secured and shipshape before dawn.

He looked over to the opposite end of the mess. Midshipman Deacon was sitting in the other small pool of light, his official diary wide open and his folder of notes and diagrams weighed down with a pair of brass dividers. Not that there was much motion to dislodge them. He had already noticed that Deacon's pen also lay untouched.

He listened to the hull murmuring around him. So familiar now, the memories of *Audacity* softened and no longer lying in wait, except perhaps at moments like these.

The ship seemed so quiet, with only an occasional intrusion, some one coughing, or rope being hauled through a block and made secure enough to satisfy the officer of the watch, or one of his subordinates, who could find no peace with his thoughts.

It was very dark on deck. No moon to mark the sea breaking away from the bows, or touch the figurehead's outthrust trident.

Simon Huxley was on watch now, with Monteith as his lord and master. At least he would have little time to brood. Young Walker would be up there with him. That should help. . . .

Tomorrow would be Walker's birthday. Thirteen years old. And he was full of high spirits at the prospect.

Napier sat thinking quietly over the day's events. Watching the schooner parting company, a prize crew waving and cheering. A stark contrast to the three burials. It had come to him then, like a shock. Half of *Onward*'s company had not seen men buried who had been killed by the violence of the enemy, or ever been under fire themselves.

They would have felt it today. Clearing for action, rigging nets to repel boarders, gun drill, all timed to the minute by Maddock and the first lieutenant.

The old hands bided their time. *I'll believe it when I sees it!* Or *Don't they know the war's over?*

Afterwards, Napier had seen Maddock the gunner, making his way to the narrow passage that led only to the magazine. He had been carrying the thick felt slippers he would wear if *Onward* was called to action. Down there in his world of fuses and packed charges, it only needed a single spark to turn the ship into an inferno, or blast her apart.

Napier had heard one of his friends ask Maddock why he had chosen his trade, if it meant being trapped below amongst all the powder and fuses.

He had grinned and retorted, 'I can't stand the noise on deck!'

But that was then.

He shivered, but not from cold.

He stared at the paper swimming in the dim light, and touched it. It was still hard to accept, but he could see the old grey house quite clearly. The faces, some of them familiar, the horses nodding from their boxes when he passed, or taking apples from his hand. The staircase and the portraits. And the admiral's sister. *Aunt Nancy.*

He touched his face, his mouth. *And Elizabeth.*

He wanted to stop, to laugh at himself. She would not even do that. . . .

He felt a hand on his shoulder, firm, insistent.

'Rise an' shine, sir!' The face seemed to be floating above the table, and he knew he had fallen asleep.

He got to his feet and saw the man grinning, satisfied that he was awake.

'Like a millpond up top, sir. No war today!' He hurried into the shadows, laughing.

Napier looked around, feeling his pockets, ensuring he would not forget anything. Deacon had disappeared, his diary and papers packed away. Unable to work, or to sleep.

He realized that a tankard was standing in the foul-weather slot beside him. It was Deacon's: he had seen it often since he had joined *Onward*, and it had his initials engraved on the side.

It was half full. Deacon must have put it down carefully, so that he would not wake him, or need to explain. It was cognac. Preparing him, and perhaps himself.

Napier sipped it slowly and stared at the blank sheet of paper on the table.

Feet were thudding overhead, but his hand was quite steady. *Dear Elizabeth. . . .*

He swallowed the rest of the cognac and reached for his hat.

It *was* today.

Adam stood in the centre of the cabin and watched the empty darkness of the sea astern, in marked contrast to the deckhead skylight, where the first red rays gave colour to the shrouds, and the hint of canvas above. He stretched until his fingers could feel the movement, the life of the ship, lifting and plunging gently as she headed into an early dawn.

It seemed quiet after the bustle of hammocks being stowed, and the shouts hurrying along some one who had not heard the pipe, or had forgotten that today was different. *Because the Captain had decided, and demanded, as much.*

He touched the back of the chair, where he had been attempting to sleep. He had gone over it again and again. Suppose he was mistaken? The whole ship's company keyed up for possible action, only to find that their captain had made an error of judgment. Lost his nerve. . . .

Perhaps the French government had rescinded the order to hand *Nautilus* over to the Aboubakr rulers, or no such order had yet been received by Capitaine Marchand and his company. In which case. . . . He shrugged. Better to be a laughing-stock than allow people to die for no purpose.

He recalled the faces of his officers, in this cabin, when he had explained his reasons and his intended course of action.

Squire had said, 'If these rebels, whoever they are, were ruthless enough to try and sink *Nautilus* before she could act as French guardship, there'll be no stopping their next attempt to control the coast. All the way to Algiers, if need be!'

Vincent had said only, 'We have no choice. It's too late for us to wait for assistance.'

Julyan had offered even less. 'That's nothing new!'

A door closed and Adam heard Jago speak briefly to somebody in the lobby.

He felt his chin: a smooth shave, as only Jago could give, and without fuss or argument, no matter the time of day or night, in storm or flat calm. Always ready.

He glanced around the cabin. His coat, hanging near the quarter windows, swaying to the easy motion, buttons and lace catching the strengthening light. Waiting for Morgan to stow it away once the crisis was over.

Like Jago, he had already been and gone. The breakfast, which he had prepared even before all hands had been piped, still lay untouched on the table.

He looked at the coat again and thought of his uncle, wearing his dress uniform that day aboard *Frobisher*, when an enemy marksman had shot him down.

He had always said, 'They will want to see you.'

And it was true. Adam had seen men's faces turning aft in

the heat and hell of battle to look for their captain, and be reassured.

Something made him turn his back and cross to the opposite side of the cabin. His sleeping compartment was still in darkness, but the door was open. He stood quite still, gazing at her face in the reflected light. Morgan must have put the painting in the cot, ready for it to be taken down to the orlop if or when the ship cleared for action.

Looking directly at him, like that day in the studio: Andromeda, chained to a rock as a sacrifice. And later, when she had overcome her fear, and had lain with her wrists tied with her own long hair, and had given herself to him.

He put his hand inside his shirt and felt the silk ribbon he had taken from her that day.

He heard the screen door again. Jago was back.

He was carrying the old sword, moving it slightly up and down in its scabbard.

'Good as new, Cap'n.' He did not look beyond the open door, at the painting propped in the cot. He knew.

He said, 'Fair an' clear. Wind's backed a piece, nor' west, they tells me.'

Adam saw it in his mind.

Jago added, 'No land in sight,' and watched Adam take the sword, and hold it to the light. *That old blade could spin a few yarns.*

'We should sight land again in an hour or so. We shall change tack if the wind holds steady.'

Jago sighed. Always planning, always worrying.

He thought of the painting, and the girl who had posed for it. The ship had a strong rival.

He hesitated, and then asked, 'Suppose *Nautilus* don't come out lookin' for a fight?' He saw him turn abruptly. Maybe he had gone too far this time.

Adam laid the sword on the table.

'Then we'll go in looking for her!' Then he smiled. 'But she will!'

They both looked up as some one ran heavily across the deck.

'Midshipman o' the watch, *sir*!'

226

It was Napier, a seaman close on his heels and panting noisily.

'Masthead reports sail to the nor' east, sir.' He almost dragged his companion in through the door. 'Mr. Squire's respects, sir, and he said you would wish to speak to the lookout.'

Adam nodded. 'Nesbitt, isn't it? A Devon man, if I remember rightly.'

The seaman grinned and ducked his head with pleasure.

'Aye, zur, Brixham!' It gave him time to recover his breath.

'Tell me what you saw.'

'Frigate, zur. No doubt about it.' He gestured. 'I 'ad a glass, zur.'

More voices, then Vincent appeared at the screen.

'I've just been told, sir!'

'Nesbitt here has good eyes.' Then to Napier, the formality abandoned, 'Take care of yourself, David.'

Then he turned and stared astern for a moment.

'I'll come up directly.' Vincent waited by the door until he had turned back, and their eyes met. 'You may beat to quarters.'

Jago watched his face once they were alone again. It was as he had expected, but, as always, it came as a shock.

He looked at the coat, hoping he might yet change his mind.

They wants to see you alive, Cap'n! But knowing that he would not, he lifted it down.

At that moment, the drums began to rattle.

227

17

In the King's Name

'Ship cleared for action, sir!' Vincent touched his hat. 'Both
cutters towing astern.'

Adam walked forward to the quarterdeck rail and stared
along the ship, seeing it as he had already pictured it in his
mind from the moment he had abandoned all pretense of sleep.
Onward's state of readiness recalled the regular drills, which
he and the gunner had timed to the minute. And yet so
different. Each eighteen-pounder with its full crew, their tools,
rammers and sponges and handspikes, and slow-matches
within reach if a flintlock misfired. He could feel the grit under
his shoes and knew that the decks had been sanded, to prevent
men from slipping if water was shipped once the ports were
opened. Or in blood, if the worst happened.

He saw the burly shape of the boatswain leaning back as he
checked the hastily rigged boarding nets. He had already heard
him once before during their recent preparations. 'Slacken 'em
off, lads! They'm supposed to *catch* the buggers in a net, not
be used as a ladder to make 'em welcome aboard!' There had
been some laughs. Not this time.

Vincent said, 'I've sent Tucker to the foremast, sir. Ready
and eager.' He gestured toward the two midshipmen waiting
by the flag locker. 'I thought Deacon might be more useful
aloft with the signals telescope.'

Adam lifted his own glass and trained it across the starboard
bow. Slow and steady. As if he had stopped breathing. Blurred
faces, taut rigging, sharp and black in the strengthening glare.
The curved edge of the forecourse. He watched the other ship

move across the lens, then stand motionless, as if trapped.

On a converging tack, leaning slightly to beat to windward. He lowered the glass and allowed his eye to recover. The rest would be guesswork. The pyramid of sails was reduced to a miniature, like the fin of a giant fish cutting the horizon. Beyond, there seemed to be haze or mist. But he knew it was the land, reaching out like a great arm. Or a trap.

He recalled what Vincent had said.

'Good thinking, Mark. Tell Deacon to go now.'

He saw a messenger run to the flag locker. When *Onward* had first arrived at Gibraltar, Deacon had been the only one to realize that the flagship had been flying a commodore's broad pendant, not an admiral's flag as listed. They had all made what was a common mistake among sailors, so long staring out to sea that they only saw what they expected to see.

He saw the midshipman striding forward, the telescope slung over his shoulder like a small cannon, and Lieutenant Monteith by one of the eighteen-pounders, watching him. Perhaps remembering when he had been like Deacon, hanging on the threshold of promotion. And little Walker taking over the signals party. Thirteen years old today. He was not likely to forget it.

Adam moved to the compass box. The chief quartermaster was on the wheel, backed up by two helmsmen. He glanced at the compass, then up at the masthead pendant, and felt the sun on his face.

'Nor' east by north, sir. Steady as she goes!'

Adam smiled. 'Thank you, Carter. So be it!'

A squad of Royal Marines was standing with their sergeant, ready to add their strength to the braces when needed. But their muskets were piled nearby. Like a warning.

He returned to the rail, unhurriedly, despite the instinct crying out to be in all places at once. Nobody looked at him directly, but he knew they were watching when he passed. Men waiting to go aloft, and claw out along the yards, to dangle over the sea or fall to certain death on the deck if they missed their footing.

The gun crews, along either side as before. But restless now. Or was he imagining that?

He wanted to lift his telescope again, but knew it was too

229

soon. He had seen some of the men at the guns turn to stare aft. *They will want to see you.*

But not if he was showing himself to be a fool.

His coat felt heavy across his shoulders, and his shirt was clinging damply to his skin. Such a short while ago, below in the great cabin, when he had seen Jago's expression. His doubts.

Together, they had experienced and shared so much. Like the prayer book Jago had fetched from the cabin when they had buried the three sailors. They had both been remembering that other time, in *Athena*, when they had committed Catherine's body to the sea. Her roses would still be blooming in their garden beside the old grey house. He touched the lapel of his coat reminiscently.

'Deck there!'

It was Tucker. Cupping his strong hands, his voice clear and steady. 'She wears *French* colours!'

Adam stared over the gun crews and across the glistening water until his eyes were blinded. Men were shouting with relief or derision, probably both.

Vincent had said something, but Adam heard only one voice. Through the brutal memories of death and its aftermath: Marchand, as they had parted. *When next we meet, there will be no flags. It will be as friends!*

He would be the last to forget.

'Pass the word. All guns load, but do not run out.'

Vincent licked his lips. 'Do we fight, sir?'

Adam looked over at Jago, and nodded.

'And we shall win!'

Napier was careful to stand clear as the foremast gun on the starboard side was hauled inboard away from its port. *Onward* was leaning slightly downwind, so that the gun crews had to use all their strength to haul their massive weapons into position. Fourteen guns on either beam; at least it would be easier when the order came to run out. Napier had taken part in nearly all the drills. A few accidents or mishaps, and curses in plenty. He could feel the tightness in his stomach, something he had taught himself to overcome. But this was not a drill. Almost like *Audacity* that day, when the

230

drums had called them to their quarters for action, and the ship's last fight.

He touched the dirk hanging against his hip. When *Audacity* had gone down and he had started to swim for the shore, this fine new dirk had still been on his belt. One of the marines who had helped carry him from the beach had told him that its extra weight could have cost him his life. He had not understood what it meant to him. Then . . . he touched it again . . . and today.

He heard Lieutenant Squire calling to one of the gun captains, making him grin as he took a ball from the shot garland, and seemed to fondle it in both hands.

Most gun captains were like that. The first broadside would be double-shotted, while there was still time to think. To react.

The charge was already loaded, with two sharp taps to bed it in place and wad to hold it steady. Then the balls, and a final wad rammed home.

Along each side the gun captains faced aft, fists raised. Only a minute or so between them.

'All guns loaded, sir!'

Napier exhaled slowly. The other guns, nine-pounders and the squat carronades, the 'smashers', were close to follow. There was a lull, and he heard a seaman at the nearest gun say, 'It's *real* this time, Dick!'

The loader turned to look at him.

'Cap'n don't want us caught with our britches down, see?'

Napier saw Midshipman Huxley hurrying along the gang-way, ducking to avoid the nets, doubtless taking a message from the quarterdeck. Across the long rank of eighteen-pounders, they saw one another and waved.

He heard Squire say, '*Walk*, don't run. We're still afloat!' But he was speaking to himself. Like some of the others nearby he was watching the boatswain and his men by the empty boat-tier, preparing to hoist out the two remaining craft, gig and jolly-boat, to join the cutters already towing astern. A wise and necessary precaution: more casualties were caused by flying splinters than iron shot. They would be cast adrift if action was joined, and recovered afterwards. It sounded simple enough, but the landmen and less experienced hands might view the procedure with alarm.

231

Without realizing it, he had reached down to feel his leg, and the ugly scar.

You were lucky.

He recalled Murray the surgeon's comment.

'He did a good job on that, whoever he was!'

But suppose some one was seeing the scar for the first time? He thought of the letter which had never begun. He was stupid even to think of it. . . .

There was a metallic clatter and he saw a young seaman stumble amongst a length of chain. They had been rigging slings to some of the upper yards, a protection should one or more of them fall to the deck. There was a dark stain across the sanded planking, where water had been tipped from the boats. He must have slipped in it.

'You clumsy, useless scum!' It was Fowler, the boatswain's mate, almost spitting with anger as he lashed out with his starter and cracked it across the man's shoulders. 'Listen to me, damn you!'

Another crack; there was blood this time.

But the young seaman seemed unable to get to his feet, or even shield himself from the blows. He was clutching at his foot or his ankle, badly twisted when he had fallen.

The starter was raised again. Napier pushed past some of the working party and tried to stop it, saw the crouching figure cringe as it slashed toward him.

He gasped, and cried out as the deflected blow caught his outthrust arm.

Fowler lost his balance and almost fell, his face torn between fury and surprise. He started to speak, perhaps to defend his actions. Napier could never afterwards remember.

Squire sounded very calm. Unemotional, as if they had never met before, and oblivious to the watching seamen. The deck might have been deserted.

'I have warned you about your behaviour, Fowler, and your readiness to administer punishment, above and beyond the line of duty!'

Fowler was glaring at him, his breathing regular again, recovering. He even managed a sarcastic grin.

'Speakin' up, are you, sir? Showin' a bit of authority at last? I was just doin' my rightful job with this clumsy waister!'

Squire smiled coldly. 'We will all have to do our duty very shortly, I think.' He reached out and grasped Napier's sleeve. 'However, you just struck an officer, Fowler. Do you deny that?'

Fowler stared from one to the other.

'Not true! Weren't like that! It weren't meant. . . .' He broke off as some one shouted, 'I saw it, sir! Call me if you need a witness!'

There was something like a growl from the gun crews and the men waiting by the two boats.

Napier could feel it as if it were something physical. It was hate.

Squire said, 'Report to the master-at-arms, Fowler. You are no stranger to threats, I think you'll agree. If you are disrated because of this, I feel sure you will hear more of them when you join the messdeck!'

Fowler exclaimed, 'If I was to tell 'em. . . .' and stared around, the fight suddenly gone out of him.

A Royal Marine, who had been posted by one of the hatchways when the ship had been cleared for action, stepped smartly forward and rapped Fowler on the shoulder.

The surgeon had also appeared, and after a brief examination of the injured man, announced calmly, 'Broken ankle.' He patted his arm. 'You'll be taken to the orlop. Best place, if you ask me!' He nodded to Squire. 'No peace for the wicked, I'm afraid.'

Napier walked back to the first gun, feeling the stinging pain in his arm. It would be badly bruised tomorrow. . . . Far worse for the injured seaman he had been trying to protect.

He turned quickly, but was too late to see who had touched his back, firmly and deliberately.

The gun captain was talking quietly with two of his crew, and another was loosening the breeching rope. Nothing left to chance.

He could still feel it, stronger and more eloquent than any spoken word of thanks. No one met his eye.

He saw Midshipman Deacon making his way aft, tar stains on his white breeches, about to report to the captain. Later the entire episode would find its place in his diary, if he lived.

He heard tackles taking the strain as the gig was hoisted in readiness for lowering. The seamen at the tackles were waiting for Jago, the captain's coxswain, to give the order, and he was standing by the gig, one hand on the gunwale.

But he was looking up, through the rigging, watching the flags as they ran up the halliard and broke to the wind.

Enemy in Sight!

The pretense was over.

Adam felt the sun, a sudden hot bar across his shoulder, as the ship leaned more steeply from the wind. Only the shadows and the sea alongside were moving, and even the sounds of rope and canvas seemed subdued.

At the guns, the crews waited in silence like groups of statuary, with only an occasional movement as some one hurried with a message or climbed on the gangway to look for *Nautilus*.

She was almost directly ahead now, and had displayed her full broadside when she had changed tack, sails in confusion as she had clawed into the wind. If any doubts had remained, they had gone from that moment. Adam saw Midshipman Deacon standing by his flag locker, with little Walker beside him. He could still see his expression when he had come aft to report on the other frigate's course and bearing. He had described the moment when the French flag had been lowered. *Cut down.* The young face and voice so deeply serious as he had motioned with his hand.

'It fell, sir. Like a dying bird.'

Vincent had said, 'They're trying to beat to wind'rd, and take the advantage.'

Adam moved slightly and saw a sliver of blue water open and widen through the shivering rigging. Almost bows-on again, sails filled and braced on her new tack, her shadow reaching over and ahead of the hull.

What kind of men were these? Rebels, renegades, maybe deserters from the old enemies, even from their own fleet. It was not unknown for men who had broken the yoke of one life of discipline and danger, only to find it was the only thing they knew and understood.

He looked away from the other ship. *What will he do? What would I do?*

234

He walked to the rail again and could feel the group around the wheel staring at his back.

They are all in my hands.

Nautilus would try and hold the wind-gage and remain on the same tack. Once abeam, she would open fire and attempt to dismast and cripple *Onward*, regardless of the range when they passed. He realized that he had punched one hand into the other. *Then reload while she crosses our stern with another full broadside.* The death of any ship which was cleared for action, decks open from bow to stern when the iron thundered through.

He said, 'Cast off the breechings and open the ports.' He turned to look directly at Vincent. 'Larboard side only!'

He saw him nod, and perhaps smile. 'Warn the starboard crews to stand by.'

He saw Julyan turn aside from the quartermaster as if to confirm his own thoughts about a trick which could so easily turn into disaster. He had been looking up at the masthead pendant, feeling the wind like a true sailor.

Adam did not. Instead he looked along the deck, the gun captains signalling that they were prepared. Breeching ropes cast off, the ports along one side open, the sea sliding briskly beneath them.

But if the wind drops?

He took the telescope and realized that Jago had joined him, grim-faced, watching the distant frigate. As for most fighting sailors, waiting was the worst part. Or so they told themselves.

But he said, 'Ready to cast off the boats, Cap'n. Just give the word.'

Adam opened the telescope. *Another hour? Less, if the wind holds steady.*

'Do it now, Luke. I'll lay odds that every available glass is trained on us at this very moment.'

He looked at Vincent. 'Run out!'

He could see it in his mind. All along one side, the black muzzles were poking into the sunlight. Like one of the drills, with extra hands from the starboard side to add their muscle and run the guns up the sloping deck.

Vincent said, 'With permission, sir?' He did not finish it, but touched his hat formally before walking to the gangway.

Squire was already making his way aft to take his place. Opposite ends of the ship. . . . Like hearing a voice from the past.

Don't display all your eggs in the same basket.

He saw Lieutenant Gascoigne, his face almost as scarlet as his tunic, moving slowly along the front rank of his Royal Marines, eyes noting every detail, making a comment from time to time. As if they were mounting guard in the barracks ashore.

Napier had come aft with Squire, calm enough, but he glanced round, startled, as the two cutters were cast adrift and were soon falling astern.

Then he stopped by the companion and said deliberately, 'I shall be here, sir.' He seemed to nod. 'I'm not afraid. Not this time.'

Adam held his arm, and thought he flinched.

'Keep on the move, David.'

Napier bit his lip, feeling the bruise left by Fowler's starter, but no longer caring. This was the closest they had been; had been allowed to be.

'You, too.' Then he did smile. 'Sir!'

Jago had returned, and Adam saw that he was wearing his broad-bladed dirk. Like *Athena* and *Unrivalled*.

He said only, 'Gig's gone adrift, Cap'n.'

Adam loosened his belt and moved the old sword into the glare. Jago gave a crooked grin.

'*Now* we'll have the bastards!'

There was a sudden explosion, a solitary gun, probably a ranging shot, the sound echoing and re-echoing across the water like something trapped in a tunnel or shaft.

Adam watched the sunlight touching the open port-lids of the oncoming frigate, then the line of guns. He thought he saw the flash of reflected sun: some one training a glass on *Onward. Perhaps on me.*

He dragged off his hat and waved it toward the men below him at the guns.

Too soon! Or too late?

'Stand by to come about!'

Calls shrilled and men who had been crouching at braces and halliards shouted to one another as they ran to obey.

236

'Helm a-lee! Hard over!'

'Open the ports! Run out!'

Some one even gave a wild cheer as the eighteen-pounders squealed against the side, the gun captains racing one another to sight and lay on the target even as *Onward* thrust into and across the wind, topsails flapping and booming while the yards braced round, as if responding to a single hand.

At that moment, *Nautilus* opened fire.

Only seconds, but it seemed forever: the intermittent flash of gunfire and the shuddering onslaught through canvas and rigging overhead, the shock of iron slamming into the hull. Adam stood quite still, his eye fixed on the bowsprit and jib-boom as it continued to swing, like a giant pointer, as if to reach out and touch the bulging canvas. *Nautilus* seemed to loom closer, as if she and not *Onward* was swinging to engage.

His muscles tensed as he felt the deck shake under his feet, expecting the sounds of broken spars, anticipating the agony that would end everything.

The ship was still answering the helm, while the headsail sheets were let go to allow her to swing unheeded through the wind.

He saw *Nautilus*, shrouded in her own gunsmoke, but no longer free to sail past and deliver another broadside. *Onward*'s agility and sudden, seemingly reckless change of tack and direction had caught her gun crews unawares. Most of the shots had passed overhead.

Here and there small scenes leaped out at him. A seaman seizing one of his companions at the gun below the quarter-deck, and throwing him aside as a massive block, severed from the rigging high above, smashed down beside them. Shock, obscenities, then a grin. Midshipman Hotham, the clergyman's son, face screwed up in concentration as he loaded and examined a long pistol, flinching as more debris fell clattering nearby. Then he handed the pistol to Monteith, who took it with a curt nod.

And the men at the braces, stiff with crouching, waiting and willing the ship to complete her tack. *And hit back.* One of them, naked to the waist, was sharing his handhold with another, younger sailor, who was not even daring to open his eyes as the smoke billowed across the water. The scars of the cat were still livid on his back, as if the flogging had given Dimmock some kind of authority.

Adam thrust out his arm and heard Julyan yell, *'Ready, sir!'*

Perhaps he had not dared to look aft, in case the helm was shot away or manned only by the dead.

'Steady as you go! Meet her!' The spokes were turning, but Adam was staring up at the masthead pendant, stark and clear again above the thinning smoke. Broken cordage jerking in the wind, and a blackened hole in the topsail, where two shots had missed both mast and yard by a few inches. There was blood too, drying on the canvas. One of the topmen. A face he would have known.

'Let go and haul!'

'Heave, me lads! *Heave!*' Guthrie's voice, powerful, unhurried, ready to send or push more hands where they were needed.

Adam heard some one cry out in pain, but he kept his eyes on the yards, still swinging in response to the men at the braces.

He watched the big arrowhead of water changing shape, the *Nautilus* very bright now in the sun, her gunports empty and with every crew trying to reload and run out again, before. . . . He shut his mind to it, surprised that he felt neither doubt nor anger. Only hatred.

'Steady as she goes, sir!'

Adam did not hear. He had drawn his sword, and held it lightly across his right shoulder.

He saw a slight movement, sunlight disturbing the pattern as the first gun to reload thrust through its port.

Too late.

He brought the sword down to the rail, and thought he heard some one cheer.

'Fire!'

Every gun fired as one, recoiling from its port and brought under control before the full impact of their combined, double-shotted broadside exploded against the enemy. They were already sponging out and reloading with fresh charges, shouting and cheering like madmen, and despite the neckerchiefs tied around their ears were too deaf to hear or share the excitement and relief after hours of waiting behind sealed ports while the larboard side had bared its teeth.

Adam covered his mouth and nose as the smoke billowed inboard in a solid cloud. The roar of the full broadside seemed to hang in the air, an echo perhaps of the double-shotted onslaught which had found its target.

Men were coughing and retching, but some were peering around in the smoke for friends. Gun crews were calling to each other, throwing their weight on tackles and handspikes, their world concentrated on the open ports before them.

Adam reached for his telescope, then waved it aside as a hand offered it through the thinning smoke.

He did not need it. The regular drills and the gun crews' patience and trust had done their work today.

Nautilus's proud beauty was broken, disfigured. Her foremast had gone completely, dragging over the forecastle and into the water alongside, the tangled mass of spars and severed rigging already dragging her round like a giant sea-anchor. The main topmast was also shot away. He thought of Maddock the gunner, down below the waterline, sealed in his cavern of explosives and instant death. He must have heard it, felt the success of his training and hard work, and been proud.

Somebody exclaimed, 'That'll make 'em put their bloody heads together an' think again!'

Squire sounded wary, impatient. 'They've got plenty of *those*, for God's sake!'

Adam walked aft to the wheel, men turning toward him, still too dazed and deafened to grasp the significance of the lieutenant's warning.

Nautilus was not responding to her rudder, and it seemed nothing was being done to cut away the burden of mast and sails which was dragging her further and further downwind.

Squire had seen it. The wind was no longer an ally.

He looked at the smoke, drifting just above the water. The wind was dropping, biding its time. The real enemy.

Napier was beside him, as if he had expected to be called.

'Ask the first lieutenant to lay aft.' He saw him touch his hat and hurry to the larboard gangway.

He heard musket shots, far-off and ineffectual. Some of the Royal Marines of the afterguard were listening, gripping their muskets, gauging the range.

They would not have long to wait.

The wind had almost dropped, but there was still enough to carry a new sound, more threatening than the infrequent report of a musket.

Voices, hundreds of them, joined together like a muffled roar.

Vincent had reached the quarterdeck, his eyes on the loosely flapping topsails, and then the men at the wheel.

'If the wind returns, I can bring our guns to bear.'

Adam shook his head. 'So might *Nautilus*. But she'll need a dockyard before she can fight and win under *any* flag.'

He saw the familiar frown, the old challenge. Then he said quietly, 'They'll try to board us, sir. Their only chance. Fight or die.'

Adam turned the old sword over in his hands.

'And ours, Mark.'

He stared along the upper deck, the men at their guns, others dragging away fallen rigging. There were two bodies lying by the empty boat-tier, already covered. Wasted.

'So be it. *Close quarters!*'

Julyan called, 'She's swingin', sir!'

Adam laid the sword on the rail and took his telescope.

Onward was answering the helm again, the quartermaster peering at the compass as a gust of air lifted the big ensign above the poop defiantly, and another volley of musket fire made some of the seamen duck for cover.

Adam stood motionless, the telescope hot against his skin.

Nautilus was turning very slowly, the sun suddenly like a mirror across the quarter, and then more slowly still over the poop itself. He felt something crack against the deck and saw splinters blown aside. More shots, this time from the maintop, some of Gascoigne's marksmen returning fire.

Adam wiped his eye and steadied the glass again. Figures running along *Nautilus*'s gangway, above the entry port, where Marchand had welcomed him aboard. More were already clambering around the cathead, trying to hack away the remaining shrouds which held the fallen mast alongside.

'As you bear!' He heard Napier, then another voice passing the order to the guns.

More shots, and a louder bang: a swivel gun, he thought. The glass remained steady, but he could feel sweat running down his spine like blood.

It was now. The crash of the first eighteen-pounder seemed sharper, louder, not double-shotted this time. The stern windows were blown aside, pieces of carved 'gingerbread' splashing and resurfacing beneath the counter even as the next gun fired, blasting through *Nautilus*'s stern.

Adam picked up the sword, the stench of smoke and charred timber searing his throat and eyes.

He saw a marine reloading his musket, and pausing to fix the bayonet, before running to join his section. He was shouting, but Adam could barely hear over the gunfire.

Julyan shouted, 'You got your wish, sir!' and turned to say over his shoulder to the quartermaster, 'Watch your helm, Carter!' Then he stepped over the man's body and added his own weight to the wheel. The quartermaster had been a trusted friend. But there was no time to think about him, even as he was trying to drag himself to his feet.

He shook his fist, swearing as more shots pounded the deck and clanged aside from one of the nine-pounders.

Adam saw the *Nautilus* looming over the side, and felt the two hulls shudder together. On deck, the gun crews were reloading, some falling, wounded or dying, as grapnels clattered on to the gangway above them.

'Repel boarders! At 'em, lads!' The marines ran to obey, bayonets gleaming, as others fired down from the main and mizzen tops. A mob was clambering on to the gangway and reaching for shrouds and ratlines, only to be trapped by the loosely rigged boarding nets.

Blade against blade, teeth bared: almost inhuman as they tried to hack the stout netting aside. No time to reload; it was man to man. Some were through the defenses, to be met by cutlass and boarding axe, and sometimes fists, as they fought and struggled above the guns.

The boatswain was using a cutlass; it looked like a dirk in his massive fist.

'They'm runnin', th' bastards!' Then, like a great tree, he fell, his own men still cheering as they ran across him in pursuit.

Adam hurried to the midships part of the gangway, where

the nettings had been hacked away completely. Men were shouting and cursing, some too exhausted even to cry out if they were cut down. There were bodies fallen and trapped between the two hulls, and Adam saw some of the attackers wilt and retreat in confusion as they were confronted by some marines and their cherished musketoon.

Wild cheers now: Vincent was running along *Nautilus*'s quarterdeck with some of his seamen, climbing back to *Onward* after pursuing the attackers.

Too late, he became aware of his own danger, and found himself face to face with a strongly built figure brandishing a double-bladed sword as if it were weightless. Perhaps he had seen the uniform, or maybe he was too crazed by the fighting and death all around him, that it was merely a final spur to his madness or his courage.

Their blades locked, and Adam thought he heard Squire yell, '*No heroics!*' then he drove his own sword into his ribs.

He staggered as his shoe slid on blood, and yelled to the gun crews below him.

The attackers had fallen back to *Nautilus*'s deck, but they were rallying, being led or driven by the same relentless chanting.

'*More men!*' Adam waved his sword. Monteith should be ready with a party of seamen and the last loaded swivel gun on the opposite gangway.

But he was lying on the main deck, his uniform impeccably clean amidst the blood and filth of fighting.

He saw Napier coming to join him, a hanger drawn and ready, and shouted, 'Fall back! Watch *yourself*, David!'

He pushed two struggling men aside, but another had climbed on to the gangway, a long knife clenched between his teeth.

Napier lost his balance, and the hanger slithered out of reach. His attacker leaped on to his shoulders, dragging him down, gripping the knife as two more of his companions hauled themselves on to the gangway.

'*No, you don't, you bastards!*' Some one was running from the side, a boarding pike held like a lance as he charged across the deck.

The pike struck Napier's attacker in the back, with such

force that Napier could see the bloodied tip protruding from his chest as he went down and over the side.

He staggered to his feet, staring with shock and dismay as his rescuer threw up both hands and fell after the man he had killed. He was bleeding badly, probably hit by a stray shot even as he watched the boarder fall from view between the hulls.

'Did you see *that*?'

Adam grasped his shoulder, guiding and pushing him toward the quarterdeck. Just a brief glimpse, as he had tried to wrench the pike free of its victim. Mouth wide in a shout or a laugh of jubilation, even as he had been shot down. Jeff Lloyd, one of the sailmaker's crew, who had repaired his old uniform.

He shouted, 'Stand by, on deck!' There was a gap now between the two ships, widening and gaining colour even as he watched. He could feel it on his face, and wanted to yell it aloud. The wind was returning, and not only in his mind. Or his prayers. *Nautilus* was already further away. He could see broken timber and corpses floating free.

More men running along *Nautilus*'s deck, but confused now, perhaps leaderless.

Adam saw a gunner's mate peering up at him while Midshipman Simon Huxley continued to tie a bandage around his arm, taking his time.

'As you bear, lads!' He saw the gunner's mate acknowledge it.

Adam walked along the gangway and saw Jago coming to meet him. The crash of the first gun seemed to swamp everything as the two ships continued to edge apart, the water clearer, reflecting the smoke like harmless clouds. *Nautilus* was turning again, and would soon expose her side, ready to reopen fire.

There was more smoke swirling from her stern, from the great cabin itself. He saw the eighteen-pounder standing inboard, its crew sponging out and tamping home another charge, a fresh ball already held, ready to follow. The gun captain was gazing at *Nautilus*, and the smoke that marked his last shot. But there was no cheering this time.

Jago turned as Napier muttered to himself, 'He saved my life,' and touched his sleeve, as he had seen his captain do many times.

243

'We needs you, for better days!' But the habitual wry grin had deserted him.

The gun was already being run up to its port, its captain staring over the breech. He did not even turn his head as the next gun crashed and recoiled, and was being sponged out before the smoke had cleared.

Adam glanced up at the topsails. They were still filled and steady. *Onward* could break off the fight and go with the wind. Who would blame him?

'Standing by, sir.' That was Squire, who was watching the gun crews impassively as they stared aft, waiting for his signal.

Adam was studying *Nautilus*'s line of ports, still at an angle, but they would soon come to bear again. No jury-rig as yet, nor any attempt to hoist one. But the wreckage had been cut away. Already drifting clear. He saw two boats close by, *Onward*'s own cutters, unlikely witnesses to a necessary killing on both sides.

He walked to the rail and saw Monteith, sitting now on an upturned box, his head buried in his hands, a crude bandage beneath his fingers. He had apparently been knocked unconscious by a piece of falling timber.

A marine, leaning with his musket against the tightly packed hammock nettings, said, 'Mister Monteith is goin' to be all right.' A pause. 'Pity, ain't it?' But nobody laughed.

Adam clenched his fist and pressed it against his side. More of *Nautilus*'s guns were visible now. A full broadside . . . he could wait no longer.

She was a much older ship than *Onward*. He thought of the empty and abandoned vessels that filled so many ports and inlets in England. Once proud, even famous names, waiting for the breakers' yards, or ignominy as hulks. But most of them would remain afloat. And still withstand a broadside if necessary.

He did not look along his ship again. She had been built for speed and agility. Endurance had outpriced itself, and stripped the forests.

'Full broadside!'

He knew that every fist would be raised, lanyards taut, ready to obey.

He reached out, not daring to take his eyes off the *Nautilus*.

It was a trick, to prolong the inevitable. The slaughter.

He gripped the telescope, still without turning his head, wasting seconds which could cost the lives of those who trusted him.

He saw part of *Nautilus*'s upper deck, guns run out, the scars and broken timbers stark in the lens. Nothing moving except the shadows of torn and blackened canvas from her mainyard, which had somehow escaped destruction.

'*Ready*, sir!' Anxiety. Impatience.

Nautilus's deck was full of people. Not standing by the guns, or crouching along gangways waiting for another attempt to board this ship. There were so many of them, they would crush any resistance by sheer weight of numbers, heedless of the cost.

Some of them were moving now, faces toward *Onward*, but without authority or purpose. Held in check, waiting.

He wanted to look away; his eye was stinging with strain and concentration. But if he did, he would lose this fragile hope, and the world would explode into nightmare.

Some one said, 'They're dropping weapons over the side!' Then more loudly: 'They *are*, for God's sake!'

Adam said, 'Aft, by the mizzen.' He rubbed his eye with his wrist, and thrust the telescope at Jago. 'Tell me, Luke, am I wrong?'

Jago took the telescope and lost precious seconds adjusting it. He would not be hurried. He *knew*, as did his captain.

A little cluster of figures beneath the mast, having climbed up from another deck, staring around now, as if half blinded by the daylight. Their progress had been slow, but the crowd around them had parted to allow them through without any attempt to prevent their passing. It was like a signal, when the swords and muskets had started to splash alongside.

Jago watched, not daring to breathe as one group lowered a tall ladder-backed chair and turned it toward *Onward*. It was a powerful telescope; no wonder Bolitho was so proud of it.

He wanted to clear his throat, but something stopped him.

He said, 'It's the Frenchie, Cap'n. A bit knocked about, but still alive.'

Adam could still see it. The tall figure he remembered, stooped over, and supported in a chair. The bandages and the

245

blood on his torn uniform, like tar in the sunlight. He could have been dead. But one of his officers had taken his wrist and raised it carefully, and held the hand up almost in a salute.

And Marchand had smiled.

Adam had thought of Deacon's *dying bird*. When Marchand must have cut down his own flag.

Squire said, 'They'll try to bargain, using him and his men.'

Adam looked at Jago. 'No bargains.'

There was a sudden burst of cheering, which drowned out every other sound. Men stood away from their guns, and some embraced one another. Even Monteith lifted his face from his hands and stared around, startled, as if he could not recall what had happened.

Some one yelled from the forecastle and Adam saw the drifting cutter nudging against the hull.

A voice shouted orders, and a marine ran to pitch a grapnel and haul it alongside.

Adam stared at the stains and the scars of gunfire. It should have been Joshua Guthrie's leather-lunged voice, but it had been silenced forever. The boatswain had fought his last battle.

The cheering had died away, and he could hear the thud of hammers and the regular clank of a pump. *Onward* had been wounded. But she was the victor.

Julyan called, 'We can't anchor here, sir! No bottom.'

He thought he had heard the leadsman's chant even as they had approached *Nautilus*, feeling their way.

'No matter. We will take her in tow until we can make her fit for passage.'

Jago said, 'Cutter's made fast, Cap'n.'

Adam walked to the larboard side, the wind at his back. *Just in time*. But too late for men who had deserved a longer span of life, to enjoy or to endure.

There was no land in sight, nor would there be until the Strait.

He saw young Walker by the flag locker, dabbing his eyes, which were red-rimmed with smoke or tears. Caught like that, he looked like a child in uniform.

Adam called, 'A birthday we'll *all* remember, Mr. Walker!'

Some of the seamen laughed and raised a cheer, and one

246

patted him on the back. His face would be remembered, too.

He tried to steady his thoughts, but they were swirling and disordered, as if they had been cut free.

He heard the cutter, manned and pulling away to recover another boat, maybe Jago's gig.

A boarding party to stand guard while a jury-rig was joisted over *Nautilus*. Wounded to be treated. He thought of the sailmaker who had saved David Napier's life. There would be more to bury in the next day or so, no matter what the surgeon and his assistants could do.

He saw Jago's eyes on his shoulder, and when he reached up his fingers encountered a jagged sliver of gold lace, severed only inches from his neck. He had not felt the ball rip past. The unknown marksman had observed him with care, but had waited too long.

He saw Vincent up forward, heard him calling names while Midshipman Huxley ticked them on a list.

He felt Deacon watching him, still smiling a little, no doubt because of his remark about his helper's birthday.

'Sir?' Alert and correct. A lieutenant's commission no longer only a dream.

'We will be making for Gibraltar. As we approach, we will be challenged, as you would expect.'

He saw him frown as he pulled out his pad.

'A signal, sir?'

'It will be a long one.' He looked across at the other frigate, a prize now. More weapons were dropping over her side, and he thought he saw a uniform walking unchecked past the abandoned guns. One of Marchand's officers, surprised to be free and alive.

He shut his mind to it. A higher authority would sift and carry the burden.

The ship comes first.

'When challenged, you will make. . . .'

He paused and looked out over the glistening water.

Ships were all different, with characters of their own. Any old sailor could name a dozen or more without stopping to think.

Maybe ships understood?

247

He spoke slowly, and knew that Jago was listening. Sharing the moment.

'His Britannic Majesty's ship Nautilus is rejoining the Fleet. God Save the King.'

Epilogue

Francis Troubridge stood on the steps below the church and tugged his dress coat into position. There seemed to be people everywhere, waiting and watching, some even pointing now that he had appeared, as if a signal had been given.

He shivered, although not from the cold. It was November, but the sun had made an appearance, and he was surprised that he could feel so unnerved, and completely alone.

All those hundreds of miles, delivering urgent despatches to the admiral at Plymouth; it was hard to recall every detail, or arrange them in sensible order.

One memory never faltered. Gibraltar, watching the two frigates entering harbour, the damaged *Nautilus* under her jury-rig, and a White Ensign clean and vivid above her scars. Then the cheering, with every ship in the anchorage alive with waving sailors, boats pulling to greet the arrivals, and cannon firing in salute from the Rock itself.

And other vignettes, clear and personal. There had been an Admiralty warrant waiting for *Onward*, for the immediate arrest and trial of one of her company. A woman had come forward as witness to the murder of Captain Charles Richmond, Adam Bolitho's predecessor. It was rumoured that both Richmond and his alleged killer, a sailmaker named Lloyd, had been the woman's lovers.

Troubridge recalled the exact moment when Bolitho had been given the warrant, when the cheers and tumultuous welcome had still been ringing in his ears. Very deliberately, he had torn it into pieces, and said, 'He fought for his ship. He will be answering to a far higher command than their lordships!'

He shivered again. Things had moved with such a speed, almost from their arrival at Plymouth. *Onward* had been taken into the dockyard because of damage on and below her waterline, and most of her company had been put ashore to await developments. And *Merlin* was to be reassigned to the Channel Fleet.

Another vivid memory, only a few days ago, when he had been granted leave personally by the admiral to come to Falmouth and attend Bolitho's wedding.

Some one gave a cheer and he saw some more uniforms approaching, and being met by an usher. A good day for smugglers; there were two revenue cutters in harbour, and these were their officers.

He thought of this morning's short journey in the carriage from the Bolitho house to the Church of King Charles the Martyr, Adam Bolitho beside him, and, sitting opposite them, his pretty aunt Nancy and Sir Richard's old friend Thomas Herrick. He had always felt that he would know them, but when the time came, he was still the stranger. Herrick had donned his uniform for the occasion, which had not helped. Looking back, it seemed the retired rear-admiral had been even more uneasy.

Some one exclaimed, 'Coming now!'

The crowd was thicker; even those he had thought only casual onlookers had pressed closer to join the others.

A smart carriage with a crest he did not recognize on its door was wheeling round to the foot of the steps.

For an instant longer he saw the girl in the untidy studio, when Adam had smashed down the door and he had found himself with a pistol in his hand, ready to shoot. To kill, given the slightest provocation. And Lowenna, the gown ripped from her shoulder, with a brass candlestick in her hand, the man who had tried to rape her sprawling at her feet. *I would have killed him*, she had said.

So would I.

The carriage stopped and some one ran up to hold the horses. The coachman had jumped down from his box and let down the step before Troubridge could move.

He thought of the coachman who had driven them from the house. Young Matthew, they had called him, although he could have been their father. . . . And he had seen the quick exchange of glances, and the smiles when Young Matthew had been ready to assist the one-armed Herrick from the carriage, but he had declined. No words had been necessary.

He stared, startled, for an instant as a midshipman stepped from the coach and turned to take the bridal bouquet, a spray of golden chrysanthemums tied with ribbon.

But the 'midshipman' was a girl, in a perfect copy of a uniform jacket, with a white skirt that skimmed her ankles. Her tall, slim figure would never pass unremarked on any gangway.

He moved toward them, his eyes on Lowenna. She was wearing a gown of heavy cream silk, the sleeves long and puffed and the bodice shirred with gold thread that caught the faint sunshine, her dark hair piled up and caught with a cluster of white silk roses and a drift of veil. The single pearl and diamond drops which had been Adam's gift flashed at her throat and ears as she stood, quite motionless, looking up at the church tower, and then directly at him.

'Francis, it is so good, so *right*, to see you today.'

He took her hand and kissed it, and there was a murmur of approval from the watching crowd. Neither of them heard it.

She lifted her chin. Pride, a little defiance as she reached out to take his arm.

Troubridge said, 'If ever. . . .' He checked himself.

She looked at him and touched his mouth with her fingers, and he caught the faint, cold, autumnal scent of the flowers.

'I *know*. And I thank you, Francis.'

They walked toward the open doors, Elizabeth, the midshipman, close behind them, her arms full of chrysanthemums.

A few steps from the entrance, Lowenna stopped and faced the crowd for the first time.

There was a man standing almost against the door frame, stiffly, propped on a crutch, his foot a wooden stump. He must have been here for hours, Troubridge thought, to have found a place so close.

With great dignity he lifted his old hat and smiled.

'God bless you an' Cap'n Adam, an' fair sailing!'

She waved and smiled back as the crowd broke into another burst of cheering.

Perhaps one of the old sailors from the waterfront, where she had walked with Adam, and found hope. But the one-legged figure had gone. A ghost, then. . . .

She looked at her escort and pressed her hand against his arm. She was ready, but the tears had been very near.

Walk with me.

Adam stood below the high altar with his back to the reflected sunlight, glad of the shadows. The church was as crowded as he could ever remember. There were even some additional benches near the nave, which had been occupied when he had arrived.

Nancy and Herrick were sitting close by, and young David Napier. He remembered his face, his surprise and obvious delight when he had told him that of course he was invited. *One of the family.*

He looked around at the carvings and the tablets. So many of Falmouth's sons were remembered here.

Like the day he had stood in this church, beside Catherine, when the flags had been lowered to half-mast, and *Unrivalled* had fired a salute to the memory of Sir Richard Bolitho. And years before, when he had escorted his uncle's bride up to this same altar. Belinda, Elizabeth's mother, who had died after a riding accident. Had she been trying to prove something even then?

And now there was Elizabeth, no longer a child. She had already proclaimed that she would never marry a sailor, who would put the sea before his wife.

He looked through the church, his eyes accustomed to the cool shadows. Like taking over a watch before dawn. . . .

He thought of *Onward*, her wounds entrusted to the care of the builders, and of the action and its aftermath, *Nautilus* now awaiting her fate in Gibraltar. And the Turk, Mustafa Kurt: killed in the whirlwind of his own sowing, or vanished in some new guise to join or ferment further rebellion elsewhere?

He heard the discreet cough, and knew the clergyman had received some message or signal.

Lowenna was arriving now.

He glanced around. All the faces, some so well known, part

252

of himself. Allday and his Unis; Yovell, spectacles balanced on his forehead, as Adam could imagine even if he could not see them. Grace Ferguson, despite all the memories this church would evoke. Perhaps she had nothing now but the Bolitho family.

There were uniforms here in plenty, naval, and red coats from the garrison. But mostly they were local folk.

He saw a hand move and raised his own to Jago, standing in his special place for today. He and Allday would have a few yarns to share before the day was over.

There were sudden cheers outside, and a few late arrivals hurried across a shaft of sunlight to be guided clear of the aisle.

Then he saw Lowenna, with Troubridge beside her, flowers on her arm, and more following close behind her in Elizabeth's hands. Every head turned to her, the air quivered as the organ breathed into life, but her eyes were on his, and remained so until their hands joined and together they faced the altar.

At the very back of the church, one of the ushers managed to find a seat in a crowded pew for a latecomer. And that was only because he was limping badly, obviously recovering from an injury or wound. And he was a foreigner, and Cornish folk prided themselves on making strangers welcome.

'Are you a guest of the Bolitho family?'

Capitaine Luc Marchand smiled, and shook his head.

'He is my friend.'

It was enough.